The Drowning of An Old Cat and Other Stories

Chinese Literature in Translation

EDITORS

Irving Yucheng Lo
Joseph S. M. Lau
Leo Ou-fan Lee

The Drowning of an Old Cat and Other Stories

· · · · ·

by Hwang Chun-ming

*Translated from the Chinese
by Howard Goldblatt*

INDIANA UNIVERSITY PRESS
Bloomington

First Midland Book Edition 1980

Manufactured in the United States of America

Library of Congress Cataloging in Publication Data
Hwang Chun-ming.
The drowning of an old cat, and other stories.
(Chinese literature in translation)
Includes bibliographical references.
CONTENTS: The fish.—The drowning of an old cat.—His son's big
doll. [etc.]
I. Title.   II. Series.
PZ4.H8747Dr   [PL2865.C56]   895.1'35   80-7494
ISBN 0-253-32452-1   1 2 3 4 5 84 83 82 81 80
ISBN 0-253-20253-1 (pbk.)

For Ah-kwei

Contents

$\cdots\cdots$

Translator's Preface

The stories included in this anthology were written over a period of approximately seven years; the most recent is dated 1973. All first appeared in Taiwan magazines and newspaper supplements and were later included in one or more of four short-story collections by Hwang Chun-ming* (see Bibliographic Note). They have been arranged chronologically here so that the reader can observe the author's artistic and philosophical development, including his movement from rural to urban themes.

Two of the translations, "Sayonara • Tsai-chien" and "The Taste of Apples" (both in modified form), were previously published in *The Chinese PEN*, a Taiwan translation journal; "Sayonara • Tsai-chien" was subsequently reprinted in the Hong Kong magazine *Renditions*. Three of the remaining stories have appeared in print by other translators, but for reasons of stylistic continuity, personal preference, and the occasional repair of a mistranslation, I have undertaken to do my own rendering, taking the counsel of my predecessors wherever necessary.

It is lamentable, though unavoidable, that one of the hallmarks of Hwang Chun-ming's fiction, the conscious, liberal use of dialect, cannot be captured in translation. The one exception is in the romanization of the main character's name in "The Gong," where Taiwanese was chosen over Mandarin. But even this will be apparent only to readers familiar with normal Mandarin spellings in the Wade-Giles romanization.

Since the two dialects spoken in Taiwan—the official language of Mandarin and the indigenous Taiwanese—are mutually unintelligible when spoken and sometimes vary in written form, the language gap among people in Taiwan is often a pronounced one. Thus, in

---

*(Huang Ch'un-ming in Wade-Giles romanization) The spelling used here is the one preferred by the author himself.

the stories, we encounter frequent references to members of the older generation who cannot comprehend what is being spoken around them. It is language and not IQ that makes them so apparently obtuse.

One feature of Hwang's writing that can be more or less faithfully recreated in translation is his humorous, sometimes racy, and highly colloquial dialogue. In my attention to fidelity, I have attempted above all to be faithful to the author's tone, especially in the all-important dialogue. Where a direct translation has not seemed appropriate, liberties have been taken with the text to realize this goal.

The reader will notice an apparent inconsistency in the rendering of characters' names—some have been transliterated while others have been translated. The rule of thumb has been that only nicknames have been translated. Some of these names may seem cruel to the reader, but in fact the acknowledgment of physical disabilities is common in rural Taiwan—there are no "closet cripples" in Hwang's fiction. I have occasionally slightly altered the spelling of a transliterated name so that the same names do not recur to confuse the reader (in Chinese, the different written characters obviate this problem); one family does appear twice—Chiang Ah-fa, his wife, and several children have starring roles in "Ringworms" and in "The Taste of Apples."

It remains only to acknowledge the encouragement and assistance of the people who helped make these translations possible. Among them are John Hu and David Steelman, whose translations proved instructive; Nancy Ing and George Kao, for their encouragement; George Cheng, who checked much of the manuscript; and the many Taiwanese friends, including the author himself, who aided in my understanding of Taiwanese expressions, customs, and attitudes. Thanks also to Professors Joseph Lau and Leo Lee, who provided much of the inspiration and support that saw this project through to completion, and to Judi Wong, who typed the final manuscript.

Introduction

It is ironic that this exposure of Hwang Chun-ming's fictional creations to Western readers occurs at a time when many of the author's Taiwan contemporaries consider the stories that make up the bulk of the present anthology passé. For someone so young and so talented, whose writings were considered almost revolutionary in subject matter and in use of language, to become so quickly a transitional figure is unfortunate though not uncommon in a world that is changing so precipitously. In Taiwan, where the ethnic dichotomy between the mainland Chinese and the Taiwanese has not disappeared—nor, it seems, will it in the immediate future— and where the future itself is very much in doubt, the process of change is even more greatly accelerated. It may be that as a writer, Hwang, whose stories of the Chinese in Taiwan were a radical (and welcome) departure from the anti-Communist fiction of the 1950s and the subsequent Western-influenced, often avant-garde novels of the early 1960s, may have fallen victim to a social process that he helped put into motion.[*]

Hwang Chun-ming writes primarily of rural Taiwan, a rather closed society. He is thus regarded as a regional writer, a term that, while accurate in the main, is somewhat limiting in describing both the contents of his stories and their intrinsic universality. Consistent, clearly defined geographical settings and character types, as

---

[*]I have discussed the stories of Hwang in detail in "The Rural Stories of Hwang Chun-ming," in *Chinese Fiction from Taiwan: Critical Perspectives*, edited by Jeannette L. Faurot (Indiana University Press, 1980).

the novels of Faulkner and others have shown, can aid an author in more fully developing his world view and in expressing his personal observations of the people and places with which he is most familiar. Hwang's characters (who are far more important than the incidents in their lives) are generally uneducated, disadvantaged men, women, and children who must cope with assaults on their traditionalism, hostility or condescension on the part of their urban brethren, and of course poverty, with all its debilitating effects. For the most part, these characters are society's rejects, people languishing on the lowest rungs of the social ladder; they have suffered at the hands of their peers or of their betters, and they quite often find life and society passing them by. Witnesses to the inexorable disintegration of the community they have known all their lives, they find themselves in the unenviable position of having to choose between obstructionism and passive acceptance of their own anachronistic existence.

Hwang could be forgiven if he were to allow his compassion and concern for these people to influence his writing in the directions of idealization or pathos. To his credit he does not. Rather, he infuses his characters with dignity and wisdom, attributes in which no class has a monopoly (a society that has embraced the likes of Will Rogers and Eric Hoffer understands this). This should not lead us to expect an uninterrupted series of happy endings to Hwang's stories, human existence being what it is; despair born of a sense of personal inadequacy or loss of livelihood, overreactions to simple misunderstandings that place too great a strain on love, and the overpowering need to be accepted and respected often lead to tragic ends in the stories that follow.

There is a definite pattern to Hwang's stories, a progression from the small-town environment of his hometown and the surrounding villages to the larger urban areas and finally to the metropolis, Taipei. The supporting roles played by the old-timers in "The Drowning of an Old Cat" and the local vagrants in "The Gong" are replaced in the later works by Japanese tourists ("Sayonara • Tsai-chien") and American military advisors and foreign-affairs policemen ("The Taste of Apples"). Pedicab drivers, gong beaters, and "admen" with sandwich boards over their shoulders give way to TV reporters and clerks in large companies. Still, the dominant characters in the stories collected here are deeply rooted in rural Taiwan; the one exception, the narrator of "Sayonara • Tsai-chien," is himself new to the big city, and is very close in background, interests, and personal situation to Hwang Chun-ming himself. In a word, rural Taiwan itself is often the central character.

Lacking an education, speaking only their native Taiwanese dialect, and unable to change their conservative, superstitious, unaffected ways, these people are the unwitting and guileless victims of changing societal values, and even when they transcend their humble origins, overshadowing all around them, their victory is but a temporary one. Certainly the greatest threat to these people, as to so many of their kind throughout the world, is the unremitting, merciless, and irreversible encroachment of "modernization," the introduction of highly appealing creature comforts and of the more efficient technology of an increasing industrialized society into increasingly remote areas.

Hwang Chun-ming is a humanist of the first order. He is a self-designated spokesman for the culturally disadvantaged and a prod for the consciences of those who would lose sight of the human costs of a blind, reckless adherence to "progress." He comes to writing instinctively and with no formal training. But what his works may lack in technical brilliance they easily gain in sheer readability and humor, and the complex sentiments of his characters and their reactions to events are faithfully and movingly captured in lively dialogue and uncomplicated narrative. Hwang does experiment on occasion, employing such devices as interior monologue in something approaching stream-of-consciousness style, or using his cinematic background in the shifting of scenes and use of flashback, but he is neither particularly innovative nor trendy where fictional techniques are concerned. The success of his stories can be attributed to his being content to let the characters tell their own stories.

Hwang, who grew up in a rural Taiwan environment, has witnessed firsthand the old and the new (including the transition from
the one to the other) and the many and varied outside influences
on his homeland, from Japan, mainland China, and the West, particularly the United States. All of this is reflected in his short stories
and novellas, and in such a way as to parallel the changes in Taiwan over the past two decades. But the reader should not assume
that we are dealing here with period literature only (a corpus of
writing that has diminished relevance and appeal), for the prime
element in the bulk of the stories presented here is the author's
basic sense of humanity. For the Western reader, the unfamiliar
aspects of setting are transcended in most of the pieces by a uni-
versal and timeless appeal in the depiction of man's role in life,
of his contradictions, his confrontations with society at large, his
struggles with poverty and prejudice, and his ability to adapt to
change. Hwang's stories are a reaffirmation of the sanctity of human existence.

In the stories that follow, the Western reader will find a good
many unfamiliar attitudes, modes of behavior, figures of speech,
and interpersonal relationships; these dissimilarities, which may on
occasion puzzle the reader, are overshadowed by the eminently
recognizable emotions, situations, and involvements that are common to us all. There is here a delicate blend of tenderness and in-
sensitivity, worldliness and idealism, love and violence, humor and
tragedy; but mostly there is honesty, compassion, and all the ingre-
dients of stories well told.

The ordinary people of Taiwan have a devoted spokesman in
Hwang Chun-ming, and the rest of us who read his stories can "discover" a new and highly talented writer and "rediscover" certain
aspects of the human condition.

The Drowning of
An Old Cat and
Other Stories

The Fish

· · · · ·

"You told me to bring a fish with me the next time I came home, Grandpa. Well, I've brought one—it's a bonito!" Ah-ts'ang shouted happily to himself as he left the little town behind him on his rickety old bicycle.

A twenty-eight-inch bike was not made for a child as small as Ah-ts'ang, and as he set out he was tempted to stick his right leg through the triangular space below the crossbar. But then he changed his mind, figuring that he shouldn't be riding a bike that way anymore. After all, he wasn't a kid any longer.

Perched on the big bike, Ah-ts'ang could not keep his rump from slipping off first one side of the seat and then the other. The cooked bonito, wrapped in a taro leaf and hanging from the handlebars, swayed violently along with the motion of the bike. Ah-ts'ang knew how happy his bringing this bonito back to the mountain would make his grandpa and his younger brother and sister. They would also be surprised to see that he had learned to ride a bicycle. Besides, by riding a bike to and from the base of the mountain at Pitou, he would save twelve dollars* in busfare. That was why he had pleaded with the carpenter to lend him the rickety old bike that lay unused in the shed.

Ah-ts'ang pedaled down the road with the single-minded purpose of getting that fish home to his grandfather as quickly as possible; not even the clanking sounds of the old bike disturbed his

---

*The exchange rate of Taiwan currency, the NT or New Taiwan Dollar, fluctuates between thirty-five and forty to the U.S. Dollar. In these translations, the word "dollar" always refers to the NT Dollar.

thoughts. The moment he saw his grandfather he would hold the fish up high and say: "Well, what do you say? I've got a pretty good memory, haven't I? I brought a fish home."

"Ah-ts'ang, the next time you come home, try to bring a fish back with you. It's not easy to get seafood up here on the mountain. Bring a big one if you can."

"But I don't know when I'll be able to come home again."

"I'm saying *when* you come home."

"That'll be up to the master."

"I know that! That's why I said to bring a fish back with you *when* you come home."

"*When* I come home? I may not have enough money *to* come home."

"I mean when you *do* have the money."

"That'll depend on the master too."

"When will he start paying you wages?"

"You should know—you took me there. Didn't he say I'd have to be an apprentice for three years and four months before I got any money?"

"That's right. You're there to learn a trade from him. How long before you can nail a table together all by yourself?"

"Nailing a table together is easy. I learned how to do that a long time ago."

"Then you shouldn't be an apprentice any longer."

"I haven't been there three years and four months yet."

"Oh? How long have you been there?"

"I still have a year and a half to go." Ah-ts'ang sighed. "Hmm, I sometimes feel I could spend my whole life there without finishing."

The old man quickly admonished him: "Hush! Children aren't supposed to sigh!"

"Why not?"

"Because they're not supposed to." He paused for a moment. "It's bad luck. You remember that."

"Grandpa." Ah-ts'ang raised his head slightly and looked up at the old man.

"Hm?"

"When you're really low, it makes you feel good to sigh."

The old man laughed loudly.

"What're you laughing at?"

"You don't look any older, but you talk like you've grown up a lot."

"I mean it! After I sigh, I always feel really really good."

"Don't walk over on that side where the road curves. The day before yesterday one of the shopowners from the foot of the mountain got a little careless while he was coming up to collect some bills and lost his footing there . . ."

"Was he hurt?" Ah-ts'ang craned his neck to look over the side.

"Of course he was hurt. The bamboo down there had just been cut so that each stalk looked like a crow's beak, and when he slipped over the side he was stuck by pointed bamboo stalks all over his body; he also broke his leg. Okay, that's enough looking down there. That bend in the road has always been a bad spot."

"Who owed him money?"

"Who up here on the mountain doesn't owe money to the flat-landers?"

They silently skirted the bend in the road.

"Where are you going?"

"Nowhere. I'll just walk you down the mountain."

"You don't have to. I'll be careful, and I'll remember to bring a fish back with me the next time I come home."

"That's fine. But if you can't, don't worry about it. Sometimes when the weather turns bad, the fishermen don't go out to sea, and then you can't get a fish even if you have the money."

"Then I hope there's no bad weather."

As they approached a narrow section of the road, the old man let his grandson go ahead of him; he gazed at the boy from behind and asked: "Is it a rough life?"

"What can I do about it? They make me do just about everything in the master's house, even wash the baby's diapers . . ." The boy was choked up.

"Then what does the master's wife do?"

The child just shook his head without saying a word.

"Huh! So that's the kind of woman she is!" Then the old man comforted the child by saying: "It doesn't make any difference. Haven't you been putting up with it all along?"

"You told me I had to put up with it when I first went there."

"Then you're doing the right thing. You have to set a good example for your brother and sister."

Ah-ts'ang looked off at nothing in particular on the mountain slope. He saw a herd of goats grazing in Heartbreak Woods.

"How're our goats?"

"Oh, they're just fine."

"We oughta raise a few more."

"That's what I've been thinking."

"Let 'em hurry up and have some kids."

"That's what I was planning to do."

"After all the time we've been raising goats, we still only have those three."

"That's because they're all males."

"Males are useless!"

"If they were all females, they'd be just as useless."

"I figure we should raise a few more goats, then later swap 'em for a set of carpenter's tools." Ah-ts'ang casually picked a blade of grass from the side of the road.

"Be careful, that grass can cut your finger." The old man quickly returned to the subject at hand: "Do you want a set of carpenter's tools?"

"Um-hm!" the child said. "I can do more than make tables—I know how to make wardrobes, doors, beds, and chests, too."

"That's wonderful!" the old man said delightedly. "I'll go ahead and raise a few more goats so you can exchange them for carpenter's tools."

"When?"

"What's your hurry? Grandpa'll take care of it right away. I'll swap two of our male goats for one female with one of the flat-landers, and we can start."

"You'd better hurry, 'cause I'll be a carpenter pretty soon!"

"That's what I mean!" the old man said, then added lovingly: "But you'll have to put up with anything that comes along for the time being. You know that, don't you?"

"I know. I'll have to be patient."

After they had passed by Heartbreak Woods they could see the bus sign off in the distance at Pitou. They fell silent. When they finally reached flat land the old man said: "Do you get enough to eat?"

". . ."

"Do they beat you?"

". . ."

"What's wrong? Why aren't you saying anything?"

The child lowered his head and fought back the tears.

"Don't cry. Why would anyone cry when he's about to become a carpenter?"

The child shook his head as he wiped away the tears with his hand. "I'm not crying." But he still refused to raise his head.

"Hey, do as Grandpa says and take this sack of sweet potatoes along for your master. Maybe they'll treat you better if you do."

"No!"

"Go ahead and take it." The old man let the sack of sweet potatoes slip down off his shoulder and set it in front of the boy. "But don't forget to bring the sack back."

"I said no! They'd laugh at me!"

"These are the best sweet potatoes anywhere around here!"

The child looked up at the old man with eyes red from crying and shook his head.

"All right then!" the old man said angrily. "I'd rather feed them to the pigs than give them to anyone who would touch a single hair on my grandson's head!"

"Grandpa, why don't you go on back now."

"All right, I'll go back after I've rested here a spell. You hurry on down and wait for your bus."

Before the child had taken more than a few steps he was called to a halt by the old man.

"Are you sure you don't want to take the sweet potatoes?"

"Let's just drop the subject."

"Who knows, they might even buy a fish for you to bring back the next time you come home."

"I told you I'd bring a fish back for you."

"Come over here." The old man took a couple of steps toward the child. "Your grandpa once carried a load of dozens of catties of sweet potatoes to sell in the market. I wanted to buy a fish for you kids to eat. Is the bus coming?"

"Not yet."

"Tell me when it is. You know fish is more expensive than most foods. That day I walked around and around those fish stalls until the fishmongers finally got tired of calling out to me. But I kept walking, trying to make up my mind. You know why?"

"You were going to steal one?"

"Nonsense!" The old man straightened up. "That's something you must never do. I could never do anything like that. I'd rather starve!" Then he bent over again and explained to the child: "I did it because fish was so expensive and the fishmongers are all crooks. If they aren't tampering with the scales, then they're padding the weight. I didn't know how to figure, and I knew if I just asked them how much the fish sold for, they'd reach in to get a fish and weigh it wrapped in a thick wet cord. Keep your eye out for the bus! Tell me when it's coming."

"Not yet."

"So I kept walking around the fish stalls looking the fish over and trying to find an honest face among the peddlers. Finally I stopped at a stall where bonitos were being sold and pointed to one of them. I told the fishmonger to give me an honest weighing and not take advantage of an old man. She told me not to worry, so I bought a three-catty bonito, but when I weighed it at home I found it was a catty and a half light!" The old man knitted his brows tightly. "I should have been able to buy a three-catty bonito with a full load of sweet potatoes . . ."

"The bus is coming! I can hear it."

The old man, having stooped over too long, straightened up with a great deal of difficulty and looked with the child off in the direction where the bus would be coming.

"If you can only hear it, then we've still got time."

"Who knows, maybe it's a Forestry Department truck," the child said excitedly.

"That's even better. Then you could hitch a ride." The old man paused. "Let's see now, where was I?"

"You were saying you should have been able to buy a three-catty bonito with a full load of sweet potatoes."

"So you've been listening to what I've been saying?"

The child nodded.

"They robbed me of my load of sweet potatoes. People like that are crooks, pure and simple. I was so upset I fretted over it for several days. To tell you the truth, even today I won't go near the fish stalls in the marketplace!" He heaved a long sigh. "Ai! It's not easy for us mountainfolk to eat seafood . . ."

"Here comes the bus."

The old man gazed off, bleary-eyed.

"Over there where the big trail of dust is."

"It probably is the bus. Okay, you go ahead now. Grandpa'll stay here and rest a spell."

"I'm going now."

"Ah-ts'ang, now don't forget . . ."

". . . to bring a fish back with me," the child finished the sentence. They both laughed.

"Grandpa, I didn't forget. I brought a fish back with me—a bonito!" Ah-ts'ang said over and over to himself, his happiness tinged with a sense of triumph. As he rode along he envisioned the wide-eyed looks on the faces of his brother and sister when they saw the bonito, and he could almost see the tips of his grandfather's trembling chopsticks as they reached out to pick up a morsel of the fish. "Grandpa, I'll be a carpenter in two more months!"

Clank! "That damned chain!" Ah-ts'ang jumped down off the bike, put the slipped chain back onto the teeth of the sprocket, then turned one of the pedals until the chain was once again engaged. The chain had slipped off the sprocket many times along the way, so he knew he shouldn't ride too fast—but he invariably forgot. This time, after brushing some of the rust and oil off his hands, he discovered to his horror that the fish had fallen off! All that was left hanging on the handlebars was the now-empty taro leaf. He quickly headed back, and a mile or so down the road he found what he was looking for, though now it was only a squashed imprint on the muddy road. The fish had been run over by a truck.

More than two hours later the crestfallen Ah-ts'ang could cry no longer over this freak accident, so he headed back up the mountain. Off in the distance he could see his grandfather sitting in the doorway weaving implements out of green bamboo. Lacking the courage to call out "Grandpa," he just quietly walked up to the old man.

The old man jerked his head up. "Hey! When did you get back?"

"Just now," the boy answered as he walked into the house.

The old man laid the things in his hand down, then rose to follow the boy inside. But between the time he started getting to his feet and the time he finally straightened up, he had plenty of time to ask the boy several questions.

"Ah-ts'ang, did you see our goats by the roadside on your way home?" No answer. "They're over there in the high grass. Your brother and sister are there watching them. I managed it for you— you'll have your set of carpenter's tools any day now."

Ah-ts'ang felt even worse now.

"Ah-ts'ang, did you hear what I said?" the old man asked as he walked into the house. Still no response. "What's wrong with you? You're acting like a bride who hides in the corner the minute she steps into the house." He walked into the bedroom, then into the

toolshed, and finally into the kitchen, where he found Ah-ts'ang
taking big gulps from the water ladle.

"Oh, here you are! Did you bring a fish home?"

Ah-ts'ang continued to drink.

"The weather hasn't been very good the past few days, so there
wouldn't be any fish for sale in the marketplace," the old man said,
knowing full well that the past few days' weather had been excellent. "You can't use our weather here as a gauge—out at sea it's
always changing."

Ah-ts'ang purposely got his face all wet so that his grandfather
wouldn't know that he'd been crying. He raised his wet face and
said: "They're selling fish."

"Well?"

"I bought one—a bonito."

"Where is it?" The old man searched the kitchen with his eyes.

"I dropped it!"

"Dropped it?"

"Dropped it!" Ah-ts'ang didn't dare look the old man in the eye,
so he buried his face in the water ladle again, though he really
didn't want any more water—he couldn't drink another drop.

"How . . . how could that have happened?" The old man was bewildered. The pain he had felt that time when he had been cheated
on the weight of the bonito returned.

But Ah-ts'ang, not comprehending what the old man was feeling,
argued defensively: "I really did! I'm not lying to you. I hung it on
the handlebars of the bike, and it just fell off."

"The bike?"

"That's right. I know how to ride a bike now!" He waited to see if
this made his grandfather happy.

"Where's the bike now?"

"I left it in the care of a shop at the foot of the mountain."

"It fell off the handlebars?" The old man spoke every word slowly
and clearly.

Ah-ts'ang's disappointment was now complete.

"I really did buy a bonito to bring home. A truck ran over it and squashed it on the road."

"Isn't that the same as not even bringing one home?"

"No! I did bring one with me!" he shouted.

"That's right, you did bring one, but you dropped it. Isn't that right?"

Ah-ts'ang was angry that his grandfather had taken such a matter-of-fact attitude.

"I really did bring one with me," the boy said angrily.

"I'm aware of that."

"I'm not lying to you! I am *not* lying to you! I swear!" Ah-ts'ang was crying.

"I know you're not lying to your grandpa. You've never lied to me. It's only that the fish fell on the road," he said in a comforting tone.

"No! You don't believe me! You think I'm lying . . ." Ah-ts'ang's sobs sounded like the lowing of a cow.

"You can bring one home next time. Won't that take care of it?"

"But I already brought one back today!"

"You say you brought a fish with you today, and I believe you, so what are you crying about? You're acting silly."

"But it never got here . . ."

"It fell off and was squashed by a truck, right?"

"No! You don't know! You don't know! You think I'm lying to you . . ."

"Grandpa believes every word you're saying."

"I don't believe you."

"Then what do you want me to say?" Beginning to lose his patience, the old man spread his hands in a helpless gesture.

"I don't want you to believe me, I don't want you to believe me . . . ," Ah-ts'ang shouted as he threw the ladle to the floor, then began to sob again.

The old man, finding himself cornered, started to fume. He reached behind the door to pick up his carrying pole, and began hitting out with it. Ah-ts'ang was struck on the shoulder and quickly darted out of the room, the old man right on his heels.

Ah-ts'ang ran through the tea orchard, followed closely by the old man. He then ran over to the bramble patch and quickly threaded his way in to a depth of five or six feet. From there he hopped down onto the road leading home. The old man stopped at the entrance to the bramble patch. Ah-ts'ang turned around and saw that the old man had stopped, so he did too. There was by then a considerable distance between the two of them.

The old man stood there gasping, one hand waving the carrying pole, the other resting on a bramble bush.

"Don't you dare enter my door again!" he shouted. "If you do, I'll beat you to within an inch of your life!"

Ah-ts'ang responded in the loudest voice he could manage: "I really did bring a fish back!"

It was then approaching evening, and the mountain was very quiet. The old man and the boy were both startled to hear the crisp echo coming to them from the valley:

". . . really did bring a fish back!"

The Drowning of an Old Cat

· · · · ·

1. The Lay of the Land

The out-of-the-way county in this story has been designated by the Taiwan provincial government as a developing area. Its urban center is a small town of forty or fifty thousand people. When the town youth are in the presence of people from the outlying countryside, they habitually put on airs of self-importance to show that they are urbanites; the somewhat older people, with their greater understanding of humility, will go no further than to nod their heads with slightly superior smiles on their faces. People from the countryside cheerfully and loudly tell anyone within earshot stories of their daughters who have married men from town. And even though the ears of the listeners ring with this barrage of talk, they feel it only proper, for were they to have an eligible young daughter, she too would leave the farm and marry a townsman (so they think). Even greater glory comes to someone whose son brings a townswoman back to the farm as his wife, for no matter how their lives together turn out in the end, at least in the beginning there is a great deal of loud, enthusiastic talk.

This urban center is only about seventy or eighty kilometers from the nearest big city, and transportation to and from the city—by train or by car—is extremely convenient. The roads are well traveled every day, for a round trip takes no more than four hours; a person can go to the city, take care of his business, and return home all in the same day. As a result, many big-city fads find their way to this urban center. Miniskirts that come to a point twenty centimeters above the knee are displayed on girls of the town, and go-go dancing is very popular at the parties held by the town's youth. As for their elders, the fear of death has become a fashionable trend, with an emphasis on the beneficial effects self-awareness has on one's health.

Someone had recently discovered a number of young children swimming in a spring in the village of Clear Spring, and before long, men with expanding pot bellies and respectable positions in society got up at the crack of dawn and drove over to Clear Spring Village to soak themselves in the spring. Later, when they discovered that they were able to take in their belts one hole after another, their numbers increased. They were so diligent about coming that not even inclement weather stopped them. After a while, in addition to soaking in the water, they were all able to propel themselves a bit through the water, more or less in the fashion of swimming. Among them were physicians, senior bank officials, lawyers, school principals, assemblymen, businessmen, and many others. Nearly every member of the local Rotary Club participated, except for David and Tom, one of whom had an artificial leg, the other a case of congenital rickets.

Clear Spring Village had gotten its name from a spring the size of two parcels of land that was in the middle of the village and was under the jurisdiction of the local Water Control Board. Actually, if one were to dig a hole three to four or perhaps five to six feet deep anywhere in Clear Spring Village, a bubbling spring of sweet water would rise to the surface in a continuous flow.

The sixty or more households who live here are as pure and simple as the spring water that flows to the surface; there is little difference between them and the unbroken gush of spring water as they diligently till the more than forty parcels of land they own, plus the side of Ku-tzu Hill. There has never been a drought over the farmland here, yet for many years the place has been an impoverished area, which is the prime reason for the people's pure and simple nature. Though no more than two and a half kilometers separate them from the urban center, since the road to town crosses the hill and is fairly steep, and since there is no busline between the two places, the townspeople feel that Clear Spring Village is a great distance away.

2. The Sky is Falling

In the year when the Temple of the Patriarch was erected, a banyan tree had been planted beside it; now that more than sixty years had passed, fully half of the more than four thousand square feet of temple ground lay in the shade of this banyan tree. On the portion of the red-tiled temple roof that stood under the shade day in and day out, year after year, a carpet of deep green moss and grass flourished, while on the other half the aged red tiles were in full, sunlit view. For this reason the people referred to the Clear Spring Village Temple of the Patriarch as the Yin-Yang Temple, or the Temple of Dark and Light. This long process of change was mirrored in Uncle Ah-sheng and four or five other old-timers who lived in the village, as they had grown old watching the gradual change take place. In earlier days they had hitched rides on the back of the oxcart that carried bricks used to build the temple, getting an occasional taste of the carter's whip. Now they were the oldest people in the village, and on every temple festival the duties and activities of the villagers were under the direction of these few men, led by Uncle Ah-sheng.

But temple festivals only came around a few times a year, and during the remaining long days these old-timers congregated in one of the temple's siderooms. In the winter they secured the door, each of them carrying a small heater to keep himself warm; in the summertime they swung the door open and availed themselves of the cool breezes that passed through the sideroom and carried up to the heavens the fragrant smoke of incense from the black joss sticks that symbolized the people's devotion. For the most part these men talked of the past, and even though their talk was very repetitious, they never tired of it. With great fondness they recalled those early days when they had struggled with poverty. Memories of the past are always fond ones, and this was especially true for these men in their twilight years for whom only their pasts gave them feelings of pride. For them tomorrow was a big question mark; who could say that tomorrow would not be the day they stopped coming to the temple? This was evident in that last year there had been seven or eight of them, and now, a mere year later, their number had been cut almost in half.

The stone block just inside the door pillar to the left had originally been Uncle T'ien-sung's seat, but it had lost its source of warmth and now just stood there in icy coldness. After T'ien-sung had departed, Uncle Huo-shu selected this seat for his own and sat on it for a single day. That night T'ien-sung appeared at the head of Huo-shu's bed in a dream, angrily demanding the return of his stone-block seat. From that day on, Uncle Huo-shu was bothered by a case of hemorrhoids, until everyone in the village knew about the incident. His hemorrhoids eventually became extremely painful; he took dozens of medications and applied dozens of ointments, but even the generations-old nostrum of the K'un-t'ien family had no effect. Finally he heeded the advice of several old friends and dragged his half-dead body over to T'ien-sung's spirit tablet, where he burned incense and offered his apologies. Uncle Ah-sheng, in his role as eldest among them, stood in front of the spirit tablet and upbraided T'ien-sung: "T'ien-sung, when you were alive you were open-minded, so why have you become such a short-tempered ghost? You and I and Huo-shu and the others are old friends who grew up together in Clear Spring Village from the time we were all wearing pants with split crotches. Now, just because he sat on your stone block, your meanness has brought him to death's doorstep. The fact of the matter is, that stone block doesn't belong to you. Since it's inside the temple, it belongs to the Patriarch . . ." At first many of the startled villagers present paled when they heard this, for it was as though Uncle T'ien-sung were actually there among them accepting Uncle Huo-shu's apologies and being scolded by Uncle Ah-sheng.

Strange as it sounds, within a week Uncle Huo-shu's hemorrhoids inexplicably disappeared. But then two months later he simply up and died. Naturally no one else ever again dared to sit on the stone block, and in the minds of the Clear Spring villagers this stone block had already been given a special name as a warning—hemorrhoid stone.

Only when he had an important matter that required his attention would one of these old-timers willingly miss passing the time of day with the others in the temple sideroom. Their number had diminished to four or five, and when they talked among themselves, no explanation of what was being said was ever needed. Their interests and topics of conversation were entirely compatible. And so, coming to the temple to chat right after lunchtime had become a big part of their lives.

On this particular afternoon, Uncle Cow's Eye, Uncle Earthworm, Uncle Yü-tsai, and Uncle Ah-ch'uan were all there; only Uncle Ah-sheng had not yet arrived. Usually he was the first on the scene, and even if he had to be late, one would think that by three o'clock at least he would have shown up. The others were soon so worried and uncomfortable that they were unable to talk about anything for more than a few moments.

"I hope nothing's happened to him," someone said uneasily.

"I saw him leading his ox out to Grass Canal to graze this morning."

"How could that be? I took my own ox out to Grass Canal this morning and I didn't see him there. But I did see you walking along the canal down to the end."

"Oh, right! That wasn't this morning, it was yesterday," the old-timer said, quickly acknowledging his forgetfulness.

"Could he be sick?"

"I don't think so. He was just fine yesterday. This morning when I was out at Grass Canal with my ox I ran into his eldest daughter-in-law with an armful of clothes she was taking out to wash. She would have told me if he was sick." He paused, then added: "But she didn't say a word, so there can't be anything wrong."

"Well, that's strange! He couldn't have just disappeared, could he?" A momentary smile appeared on Cow's Eye's face, but then faded away as a brief silence fell over the group of men.

"Oh shit, that's right!" Earthworm suddenly blurted out. "Didn't he say just the day before yesterday that he was going into town to find a divinator to select the right date to rebuild his stove? He said that the firewood burned too hot."

"Ah-ha, now I remember!" Ah-ch'uan's lips parted momentarily into a broad grin before he continued: "This old noggin of mine's like a stone in the field—it oughta be thrown away. This morning I bumped into him by the well just as he was setting out for town."

"Well I'll be damned! Is that the truth?"

"You said it—just another stone in the field!" Uncle Yü-tsai cursed him, half in jest.

"Still, if he went to town to select a date he should have gotten back by now!"

"Do you think he might have dropped dead on some whorehouse bed?" Earthworm asked with growing interest.

"Shit! That'd be the way to go—the old fart."

"You're not so young yourself."

"That's right! I'm saying we're all old farts—right?"

Without Uncle Ah-sheng in their midst it was as though they were missing their leavening agent, so their conversation never really got started. Most of what they had talked about in the past had been subjects he had introduced. As the day grew later they all dozed off in the refreshing cool breeze.

On the magnificent tree that stood near the west sideroom—that large banyan tree—the ripe figs were bright purple, since it was just in the fruit-bearing month of June; the slightest bump sent them falling, splattering as they hit the ground. Beneath the tree there was already a blanket of crushed figs that gave off a sickly sweet, slightly acrid but generally pleasant aroma. A group of lively

birds was hopping from branch to branch singing songs that
sounded like delicate fingers flowing across piano keys in a musical
run. The ripe fruit beat out a rhythmical background as it fell to the
ground—*splat, splat*. The twin six-year-old grandsons whom Earthworm had brought along with him each sat astride one of the stone
lions at the temple entrance, both of them fast asleep, their arms
draped tightly around the lions' necks.

Uncle Ah-sheng was hurrying home from town. His heart felt as
though it were burning a hole in his chest, and the faster he tried
to make the return trip to Clear Spring, the longer the road seemed,
as though there were something deliberately delaying his return.
He grumbled to himself along the way: "Won't this be the end of
Clear Spring? I won't let them get away with this, I absolutely
won't allow it! I'll hurry home and tell the others." He went down
the road as fast as he could; after K'un-ch'ih's farm came Mute's
farm, followed by Red Turtle's farm. After Red Turtle's farm there
was Dragon-Eye Well and Clear Spring's public school. When
Uncle Ah-sheng drew up alongside Dragon-Eye, the village's natural spring well, after having made a point of cutting across to take
a look at the well and the area surrounding it, he muttered angrily
to himself: "If we let the people in town get away with this, it'll be
the end of Clear Spring's geography. What a mean, vicious thing
to do! This is a matter as great as heaven and earth itself, and
they've made up their minds just like that! Damn!" He quickly
turned on his heel and ran to the temple.

The moment Uncle Ah-sheng strode into the western sideroom
of the Temple of the Patriarch he shouted at the top of his lungs:
"Hey! Let's see how long the Demon of Sleep can keep you in his
power!"

The men were startled to their senses by this unexpected and
unusual shout. Then when they saw his appearance they knew that
something important and inauspicious was in the air; otherwise,
that red birthmark on the side of his face would surely not have
lost color like that. A quick glance showed that he was so winded

that his nostrils could not handle his breathing, and his parted lips were trembling wildly.

"Why the hell do you have to yell so loud?" Earthworm said angrily after having been frightened awake. But when he saw that Ah-sheng's expression was different than usual, he changed his tone to say with growing interest: "We thought you'd wound up in the whorehouse on the other side of town and decided not to come back." He wiped the saliva that had run down the side of his mouth while he was asleep.

"What took you so long?" Ah-ch'uan asked.

Ah-sheng suddenly spread himself out in a bamboo chair, but the moment his back touched the back of the chair he sprang up into a sitting position and said: "We simply cannot allow them to do this—it'll be the end of our Clear Spring." This time he spread open his arms and lay all the way back in the chair, giving the impression of one who had expended his last bit of energy in uttering these few words.

The others just looked at one another until Earthworm said anxiously: "What's going on with you, old man? Since you've brought home some bad news, you'll have to make things clear to us if you want us to share your concern! Isn't that right? All you did was say two words—'the end!'—then just stretched out there. What's happened?"

The several pairs of eyes that had been riveted on Earthworm shifted over to Uncle Ah-sheng, who breathed a long sigh.

"The people in town want to come out and dig up Clear Spring's Dragon-Eye." Everyone froze when they heard this.

"What does that mean?"

"It means that those people who come here every day to swim in our spring have scraped up three hundred thousand dollars to build a swimming pool next to our village well." Ah-sheng looked at the others, who had been stunned just a moment before, only to observe that his revelation had produced no effect at all. Quickly growing irritated, he said: "What's this! Aren't any of you concerned?"

"What's wrong with having a swimming pool?" Ah-ch'uan asked.

"What *isn't* wrong with having a swimming pool? First, it'll ruin our geography here. Have you forgotten that the only reason this Clear Spring of ours is such a terrific place is because we've got Dragon-Eye Well? My grandfather told me so when I was just a boy."

"Sure, everyone knows that. But what difference will it make if they build a swimming pool alongside the well?"

"You see what I'm saying! Cow's Eye, you've got no reason to be angry when people laugh at you for being a fool. Just think! They'll have to draw water for that swimming pool from the well by motor, and if they draw it dry, what are we gonna do with a dried-up well? Won't that be the end of Clear Spring?"

They all looked at one another and nodded their heads.

"That's right," Cow's Eye said. "This is a serious matter."

"Have you all forgotten that year when the big typhoon hit and somebody threw a bale of straw down the well? Don't you remember how the eyes of everyone in the village, young and old, began to hurt as a result? Luckily that time it was only some straw. If it had been balls of thorns* probably everybody in Clear Spring would have dropped dead!" Observing that looks of distress were beginning to show on their faces, Ah-sheng began to experience the grim satisfaction he had expected. "You see what I'm saying." Ah-sheng had a habit of prefacing his remarks with this phrase or uttering it whenever he was about to make a positive concluding remark. "How'll we ever be able to put up with a motor in Dragon-Eye?"

"Are you telling us the truth?" Ah-sheng was the focus of attention. As they became convinced that he was telling the absolute truth, a mood of grim concern began to settle upon them. Still they were hoping desperately that the answer might be negative, and it was this hope that had prompted Uncle Earthworm's question.

---

*Steel barbs formed in the shape of a ball and used in Taiwanese temples.

At this stage Ah-sheng grew decidedly more relaxed, sensing that the heavy burden this news had placed on him was starting to be shared by the others. "Some time ago—just when, I'm not sure," he said, "they tested some of our water and concluded that it was special. The fools! Of course the water from Clear Spring's Dragon-Eye Well is good. We didn't need any stupid tests to tell us that! But just because the water's good doesn't mean they can come and dig a swimming pool!"

"Then we're going to have to fight this all the way," Uncle Yü-tsai said, so greatly aroused that he sprayed saliva onto the others' faces.

Cow's Eye, unflappable as ever, gently wiped the spit off his face and said: "Well, of course we will. We won't stand for this!"

Uncle Yü-tsai also reached up and wiped his face.

"And there's another reason. Rest assured that if the pool opens, the people who come from town to go swimming will be mixing with each other, wearing almost nothing. Who knows what'll be going through their minds? Here in Clear Spring we've always been simple, decent folk, but this could bring ruin to our sons and daughters and corrupt the entire village!"

Ah-sheng noticed the others nodding their heads in silence, so he added: "You see what I'm saying, we've got every reason to fight this."

Just then Ah-ch'uan, in whose heart anger had been building, gave yet another reason: "Not only that, it wouldn't be right to let Dragon-Eye see all those girls and boys with their indecent clothing. The dragon's whole body would grow restless."

"That's right! So now we have three good reasons. Let's think now, are there any more?"

Earthworm jumped angrily to his feet: "What other reasons do we need? With these three it's the same as saying the sky is falling!"

Just then one of his grandsons fell off the stone lion and began to cry. The timing of the tail-end of Earthworm's comment—"the sky is falling!"—made it seem like a reaction to seeing his grandson fall to the ground.

3. *The Fundamental Knowledge In Democracy**

Never before had these few old-timers attended one of the village meetings, but on this particular evening they arrived very early at the makeshift meeting grounds at Village Chief Hsieh's grain-drying yard and seated themselves on front-row benches. Everyone in the village knew that they had been waiting impatiently for this evening's meeting, and in fact were anxiously waiting to see whether their opposition to the construction of a swimming pool next to Dragon-Eye Well would have an effect. Consequently, those who came to the meeting were much more enthusiastic than usual. Some families were even represented by several members.

The people responsible for conducting and witnessing the village meeting had still not arrived by the time the meeting site was crowded with villagers; from Village Chief Hsieh's house came the sounds of a local opera on his radio, which had been turned up full blast. Normally so little significance was placed on such meetings by the people who had gathered there this evening that if each household hadn't been required to send a representative to stamp the attendance sheet with a personal seal at the beginning and end of each meeting as proof of attendance, no one would ever show up. It was normally the children who took the heads of household's seals to the meeting, where they simply played the whole time. This satisfied the adults as well as the children, who earned fifty cents for their efforts. But this time it was different. Everyone felt that the meeting was absolutely necessary to solve this problem of theirs, one that had been rapidly growing more pressing each day. Everyone in attendance was emotionally stirred up to the point that the slightest additional stimulus might just turn them into a mob.

---

*A book dealing with the procedure of parliamentary rule, written by Dr. Sun Yat-sen.

Uncle Ah-sheng and the others turned their heads back repeatedly to look at their fellow villagers who were crowding in behind them; their smiles showed that they were pleased by what they saw. Never before had these few men felt as secure as they did on this evening, for at this moment at least, all their fellow villagers were standing beside them in support. The feeling of superiority they had could be likened to someone on a battlefield fearlessly facing the enemy and shouting: "Come on ahead, damn you! Anyone who turns and flees is a son of a bitch!"

Cow's Eye turned to his cronies and said: "Hey, let's not let these youngsters think that we're all over the hill. Tonight we old-timers can give them a real show." The others nodded their heads simultaneously, determined to do just that.

After the village secretary had raised the flag, he disappeared, following which the village chief also vanished. The meeting had originally been scheduled for seven-thirty, and although it was already more than twenty minutes late, you couldn't have told it from the people's faces, for they were all listening with keen interest to the Taiwanese opera radio program. Suddenly, just before eight o'clock, someone turned off the radio, bringing the crowd up short. The village secretary and village chief emerged from the front door of the house, panting as though they had been running. As someone in the crowd yelled that it was time to start the meeting, the village chief got up onto a crate and announced with a slight stammer that it would begin in a moment. He asked everyone to quiet down.

The village secretary kept glancing down the road, and when he finally spotted some figures walking toward them he shouted excitedly: "Here they come! Here they come!" All the villagers turned their attention to the road. Some even stood up, throwing a momentary fright into the approaching people, who stopped in their tracks, surveyed the situation, then slowly began to approach the meeting site. The village chief quickly jumped down from the crate, went over and shook hands all around, then led the people over to the speaker's area.

To the crowd's surprise, even the district chief had shown up, but what made them feel that something highly unusual was afoot was that Constable Liu had brought five unfamiliar policemen with him. As usual, there was a smile on the constable's face, but there were disagreeable looks on the faces of the five policemen. There were in addition three members of the gentry, who wore Western suits and carried paper fans, all nearly identical. It became clear after they were introduced by the village chief that they were special invited guests.

It was eight-thirty by the time the official party was seated; everything this evening was extraordinary, for under normal circumstances the officials were the ones who waited for the villagers to arrive. The village secretary kept his eye on the three gentlemen, and when he saw the fat one nod his head he yelled out at the top of his lungs: "The village meeting will come to order!"

Before the secretary had even requested the chairman to take charge of the meeting, Earthworm nudged Uncle Ah-sheng to get up and have his say. So Uncle Ah-sheng stood up and began to speak in a loud voice: "I have something to say . . ."

Wanting to preserve the decorum of the meeting, the village secretary ignored Uncle Ah-sheng's remark and continued with his parliamentary command in an even louder voice: "The chairman will please take charge!"

When Uncle Ah-sheng saw that he was being ignored by everyone on the platform, he called the village chief by his nickname: "Hey! Gander K'un-tsai, before we begin the meeting, I want you to know that I've got something to say tonight."

Several people began to laugh despite themselves and even the five policemen with tightly set faces smiled briefly. Village Chief Hsieh Ah-k'un turned to look down from the platform at Ah-sheng, giving him an angry and exasperated stare. But Ah-sheng thought that this constituted an unjust rebuke by the village chief, so he continued: "I really do, damn it! I already told you I did!" This elicited another outburst of laughter.

The village secretary quickly walked over and put his mouth up to Ah-sheng's ear; upon being told that the right ear was no good and that he would have to speak into the left one, he whispered to Ah-sheng: "Don't you know that fat guy is a big shot? You shouldn't try to break up the meeting with a lot of funny remarks."

This sort of threat greatly displeased Ah-sheng, so he shouted: "What's this? You call it breaking up the meeting just because I want to say something?"

In obvious embarrassment, the village secretary whispered again into his ear, this time saying very politely: "You've got us all wrong. We want you to talk in a moment, but we're not ready for you yet. I'll tell you when your time comes."

Ah-sheng nodded, but added loudly: "How was I supposed to know it wasn't time to talk yet?" Then he gave Earthworm a jab: "Damn you, it's all your fault 'cause you told me to stand up and talk."

"How was I supposed to know?" Earthworm answered in an equally loud voice.

An argument nearly broke out between the two of them, but the village secretary stepped in quickly to calm them down: "Okay, okay now. Whatever it is you have to say, I'll let you have your turn in a little while."

The whole episode produced a good deal of laughter among the villagers, and each time his actions drew laughter from the crowd, Uncle Ah-sheng turned around to survey the laughing faces to see if the people were still standing by him. Evidently he was encouraged by what he saw, as anyone could tell by his rustic, somewhat foolish manner.

The village chief opened the meeting with a speech in Mandarin that left our old-timers feeling terribly dissatisfied, simply because they didn't understand a word he said. Next the three gentlemen came up and gave speeches, though in the eyes of the oldsters it was nothing more than an unbearable series of gestures. The same thing happened with the district chief and the village chief, and finally even the constable got up and said a few words. Ah-sheng figured he'd have to wait until each of the five policemen had his say before his own turn finally rolled around, so he turned to Earthworm and said in a grudging voice: "Shit! We might sit here until our backs are hunched before our turn to talk comes."

But before too long, just prior to inviting Uncle Ah-sheng up to speak, the village chief recapped in Taiwanese what had been said. He explained that the chief representative had described in detail how all sides concerned had enthusiastically promoted the construction of a swimming pool alongside the well in the interest of developing Clear Spring, and how he hoped that the local people would synchronize their efforts to realize this goal. After the swimming pool was completed, there would be vehicular traffic, the local school would gain independence, and Clear Spring Village would soon prosper. As he finished his announcement, not a single villager below the platform applauded, but when Ah-sheng eventually stood up, he was greeted by a burst of enthusiastic applause. He turned to look at the villagers, then faced the platform and clearly voiced his opinions in a challenging tone:

"I would like you to go back and tell the people in town that Uncle Ah-sheng of Clear Spring says that if they want to go swimming to please go home and take a dip in their bathtubs!"

Not only did this provocative statement produce an outburst of laughter and an almost deafening round of applause, even Uncle Ah-sheng himself was at a loss to understand just where his inspiration had come from. He continued: "Don't be fooled into thinking that Clear Spring is the place for you to build your swimming pool —the water in Clear Spring is for our use in the rice fields, not for you townspeople to take baths in!" The waves of applause increased the pitch of excitement in the old man's words: "The people of Clear Spring have no use for your 'vehicular traffic'—all anyone needs is two good legs. We're concerned only about our fields and our water. As for the lay of the land, Clear Spring is a dragon's head. The village exit leading to town is the mouth of the dragon, and the well beside the school is the eye, which is why we call it Dragon-Eye Well. Ever since the time of our ancestors, the people of Clear Spring have been protected by this dragon, which is why we've been able to live our lives in peace. Now suddenly someone wants to bring harm to our dragon's eye, and the people of Clear Spring are not going to just stand by and let that happen." He turned around. "Isn't that right?" he asked the crowd. They all jumped eagerly to their feet. The people sitting on the platform were shocked by Uncle Ah-sheng's ability to incite the crowd.

Cow's Eye leaned over to Uncle Ah-sheng: "Say, old pal, has the revered Patriarch adopted you as his spokesman?"

"I don't know," Uncle Ah-sheng answered him. "Somehow everything seems as clear as a bell to me."

After the meeting ended, Uncle Ah-sheng was invited by the village chief to his house, where he met several of the special guests in the reception room. The village secretary interpreted what they were saying for his benefit. The chief representative said to Uncle Ah-sheng respectfully: "Old uncle, I sure admire your ability to speak."

"You flatter me. I've never been to school and can't even write the simplest character."

"To be able to speak like that without ever having been to school is even more amazing."

"Don't talk like that. You're embarrassing me," Uncle Ah-sheng said. "I've heard people quote some of the things the master Confucius said, and that's more than enough for my use."

The chief representative then exchanged some words with the people around him, which Uncle Ah-sheng asked the village secretary to interpret for him.

"He's commenting on your speaking ability."

"There's no need for that kind of talk. I'm only being reasonable, taking the truth as I see it and speaking as honestly as I know how. The more you speak common sense, the clearer everything becomes. The truth can stand any test, or as they say, 'true gold fears no fire.' Isn't that right?"

"Old uncle, I want to ask you something, and I hope you'll answer me honestly. Just what is it that makes you so brave, and why do you oppose this matter so strongly? Is someone in the background goading you into doing this?"

"No!" Ah-sheng was angry.

"Then why are you so set against it?"

Uncle Ah-sheng responded without a moment's hesitation, and with considerable pride: "Because I love this piece of land and everything on it."

4. The First Round

On the very day that the Reliable Construction Company erected its sign over the twenty-five-by-fifty-meter swimming-pool site in Clear Spring Village, they ran into trouble, for they were unable to find a single temporary laborer anywhere in the village to dig the hole. On the second day they hired fifty laborers from elsewhere to come and carry off the dirt from the hole.

Uncle Ah-sheng and the others spent the whole of every day at the work site obstructing the construction company workers, until finally the police had to step in and warn them that they were breaking the law. This greatly upset Uncle Ah-sheng. He could not understand why others received the protection of the law for coming and interfering with his and the others' actions, while the righteousness of his behavior was considered illegal.

The old-timers split up, each recruiting a group of men who returned to the construction site with poles and knives. When the laborers saw this turn of events they threw down their carrying poles and baskets and fled from the work site. The group of men Uncle Ah-sheng had brought with him then piled up all the abandoned tools, set a torch to them, and watched them burn. As the flames burned fiercely, the men gathered around the bonfire, the thrill of victory instilling them with a feeling of freshly gained glory. Before long a circle of village women and children formed around them, their admiration causing the men to experience a heroic dignity that showed on their faces.

From the midst of the crowd came some loudly voiced comments by Uncle Ah-sheng: "Since they've fled, well and good. That way they can keep their scrawny hides. We've given them a taste of what the people of Clear Spring can do, now let's see if they dare to come back after this and move even a blade of our grass!"

Just then they heard shouts off in the distance: "Here they come! Here they come!" And before they knew what was happening, a fire engine carrying a dozen or so armed policemen had arrived in their midst. The policemen jumped down from the truck and quickly penetrated into the heart of the crowd, after which they turned and began forcing the people back, scattering them before them. The farmers were disarmed and herded one by one into the fire engine. The whole procedure was carried out with the precision of a military exercise.

After Uncle Ah-sheng got into the fire engine voluntarily, the whole lot of them were delivered to the town's station house. Several of the armed policemen stayed behind to calm down the remaining villagers and smilingly urged everyone to quietly return home.

The village and district chiefs ran from place to place over this incident; the construction company officials said they wanted assurances that this sort of thing wouldn't happen again and guarantees for the safety of the laborers at the work site before they would be willing to work out a settlement.

Late that evening the word came down to release the men, each of whose tightly drawn face showed the effects of the scare he had been given.

The apprehensive mood they were in remained with them even after they had returned to Clear Spring, and their minds were still on the written depositions and fingerprints they had left behind at the station house. They wondered what kind of trouble this might mean for them later on. This somewhat terrifying consideration hit them even harder when they reached home and looked into the faces of their family members. Regret set in, and no matter what thought of Dragon-Eye or, for that matter, of the entire village of Clear Spring came to them, they were powerless to muster the slightest feeling of resistance. In fact, some even lacked the will to resist that was normally hidden in their subconscious.

When they thought of the incident they couldn't imagine how they had gotten so stirred up; all Uncle Ah-sheng had done was sound the call and everyone had joined the charge like a swarm of bees. They could not know how proud Uncle Ah-sheng was that they had dared to throw out their chests and come forth on behalf of Clear Spring.

Although Uncle Ah-sheng had been declared the ringleader of the mob and was kept overnight at the station house, the reassurance he felt in his heart gave him the appearance of a religious soul completely at peace with himself. From the moment he had allowed his actions to be dictated by his ardent love for Clear Spring, he sensed that he had changed somehow, and he no longer considered himself a man devoid of purpose. In fact, this matter had taken on a greater importance than his own life. If he didn't do it, who would? It was as though a kind of faith had attached itself to his body and had thus become personified; somehow others too had the feeling that he was enveloped by a layer of something that shielded him from outside forces. The rustic airs that had always been with him began to fall away, and the gap between him and other people grew to vast proportions. This feeling was shared both by those who knew Uncle Ah-sheng well and by others who had at one time or another had a serious chat with him. But Uncle Ah-sheng was aware only that he spoke altogether differently than before. He was amazed by almost every sentence he uttered. For example, when someone who was sent specifically to change his mind asked what was so good about the water of Clear Spring, a mystical look came to Uncle Ah-sheng's eyes as he said, as if he were in a completely different world: "If you can speak to fish, then you ask that question of the fish in Clear Spring. Otherwise, just take a look at how happy they are and you will get the answer you seek. And it won't be your Uncle Ah-sheng who gave it to you."

The people around Uncle Ah-sheng were just as confused by all of this as he was; the sensitivity with which he felt the changes in himself gradually diminished. The extraordinary mystery of faithful devotion to a belief can cause a man to approach godlike sublimity. This was probably the case with Uncle Ah-sheng—he had already begun the process leading to that plateau where man and God exist together as an apostle.

In the middle of the night Uncle Ah-sheng was taken to a larger room, and the moment he entered he spotted the honored guest from the village meeting of the previous night—the fat man who had been sitting in the middle. Everyone was very polite to Uncle Ah-sheng, inviting him to sit in a rattan chair in front of a table, pouring him a cup of tea, and offering him a cigarette. They wanted to take down his statement, but before they began, the fat man explained to Uncle Ah-sheng that he was not being detained by the police, that they only wanted the "elderly gentleman" to cool down. As far as they were concerned, the whole incident had started out as a simple matter, even though inciting the superstitious masses and nearly turning the whole thing into a violent affair was something the law could not tolerate. But since the "elderly gentleman's" motives were pure, they were willing to turn a major affair into a minor one, and a minor affair into none at all, with the hope that the "elderly gentleman" would go home and enjoy his grandchildren. Uncle Ah-sheng thanked them unenthusiastically and began to answer their questions for the written statement.

"What's your name?"

"Hsü Ah-sheng."

"How old are you?"

"I'm seventy-nine, not counting intercalary years, and I won't live many more."

The others laughed at this comment, and one of them said: "Then you ought to take it easy and enjoy your twilight years. Why bother yourself with matters that don't concern you?"

Uncle Ah-sheng answered him in a very relaxed manner: "For the simple reason that I won't be around too many more years, and if I don't concern myself with such matters now, I won't have the chance to do it later." He suddenly turned very serious as he continued: "Whether a matter concerns a person or not depends on your point of view. And I . . . I don't agree with you."

The man who was taking down the deposition responded nervously: "Why do you oppose the construction of a swimming pool in Clear Spring?"

Uncle Ah-sheng gave the three major reasons, embellishing upon them quite a bit.

"Then why did you organize such a big crowd to disturb the peace?"

"I could hear Clear Spring moaning with each bit of earth those people's hoes took out of her to build the swimming pool, and since I didn't have the power to come to her rescue alone, I had to gather the villagers of Clear Spring around me to stop what was happening."

"Do you realize what sort of criminal act this constitutes?"

"What does that have to do with the geography of our village?"

"I wish you'd just answer my questions. I'll ask you one more time. Do you realize what sort of criminal act this constitutes?"

"No, I don't."

" . . . "

" . . . "

Uncle Ah-sheng was still full of vigor as dawn broke in the morning and they quietly sent him back to Clear Spring by jeep.

5. Old Master Chen's Grandson

The construction work proceeded apace, as Uncle Ah-sheng had by now lost the active support of his fellow villagers. His isolation and worries had aged him considerably, and even though his family had tricked him into leaving Clear Spring for Taipei to visit some relatives, owing to his unfamiliarity with flush toilets and a mental block against using them, that night he returned to Clear Spring with a growing pressure in his gut. He entered his home without saying a word and headed straight for the outhouse located in the pigsty.

Several of his old friends had grown very passive over this whole matter, and as he witnessed the work on the swimming pool moving along day by day, he knew that somehow he would have to stop it soon, for even if he managed to stop the work after all the earth had been scooped out, the refilling of the hole alone would be a taxing job. He thought things over, deciding that rather than trying to interfere directly at the work site, he would use the more indirect method of enlisting the aid of a friend. If only he could find someone with some real clout, that would solve all his problems.

But considering Uncle Ah-sheng's circumstances, there could not possibly be any bigwigs with whom he had a personal friendship. Then in the midst of his dilemma, he suddenly thought of County Chief Chen. He could still vividly recall how County Chief Chen had come to Clear Spring during the election campaign, sweating profusely, and had pumped his hand enthusiastically, begging over and over again for his support. He had promised that if he was elected, Ah-sheng could come to him any time with his problems.

One of County Chief Chen's campaign workers had told Uncle Ah-sheng that people who voted for County Chief Chen were folks with insight, for Chen was not a man to make empty promises. So not only did Uncle Ah-sheng vote for Chen, he also urged others to do the same. At the time, he had been genuinely moved that the owner of that plump, delicate hand had been willing to let it be shaken by his coarse, rustic one.

"That's it!" he thought. "Why not go to see County Chief Chen? He once promised me that I could bring him any problems I had. During the Manchu dynasty County Chief Chen's grandfather was known as Old Master Chen, and my grandfather was one of his tenant farmers. In the old days, whenever the provincial governor came to recruit soldiers and collect taxes, my grandfather and my father always volunteered their services as provisional soldiers. All I have to do is go see County Chief Chen and tell him that our family used to be his family's tenant farmers, then he'll be obliged to help." This thought brought a new flicker of hope to Uncle Ah-sheng.

Early the next day he changed into a set of clean clothes and went into town to the county office to look up County Chief Chen.

Only after going to several offices did he finally manage to present himself at the outer office of the county chief, and after surveying the stylish surroundings, he inwardly felt very pleased. The county chief must certainly be a big shot: his office was so hard to find, and was such a solemn place, that he must oversee a lot of people. As long as he gave his approval, anything was possible.

The secretary informed him that since the county chief was in a meeting inside, he should return in the afternoon, but he told her he was willing to wait until the meeting was over; in fact, he was happy to wait, for in his estimation, the harder a person was to see, the greater his stature.

When he finally got in to see the county chief, he gave a deep bow, which, however, was not returned. When the girl had told him in the outer office that he could have no more than ten minutes of the county chief's time, he had experienced some feelings of apprehension. Where should he begin if he hoped to make this matter clear to the county chief in ten minutes' time?

He thought it best to first make the county chief aware of their relationship, so after the county chief asked him to take a seat, he began by saying: "My family, the Hsü's, used to be tenant farmers of Great Master Chen's." He cast a hopeful glance at the county chief's face to see if there was an expression of appreciation, but he merely heard him give a grunt and saw him lower his head to leaf through a tall stack of red-lined official documents. Uncle Ah-sheng lapsed into silence, but the county chief raised his head and urged him to continue with what he had come to say. Yet all the time Uncle Ah-sheng was talking, the county chief's head was buried in the stack of official documents, as he mechanically affixed his seal to one after the other. It was apparent that he didn't even have to read them—there were so many that it took all of his time just to affix his seal on each one.

After Uncle Ah-sheng had mentioned all the important points and was awaiting a reply, the county chief was still hurriedly stamping the documents. As for the matter at hand, the county chief felt that it was a dispute involving land and developers, so he pondered over which agency he should assign to settle the matter —the social services administration, the civil administration, or the construction bureau.

While he was still giving the matter some thought, he rang for his secretary, who then led Uncle Ah-sheng over to the construction bureau.

As things turned out, Uncle Ah-sheng was the butt of a number of jokes in the construction bureau before finally being turned down; since there was no place else he could go, he returned wearily to Clear Spring, his original impression of County Chief Chen now completely shattered.

On the road home, he reflected on what had happened, cursing inwardly: "Damn! So that's Old Master Chen's grandson! Old Master Chen would certainly weep if he knew this."

6.   A Cat Is Not a Dog

After Uncle Ah-sheng lost the support of his fellow villagers, he found he was no longer able to translate his beliefs into action. He gradually lost that religious aura that had surrounded him at the beginning, so that on the day when the swimming pool was completed, he had completely reverted back to his old rustic self.

A great many people were gathered outside the chain fence around the swimming pool watching the splashing and hilarity inside. Many of the local children ran home, raising a big fuss until they were given a dollar to go swimming. Young people who should have been out working in the fields had put their hoes aside and were staring, as though mesmerized, at the bras and short red pants of the swimsuits, their desires aroused. Seeing all of this, Uncle Ah-sheng was greatly troubled. He paced back and forth outside the pool enclosure agonizingly stewing in his own juices. Finally he rushed crazily into the pool area and shouted at the top of his lungs: "If you're gonna take your clothes off, why don't you just go all the way, like this?" With that he stripped right in front of everyone. The young girls were so shocked they scrambled out of the pool shrieking, while the young boys laughed hilariously and applauded. Uncle Ah-sheng bent over at the waist and dove head-first into the deep end of the pool, even though he didn't even know how to dog-paddle. When he didn't surface right away, the people who were watching no longer thought it was funny. Two girls dove in with a sense of urgency and pulled him to the surface, but they were just a moment too late—all that now remained of Uncle Ah-sheng was his name.

7. The Sound of Laughter

On the day of the funeral, Uncle Ah-sheng's family had requested that the swimming pool be closed down for the day—after all, it had been the cause of his death. The procession with Uncle Ah-sheng's coffin had to pass right by the entrance to the swimming pool, so the manager of the pool had given his consent to drape some black bunting across the entrance. But even before the coffin had passed by, many of the children of Clear Spring, not to be denied, had sneaked into the pool area, and the peals of laughter that accompanied their frolicking in the water poured across the walls like waves.

His Son's Big Doll

·····

In foreign countries there is an occupation called the "sandwich-man."° This line of work one day suddenly made its appearance in the little town, but no one could come up with a fitting term, nor knew what it was supposed to be called. Eventually, someone— just who is not known—coined the term "adman" for a person engaged in this work, and once the term became known in town, everyone, young and old, quickly grew accustomed to saying "the adman." Even babies cradled in their mothers' arms would stop crying and fussing and raise their heads to look around whenever their mothers called out: "Look, here comes the adman!"

The sun, like a fireball rolling along overhead, followed the people below, causing the perspiration to flow freely. For K'un-shu this sort of hot day was particularly unbearable, for he was attired from head to toe in a strange costume that made him look like a nineteenth-century European military officer. He was the center of attention not only because of the way he was made up, but even more so because of this heavy costume. But then that was what this job of his was all about—attracting attention. The sweat coursing down through the black makeup on his face gave him the appearance of a melting wax statue; the false moustache stuffed up into his nostrils was soaked with sweat, making it necessary for him to breathe through his mouth. Only the waving feathers atop his high conical hat gave an appearance of coolness. He longed to escape the heat by walking under the arcade, but the movie ad-

---

°English in the original.

vertisements he was carrying over his shoulders made this impossible. Two more adboards had recently been added below the original advertisements: the one in front proclaimed the virtues of Hundred-Herb Tea, the one behind plugged a tapeworm medicine. As a result, when he walked down the street, he looked like a puppet on a string. The added load was more tiring, of course, but he consoled himself with the thought that the additional money was worth the increased fatigue.

He had regretted going into this line of work from the very first day, and he was eager to find another. The more he thought about what he was doing, the more ridiculous it seemed. He laughed at himself, even if no one else did, and this self-imposed mental torment was forever on his mind, increasing in intensity as his fatigue grew. He'd better find a new line of work. But then he had had the same thought for more than a year.

In the heat, the glare of the asphalt road ahead made it impossible for him to see anything. Off in the distance everything was shrouded in a bile-colored haze, which he dared not even try to look through. For if he were to actually collapse there, as he feared he might, that would be the end of it for him. He summoned up all his willpower to struggle against the pall of color before his eyes that seemed bent on hounding him to death. *Damn it! This is no job for a man.* But whom was he to blame?

"Say, boss, since this moviehouse of yours just opened, it won't hurt to give it a try. Try it for a month, and if I don't produce results, you don't have to pay me. I can take your movie ads to the people far better than any billboard. What do you say?"

"What sort of costume do you have in mind?"

It wasn't so much what I said as it was my pitiful look that aroused his sympathy and made up his mind.

"If you'll give me the go-ahead, you can leave everything to me."

Getting this damned job was the most exciting thing that had ever happened in my life.

"Well, you got yourself a job."

Damn it! Ah-chu was so happy about this job she was in tears.

"Ah-chu, now you don't need to get an abortion."

It's only right that Ah-chu was in tears about this. She's a strong woman, for that was the first time I had ever seen her cry with such helpless abandon. I knew she was very happy.

At this point in his thoughts K'un-shu couldn't keep from shedding tears himself; they flowed unchecked, partly because he didn't have a hand free to wipe them away and partly because he was thinking. *What the hell, no one can tell if it's sweat or tears anyway!* Under the scorching sun he felt the two lines of hot tears flowing down his cheeks, and for the first time in his life he experienced the satisfying relief of an unrestrained cry.

"K'un-shu, just look at yourself! What in the world have you turned into? You don't look like a proper man *or* a proper ghost! How could you let yourself come to this?"

On the evening of his second day on the job, Ah-chu told him that his uncle had come several times that day. He was changing his clothes when his uncle came shouting his way in.

"Uncle . . ."

I should have stopped calling him Uncle long ago. Uncle! Uncle be damned!

"Don't you call me Uncle, the way you're made up!"

"Uncle, hear me out . . ."

"What's there to say! Is this the only job around? I believe anyone willing to be an ox can find a plow. I'll tell you to your face— I want you to get the hell out of here and not bring disgrace down on your community. If you don't heed my warning, don't be surprised if you're disowned by your own uncle!"

"I've been looking everywhere for a job . . ."

"What? You looked everywhere and you came up with this ridiculous dead-end job!"

"There wasn't anything I could do. I tried to borrow rice from you, but you wouldn't . . ."

"What? Is that my responsibility? Is it? I don't have rice to spare. I bought that rice little by little. Besides, what does all this have to do with that ridiculous job of yours? Stop talking nonsense! You . . . !"

Nonsense? Who's talking nonsense? That makes my blood boil! Uncle! So what? Screw him!

"Then just leave me alone! Leave me alone leave me alone leave me alone!"

He's driving me crazy!

"You dumb beast! Okay, you dumb beast, if you want to defy me, go ahead and defy me. From now on I am no longer K'un-shu's uncle! We're through!"

"If we're through, we're through. With an uncle like you, I'd starve to death anyway."

A good reply. How did I ever think of a reply like that? As he left he was cursing a blue streak. I really didn't feel like going to work the next day, not because I was afraid of offending my uncle, but because for some reason I was in the dumps. If I hadn't noticed the tears in Ah-chu's eyes, reminding me of my promise to her— "Ah-chu, now you won't have to have an abortion"—and how I had already thrown away the two packets of medicine, I'm sure I wouldn't have had the courage to walk through the door.

Thoughts. They were the only things that helped K'un-shu get through the day; without them, the passage of time would have been agonizingly slow as he made his dozen or so rounds every day, from early morning till late at night, up and down every street and lane in town. His mind was active as a natural result of his loneliness and solitude. He seldom thought about the future, and even when he did, it was only about the practical problems of the next few days. Mostly he thought of the past, a past that he judged by present-day standards.

The blazing fireball overhead followed him as he left the asphalt street. The bile-colored pall was still there a short distance ahead of him, and he was troubled by the sinking feeling that engulfed him. The mood of anxiety thus forced upon him was a little like the feeling he had every morning at dawn: as he lay on his bed, watching the first rays of the sun seep in through the cracks in the wall amidst the surrounding darkness, the stillness, and that dampness peculiar to this house, his mood would change suddenly from one of tranquility to one of fear. Though this was something he had grown accustomed to, it was almost like a brand new experience each day. His monthly income didn't amount to much, but it was certainly no worse by comparison than the income from other jobs. It was the tedium and the ridiculous nature of the job that nearly drove him mad. But without the money it brought in, his family's rudimentary livelihood would have presented an immediate problem. So what was he to do? Finally he would force himself to climb out of bed uneasily and, with a certain sense of shame, sit down at Ah-chu's little dressing table, take some face powder from the drawer, and rub it onto his face before the mirror. Looking in the mirror with only half of his face painted, he would smile sorrowfully as waves of vague emptiness surged through his mind.

He felt that all the water in his body was gone—he had never been so thirsty! The prostitutes in the red-light district next to the elementary school were standing around food stands snacking in their pajamas and wooden clogs. Others were sitting in doorways making up their faces or just leaning in the doorways, their heads buried in comic books as they passed the time. The few families that lived in this red-light district either barricaded themselves behind tightly closed doors or had put up fences in front of their homes; as an added measure, each house sported a sign alongside the door with the words "Regular Household" painted in large red letters.

"Hey, the adman's coming!" one of the prostitutes called out from a food stand. The others turned their heads to look at the signboard hanging in front of K'un-shu.

He mechanically approached the food stand.

"Hey! What's playing at the Palace Theater?"

He mechanically walked over to them.

"Have you lost your marbles? That guy never talks," one of them said sarcastically to the prostitute who had asked the question.

"Is he a mute?" The prostitutes began chatting among themselves.

"Who knows what he is?"

"I've never seen him smile either. His face is always lifeless."

He was only a few steps away from them, and their words pierced his heart.

"Hey! Adman, come here! I'm waiting for you," one of the prostitutes yelled, running after him. Amidst the ensuing laughter, someone said:

"If he really does come to you, it'll be a wonder if you don't die of fright."

He continued walking away from them, but he could still hear the prostitute's provocative comments. At the end of the lane he smiled.

I'm willing. If I had the cash I'd be willing. I'd choose the day-dreamer leaning up against Hsien-lo's door.

Passing through this red-light district helped him forget his fatigue for the moment. He saw by a clock on the street that it was nearly three fifteen. He had to hurry to the train station to meet the passengers coming in from the north. This was all part of his arrangement with the boss: he had to mingle, for instance, with the factory workers as they left work and the high-school students when school was out.

He had managed his time so that he didn't have to rush or take any shortcuts. As he emerged from the Eastern Lights area and turned toward the train station, the passengers he had come to meet were just then filing out of the exits, so he approached them from the shady side of the street. This was one of his methods of operation: the heat was still so intense it could bake a potato, and the departing passengers scooted across the open area and quickly moved under the sheltered arcade where the transport company was located. The only people who were at all interested in him were a few out-of-towners. He wouldn't have known what to do if it hadn't been for the encouragement he received from those few unfamiliar, curious faces. He was confident that he could look at any of their faces and tell you exactly where and when they had first shown up.

But no matter how things looked, he could not hold onto this job by relying solely on these few unfamiliar faces. Sooner or later the boss was bound to find out. The reaction of the people in front of him made his heart sink.

I've got to think of something else.

A conflict was raging in his heart.

"Look! Look over there!"

During his first days on the job, everyone had looked at him with the astonishment of someone seeing a ghost.

"Who's he?"

"Where'd he come from?"

"Is he from our town?"

"Can't be!"

"Yo! It's an ad for the Palace Theater."

"Where in the world is he from?"

I'll be damned! What's so interesting about me? Why don't they pay more attention to the ad? In those days I was an object of real interest to them—I was a riddle. Their mothers'——! Now that they all know I'm K'un-shu, and the riddle has been solved, no one pays me any more attention. What's it all got to do with me anyway? Isn't the ad changing all the time? But the gleam in those cold, curious eyes!

It was all the same to K'un-shu—being the center of attention and being ignored were equally painful to him.

He made a sweep around the train station, then meandered back to the street in front. Unable to reconcile the conflict of an inner cold and an outer heat, he reacted only with a few inward curses. The bile-colored pall reappeared some five or six meters ahead of him, and his throat was so parched it seemed about to crack. At that moment his home exerted a powerful pull on him.

She won't fail to make tea for me today because of what happened last night, will she? Ai! I was wrong not to go home for lunch, and I should have returned home for tea in the morning. That'll only add to her misunderstanding. Damn it anyway!

"What are you so mad about? And why take it out on me? Can't you lower your voice a little? Ah-lung's sleeping."

I shouldn't have taken my anger out on her. It's all the fault of that cheapskate—he wouldn't go along with my suggestion to change the costume. "That's your affair!" he had said. My affair? That damned dog-turd. This costume, which I made out of a fireman's uniform, has lost its appeal. Besides, it's not the sort of thing to be wearing in scorching weather like this!

"I'll talk as loud as I please!"

Whew! That was going too far. But what was I to do with all that anger inside me? I was bushed, and Ah-chu wasn't using her head. Why couldn't she put herself in my place instead of arguing with me?

"Are you trying to pick on me?"

"What if I am?"

Damn it, Ah-chu, I didn't mean it!

"Really?"

"Let's drop the subject!" Then he had added gruffly: "Shut up or I'll ... I'll slug you!" He had clenched his fist tightly and slammed it down hard on the table.

It must have worked, because she shut up. I was worried that she would try to stand up to me, and I wouldn't be able to stop myself from hitting her. But I really didn't mean it. Honestly, I shouldn't have frightened Ah-lung awake. The way Ah-chu held the crying child tightly in her arms was enough to tug on anyone's heartstrings. My throat's so dry I can't stand it, and it doesn't look like I'll get any tea today. Serves me right! No, I'm too thirsty.

Occupied with thoughts of what had happened last night, before he knew it he was standing in front of the door to his house. He was shocked back to the here and now. The door was slightly ajar, and as he nudged it with his foot it swung open lightly on its hinges. He laid down his adboard, tucked his hat under his arm, and entered. The big teapot was on the table beside a bamboo food cover, a big green plastic cup covering the spout. She had made tea! A warm feeling flooded K'un-shu's heart—he was greatly relieved. He poured himself a full cup of tea and gulped it down. It was the ginger tea with brown sugar that Ah-chu had been preparing for him every day since the beginning of summer, and which was waiting for him each time he passed by the house. Someone had once told Ah-chu that ginger tea is a good tonic for a tired man. He was so thirsty he filled the cup again, but he felt his heart filling with anxiety. Normally it didn't bother him if Ah-chu wasn't there when he came home for tea, but thoughts of his unreasonable loss of temper with her the night before unsettled and distressed him. He put down the cup and looked under the food cover and into the rice pot, discovering that nothing had been touched. Ah-lung was not asleep in his bed, and the clothes Ah-chu had washed for others were neatly folded—Where was everybody?

When K'un-shu left that morning without eating breakfast, Ah-chu was unable to check the deep concern in her heart. At first she wanted to call him back to eat breakfast, but she hesitated a moment, and before she knew it, he was already across the street. They hadn't spoken a word. As always, she strapped Ah-lung onto her back and went out to wash other people's clothes. She was so disturbed she didn't know what to do with herself, so she scrubbed the clothes extra hard—so hard that the movements of her body made it impossible for Ah-lung to cram the soap dish he was holding into his mouth to satisfy his sucking instinct. He threw the soap dish away and cried angrily. Ah-chu continued to scrub the clothes hard, evidently unaware that the child was crying more and more loudly; in the past she had never let Ah-lung cry so pitifully without paying him any attention.

"Ah-chu," the mistress called to her through the bathroom window overlooking the washroom.

Her head lowered, Ah-chu continued to scrub the clothes.

"Ah-chu!" The amiable woman was forced to raise her voice.

Startled, Ah-chu stopped her work and straightened up to hear what the mistress had to say. Then she suddenly became aware of Ah-lung's cries and reached back to gently pat his bottom with a wet hand. She cocked her head to listen to the mistress.

"Didn't you know your baby was screaming?" Her voice, while mildly reproachful, was as amiable as ever.

"This child of mine . . ." There was really nothing she could say. "Even with a soap dish to play with he still cries!" She lowered her left shoulder and looked back at the child. "Where's your soap dish?" Quickly discovering the cast-off soap dish on the floor, she bent over, picked it up, rinsed it off, and handed it back to Ah-lung. Then she stooped down again and picked up the clothes, but before she could begin scrubbing, the mistress spoke to her:

"That's a brand new dress you have in your hands, so don't scrub so hard."

Ah-chu could not remember how she had been washing the dress, but there didn't seem to be any call for this reminder by the mistress.

After finally managing to hang up all the clothes, Ah-chu rushed out onto the street with Ah-lung on her back. She threaded her way through the marketplace and the main section of town, looking up and down the streets anxiously, searching for K'un-shu in vain. She racked her brain thinking of places where she might find him. Finally she caught a glimpse of him off in the distance, carrying his adboard high as he walked down People's Rights Road toward the Town Hall. She ran after him in high spirits, and before long his back was fully visible to her. She lowered her left shoulder and put her face up close to Ah-lung's.

"Look, Ah-lung, there's Daddy." The way she pointed at K'un-shu's back and her tone of voice had the qualities of cringing inferiority. There was too great a distance separating them for Ah-lung to know what was going on. Ah-chu stood by the side of the road and followed K'un-shu's back with her eyes until it disappeared at the crossroads. At that moment the outermost layer of anxiety was stripped from her heart. She wondered what K'un-shu was thinking, for there had been a message in his not eating. Still she received some consolation from the sight of him carrying his signs as usual. But the mixture of this relieving thought with those other disturbing elements produced a confusion in her mind even more unbearable than her original fears. Seeing K'un-shu like this only changed her mood—it did nothing to lessen her anxiety. She decided to go over to the next home and wash their clothes.

The moment she came home after finishing her work, she went over and removed the lid of the teapot: the pot was still full and the rice porridge had not been touched, proof that K'un-shu had not been home today. Something was definitely wrong. Or so she thought. She had intended to put the sleeping Ah-lung to bed, but now she could not. She rushed back outside, closing the door behind her.

The heat of the fireball overhead was intense, and most of the pedestrians had sought refuge under the arcade, making it much easier for Ah-chu to look for K'un-shu. At each cross-street she stood in the intersection and looked both directions until she determined that he was not there. Finally she spotted him near the lumber yard on Chiang Kai-shek Avenue North heading toward the Temple of the Goddess of the Sea. She followed him discreetly at a distance of seven or eight houses, being careful lest he turn around and see her. Noticing nothing out of the ordinary about his behavior from the rear, she hid herself behind arcade posts several times, closing the distance to two or three houses, and continued to watch him. Still nothing out of the ordinary. Nonetheless she felt very uneasy over his refusal to eat or drink. And she was not reassured by what she was seeing. Convinced that something was wrong, she feared that something had come between them.

She suddenly felt a need to see him from the front, figuring that a look at his face might tell her what she wanted to know. So she followed him to an intersection, and when she saw that he continued walking straight ahead, she ran on ahead several blocks and hid herself behind a peddler's stand near the Temple of the Goddess of the Sea. There she waited for K'un-shu to appear. The pounding of her heart increased as she impatiently awaited his approach. When he drew near, she quickly squatted down behind the peddler's stand, ignoring the inquisitive looks on the faces of bystanders, and looked around the stand to see K'un-shu as he passed in front of her. In that brief instant all she could see was the profile of his sweltering face, the tracks of perspiration reminding her that she too was sweating profusely. Even Ah-lung was bathed in sweat.

This pursuit had stripped away some of the layers of worry inside her, but the innermost layers were so sensitive that the slightest touch was painful. Ah-chu now placed all of her vague hopes on the noon meal. After finishing her washing at the last house, she went home and prepared lunch. Then she sat down to wait for K'un-shu, the baby Ah-lung at her breast. But she began to grow restless when he still had not appeared after the passage of a considerable amount of time.

With Ah-lung on her back, she went out and found K'un-shu on the road leading through the park. More than once she nearly found the courage to go up to him and beg him to come home to eat, but each time, as she started to draw near to him, this courage left her suddenly and without a trace. So she just kept her distance and tagged along behind him, quietly and forlornly. Street after street, lane upon lane she followed him, blaming herself for having talked back to him the night before, which had so far cost him two meals and his tea as he walked the streets on this sweltering day. Every few steps she had to wipe away her tears with the end of the carrying cloth strapped around her back.

When she finally saw K'un-shu turn toward home, she was so happy she grew somewhat tense. Taking a different road, she arrived ahead of him and stationed herself at the mouth of the lane opposite their place, where she could observe how he approached the house and see whether or not he ate lunch. Here came K'un-shu. He stopped for a moment in front of the door. When Ah-chu saw him finally enter the house her tears were flowing so heavily that she covered her face with her hands and leaned her head against the wall for support, feeling a great surge of relief. She could see his every movement inside the house and could guess what he was feeling at the moment—he was probably looking for her anxiously. This thought gave her a sense of well-being.

Just as K'un-shu was about to leave the house, feeling depressed and unable to wait any longer, Ah-chu, with Ah-lung on her back, entered quickly, her head downcast. (At the very moment she was bounding across the street filled with the happiness of having seen him drink some tea from her vantage point across the street, his feeling of depression had been almost overwhelming.) The two of them seemed to shed a heavy emotional burden simultaneously—he having seen his wife walk through the door, she having seen her husband drink some tea. Ah-chu kept her head lowered as she busied herself with removing the food cover and filling K'un-shu's ricebowl. He slipped the signboards over his head and placed them off to the side, then sat down at the table after unbuttoning his shirt. He ate his food in silence. Ah-chu filled her own ricebowl, sat down opposite him and began to eat. Since they did not say a word to one another, all that could be heard in the room was a munching sound like that made by hogs at the trough. When K'un-shu got up and refilled his ricebowl, Ah-chu quickly raised her head to catch a glimpse of his back, then just as quickly lowered it again and resumed eating. When she in turn got to her feet, he caught a hurried glance of her back before looking away as she turned back around.

Finally he could stand this oppressive silence no longer:

"Is Ah-lung asleep?" He knew quite well that Ah-lung was sleeping on his mother's back.

"Yes." Her head remained bowed.

More silence.

He looked at Ah-chu, but when he thought that she was about to

raise her head, he immediately looked away. He broke the silence
again:

"The blacksmith shop at Red-Tile Corners caught fire early this
morning. Did you know that?"

"I know."

Her answer cut short what he was going to say. He paused for a
moment.

"Two children were killed on the street this morning right in
front of the noodle shop."

"Huh!" Her head shot up, but she quickly lowered it again when
she saw that he was just about to raise his head from his ricebowl.
"How did that happen?" She was eager to know, but her tone of
voice lacked the excitement of her initial exclamation.

"Some sacks of rice fell off an oxcart and crushed the kids hanging onto the back."

Ever since beginning this line of work, K'un-shu had more or
less become Ah-chu's exclusive reporter of local news. He re-
ported to her daily and in great detail everything that occurred in
the town. Sometimes he came to her with an extra news flash like,
for instance, the time on Park Road when he saw a long line of
people stretching from the side entrance of the Catholic church all
the way to the street. He rushed back home to tell her that the
Catholic church was distributing free flour, then returned that
evening to find two large sacks of flour and a can of powdered milk
lying on the table.

Though a note of awkwardness was discernible in their conversation, they had now reestablished a line of amicable communica-
tion. K'un-shu buttoned his shirt, checked his equipment, and, to
keep the conversation going, asked: "Is Ah-lung asleep?"

What a dumb question. I already asked that!

"Yes," she answered.

But K'un-shu, utterly embarrassed by his own question, didn't
even hear her response. Wanting to get out of there in a hurry, he
left hastily without even turning his head back. As Ah-chu walked

over and stood in the doorway to watch her husband walk off, she rocked the baby on her back and gently patted his behind with her hand. The whole reconciliation process had taken about half an hour, during which time their eyes had never once met.

The wall of the Farmers Association granary was not only high, but it also seemed to people to be uncannily long. Because of this huge wall the winds swirled round and round the area. The wall also cast a great shadow over the low houses across the way, and this was where K'un-shu was headed. He was feeling much better now, and there was no longer a bile-colored pall anywhere in front of him as far as he could see. With the numbness gone from his shoulders, he could once again feel the weight of the ads draped over his head. Calculating the time of day, he cursed the length of time remaining before nightfall, for he wanted very badly to take Ah-chu to bed. Experience showed him that that was all they needed to remove any bad blood between them. Actually, the removal of these marital ill feelings was an incidental benefit; he didn't know why, but whenever the animosity between them grew to a certain level, his sexual desires were aroused. The sun-drenched day became the object of his curses.

As sparrows chirped incessantly around the granary, he thought back to his childhood, when the land beneath this row of low houses had been completely vacant. He remembered how he and several of his playmates had often come here to shoot sparrows— he had been an excellent hand with a slingshot.

He was being scrutinized by several sparrows perched on the telephone wires, and though he turned his head to look at them, he didn't slacken his pace, so that the angle of his head and eyes changed with each step. He was suddenly brought up short by the sound of running footsteps approaching him from behind. He turned his head, just as he had done in years past when he was watching out for the old man at the granary. This reflex amused him. The old man had died long ago, when K'un-shu was still shooting sparrows, and they had found his body near the well beside the granary. With these thoughts in mind, he gradually left the sparrows on the telephone wires behind him.

A group of children playing in the mud by the side of the road left their games and ran toward him giggling and laughing. They kept a safe distance from him as he walked along, those in front walking backwards and facing him. Prior to the birth of Ah-lung, he had been angered by the constant pestering of children on the street. But now things were different: now he would make faces at them, which not only delighted the children, but somehow also gave him great pleasure. It was the sort of feeling he had every time he played with the laughing Ah-lung.

"Ah-lung——Ah-lung——"
"Go on, get out of here. You don't have to be cute with him."
"Ah-lung, bye-bye, bye-bye . . ."
This is how K'un-shu took his leave of them nearly every day. Whenever Ah-lung saw his daddy walk out the door, he would cry and make a scene, sometimes trying to keep him from leaving by bending over backwards in his mother's arms. Then it would be up to Ah-chu to say things like, "He's your child, and he'll still be here when you get back," before K'un-shu would reluctantly drag himself away.

The boy really likes me.

K'un-shu was very happy. This job had enabled them to have Ah-lung, who in turn enabled him to endure the hardships the job forced upon him.

"Don't be silly! Do you think it's really you that Ah-lung likes? What he thinks he has is somebody who looks like you do now!"

At the time I nearly misunderstood what Ah-chu was saying.

"When you go out in the morning, he's either asleep or else I've put him on my back to go out and wash clothes. During most of his waking hours you're made up like you are now, and when you come home at night he's asleep."

It's not as bad as that, is it? But the boy is shying away from strangers these days.

"He likes the way you dress up and make faces at him. It's no secret that you're his big doll."

Oh! I'm Ah-lung's big doll, his big doll!

The child walking backwards in front of him pointed and yelled: "Ha-ha, look here, quick. The adman, he's smiling. The adman's saying something and his eyes and mouth are all twisted!"

I'm a big doll, a big doll.

He was smiling. The long shadow he cast ahead of him did not seem at all like a man's shadow, because of the adboards over his shoulders. The children were making a game of stepping on his shadow. One of the children's mothers was calling to him from somewhere far behind K'un-shu; the child reluctantly stopped what he was doing and looked up, then enviously looked at his playmates, whose mothers were not calling an end to their play.

K'un-shu inwardly admired Ah-chu's cleverness, musing over her metaphor: "A big doll, a big doll."

"Born in the year of the dragon, what better name for him than Ah-lung—Little Dragon?"

If Ah-chu had had any schooling, she would have been a good student. But then if she had had schooling, she wouldn't have married me.

"Hsü Ah-lung."

"Is this the way you write 'lung'—dragon?"

That fellow who handled birth certificates was really something —he knew perfectly well that I only asked him to fill in the form because I don't know how to write, so why did he have to ask that in such a loud voice?

"It's a dragon, like in the solar cycle."

"He was born in June. Why didn't you come and report it earlier?"

"We only named him today."

"Since you didn't report the birth within three months, there's a fine of fifteen dollars."

"We didn't even know we were supposed to register."

"You didn't know? I'm surprised you knew how to make a baby."

He really shouldn't have made fun of us like that. He said it so loud that everyone in the Town Hall was looking at us and laughing.

High school students on their way home from school, more curious than adults, carefully read the movie bills on his board. Some even discussed the movies, though one of them remarked: "What's the use? The teachers won't let us go see them!" K'un-shu didn't comprehend what the boy meant, but he was happy just looking at their bulging book bags, and his mood changed from sadness to admiration.

No one in our family has been to school for three generations. But Ah-lung will be different. The only thing that worries me is that he might not do well there. I've heard it costs a fortune to put a child through school! What a lucky bunch of kids they are!

Two rows of trees lined the sidewalks, one of them throwing spotted shadows onto the street. The workers emerging from the industrial district at the far end of the street lacked the enthusiasm of the high school students; fatigue written plainly on their faces, they walked in silence, the few conversations among them carried on in hushed tones, the rare laughter subdued. Before taking on this job, K'un-shu had applied for work in a paper factory, a lumber factory, and a fertilizer factory, and he envied these people their work and the regularity with which they walked down this cool tree-lined road at the same time every day on their way home to rest. Not only that, they had Sundays off. He didn't know why he had been turned down for a job. He had thought long and hard about it, but the answer escaped him.

"How many in your family?"

"Only my wife and me. My parents are both dead. My . . ."

"Okay, okay, I know."

That's odd. How could he know? I haven't finished. Damn him! After waiting in line all that time for an interview, is that all I'm going to get—two or three questions? Some of the men weren't even asked anything. He just nodded his head and smiled, and they walked off looking very satisfied.

Dusk.

K'un-shu looked up at the sun, which was sinking into the sea. The sight quickly filled him with happiness. When he returned to the Palace Theater, the manager was outside looking at the movie notices. He turned around and said:

"Ah, you're back. Good, I've been looking for you."

This came as a shock to K'un-shu; finding himself momentarily speechless, he finally managed to say: "What's up?"

"I want to discuss something with you."

K'un-shu quickly tried to grasp the intent of the manager's words and the significance of his cold manner. He carefully leaned the ad signs against the bare wall below the theater announcement, then removed the boards that sandwiched him. The hand in which he was holding the tall hat was trembling. He wanted desperately to postpone what was coming, but he had exhausted his supply of delaying tactics, and it was time for him to say something. He turned around with great apprehension; his hair, which had been wet but was now dry, stuck to his scalp, and the white powder that had covered his forehead and cheeks had run with the perspiration and was now caked in his eyebrows and the hollows of his cheeks. The skin that showed through was so rough it looked diseased. Finally, he unmindfully removed his false beard and stood there staring blankly ahead, like a strange muted mannequin.

"Do you think this sort of advertising is producing any results?" the manager asked.

"I, I . . ." He was so nervous he couldn't speak.

I should have known. This is it!

"Maybe we should try something else."

"I think so," K'un-shu responded without knowing what he was saying.

If the damn thing's finished, that's just as well. What future is there in this line of work anyway?

"Can you handle a pedicab?"

"A pedicab?" He was crushed.

Shit!

"I, I don't think so," K'un-shu continued.

"There's nothing to it. You'll get the hang of it in no time."

"Uh-huh."

"I'm thinking of switching to a pedicab for advertising. In addition to riding around on the pedicab, you'll continue to help out until we close at night. The same wages."

"Right."

Whew! That was close! I thought I was washed up.

"Tomorrow morning you go with me to the shop to fetch the pedicab."

"What about these?" He pointed to the signs leaning against the wall, but what he really wanted to know was could he stop using makeup.

The manager pretended he didn't hear him and walked inside.

Stupid! Why did I have to ask that?

He felt like laughing, but didn't know just what was so funny. He hadn't a clue. He opened his mouth wide as though to laugh, but no sound emerged. On the road home he casually carried all of his equipment over his shoulder, which unexpectedly drew astonished looks from passersby; the townspeople had never seen him like this before, with his tall hat tucked under his arm.

"Take a good look, it'll be your last chance." He was so exhilarated he felt he could actually fly.

What a ridiculous job! He remembered when he was a child, and a traveling moving-picture show had come to town from somewhere—oh, right, it was a show at the steps of the church—and he, Ah-hsing, and some other friends had climbed up an acacia tree to watch. One of the moving pictures had shown an adman dressed up just like him being pestered by a crowd of children. It had left a deep impression on their young minds, and afterwards they had often dressed up like that to play games. *Who would have thought that as an adult those games would turn into reality for me? That's really funny.*

"Damn that short movie scene and its damned consequences. It's damned funny." As he walked down the road with his thoughts, he mumbled incessantly to himself.

Scenes of past events came to his mind one after the other.

"Ah-chu, if I don't find a job soon, you'll have to get rid of the baby you're carrying. This medicine is supposed to work during the first month of pregnancy. Don't be afraid—it'll all just come out in the form of blood and water."

That was close!

"Ah-chu, now you won't have to have an abortion."

If that's the case, then if I hadn't seen the outdoor movie, Ah-lung might not be here today! It's a good thing I climbed that acacia tree.

The strange thing was, this job that he had tried so unsuccessfully to give up and which had been the object of his curses, he now viewed with a certain degree of affection. But affection is all it was. The inner happiness he was feeling now easily won out over all other emotions.

"K'un-shu, you're back!" Ah-chu called out loudly with an uncharacteristic exuberance as she saw her husband off in the distance making his way home.

This took K'un-shu completely by surprise. How in the world could Ah-chu have found out? If he weren't so preoccupied, K'un-shu would have viewed this display of affection by Ah-chu as too sudden and too bold; usually, this sort of thing caused him prolonged embarrassment.

As he drew nearer, but not yet near enough to say anything, Ah-chu blurted out: "I knew your luck would change." She seemed unwilling to hold anything back. This time K'un-shu was really stunned. "Can you handle a pedicab?" she continued. "It doesn't make any difference anyway. You'll get the hang of it in no time at all. Chin-ch'ih wants to sublease his pedicab to you. As for the details . . ."

Now he understood the coincidence, and he decided to play a

joke on her. "I know everything," he said.

"I figured as much when I saw the way you were walking home. What do you think? It doesn't sound bad, does it!"

"No, it doesn't sound bad, but . . ." He was barely able to keep himself from telling her the happy news. He stopped just as the words were about to tumble out.

Ah-chu pressed him anxiously: "What's the matter?"

"If the manager doesn't want us to do things this way, I don't think we ought to accept Chin-ch'ih's offer."

"Why?"

"Just think: if it hadn't been for this job, I'd hate to think what our lives would be like. Ah-lung might not be here today. Now if I give up this job the moment a better one comes along, that's going a little too far, isn't it?"

He had thought this up on the spur of the moment, but once it was out, the seriousness and importance of what he was saying came to him in a rush, and he grew dead serious. Ah-chu, in turn, was gripped by fear, not because she understood what he was saying, but because of his change in demeanor. Obviously disappointed, she nonetheless gained support from her sense of right and wrong. She followed her husband into the house in silence, feeling, in the midst of her bewilderment, a newborn respect for him. Perhaps she was able to accept his explanation so readily because of what he had said about Ah-lung.

They ate dinner that night together as usual, the only difference being the silent, mysterious looks K'un-shu gave Ah-chu from time to time. Though somewhat puzzled by these looks, she was completely reassured by the twinkle in his eye. She was very conscious of the fact that she had already planned their whole future after he once began riding a pedicab, without any thoughts for the well-being of the man who was making it all possible, and she felt terribly guilty about this. K'un-shu decided to wait until he came home at night following the last show to give Ah-chu the good news. He put down his ricebowl and walked over to look at Ah-lung, who was fast asleep.

"That child sleeps all day long."

"It's a good thing he does. Otherwise, I wouldn't be able to get a thing done. The Goddess of Childbirth has been a big help by giving us such a good child."

He left to go to work at the theater.

He regretted not having told her the truth right away, because now he didn't know how he would be able to stand the long three-hour wait until closing time. Maybe for other people this was just a commonplace matter, but to K'un-shu, who could no longer contain himself, anxiety was bubbling up inside him.

I nearly told her while I was taking my bath. Wouldn't it have been better if I had?

"Why have you flattened out your hat?" Ah-chu had asked him.

Ah-chu has always been clever, and she knew there was something in the air.

"Oh! Have I?"

"Do you want me to straighten it out for you?"

"No need."

She was trying to look right through the hat to see if she could discover some secret.

"Oh, all right, straighten it out."

"How could you be so careless as to ruin the hat like this?"

Go ahead and tell her and be done with it!

Musing over past events like this had already become a habit with K'un-shu. He couldn't have changed if he had wanted to. He sat listlessly in the office, thinking about isolated incidents in his life. Even thoughts of events that had caused him pain and discomfort at the time today somehow brought a smile to his face.

"K'un-shu."

Lost in his thoughts, he didn't move.

"K'un-shu." This time it was louder.

He turned around in surprise and smiled awkwardly at the manager.

"The show's about over. Go open the exits, then give a hand at the bicycle rack."

The day was finally coming to an end. He no longer felt tired. When he arrived home, Ah-chu was outside walking around with Ah-lung in her arms.

"Why aren't you in bed?"

"It's too hot in there. Ah-lung couldn't sleep."

"Here, Ah-lung, let Daddy hold you."

Ah-chu handed him the child and followed him inside. But to their surprise, Ah-lung began to cry, and no matter how K'un-shu rocked him or played with him, he wouldn't stop. Indeed, the crying grew progressively louder.

"Silly child, what's wrong with Daddy holding you? Don't you like Daddy? Be a good boy and don't cry, don't cry."

But not only was Ah-lung crying hard, he was bending backwards, struggling to get out of his father's arms just as he had tried to twist out of Ah-chu's arms that morning when K'un-shu was leaving for work in his costume.

"Naughty boy, why are you crying? Daddy's holding you. Don't you like Daddy anymore? Silly child, it's Daddy! It's your Daddy!" K'un-shu kept reminding Ah-lung. "It's your Daddy. Daddy's holding Ah-lung—look!" He made faces and funny sounds, but all in vain. Ah-lung was crying piteously.

"Here, I'll hold him."

As K'un-shu handed the baby back to Ah-chu, he felt his heart suddenly sink. He walked over to Ah-chu's dressing table, sat down, and hesitantly opened the drawer. He removed the powder and looked deeply into the mirror, then slowly began making up his face.

"Are you crazy? What are you making up your face for now?" Ah-chu was completely mystified by K'un-shu's actions.

A momentary silence.

"I . . ." K'un-shu's voice was trembling. "I want Ah-lung to recognize me . . ."

The Gong

· · · · ·

Prologue

Kam Kim-ah had not beaten his gong for quite some time now, probably eight or nine months, or perhaps as long as a year. He wasn't sure himself. He knew only that it had been a long, long time. Whenever this fact crossed his mind a great anger filled him: here he was, the only remaining practitioner of the unique profession of gong beating, and no one ever came to hire his services. By the time he became aware of what was happening, it was already too late to do anything about it. The brass gong upon which his carefree existence had depended for more than half a lifetime now suddenly lay there like something that had been frightened out of its wits, resembling the vacantly opened mouth of a mute. It had lain upside down under his bamboo bed since his last job, serving as a catchall.

That doesn't mean that there were no longer any lost children in the town, or that there were no more calls for the Buddhist faithful to offer prayerful thanks on the various temple days, or that the need no longer existed to announce publicly for the people to pay their taxes, or that smallpox vaccinations for the children were no longer given. But now these announcements were the function of a young man who pedalled his loudspeaker-equipped pedicab up and down the streets. This sight produced more than just loathing in Kam Kim-ah; there was also an ineffable, persistent pain that gripped his heart. There was something terribly incongruous, he thought, about having such a bizarre contraption anywhere in his little town. The appearance of this *thing* could not but destroy the town's social fabric—it represented an extreme absurdity.

Back in the days when Kam Kim-ah's gong was still in use, every third day witnessed a minor event, every fifth a major one. So among the town's old-timers, he drank wine more frequently than all the others, and sometimes when he had a little more money he would even splurge and buy some of the more expensive Shaohsing wine. And in the matter of names, why, even among people of distinction there was no one whose named carried the weight of Kam Kim-ah's. You had only to say the three words, Kam Kim-ah, and anyone—literate or illiterate, man, woman, or child—would have known at once of whom you were speaking. But were you to mention the mayor of the town, Brother Fu-tung, or refer to him even more precisely as the old doctor's grandson, well, old doctor's grandson or not, there were no guarantees that everyone would recognize the name. Yes, in those days Kam Kim-ah could truly lay claim to both fame and fortune.

But ever since the pedicab with the loudspeaker had come to town, quickly monopolizing the public announcement business, the group of old vagrants that congregated beneath the kadang tree opposite the coffin shop at Southgate was increased by the addition of one Kam Kim-ah. In order to secure his position in the group, he had very methodically and deliberately planned his every move, as though it were an intricate game of chess. For now that fortune was missing from his life, he was left with only his reputation. It was important not only to win this game, but to preserve face as well. In his heart he knew that he was going to hang around there one way or the other, and that sooner or later he would have his place beneath the kadang tree. *But I—Kam Kim-ah—am not that stupid! I still want to take my place in society with other people!* He knew that it was important for a man to play a role in society. So whenever he had the feeling that he somehow belonged, no matter to what depths his spirits had sunk, they would be given a momentary boost.

The Ghost Sighting*

By now a considerable amount of time had passed since Kam Kim-ah had last beat his gong. He had lost his source of income, and although there was only himself to look after, even a marginal existence was proving difficult. He could do without wine, but not food!

Of the ten or so roads in town, only two or three did not give Kam Kim-ah a sinking feeling as he walked down them, for on the other roads were general stores where he had run up bills for wine and tobacco. Times being what they were, he felt as though he were being squeezed into a long, deep fissure in which he was powerless to budge an inch. For days he had thought of little else, and he could come up with no more practical plan than to squeeze himself into the group in the shade of the kadang tree opposite the coffin shop.

Bright and early every morning he went over to the yam patch in the Ah-li-shih area alongside the stream to steal some yams. By now he was sick of the things; in fact, he had recently been bothered by indigestion, which caused his throat to grow parched and hoarse. As he saw it, the shade of the kadang tree opposite the coffin shop offered him his only hope for survival. Once made, this decision gained the force of a mandate.

With a jolt he sat up in bed. The bright light shining in through the opening of the air-raid shelter at that moment brought with it revitalized hope. In the brief moment that his gaze was fixed straight ahead, he felt as light as a feather and imagined himself to be flying away on the rays of light.

Before walking out of the small park, he washed his face at the fountain, then carefully went over in his mind once more the route

---

*This is a literal translation of the term *huo chien-kuei*, which is normally rendered "nonsense" or "absurd(ity)." As will be seen below, the author has introduced a pun with this term, and the literal meaning is more relevant to the story.

he had planned: leaving the park, he would cut across the Lan's vegetable garden via the narrow, dark path. No problems there. When he reached the Utopia Hospital, he would skirt around the marketplace, taking the alleyway in back of the Revival Movie-house. He would be careful to avoid the metalworks shop, for it was likely that Stony and the others, whose shop was nearby, might be around. Kam Kim-ah made a mental calculation: this route would certainly take him to Northgate, to the train station. He'd walk along the canal, and from there it would be best to cut across the Yü-ying Public Elementary School playground. Once he had reached the train station, he would cross the tracks and take Ah-shu-she Road, which would put him on the outskirts of town. *If I ran into any of them out there, I'd be doomed.* From there he would follow the road back to the Buddhist temple at Point Sixteen, cross back over the tracks to the west side of town, then turn south at the rice shop beneath the melia tree.

When his thoughts reached this point, he sucked in his breath. *Wow! If I stayed on this road, wouldn't I be leaving the area al-together?* He smiled. Taking such a roundabout route just to get to Southgate was like taking off your pants to fart!

He scratched his head hard and twisted his mouth. It suddenly dawned on him that he had become very clever. Clever? Crafty, he thought. *Well, since crafty is the same as clever, isn't clever the same as crafty?* He gleefully embraced this feeling of self-respect, then crisply spat on the ground. He looked up with a squint to lo-cate the sun's position in the sky: it was slanting above his head. He felt terribly hungry. It must be past noon already, he thought, probably after two o'clock.

There was a breach in the northern wall of the small park, which most people called "the dog door," but the people who actually made use of it called it "the side entrance." There were but three formal entrances to the small park; this breach in the wall, "the dog door" or "side entrance," had been opened up by the beancurd makers at Red-Tile Shelter as a shortcut for their trips to the marketplace. With the exception of their early-morning passages through the opening, few people took advantage of this shortcut. That was because, in order to make your way through Mr. Lan's vegetable patch, you had to walk along a narrow, fenced-in lane in the middle of which were two manure pits hidden in the shade of a large banyan tree. And there, from that very tree, one of the Lan family women had hanged herself one day, and the townspeople were convinced that her ghost often appeared there.

Kam Kim-ah's heart was heavy as he drew up to the breach in the wall. For some reason an old town saying came to him: "The hungry ghost is king of the ghosts, the full-bellied ghost is startled by the winds." And yet he grew bold, repeating this saying aloud over and over, as though it were a chant of exorcism, as he walked along. As he neared the manure pits, his eyes were suddenly attracted by several papaya trees nearby. Three or four huge papayas hung from one of the trees, their stems a pale yellow. What a waste, he thought, as he looked carefully around him, forgetting all about his chant. Standing on the edge of one of the manure pits on his tiptoes, he stretched out his hand to gauge the distance to the nearest papaya. If the manure pit weren't right in the way, he would only have to knock the papaya to the ground with a bamboo branch. But, stymied by the manure pit, he looked around until his gaze stopped at the bamboo fence: a branch that had fallen over until its tip was touching the ground gave him an idea. He walked over and unhooked the fence wire, thinking as he did so that once he had knocked down the papaya, he could use the bamboo branch for a cook fire. The butterfly bushes alongside the fence were as tall as a man. Closer to the ground there was a thick undergrowth of canna plants, and this wild growth of wattle had already replaced the original bamboo fence—there was no evidence of any repair work by the owner of this rotting fence. Kam Kim-ah removed the last coil of wire, then happily grabbed the branch in both hands, but just as he was about to reach out and knock down the papaya, he sensed that someone was coming. Quickly throwing the branch into the bushes, he ran over to the edge of the manure pit, pulled down his trousers, and squatted there to wait and see what the person would do. But nothing happened.

That's strange, I'm sure I heard someone coming. Why can't I see anyone? Could he have spotted me first? Maybe he's lying in wait to nab me. To hell with him. I'll just squat here a while longer and see what happens. After all, it's no crime to come here and relieve myself. He chuckled to himself. *If I don't get my hands on the papaya, that'll make five meals I've missed, and soon there won't be anything left to relieve myself of. Shit!* He laughed again.

His thoughts returned to a few days earlier when he had gone to steal some yams at Ah-li-shih. He had been discovered by the owner just as he was about to dig into the patch. The man had started yelling as he ran over from some distance away, so Kam Kim-ah had quickly dropped his trousers and squatted there casually without moving. When the other man was no more than ten steps away from him, Kam Kim-ah had started to rail at him: "What's this? You coming over here to eat shit? How can you recklessly accuse me of being a thief? Wait till I'm finished here, then if I don't rub your face in my shit, you'll be gettin' off easy! Anyone who accuses someone of being a thief doesn't know right from wrong. What kind of loot do you think you're going to get here? What rotten behavior!"

The young farmer had answered him doubtfully and almost apologetically: "What's the big idea of coming here to crap?"

"What's that? Are you complaining because I deliver it right to your door? Don't you go into town every morning before sunrise to pick the stuff up?" The young man had turned on his heel and walked off without another word. Kam Kim-ah had left that day laden with booty.

At this point his mind was brought back to the present; he carefully sized up the situation. He still could hear no sounds of anyone drawing near. It struck him that whoever was trying to nab him might just be very crafty. *All right, I'll just squat here a little longer.* He laughed to himself again. This was all very funny to him. *There's nothing easier than getting the best of one of these hicks. The people who plant yams in Ah-li-shih just serve them right up to people like me. If you get caught stealing some, all you have to say is that you're from the Fu-lun-tsai area, and that we're all members of the same group. Then the man who's caught you will just say politely: "These out here are no good; I've got better ones in the house." Then he'll take you over and let you help your-self to as much as a hundred catties if you want that much, and might even have you stay over for dinner. Naturally, if you tell him that you belong to one of the other groups from Ah-shu-she, he'll beat the hell out of you right on the spot. Um!* He heaved a long sigh. In a matter of just a few years a whole new era had begun.

He knew he couldn't squat there much longer, since his legs were getting sore as hell, so he stood up and looked around, appre-hensive that he wouldn't be able to see if there was anyone else in the patch. He parted the clumps of butterfly bushes in several places, taking care not to let down his guard. Then he hit upon a plan. He called out, not too loudly: "Someone's stealing papayas! Someone's stealing papayas!" That way, if anyone came asking questions, he could say that he'd seen a couple of kids, but that they must have run away. He waited a moment—no response. Now he knew that there was no one around. Picking up the branch from the butterfly bushes where he had thrown it, he tried to knock down the papaya. But he had grown so weak from hunger that he couldn't handle the eight- or nine-foot-long branch, which kept whipping back and forth in the air. The harder he tried to hit the papaya, the worse his aim became, until he began to grow anxious and frustrated.

As he saw it, there were some things that required a certain amount of cursing if they were to be done properly. "You fucking thing!" A burst of effort, and he actually hit it. But the big papaya he had in his sights fell with a thud onto a layer of dried excrement atop the manure pit, and began to sink slowly to the bottom. Kam Kim-ah stood there like a man who has just parted with his lover, woodenly following the sinking papaya with his eyes. He swallowed a couple of times to somehow lessen the painful pangs of hunger.

When this papaya that had so tantalized him sank to just beyond the halfway point, the bumps and hollows of the skin and its general shape made it look like a human head, with eyes, a nose, and even a mouth. Kam Kim-ah's heart raced violently, and he blinked hard to clear his vision. Suddenly the heavy end of the papaya sank below the surface, as the lighter end bobbed straight up. Terrified, Kam Kim-ah fled down the lane, screaming out to heaven, earth, and mother. Some people walking on the road adjoining this darkened lane were startled by his shouts and cursed out at him.

"Damn you, have you seen a ghost or something?"*

"Yes . . . Yes, I . . . I saw a ghost!" Kam Kim-ah stammered in response. On this harvest day in June, Kam Kim-ah was actually shivering uncontrollably.

Kam Kim-ah had always been a believer in ghosts and spirits, and this experience caused his superstitions to become more deeply entrenched. Seeing a ghost is a very unlucky omen, he thought to himself, especially in broad daylight. He temporarily postponed his plans of going over to the kadang tree opposite the coffin shop at Southgate. What with his food problems of the next few days, no matter how uncomfortable his stomach was, he would have to go ask for some yams from someone at Ah-li-shih to stay his hunger, then take it from there.

Beginning from the day Kam Kim-ah saw the apparition, the ghost of the girl named Lan, which had all but been forgotten by the townsfolk, began once again to nightly infiltrate the minds of those most fearful of ghosts, the town's children in particular.

Since Kam Kim-ah had seen the ghost, over the next few days many idlers came up to the air-raid shelter whenever they were in the park to ask him about his ghost sighting. He never wearied of

---

*This line would normally be rendered "Are you crazy?" or something along that order. See previous note.

giving a highly animated account, usually winding up by painting a heroic picture of himself. He naturally avoided any mention of stealing papayas. Some of the children hung around the air-raid shelter all day long listening to him answer the people's questions and describe his encounter with the ghost; they never tired of hearing it. Sometimes they would ask him all sorts of questions about ghosts.

"Was her tongue this long?" a child asked, sticking his tongue out as far as it would go.

"That's nothin'!" Kam Kim-ah put his hand down on a level with his navel and said: "It came down to here, all the way to her belly button."

"Wow!" The child's face grew pinched and small, though his staring eyes were larger than ever.

"Her ... her ..." Another child wanted to ask something. "Whew! I'm afraid to say it."

"He wants to know what the ghost's eyes looked like." One of the other kids said it for him.

"Her eyes! Wa! They were this big." He made circles with his fingers the size of eyeglass lenses. "But I couldn't see the pupils—the eyes were all white, with blood-red lines running through them."

"When she walked did she float above the ground?"

"Of course she did!"

"Were her nails long?"

"This long. And there was poison on every one of them. Any place they touched a person it turned to blood."

"Aiyo! Weren't you scared?"

"Me? Not too scared. If I had been, she would have snatched me away then and there!"

Thus earning looks of respect and admiration from the children around him, Kam Kim-ah grew more and more expansive, eventually convincing himself that everything he was saying was true. Once he had gained the respect of these children, for several days they went out and fetched the firewood and water he needed. As a result, he experienced an incomprehensible sensation of floating in air.

A Blade of Grass, A Drop of Dew*

A week or so later his stomach had reached the point where it could not tolerate another sliver of yam. He looked down at the pile of yams on the floor by the head of his bed—there were enough left for three or four more days—then, with his hands on his hips, he stepped toward them, touched them with his toe, and said: "So that's the way it is. I always thought the Ah-li-shih folks were generous people who would just let me take all I wanted."

He thought back to his sighting of the ghost—it had already been eight or nine days at least. What was so unlucky about it? This ought to forestall any calamities for the time being. He could now no longer postpone his plan to go over to the spot opposite the coffin shop at Southgate.

He awoke from a somewhat troubled nap, sat in bed, and dully scratched himself all over. He was fully awake by the time he was scratching his head hard with both hands, thinking of the one important matter he had not yet taken care of.

With extreme care he took a circuitous route to the Southgate area. When he reached the Buddhist temple on Ah-shu-she Road, where there was a small general store, in front of which a pot of tea had been placed for thirsty passersby, Kam Kim-ah walked quickly over to it. Actually, what had aroused his interest was the tobacco and wine sign hanging under the eaves. He couldn't actually *read* the words, but he knew that any store that displayed one of those round lacquered metal signs was a tobacco and wine outlet. He walked up to the place, poured a glass of tea, and held

---

*A Taiwanese expression which means that there is substance for everyone; even a single blade of grass has its drop of dew.

it in his hands. As he drank the tea, his eyes were constantly scanning the inside of the store. He noticed an old man dozing behind the counter, who raised his head as Kam Kim-ah walked up closer to get a better look.

"Hey, boss, this is quite some tea you have here." He took another swallow. "It must be from Wu-lao-k'eng."

The old man smiled and said: "How could we have tea as fine as that? We grow this in our own tea garden."

"Really?" He drank another mouthful. "Where is this tea garden of yours?"

"Over on Thirteen Hills."

"Aha! Wu-lao-k'eng is just on the other side of Thirteen Hills. I'm an expert where tea's concerned." He took another drink. "Not bad, not bad at all. This tea's every bit as good as Wu-lao-k'eng." As he was talking he walked into the store and plopped down on the wooden bench in front of the counter.

Hearing someone praise the tea he had set out for pedestrians, the old man was naturally quite elated.

Kam Kim-ah had spotted the pastries inside the glass-enclosed counter right off; the sight of them made his stomach growl. But each time he was about to ask the old man to let him buy something on the cuff, he stopped himself. The opportune moment hadn't yet arrived, he calculated, so he racked his brain for something to chat with the old man about.

"Shit!" Kam Kim-ah cursed out of the blue. Before the old man even had time to puzzle over this, Kam Kim-ah continued: "I saw a ghost a few days ago. My bad luck!"

"Yeah, I heard people talking about it. They said it was at the Lan's vegetable patch."

"That's the goddamn place!"

"That's always been a bad piece of land."

"I know. But I had something important to do that day, so I cut across there to save some time."

"I heard it happened in daylight."

"That's exactly when it happened! Right after lunch."

"Wow, that was some evil ghost to actually appear in the daytime."

"You're right there. Who'd have thought it!" Kam Kim-ah tilted his head back and drained the cup of tea. "I think I'll have another cup," he said as he rose to walk outside.

"A connoisseur like you should drink some of this—it's hot." The old man reached over beside his chair and took a pot of steaming hot tea from a carrying case; he started pouring it into Kam Kim-ah's cup.

"Oh, that's great. Lucky, lucky me. Whoa! That's fine, that's fine. It's full."

"Think nothing of it, and if you want more, just help yourself."

"That's plenty." Seeing the happy expression on the old man's face, he quickly added: "It's always best to have a little pastry to go with fine tea like this."

"That's for sure. These pastries here are real fresh—delivered today."

"I've never done any business in this store of yours—too far from where I live. How about the Prosperity and Longevity stores in town—do you know them?"

"Of course I know them! But how could a little store like mine compare with the likes of them?"

"I get all of my tobacco and wine and other things at those two places. If it's not Prosperity, then it's Longevity. I always buy on credit, then pay them off all at once. The day before yesterday I paid off a pretty big bill at Longevity."

The old man walked over to the counter, opened the glass case, and asked him: "How many do you want? Round ones or twists?"

"Forget it. I'll go over to the Buddhist temple in a moment and collect a debt, then I'll come back."

"It's no big deal. Why don't you eat them first."

Kam Kim-ah thought about politely refusing again as a disarming gesture, but to his own surprise he blurted out: "Okay, then give me four of the round ones." He was feeling a little guilty, but when he saw how willing the old man was to extend him credit he felt relieved.

Altogether he ate six of the round pastries and drank three cups of tea. He was feeling considerably more comfortable now. But he still wasn't completely satisfied—he longed for a smoke. Looking up at the cigarettes in the glass case behind the counter, he turned his thoughts to ways to keep the conversation going.

"It's been a long time since I saw you beating your gong," the old man said.

This threw Kam Kim-ah into such a panic that he could only mutter in response. If he couldn't steer the conversation in the direction he wanted, it would be very difficult to have his way with the old man. He hurriedly put the empty cup up to his lips and pretended to be drinking so he wouldn't have to answer at once. Suddenly he knew what to say.

"Tsk-tsk. So you want to know about me and the gong, eh?"

"You haven't beat it for some time, have you?"

"No, I still do it, but it's awfully tiring. Sometimes I get a young-ster to come and do the shouting for me, but at other times I do it all myself."

"I haven't seen you out there for a long time."

"I was out just the day before yesterday."

"Not over here."

Kam Kim-ah smiled, then said: "It wasn't good news, so I knocked off after a while."

"What was the job?"

"Taxes!" He smiled again. "If it had been some good news, I would've made sure everyone heard it." Then he added the punch line: "Say, boss, how about giving me a couple of packs of Long Life cigarettes? I'll pay for it all later."

The old man took a look at his cigarette supply. "How about a pack of Red Paradise instead? I only have two packs of Long Life left."

"I'm used to smoking Long Life. It won't make any difference, since I'll probably be back to pay you for them in a little while."

Kam Kim-ah's belly was now full and his pockets were stuffed with two packs of Long Life cigarettes. Everything's going right today, he thought. He headed over toward the Buddhist temple, figuring that within a quarter hour or so he would reach Southgate. He rubbed his slightly protruding belly, now stuffed with pastries and several cups of tea. Looking off into the horizon, he mumbled to himself: "Hai! The old saying is right on the mark: 'A blade of grass, a drop of dew.' Damned if it isn't true—'A blade of grass, a drop of dew.' " He very cautiously puffed on the cigarette, which was now as short as it was ever going to get, as though he were engaged in a parting kiss. When he could no longer put off throwing it away, he pinched the tiny remainder between his fingers, then looked down at it; there was no way he could put it back to his lips. He blew out the last puff of smoke. Totally relaxed and at ease, he felt like leaping into the clouds and flying over to Southgate.

The Narrow Road

Usually there were eight or nine old vagrants squatting beneath the kadang tree opposite the coffin shop at Southgate. Whenever a family of mourners came to buy a coffin, these vagrants would go over to hang around the coffin and assist the family in its mourning duties. They would do things like carry banners and floral wreaths in the funeral procession, or whatever other sundry jobs were required. This would earn them the right to join the funeral banquet for two or three days, and sometimes even a week or so. They would also divide up a little pocket money. These old vagrants were men with no families or involvements who for a long time had passed their days squatting under the kadang tree. There was even a system of rights and privileges that had been established within their small circle. Naturally they were well versed on the quality of coffins. If, for instance, two grieving families came to buy lacquered coffins at the same time, one made of cedar, the other made of the more expensive cypress, they would immediately catch the scent of the cypress and fall in behind it. If it was a wealthy family, there was always a great show of pageantry, and always the possibility that there would be food and drink for more than a week, plus a substantial amount of pocket money. But once in a while there was an exception. Kam Kim-ah knew just about everything there was to know about these men, so when he gave up his job of beating the gong, it was only natural that he should decide to throw in his lot with them.

Only a stretch of road separated the coffin shop from the vacant ground beneath the kadang tree. The rhythmic, even sounds of the axe chopping and the two-man saw being pulled by the two coffin shop apprentices lulled the group of men into a midday nap. Some of the old vagrants slept soundly in the shade of the tree, their faces covered with their wide rainhats; they looked like the red and gray stones of the chess game that they played before their nap, which were scattered freely about. Others were sitting in their customary places chewing the fat with one another. But their conversations were so lacking in compatibility that it often seemed like each of them was talking to himself. Every once in a while a truck would roar past them down the road, causing them to reflect that there was a big world out there, one which they had no desire to belong to.

Kam Kim-ah walked up to a spot beneath the tree, where he saw this group of carefree vagrants spread out in all positions—seated, standing, supine. He was struck by a sense of disappointment as he realized that if he joined up with them, one of those scattered bodies would then be his. He had been able to conjure up visions of what their lives were like, but seeing them like this dealt a blow to his self-respect. He had to strain to think of any redeeming features they might have. Finally, pulling out one of his packs of Long Life cigarettes, he walked over to the man called Scabby Head, who was having a smoke, to bum a light. He made a point of showing off the pack of Long Lifes, which elicited from the sleepy vagrants wide-eyed looks of envy—their attention had been captured by the cigarettes. He handed the matches back to Scabby Head, then offered cigarettes to the others. His heart was pained to see four or five hands quickly stretch out toward him.

"How come we haven't seen you out with your gong?" Scabby Head asked him.

"That's right, it's been a long time," someone else commented.

"I quit!" Kam Kim-ah answered nonchalantly, blowing out a puff of smoke. "Beating a gong doesn't interest me anymore."

But someone else asked him in a doubting tone of voice: "Don't you mean that the loudspeaker pedicab took your ricebowl away?"

This comment grated terribly on his ears. He glared at the man who had said it; seeing that the man was smoking the cigarette he had given him, he felt even worse. Wanting to forcefully squelch the effect of the man's statement, he said very disdainfully: "What's so great about a grotesque thing like that? It just so happens that old Kam Kim-ah here didn't want to beat the gong anymore, and that other guy just picked up the slack. Shit! A lot of people are under the impression that this old hand, Kam Kim-ah here, had his ricebowl smashed by some young punk!"

"Actually, beating a gong's not a bad job."

"Not bad?" His brow furrowed as he took a deep puff on his cigarette. "How would you know? You've never done it. Sometimes I was out there so long I lost my voice, and my legs were sore for days. But all that wouldn't have mattered if they'd always paid me for my efforts! Wouldn't that make your blood boil! Good? It's about as good as a fart, that's how good it is!"

"Are there really deadbeats like that?"

Kam Kim-ah saw that several of the old vagrants smoking his cigarettes were shaking their heads indignantly, which secretly pleased him.

"Lots of 'em!" he said. "If I told you their names, I wouldn't be much of a man. Some of them had me beat my gong to find their lost kids, then when I found the kids, they refused to pay!"

"Would it have been okay not to pay if you hadn't found the kids?" someone asked.

"Hell no! If Kam Kim-ah beats his gong, he's got money coming." Now, although he was a small man, owing to his lifetime of shouting as he beat the gong, once he got excited, his every word became a virtual shout; but the louder he shouted, the hoarser he grew and the less clearly people understood him. As they talked there, the men unconsciously began to move closer until they were all gathered around him.

Scabby Head, in sympathy with Kam Kim-ah, said: "That's how it should be. Whoever heard of a matchmaker who was expected to guarantee a bunch of kids in the deal?"

"If everyone was as good as you fellows, we'd never have to talk about conscience," Kam Kim-ah said to the others. "There's nothing false about what the ancients said. 'There are two men of conscience: he who has died, and he who hasn't been born.'"

The smiles that Kam Kim-ah had anticipated appeared on the faces of every man present; not only were they interested in what he was saying, they were also feeling respect for him.

"Old Kam Kim-ah here is no fool. If beating a gong was such a good life, do you think I'd just hand my ricebowl over to someone else?"

The others all smiled and nodded their heads.

As he spoke he was always saying "Kam Kim-ah here, this, that, and the other," and he would thrust out his chest or tug on his sleeve—each sentence was accompanied by some sort of action. Scabby Head and the others, feeling that he was something special, were filled with envy.

Kam Kim-ah then turned the conversation around: "But when all's said and done, what you fellows have here is the good life."

"Good?" Scabby Head, who was leaning up against the kadang tree, straightened up and shouted: "Good like hell! Good, you say?"

The others all laughed.

Just as Kam Kim-ah was about to say something, he was cut off by one of the other men:

"If it stays like it has the past few days, we'll all die of starvation!"

It had been several days since anyone had visited the shop across the way to buy a coffin.

"It's still too early to be talking about any of us dying!" Kam Kim-ah stressed the word "us." "What're you fretting about? None of us has come to the end of the line. There's no need to worry, sooner or later someone's bound to die—if not today, then tomorrow. Who knows, maybe the day after tomorrow a bunch of people will come to buy coffins all at once!" He felt that this was just the right thing to say.

"God, no, not all at the same time! One a day is just perfect." This was Turtle's opinion.

"Is that what you really think?" Know-it-all asked critically. "One a day? I don't know how you'd handle it all. Each one is good for two or three days, so one every two or three days is just about right. That way, as soon as we finish up with one, we can move right on to another . . ." Before he had a chance to speak his piece, Fire Baby piped up angrily:

"Don't be stupid! Do you think you're King Yama of Hell or something?"

Know-it-all was stunned by the severity of Fire Baby's tone of voice. Fire Baby took the roar of laughter from the other men as approval, so he proudly hammered his point home: "Don't you interfere with the business of King Yama. You're talking like a fucking idiot!"

Blockhead, who had been sitting there listening to the conversation, grinning from ear to ear and looking like the potbellied Maitreya Buddha, suddenly stood up excitedly and began to babble like a child: "Go ahead and have everybody drop dead! Go ahead and have everybody drop dead!"

His outburst drew curses from the others:

"Fuck you, Blockhead!" one shouted.

"You drop dead yourself!" said another.

"Children should be seen and not heard, Blockhead!" shouted yet another.

But Blockhead had thoughts only for his own laughter, and for the cigarette butts in the hands of his cronies. He reached down and picked up the butt Kam Kim-ah had just discarded. These men always pinched the tips of their cigarettes lightly between their fingers. They had smoked cigarettes this way so long that the nicotine stains on their fingers had turned from yellow to a dark brown. And even though the nearness of the lit ends burned their fingers, they continued to smoke them unhurriedly, as though there were absolutely nothing to be concerned about. It was indeed a rarity for this group of men to smoke cigarettes of Long Life quality (Kam Kim-ah included). The mildness and aromatic smell of the smoke coupled with the feelings of grandeur he was experiencing had Kam Kim-ah in their spell. But then the image of five or six hands stretching out to him ruined the moment, and all he could do was swallow hard a couple of times.

The only effect of everyone's curses on Blockhead was a continuous peal of idiotic giggling emanating from his nostrils, since his mouth remained closed the whole time. It was a weird snorting sound. The others' response was a mixture of hilarity and anger. Fire Baby ran over and pulled Blockhead's whiskers, but the idiotic giggling continued, and even when his whiskers were pulled hard enough to hurt him, Blockhead would only say dispiritedly: "Don't do that! Don't!"

Scabby Head took a final puff on his cigarette and flipped the butt away. Blockhead, paying no attention to Fire Baby, casually edged his fat body over to the spot, but Fire Baby jumped in ahead of him and stepped on the butt. Blockhead merely tried to shove Fire Baby out of the way, his action more symbolic than substantial.

"If you promise to wash your ass nice and clean tonight, Fire Baby'll move his foot," Scabby Head said.

Blockhead, still in control of his temper, continued shoving Fire Baby and saying: "Don't say that! Don't! Scabby Head, don't say that!"

"Call me daddy. If you'll call me daddy, I'll move my foot."

"Don't do that! Daddy, don't . . ."

Hearing him call Fire Baby "Daddy," the others squealed with laughter. Just then, the sounds of chopping and sawing from the coffin shop stopped, and this cessation of activity across the street brought the merriment of the group of men under the kadang tree to a halt; Kam Kim-ah's laughter, alone, hung in the air for an instant, as the other men all turned their gazes to the coffin shop. What they saw was three pairs of surprise-filled eyes staring back at them. The silence of this moment was broken by Blockhead's childlike speech and intolerable giggling. Amidst the ensuing laughter the voice of the owner of the coffin shop was still discernible: "Drop dead, you fucking Blockhead!"

The few men who had been sleeping soundly through all of this were rudely awakened by this extraordinarily raucous laughter.

Kam Kim-ah's chatter was well received by one and all. In fact, Scabby Head told him that whenever he had nothing to do to come over and pass the time with them. Kam Kim-ah was already aware that Scabby Head was the leader of the group, so he carried a secret happiness with him on the road home. The knowledge that he too would someday have his spot under the kadang tree wiped his mind clean of worries and anger over his loss of a livelihood, and even his concern over his outstanding debts. He nonchalantly turned his steps toward the road on which the tobacco and wine shop whose owner pressed him the hardest to clear his bill was located. He was making mental calculations: if he returned tomorrow and his luck was good, a customer might show up at the coffin shop, and he could take part in the funeral procession; with food to eat and a handout as well, he would be in seventh heaven! The more he thought about tomorrow, the greater the possibility loomed. It had been a long time since anyone had bought a coffin, a situation that could not last much longer. His only fear had been that a coffin might have been sold the day before he showed up, which would have meant a delay of several days for him.

So engrossed in his thoughts was he that the sudden appearance of the Temple of Matsu, the Goddess of the Sea, brought him rudely back to his senses—he had inadvertently walked right up next to Longevity General Store. He was about to turn on his heel and get out of there, but just then someone inside the store spotted him. The jig was up. He had a sinking feeling. Quickening his pace, he turned his face away from the store, steeled himself, and walked on. But it was too late. He distinctly heard someone behind him call out "Kam Kim-ah," though he ignored the shout and kept on walking, hoping that the other man would think it was a case of mistaken identity. But the fellow was not fooled. He not only continued to shout Kam Kim-ah's name, but he ran after him. Grabbing him by the shoulder, he pulled Kam Kim-ah to a halt and cursed him angrily: "Fuck you and all your ancestors! Come on, run— let's see you run away now. I'll bet you can't sprout wings and fly off."

Kam Kim-ah had been jerked to a stop so abruptly he nearly stumbled to the ground.

"I wasn't running away," he said innocently, "I wasn't."

"You weren't running away? If you weren't running away, why didn't you stop when I called you?"

"I didn't hear you call me."

"You didn't hear me! Hah! Are your ears plugged up with shit? Huh?" With each sentence, Longevity gave Kam Kim-ah's shoulders two or three rough shakes so that his frail body rocked back and forth in the man's hands as though he were suspended in air. "You want me to clean them out with the manure spade? Huh? What do you say?"

"Brother Longevity, let me go! Please, I beg you." Kam Kim-ah cast embarrassed looks around him at the crowd that was gathering, then said to Longevity in a soft voice: "Let me keep a little face in front of all these people, okay? Please let me go."

"Hah! A man like you worrying about *face!* Did you all hear that?" Longevity smugly turned toward the crowd of people and, with a laugh, said in a loud voice: "This is what's called 'putting face before life itself!' "

Kam Kim-ah, with his frail body, was like a mouse caught in the grasp of a cat, tossed around so violently that onlookers were concerned that his innards might be all jumbled up. Sensing that the people gathering to watch all this commotion had formed a huge crowd that covered the handcar turntable, Kam Kim-ah was so embarrassed he wanted to crawl into a hole and hide. He had always felt that he had some status in this town, but now that was erased. On top of that, what remained of his will to implore for the return of even a little dignity had crumbled. His spirits were paralyzed, his most instinctive behavior consciously repressed; if it was necessary to lose face, all he had to say was: "So what? If I'm broke, I'm broke! My flesh has a salty taste, so what can you do about it?" But he figured he'd beg one more time, and if that didn't work then he'd go ahead and blurt it out and let that be the end of it.

"Brother Longevity, I'm not your senior, though I am older than you. Let me go, please. If I had the money I'd pay you," he said softly, a weak smile on his face.

"If you had the money?" Longevity laughed as though he were on the verge of hysteria. "If you had the money, then everyone in the world would be rich!"

Kam Kim-ah could stand it no longer; he was about to wrench himself free of Longevity's grasp and shout out savagely: "My flesh has a salty taste, so what can you do about it?" when he heard someone in the crowd say: "That's Kam Kim-ah, the gong beater." Suddenly, he grew weak, sensing that if he were to take a truculent attitude, this thing called "Kam Kim-ah" would surely be beaten to a pulp.

"Uncle Longevity," he said, "have a little compassion. Until I pay back the money I owe you, let all my luck be bad. Okay? Worthy Uncle Longevity . . ." He was about to ask Longevity once more to let him go, but he guessed that the more he pleaded to be released, the more Longevity would be inclined to hold fast, so he made up his mind not to ask him again. He merely repeated himself: "Worthy Uncle Longevity . . ."

All of this evoked peals of laughter from the crowd of onlookers.

And finally, Longevity, seeing no alternative, released his grasp.

"If you don't pay me next time, I'm not going to let you off so easily! Next time I'll rip the clothes right off your back."

Amidst the laughter from the crowd, someone said: "Longevity is quite the fellow—look how big a grandson he's got!"

"My luck isn't that bad!" Longevity commented in obvious high spirits.

Standing off to the side, feeling very embarrassed and at a loss for what to do with himself, Kam Kim-ah merely examined his wrinkled clothes and tried to smooth them out with his hand. He didn't hear a word of the clamor coming from the crowd. Now that the affair was closed, he didn't even have the good sense to leave the scene.

Longevity returned to his store, while the crowd of curious spectators surrounded Kam Kim-ah as he stood there with a vacant stare on his face. Then the whole scene began to resemble a strange type of fruit: the people were the skin, which at this moment began to peel itself off, layer by layer, until all that remained was the pit—Kam Kim-ah—cast aside there at the turntable. He was still absentmindedly smoothing a wrinkled spot on his clothing with his hand. Chagrin filled his heart. *I shouldn't have let him do that to me! I should've told him right off the bat: "My flesh has a salty taste, so what are you going to do about it?" Now that he's let me go, I can't look anyone in the face. I really shouldn't have called him "worthy uncle" or "worthy elder brother!"* Worthy, hah! His feelings of regret increased. He knew that no one was watching him any longer, but he simply could not raise his head, which seemed to weigh a hundred catties.

Way off in the distance some people were pushing a handcar toward him. They were on their way here to the turntable to get on the track heading toward the ocean. The driver was shouting. Finally coming to his senses, Kam Kim-ah left the scene in a hurry. As cautiously and alertly as a mouse, he quickly made his way back to the air-raid shelter in the park.

The moment he entered he threw himself noisily onto the bed, and before he knew it tears started coursing down his face. He began to sniffle, and was soon crying. Never before, in the twenty or thirty years of his adult life, had he shed a single tear. After somewhat regaining his composure, he sat up, cursing over and over in a heavy voice: "Fuck your old mother, fuck your old mother . . ." After a while he reached over to get the rag that was draped over the head of his bed, with which he wiped his tear-streaked face. Sensing a warmth and soreness on his right cheek, he reached up to touch it and discovered that he had two scratches. He paced back and forth about the air-raid shelter until he happened to notice his gong lying beneath the bed. He took it out and looked it over.

"All right!" he said resolutely. "If I ever get another chance to go out on the streets and beat this gong again, I'm definitely going to start saving some money."

It's All Right To Watch People Drink Tonics, but Don't Watch Dogs Fight over a Bone

By the following day, Kam Kim-ah had put together a story of how he had received the two scratches on his right cheek. As soon as he saw the men under the kadang tree he said to them: "There's truth to the saying that lightning only strikes good men." He rubbed his cheek. "After I left here yesterday, just as I was passing the Cultivation Pharmacy, I picked up some peanuts from the ground to feed to the two monkeys, and who would have thought that as I raised my head one of them would grab hold of my head and scratch my face? I hope the damned beast dies an early death!"

"That's for sure! The two monkeys at the Cultivation Pharmacy are famous for their pranks. Not long ago a woman was walking past there when the same thing happened to her—one of them grabbed hold of her head and wouldn't let go," Fire Baby said.

"What happened to the woman afterwards?" Know-it-all asked, his interest piqued.

"You're the horniest guy around. You wake up as soon as anyone mentions a woman," Fire Baby said, his mouth cracked in a wide grin, as he led the others in a round of laughter.

Know-it-all, apparently somewhat intimidated by Fire Baby, responded: "Then . . . then, why did you bring it up?"

"You want to know, do you?" Fire Baby said. "Well, since you want to know, I'm going to tell you." He puffed himself up affectedly and even his words had a ring of affectation: "Afterwards, afterwards, uh, the woman got married and had some kids . . . ha-ha!"

Kam Kim-ah squatted on his haunches, and when the laughter had just about died out, he said, rubbing his scratched face: "Damn him, I hope the hand that scratched me rots away!" He was thinking about Longevity, but what he said was: "A pharmacy ought to gain a reputation by selling quality medicines, not by having its monkeys scratch people."

"That's right," said Fire Baby, who was now sitting beside Kam Kim-ah. "Do you have any of those Long Life cigarettes left over from yesterday?" There was a marked contrast in the tone of the two separate utterances. He thrust his neck out as would a throat specialist looking down the throat of a patient. His eyes were glued to Kam Kim-ah's shirt pocket.

Kam Kim-ah patted the pocket of his shirt and, with a wry smile, said he didn't.

"Does a chicken with a crooked beak get any of the good feed?" The man named Mongrel, who was sitting beneath another kadang tree, suddenly spat out.

"What's that got to do with you?" Fire Baby leapt to his feet. "What are you thinking, you damned ingrate!"

"What's it to you? You looking for trouble?"

Mongrel's response was quite strong; he got to his feet and said with a cunning sneer: "Aha! So you've finally found a pretext."

"Come over a little closer if you've got the guts."

This was said so loudly that the speaker's voice seemed about to explode.

Laughing lightheartedly, but with anger in his eyes, Mongrel took a few steps forward, his glaring eyes never leaving the other man's face.

"What's this? Are you going to stand there and let me beat the shit outta you, or are you gonna mix it up? You'll treat me for free or you'll have it delivered to my door."

Fire Baby's hands were already clenched into fists, his arms hung stiffly to his sides; he took two or three steps forward to show he wasn't backing down.

Only a single pace now separated the two men. Seeing this state of affairs, Kam Kim-ah began to tremble. He was hoping that someone would step in and break it up, but when he looked back at the others, he discovered that they were all sitting or reclining on the ground, so hot they all looked a bit dopey. Their eyes were glued to the two men squaring off with each other, and they were enjoying the prospect of a fight that loomed before them. It looked like it was going to start any second now.

"Isn't anyone going to help settle this?" Kam Kim-ah asked anxiously, his eyes sweeping their faces. "Hurry, someone hurry up and do something!" As he made his plea he walked up close to the two men.

"Why trouble yourself, Kam Kim-ah? When the weather's as hot as it is today, it takes too much energy to try to break up a fight," someone said.

Fire Baby and Mongrel were already pushing one another back and forth. Their anger was no longer as strong as when the incident had begun, and when they heard Kam Kim-ah coming over to make peace between them, saying "Come . . . come on, listen to me now," they decided to take advantage of these peacemaking attempts to gain a moral victory before the fight was called off. There wasn't going to be any fight now, anyway, they thought, so their pushing and shoving grew more heated, to the point that they were both grunting. Kam Kim-ah, who had thoughts of stepping in and breaking things up, moved off to the side when he saw how hard they were shoving each other. His mediations were limited to the vocal, not the physical variety:

"Ai! Ai! Don't fight, don't fight. Someone hurry up and pull 'em apart!"

"Don't pay any attention to 'em, Kam Kim-ah. Don't spoil their fun," Scabby Head shouted.

Kam Kim-ah just stood there, not knowing what to do.

Both Mongrel and Fire Baby were scrawny men, so that everywhere you looked they were small, except for their joints—knees, elbows, chins, cheeks—all of which jutted out almost frighteningly. This was particularly true with their shoulders: a loose layer of skin covered sharply jutting shoulder bones, and as they forcefully bumped one another, not only did they make sounds like stones banging together under water, but the sharp pains reached down to the marrow. It was too late to lessen the force of the bumping shoves—having mounted the tiger, it was hard to climb down. Matters having reached this stage, the two could only bump each other even harder to determine who would be the victor, thereby bringing this standoff to its conclusion. Their thoughts were identical. They bumped each other once more, then stepped back before going at it again; this time they both lowered their center of gravity and were almost crouching as they faced each other—this would really do the trick. The stinging pain from the last encounter was most severe in Mongrel's shoulder, but he couldn't stop now. Just as they lurched at each other this time, Mongrel twisted his body slightly, and Fire Baby brushed past him, looking like a catapulted missile as he crashed headlong to the ground, where he was stopped by a kadang tree.

Everyone burst out laughing as they saw him sprawled there. "That's a force of a thousand catties," one of them said. "Look at all the leaves he's knocked down from the kadang tree!" Fire Baby was fiery mad. He turned around, fists waving menacingly in the air, and without a thought for how things would turn out, rushed forward like a madman. Kam Kim-ah was more frightened than ever, but before the charging Fire Baby could get to where they were standing, Kam Kim-ah placed himself in front of Mongrel, spread out his hands, and shouted: "For God's sake, don't! For God's sake, don't! For God's sake . . ." The wild anger of Fire Baby had produced a similar reaction of anger in Mongrel. Ignoring Kam Kim-ah's attempt to place himself as an obstacle between the two of them, Mongrel tried to push him out of the way, but it was too late—Fire Baby was upon them. With Kam Kim-ah standing between them, they swung their fists and the battle was on. Kam Kim-ah couldn't get out of the way. When one of them kicked, the other kneed; when one of them clawed, the other ripped and tore, until they all tumbled to the ground in a pile.

Neither Mongrel nor Fire Baby could get the upper hand, but as they were rolling on the ground in a stalemate, they both suddenly felt comfortably rested. They were still grappling with one another, but a mutual agreement to stop the fisticuffs had been silently reached, and neither wanted to strike the next blow. They puffed and panted as sweat poured down their faces, then suddenly feeling how ridiculously funny it all was, their mouths parted as the laughter welling up inside them began to burst forth.

The person who got the worst of it all was Kam Kim-ah. With the two men on top of him, pinning him to the ground, he lay there covering up his head, not daring to move. His eyes shut tightly, he just kept mumbling over and over: "For God's sake, don't! For God's sake, don't!"

"That's enough, now, that's enough!" Scabby Head said as he lazily got to his feet. "You've nearly squashed Kam Kim-ah to death!"

Mongrel and Fire Baby reacted as though they had been waiting for someone to call them to a halt, for as soon as they heard Scabby Head's shouts, they let go of each other and stood up. When they saw the shape Kam Kim-ah was in they started to laugh.

"Ram it up your . . . ! Go ahead and fight! Show me how you can fight! Old Scabby Head here will treat you both to some fried noodles if you're still able to slug it out!" Scabby Head lectured them with the airs of the head of the group.

Kam Kim-ah still lay on his side, mumbling over and over: "For God's sake, don't!" unaware that he should be getting up off the ground.

"You've squashed his soul right out of his body," Scabby Head said, walking over to take a look.

The smiles disappeared from Mongrel's and Fire Baby's faces. They just stood there dumbly looking on, while the others crowded around to watch Scabby Head looking Kam Kim-ah over.

"The poor old guy," Scabby Head said. "Does anyone know how to locate his revival tendon?"*

No answer. The men just stared dumbly into each other's faces, their eyes opened much wider than usual.

Scabby Head lifted up Kam Kim-ah's black shirt and felt around under his armpits; he stopped suddenly, as though he had found something, then pinched down so hard that even his own mouth was twisted sharply. Kam Kim-ah let out a yelp, which instilled Scabby Head with confidence. "So that's all there is to locating the revival tendon!" He pinched again, hard, which elicited a "What the fuck!" from Kam Kim-ah. This quickly put everyone at ease, and their eyes returned to normal size. Blockhead was the first to break the stifling atmosphere the incident had produced with his unbearable giggles. Know-it-all, childishly hopping around like a sparrow, dashed over behind Blockhead, reached his hands around him, and squeezed his fat, slightly sagging breasts. Life had returned to this tiny section of the world.

Kam Kim-ah's every movement, from sitting up to getting to his feet to starting to talk, was carefully scrutinized. All of this made him feel as though he were invested with some special privileges. The other men watched him with smiling eyes (no, in One-eye's case you would have to say smiling *eye*—his left one—for his right eye never opened and, in fact, was inset deeply into its socket), waiting to see just what he would do.

Kam Kim-ah felt and rubbed himself all over, squealing with

---

*By pinching a particular tendon under the armpit or on the face of a person who has suffered heatstroke the excess heat will be released from his body.

pain and filling the air with four-letter words as he did so. More rubbing and feeling, until there was no place he had missed. During his self-examination, every shout and every curse was received with sympathy and good-natured laughs by the other men. And their sympathy was no less generous just because there was a little exaggeration on his part. As a result, he did not feel too strongly that he had been abused. He did sense, however, that he must take advantage of this moment, now that they were all on his side. Brushing the dust off his clothing, he was of a mind to blow his stack and show them that he was no one to fool with, but after some reasoned reflection, he said fatalistically:

" 'It's all right to watch people drink tonics, but don't watch dogs fight over a bone.' " He smiled. "Hai! The ancients sure knew what was what. We can follow their lead. Me, I'm all muddleheaded. Ai! A real muddlehead."

"I think you ought to take some medicine in case you have any internal injuries," Fire Baby said. "I'll recommend some herb medicine for you." He cocked his head. "Horsewhip grass is the best. After it's ground into a pulp, if you're a drinking man, you can add some wine; if not, you can take it with some brown sugar. It's guaranteed. I've cured a lot of people with it."

"Mixing up some horsewhip grass is easy. You can find all you want at Graveyard Harbor."

Kam Kim-ah turned around quickly to look at the person who was making suggestions for his well-being.

"There's somethin' else that's not bad," Scabby Head said. "Banyan bristles pounded into a pulpy liquid and drunk straight is good for internal injuries. It doesn't taste as bad as horsewhip grass and there's no smell."

"If you're gonna take something, do it now."

"Right, right," Kam Kim-ah said.

"It's only fair to have Mongrel and Fire Baby go pick the grass."

"That's all right, I'll get it myself. All they need to do is buy the wine."

"Sure, sure, that's being fair."

Several of the men voiced their agreement.

"But I don't have any money now," Mongrel complained, scratching his head. "We haven't had a funeral banquet for a long time."

It *had* been a long time, probably a week since they had last seen a customer at the coffin shop. But it seemed to take Mongrel's comment to force home the seriousness of this dilemma. The sweltering heat had their nerves on edge. Anxieties flooded their minds, and Kam Kim-ah's injuries quickly faded into insignificance.

"We're not heartless, but it's really been a long time since anyone died."

"What are you so worried about? There's a meal coming right around the corner," Kam Kim-ah said.

"Who?" Their eyes lit up.

"Scholar Yang. It's a sure bet."

"Balls! They were making noises about him breathing his last years ago, and they're still making those noises today."

"That old fart is holding on for dear life," Fire Baby said.

"Eleven of his twelve souls are already gone, and the last one won't let go of the threshold—you'd hold on for dear life too!"

"Ai! It oughtta give it up. The old guy isn't very smart—by hanging on like this he's lost the filial respect of the younger ones. What good does that do anybody?"

Kam Kim-ah's mention of Scholar Yang led to a lengthy discussion, but nothing came of the talk, and with the weather as hot as it was, the longer the discussion lasted, the less spirited it grew.

The clamor of a moment before and their light mood gradually began to settle earthward like dust. One by one they took up their favorite positions and settled into a dull-witted immobility. Kam Kim-ah was not accustomed to this sort of reticence. After racking his brain for a few moments, he came up with a subject for conversation. Tossing a pebble over Scabby Head's way, he said:

"Hey Scabby Head, some people say that if there's no business at the coffin shop, all you have to do is strike a coffin three times with a broom, and the next day someone will come over to buy a coffin. Do you believe that?"

"I've heard that, but I never tried it myself."

"I wonder if the owner of the coffin shop knows about it."

"Everyone knows. If it worked, he'd try it before he'd just let his business peter out like this."

"Maybe he's never tried it," Kam Kim-ah said, holding out a ray of hope. "So whaddya say?"

The others didn't want to be left out of this discussion, and although they didn't actually say anything, they had at least snapped out of their gloomy mood.

"Let's give it a try," Kam Kim-ah said excitedly.

"Who's going to do it?"

"Any one of us, including me."

"Well, speak up."

The others all shrunk back, their smiles showing that they wanted to be excluded. They cast glances back and forth.

"Look," Kam Kim-ah whispered, "the coffin shop owner and his two apprentices have knocked off for lunch. And look over there, to the left: there's a broom standing against the wall. If we're gonna do it, now's our chance."

"Who's going?"

"Let's draw straws," Mongrel offered.

"Draw straws! They'll be back outside before you've got the straws cut and drawn." Kam Kim-ah wanted very badly to try it himself. This was just what the doctor ordered to get on their good side.

"So what'll we do?" Mongrel was getting a little anxious. So was Kam Kim-ah. He was afraid that if he allowed Mongrel to be the first to volunteer, he would lose a ready-made opportunity to distinguish himself. Observing the expression on Mongrel's face, and afraid that he was about to open his mouth to speak up, Kam Kim-ah blurted out:

"I'll go!" He looked at the others. "By the time you guys get around to doing anything, you've missed your chance!"

As the others looked at Kam Kim-ah, the volunteer, respect was written all over their faces, which redoubled his boldness. Taking a deep breath, he made ready to dash across the street.

"Keep an eye on the road for me. If anyone comes, give a yell." With that, he headed across the street. Looking back over his shoulder, he saw all the men under the kadang tree holding their breath and watching his every move in motionless silence; they were so still they seemed about to pop.

Kam Kim-ah walked over beneath the eaves of the building, then looked up and down the street before darting on ahead. He picked up the broom, carried it over to the nearest coffin, rapped on it three times—*bang, bang, bang*—then scurried back across the street, still holding onto the broom.

The men had started to roar with laughter the moment they saw him pick up the broom, and the sight of him rushing back across the street, broom in hand, had them holding their sides with laughter.

"You guys are real losers. I just risked my life for you!"

They were by now laughing uncontrollably.

"You're a bunch of ignorant pigs!" He was waving the broom in the air as a symbol of his contribution.

Scabby Head was holding his sides laughing at the sight of Kam Kim-ah with the broom in his hand.

"Aiya! Mother! The . . . the broom . . . oh, it's killing me! . . ."

Everyone there was now aware of the humor of the situation. The waves of laughter reached the ears of the two apprentices at the coffin shop across the street, who emerged to see what was going on, their ricebowls still in their hands.

"Hey, Kam Kim-ah, your broom . . . ," someone said softly.

By this time the laughter had stopped completely, as the men glanced back and forth across the street, then at Kam Kim-ah. He had been completely in the dark until the word "broom" was mentioned. When he came to his senses and saw what was happening, he froze on the spot.

"Hide it—hurry, they're looking at you."

As he jerked his head around to look across the street, someone came up and yanked the broom out of his hand, threw it to the ground, and sat on it along with one of the other men.

The two apprentices continued to shove rice into their mouths as they watched the activity on this side of the street. But seeing that nothing much was going on, they went back inside. Kam Kim-ah breathed a sigh of relief, then began to sense the humor in the situation.

"How could I have carried the broom back with me?" he said. "What a lunkhead I am."

"I think you were giddy."

"Where's the broom? I'll take it back over."

"Since nothing's happened, just forget it. We'll toss it away later."

"Ai! How . . . how can we do that?"

"Don't worry about it," Scabby Head said. "Tomorrow we'll see if your plan's worked."

"Well, I . . . I've already done my part."

Although no one said anything in response, Kam Kim-ah could tell from their smiling faces that they had accepted him and that he was covered with glory.

But then, just as he was receiving their accolades, his heart was troubled by a nagging anxiety. He began to regret what he had just done, for if someone were to actually come to buy a coffin on the following day, wouldn't he—Kam Kim-ah—be responsible for the person's death? *I've already lived half a lifetime, and although I might not be considered a particularly "good" man, I've never been a particularly "bad" one either—and certainly not one to cause someone's death. I can only hope and pray that the whole experiment falls through.* He sat down on the ground with his eyes closed, his back resting against the kadang tree, as he thought about his situation.

He was completely oblivious to the words of praise, meaningful or casual, with which the group of men were rewarding him, and to their recounting of the rollicksome effects his daring venture had produced. He didn't even feel like bothering with them; he was too wrapped up in the feeling that he had sunk into a deep, dark abyss. He just sat there and thought. A stream of fond memories of events from his past, even those of little consequence, filled his mind. He now no longer had to feel badly about his loss of income, but he did lament with considerable pain the cessation of the jobs he had been given, jobs that had filled him with a sense of esteem rather than subjecting him to ridicule.

A mother stood at the entrance to the air-raid shelter calling out in mournful tones: "Gong beater! Gong beater!" Then a pause. "Is the gong beater here?"

"Yeah! Here I am!" Kam Kim-ah awoke from his nap and jumped to his feet.

"Please come outside."

"I'm coming! I'm coming!"

As he stepped out through the shelter entrance he was temporarily blinded by the bright sunlight. The woman started to talk to him before he could even make out who she was.

"My child, Ah-hsiung, is lost." After saying the words "my child," the woman began to choke up and her speech was barely intelligible.

Kam Kim-ah knew exactly what this young mother whose child was lost was feeling. He consoled her: "I know, I know. Your child is lost, isn't he?"

The sobbing woman nodded.

"Don't worry, just tell me slowly how big he is, how I can recognize him, what he's wearing, and where you think he might be. When did you notice he was missing? That should do it."

"He ... he ..." The woman was trying very hard to speak, but all she could do was sob.

"That's all right, don't worry. There isn't a lost child anywhere that I can't find. You go ask around and see if I'm not telling the truth. And I can find yours just as easily."

The young mother was greatly reassured. "His name is Ah-hsiung," she said. "He has big eyes, and he's very cute. We say he's three, but he's actually only two." She stopped and thought a moment, and as she did, her mournful appearance suddenly gave way to a look of sheer loving. "I took him with me to buy a piece of material to cut up and make some diaper pants for him. While I was looking over the material in the shop, he was fussing to get down and play, so I told him not to go into the street—he even made a sound that he understood me." The mournful look reappeared.

Kam Kim-ah took advantage of the break in her narration to ask some questions, until he finally got all the information he needed.

"Okay, that's all I need to know. You go back and look for him. Your best bet is to go down to the big drainage ditch and look around there. I'll start with the gong right away, and everything will be fine."

He turned on his heel and picked up his gong, then fell in behind the young mother and started beating the gong.

> *Bong! Bong! Bong!*
> "The gong beater's coming your way—
> "Listen everyone, here's what I have to say—
> "A child, his name is Ah-hsiung—
> "Three years old, but really only two—
> "His eyes big as flower buds, cute as a bug's ear;
>   Barefoot, black open-crotch pants, a white shirt—
> "Anyone seeing him take him to the police station right
>   away—
> "Or to the quilt shop beside the Temple of the Patriarch—
> "Ah-hsiung's mother is on pins and needles—"
> *Bong! Bong! Bong!*

No one in the entire town escaped the sound of Kam Kim-ah's gong that afternoon. Around dusk, the mother came running up the street, Ah-hsiung cradled in her arms, to catch up with Kam Kim-ah. She expressed her gratitude over and over, then thrust a red envelope into his hand. There hadn't been much money in it, but as he thought back to it now, it had impressed him as a rich recompense.

Ai! I hope and pray I haven't killed anyone, and I wish I hadn't done that stupid thing. The feeling that his heart was bobbing around in a deep, dark abyss would not go away.

It was obvious to the others that the expression on Kam Kim-ah's face was vastly different than the heroic look of a moment before.

"Kam Kim-ah, what's wrong?"

He heard them, but did not feel like answering.

"He probably really was injured," Scabby Head said, his eyes scanning the faces of Mongrel and Fire Baby.

"I, I'll go get some horsewhip grass for you, okay?" Fire Baby volunteered apologetically.

A smile suddenly appeared on Kam Kim-ah's face and his eyes flashed open. The pale faces of the concerned men who had gathered round him lit up immediately. He had obviously gained acceptance into the group, just as he had planned, except that it had happened more quickly than he had anticipated. He was not alarmed; he just felt a bit degenerate. It was the sense of degeneracy that by rights should have alarmed him, for this indefinable degeneracy was the one thing he had not anticipated. And this unexpected development was fearful enough to alarm him, as it began to crush down on him with deadening force. For Kam Kim-ah, this was the first time he had come face to face with the specter of degeneracy. "It's nothing, just an old disorder. I'll be all right after I've rested a moment."

"But don't take it too lightly. You don't want something like this to turn into a chronic injury. That's a real problem."

He sensed that he was too easily deceived. The scorn in which he had so recently held these men had been completely and immediately obliterated by a few kind words.

"I won't. I'll go get some horsewhip grass in just a moment." There were no pains anywhere on his body; casually stroking his chest, he said: "I don't think there's anything wrong."

Everyone smiled very weakly.

Cockcrow Signals a Happy Event

He had experienced a feeling of light-headedness as soon as he got up from under the kadang tree, and he never could have gotten to his feet at all if he hadn't been able to close his eyes and hold on to the tree trunk. He sat down on the cement block at the entrance to the air-raid shelter, his face buried in his hands. He figured it was probably because of his yam diet; otherwise . . . *Oh-oh! Here it comes again.* A brightness suddenly replaced the haziness in his brain; it gradually turned yellow, then green, then red, then the encircling haziness returned. At this instant his entire being seemed to be a mere shell after having something drained from it. Fortunately he was sitting down at the moment, or he would surely have collapsed. He readied himself for the next attack, which he knew would come. He continued to hold his head in his hands, his body was tense and coiled—even his toes were curled inward. These dizzy spells had troubled him a great deal of late; sometimes he was able to bring one under control through sheer willpower alone, while at other times the force of his willpower had the effect of increasing their severity. He had gradually learned to cope with these two situations by trial-and-error: when the oncoming spell was controllable, he would increase the force of his willpower very gradually; when control was out of the question, he would gradually slacken off, for if he were to let the dizzy spell take complete control of him with a rush, he would immediately begin retching or, even worse, crumple to the ground like a man on the losing end of a judo match. After a long while, and then an even longer while, before the second attack hit him, his muscles began to relax and loosen like lumps of kneaded dough. Once they were relaxed, the spell had passed, but still he raised his head very gingerly, the chill sweeping over his body making him realize that he was sweating. The scene before him was too bright, like an overexposed photograph. He propped himself up on the cement, then steadied himself with the aid of the damp wall and placed his hand on his bed; a current of warmth ran up along his arm all the way to his heart. Once he lay down on the bed this current of warmth flowed out of his body.

An oppressive darkness surrounded him, which, by comparison, made him fade into infinite insignificance. He was powerless to move. It was as though he had been placed there expressly to lie on his side and sleep facing the wall. He was totally alert. Amidst the darkness, beads of water on the damp wall slowly came into view, reflecting the light seeping in through the entrance as they slithered down the wall, drop by drop. Kam Kim-ah, who had no concept of time, suddenly felt very keenly time's swift passage. *Tomorrow will be here very soon. Have I killed anyone? I'll know tomorrow.* He was deeply superstitious. He had gone through life comforted by a conviction that the gods were protecting him. Wasn't it true, he thought, that on the day before the birthday of every temple god, it was he who beat his gong to inform all of the town faithful of this fact? And on each of the festive temple processions or excursions of the gods, it was he who led the way, waving his red-festooned mallet and beating his gong. *Shit, now I don't even have this to fall back on.* He was seeing a tradition crumble right before his eyes, as though it were a gigantic statue crashing to the ground. And since it was crumbling through his fingers, the guilt, he felt, was his. Yet all he could do was curse the cause—which was not at all clear to him. "Shit!"

Much of the light from the entrance had faded, until the drops of water on the damp wall were no longer visible. Mosquitoes buzzed around his ears, sounding like the fading resonance of a struck gong—as though the gong that lay beneath his bed and served as a container for odds and ends were making sounds: *bong, bong, bong.* Beneath the scorching sun the gong was reverberating. He wiped his sweat repeatedly with the hand that had held the mallet. He screamed at the top of his voice—the salt from his sweat was stinging his eyes. Golden flashes of light from the surface of the gong were blinding him. He screamed once more at the top of his voice. He still could not hear the sound of his own screams. Sweat continued to ooze from his pores. He tried again: the faces of passersby crushed in on him, huge and threatening, and he ran like a madman, with many people chasing wordlessly after him. He could run no farther; holding the gong tightly to his chest, he squatted down on his haunches, exposing his back until it was chilled, but when he turned around, there was nothing. The drops of water on the wall were still not visible. He could hear his heart thumping so hard that it seemed about to burst through his chest wall.

He wiped the perspiration with his clothing as he lay there gazing intently up at the shelter's ventilation opening. Originally a smokestack that had been carried over and buried deep in a mound of earth, this opening now served as the shelter's source of ventilation. Strangely, no matter how hard it rained, the water had never seeped in through it. Sometimes Kam Kim-ah would use a brick to plug up the opening, but not today.

Through it he could see a circular patch of blue poking through the pitch blackness above him and moving with his gaze. If he could have seen a bright star up there in this patch of blue, then he would have known that the night was still early. But he saw nothing, only the patch of blue that filled the space above him and kept floating past. It did not capture his attention. Instead, he rolled over and lay facing the wall, thinking about the coming day. *They're a bunch of disgusting pigs.* He yawned and his eyes watered. He closed his eyes and wiped the moisture away; he didn't feel like opening his eyes any more. *The fucking pigs!* He could hear Blockhead's inane giggles. *That guy can go to hell!* Know-it-all's grimy, protruding navel—*Whew!* One-eye's sunken eyelid; the hernia that bumped on the ground whenever Gold Clock squatted down; Scabby Head's pate, which looked like it had been gnawed on by a dog, plus his runny nose and rotting ear lobes. *A bunch of pigs!* He drew his itchy leg up to scratch it. *I never knew what scabies were, but whenever you fall on hard times you run up against just about everything.* He snapped his fingernails, yawned, wiped his watery eyes, made clicking noises with his mouth, and finally swallowed. *I hope and pray I haven't killed him.*

The shelter was hot and stuffy, and by rights he should have been sleeping in the entranceway. But now piled in front of it were several bamboo brooms and scoops. *Damn them!* He had talked to the men who swept up the park about this, telling them to put their equipment inside, for it was only on hot nights that he slept outside. They had said that if he wasn't going to sleep inside, then he should get out, because they were going to put a door and a lock on it. *Who said I wasn't sleeping there? Damn them!* He yawned again. "Go to sleep now." He said this as though he were coaxing a child to sleep. He rolled over; there were still no stars in the patch of blue above him. He listened intently and with total concentration. *Damn it, it's still early for sure.* The only sounds came from the worms, the frogs, and the water in the fountain. A happy thought suddenly struck him: *If it's not the first watch, it must be the second by now, and I haven't heard the crow of a rooster. The old saying goes: "The first and second watches signal death, the third and fourth signal happy events," and that's right.* That thought led him to another: *I haven't killed anyone, I haven't.* He looked up again and searched the patch of blue. Still no stars. *It must be the first watch. Otherwise it's the second, and not a single crowing sound.*

He rolled back over and faced the wall, yawned, squeezed his watery eyes, then noisily licked his lips a couple of times and swallowed. He did not open his eyes again. *Now go to sleep; it'll be light soon.* But he was too excited to sleep. His escapades involving the desperate search for yams and the debts he had accumulated were cast out of his mind as though they had never existed. *I don't have to wait till tomorrow—I know now that I haven't killed anyone! I'm not a bad person after all.* With happiness filling his heart, he uttered: "Even if someone actually goes over and buys a coffin tomorrow, that doesn't prove that it was my doing. Through the first and second watches there wasn't a single rooster's crow." But a nagging doubt persisted even in the midst of this joy: "I *didn't* hear a rooster's crow! I was awake the whole time!" He listened intently once more. He could no longer detect the sounds of worms or frogs, though the sounds of the water fountain and the wind in the trees sent a chill through him. *I'm going to go to sleep. If a rooster's going to crow, then let him.* He yawned. *It's past the second watch by now.*

Just as he was comforting himself with this thought, from way off in the distance came the faint sounds of a rooster's crow. This threw a scare into him; then he heard the answering crow from nearby. He rolled over to look up through the ventilation opening, where he saw a star woven into the edge of the patch of blue above him. He smiled at the star. The cold rays of light from this pre-dawn star seemed more lustrous than ever to him. *Here comes another fellow.* He heaved a long sigh. *How can I avoid aging at this rate?* A weak smile, looking like the trail of a meteor, appeared on his face.

In the oppressively dark shelter, the last hint of a thought had disappeared. His even breathing was at one with the darkness and the tranquility of the night. This was the most blissful time of day for him: all his fears, self-doubts, remorse, contradictions, and miseries seeped from his heart and melted into the darkness, leaving him to return to his beginnings, to the womb, where he was just like everyone else. He was oblivious of everything.

Good News

As dawn broke, Kam Kim-ah heard the men who swept the park come and pick up their equipment, and he heard them put it back some time later. He was just too lazy to get out of his snug bed. If he could just sleep a while longer, he thought, then he wouldn't have to go out so early to wash up and scrounge something to eat. It would have to be yams anyway. He wasn't at all anxious. *If I can hold off feeding my belly for a while and make it past noon,*

I'll have saved myself from a couple of meals. He smiled wryly.

It never occurred to him that if he went back to sleep he wouldn't wake up until way past noon. He sat groggily on the edge of the bed for a moment, then reached down and fished the Long Life cigarettes out from the gong. Since he had cut each of them in half in order to make them last as long as possible, he still had about a pack left. While he was at it he took a look at the gong. It just lay there, resigned to its fate, a receptacle for old nails of various sizes, a big red button he had found, and a ball of twine. The cigarettes were slightly damp and a little harder on the draw than usual. He decided to go over to the kadang tree and see what was up. Taking out two of the half-cigarettes, he put one behind each ear and walked out of the shelter, making some minor repairs on his conical bamboo hat before putting it on.

When the canopy of the kadang tree came into view in the distance, he could hear unusually joyful sounds coming from beneath it. By the time the men came into view he was surprised to see that they weren't sitting or lying on the ground. All eight or nine of them were standing up discussing something. Just then one of them spotted him. They all spun around. "Here he comes! Here he comes!" Kam Kim-ah was put on his guard and slowed down, being careful to take very quiet steps so as not to interfere with his hearing, but taking care also not to let on that he was on his guard. He looked the situation over very carefully: there didn't seem to be any evidence of indignation among the gathered men; in fact, he noticed that one of them was waving to him. It was immediately obvious from the motion of the man's arm that this was a wave of welcome. This put Kam Kim-ah at ease, and he began walking at a quickened pace.

"Hey! Kam Kim-ah . . . ," Mongrel called out to him when he was about ten steps away.

"Shh!" Scabby Head warned Mongrel, his back to the coffin shop. He pointed surreptitiously across the street: "Don't let on to them."

Encouraged by the smiles on their faces, Kam Kim-ah walked in among the men, who immediately crowded around him.

"Kam Kim-ah," Scabby Head said, "you did it!"

"Fuck him . . . " It was not an angry curse; quite the contrary, it was said in praise. They had taken this insulting epithet and turned it into a catch-all phrase. "It's a good thing you thought of it. Scholar Yang died! Fuck him!" He pounded Kam Kim-ah on the shoulder.

Kam Kim-ah slumped the shoulder that was being pounded and rubbed it with an exaggerated motion. "Hey! Are you crazy? Tsk-tsk-tsk." He laughed. *That's all right, let 'em go ahead and give me the credit, as long as I know the truth, that it wasn't me who killed Scholar Yang. I was awake through the first and second watches, and not a rooster anywhere crowed.* Putting the respect he was being shown to advantage, he commented: "You should have done the same thing a long time ago yourselves, instead of letting him starve to death."

"You're absolutely right."

"Actually, everyone knows you can drum up business by beating on a coffin with a broom, but no one ever thought of doing it."

"Who would have thought of doing it? We all figured that it was the coffin shop owner's affair."

As always, before he spoke, One-eye rolled his sunken eye inward, then blurted out: "Oh yeah! Well, Kam Kim-ah thought of it!"

"You said it!" Hernia waved his hand and said: "We're all a bunch of dumb blockheads."

Everyone laughed at this, as though no one took exception to his comment.

As soon as Blockhead heard that everyone there was a block-head, he resumed his interminable giggling.

They all sat down, drawing their respect for Kam Kim-ah back within them, and listened attentively to Scabby Head as he handed out their work assignments. Actually, there wasn't much difference among the various jobs, except that the ones who helped out in the kitchen made out a little better in the food department.

"Last time," Scabby Head was saying, his memory temporarily failing him, "last time where did we go?"

"That was when Te-wang's son-in-law was crushed under the pile of firewood."

"No," Fire Baby corrected him, "there's been another since then."

"Right. It was when Hsi-shui the fish peddler's mother died."

"No, that was even earlier," Mongrel said.

"What do you mean, no? That's when there was all that fish. Huh, Blockhead here almost croaked with an eel bone in his throat. I remember very clearly," Fire Baby said.

"You guys love to argue," Mongrel interrupted, spraying the area with saliva. "If I said it's not, then it's not. You'll drive everybody nuts!"

"All right, that's enough! If you two want to fight it out, go somewhere else and do it." Scabby Head was getting irritated. "Shit, we haven't had a funeral banquet for a few days, and everyone's gone buggy with hunger."

Blockhead stood over to the side muttering to himself: "Tailend was crying like a baby, hee-hee . . ."

"Ah, that's right, it was when Tailend's wife over at Westgate died."

"Right! It was when Tailend's wife died." A smile appeared on Scabby Head's face; now the others had all remembered too. "Well! Blockhead's not such a blockhead today!"

Blockhead just giggled, pleased as he could be.

"Who was in the kitchen when Tailend's wife died?" Scabby Head's glance swept past all of them. "Which ones? Whoever it was, speak up."

Still no answer. They all just looked back and forth.

All of a sudden Know-it-all shouted: "Gold Clock, it was you!"

"Me?" He pointed to himself with the airs of one wrongly accused. "Was it me?"

"It sure was, so no funny business." Know-it-all glared at him.

"Your mouth was crammed so full of fish-paste balls you couldn't even talk. Am I right or wrong?"

"Ah—," he said embarrassedly. "You know I've got a bad temper, so I'm not about to argue with you."

Everyone knew that this was Gold Clock's way of admitting the fact.

"Fuck your ancestors! You big bag of piss! So you wanted another turn in the kitchen! Aren't you afraid we'll slice your hernia off and fry it up as a dish of tripe?" Scabby Head shouted.

Gold Clock muttered angrily to himself: "Big bag of piss? I'll give it to you if you want it." His mutterings were so indistinct that not even the men sitting beside him could tell for sure what he was saying.

Kam Kim-ah sat there listening to their conversation, at the same time pondering the death of Scholar Yang, and wondering if there was any link between it and his broom work of the previous day. But no matter how he looked at it, the finger of accusation never pointed to him. He felt like joining the conversation.

"Hey, hold on a minute, all of you. I've got something I want to say. At the moment I don't have a suitable job, so for the time being I'm throwing in my lot with you. But as soon as I find a job I'll be leaving. Do you all understand? This is only temporary. I might even be leaving tomorrow. Since it's only temporary it's hard to make plans." He kept stressing the word "temporary."

"As long as you're willing to join up, there's no problem," Scabby Head said.

"We don't have it so bad here."

"Um! No, I told you—it's just temporary." Kam Kim-ah shook his head forcefully, like a man who was trying to shake loose something that had stuck onto his face.

"He's right! Nobody who's got a decent job would hang around here."

"To tell you the truth, the brothers here are happy to have you along." Fire Baby was saying what all of them felt. Their smiles were warm and friendly.

"No, no, no, it's temporary, I say. When the time comes for me to leave, I don't want you to accuse me of having no feelings. I've told you that it's only temporary." He was feeling very complacent now, for he had given himself a great deal of face.

At Peace With the World

As the group of men approached Scholar Yang's bier, Kam Kim-ah stayed behind for a moment. "He was going to die anyway. I didn't . . . ," he quietly consoled himself, though it was hard to strip away all of the fear in his heart. Not really wanting to enter the main hall, he managed to force himself to get across somehow. At first he had wanted to turn his face away, but he found himself turning to look at Scholar Yang's likeness on the image altar. In the shop of the one and only town artist, a great number of por-traits, minus faces, were placed in readiness until needed. This portrait of Scholar Yang had been one of those paintings, to which the artist had now added Scholar Yang's features. It was hard to say whether or not it looked like him. Perhaps in his younger years, or if he had gotten a bit older, there might have been some re-semblance here and there. When Kam Kim-ah looked into those eyes, which were at peace with the world, he breathed a lot more easily. He was willing to stop and take a closer look. But no matter where he looked, his eyes always came back to that other pair of eyes, which were at peace with the world. He brought his hands together and bowed before the portrait: "Scholar Yang, you're the lucky one. Please look after me."

Scabby Head and the others were told that since Scholar Yang's family already had a lot of help, their services wouldn't be needed for very many days, so they sat on their haunches beneath the eaves of the house waiting for the funeral to begin, at which time they could start out with all of their paraphernalia. They were cursing in lowered voices, particularly Mongrel and One-eye, who had been assigned kitchen duties. Since Scholar Yang's was the most respected family in the entire town, and the rites for him should have been splendid, they had decided to add one man as a kitchen helper. At the time, Mongrel was in violent opposition, feeling that two was plenty. Everyone knew what he was so nervous about, and his arguments were blocked by the others. In a burst of anger, he said: "Just a rich person who lived like a damned beggar!"

Kam Kim-ah didn't want to squat there alongside the others for fear that someone might see him; even though he wasn't sure what they would think, he knew that he would feel uncomfortable. So he just walked back and forth beside the bier. The local dramatic troupe, the funeral musicians, and the beggars were all waiting nearby. He could even see the town lunatic, Crazy Ts'ai, standing alone by the rubbish heap laughing to herself for no apparent reason. He walked a few steps, then turned his head back to look at her. "What a fucking shame!" In the days when he was beating the gong, this is what he had said whenever he gave Crazy Ts'ai a fleeting glance.

He walked a little farther off, then took another glance on the sly. She wasn't a bad looking woman at all: milky white skin, long legs, firm breasts, nicely rounded buttocks. *What bewitching eyes!* Kam Kim-ah pretended to be looking elsewhere, then fixed his attention on Crazy Ts'ai. *This summer she's really blossomed out, almost overnight, into a young woman. I always knew that, mad as she was, she would turn out to be a beautiful woman.* His throat was feeling a little dry and he tried to swallow. But there wasn't a drop of saliva in his mouth, and his desire made him uneasy. "Fuck her!" With this brief curse, he walked off as though he were in pain.

Some members of the dramatic troupe were tuning their strings and practicing their wind instruments, the funeral musicians were sounding a few tentative notes, and the whole area started to come to life. Kam Kim-ah walked over under the eaves and said to the others: "Looks like it's about time to start out."

"Scholar Yang's own porters are going to carry the coffin out themselves," Scabby Head said, obviously displeased.

It seemed to Kam Kim-ah that Scabby Head was blaming *him* for having the corpse turn out to be Scholar Yang, as though it were something he never ever should have done. "What's up, anyway?" He asked this forcefully without really raising his voice. "It's better than nothin', isn't it?"

No one knew what he was talking about. Propped up behind them were colorful banners made of coarse red, blue, and white material. Since there had been five generations of Scholar Yang's family living under one roof, these long cloth banners, slightly more than a foot in width, were fastened to lengths of bamboo that were a bit longer than the width of the banner. They hung in profusion from bamboo poles on which there were still some leaves. The men's appearance as they sat there was strikingly similar to those limp banners.

Kam Kim-ah squatted down across the street directly opposite the other men, still unwilling to be publicly associated with them. But since the procession was about to begin, he couldn't go off too far, or else he might miss the chance to carry one of the banners and share in the handout. He couldn't imagine what had gotten them so steamed up. All they had to do was join the procession, and at the very least they'd get a couple of free meals and some pocket money for their troubles. If they watched their money closely, it would surely be enough to keep them from going hungry for three days or so, until another stiff came along. So what's wrong with that? "Ptui! Just a bunch of pigs."

One-eye—the herniated Gold Clock and Mongrel right behind him—walked purposefully over to Kam Kim-ah and sat down next to him. Kam Kim-ah felt as though he were on a see-saw, for the moment they sat down, he wanted to get to his feet. He was growing tense. Afraid of causing them a loss of self-respect, he had no recourse but to keep sitting where he was. Know-it-all and Fire Baby came over and joined them.

"A wealthy household like this shouldn't provide such meager offerings for people like us. We depend on these handouts." The sunken eyelid was quivering violently. "The death of the renowned

Scholar Yang isn't as big a deal as the death of the mother of Hsi-shui from the marketplace," One-eye said.

"If they're gonna carry Scholar Yang out this way, they're sure gonna be criticized by people on the street," Mongrel said, pressing his face right up against Kam Kim-ah's nose. Kam Kim-ah didn't move a muscle. "Everyone knew Scholar Yang."

"As I see it, this is the fault of whoever's in charge. We shouldn't be blaming Scholar Yang," Hernia paused. "Kam Kim-ah, how do you feel about it?" After he had said his piece, he reached down and rubbed himself.

Kam Kim-ah just smiled, without saying a word. "This isn't just a loss of face for Scholar Yang's family—people from fifty li away will be laughing at us folk from Lotung." One-eye said this with even greater enthusiasm.

"They're all nuts! Young folks nowadays never consider the consequences of their actions."

"It's the times. As long as they have money in their pockets, they do what they please, and no one can do a thing about it."

"You there, Know-it-all," One-eye spun around to face him, "you've got it all wrong. Anyone who wants to live with other men in this society has to make sure he does things with other people in mind." He turned back to Kam Kim-ah, his sunken eyelid fluttering: "Kam Kim-ah, you've got no axe to grind—am I right or not?"

Kam Kim-ah smiled and looked at One-eye's single eye, which seemed almost capable of talking. One-eye interpreted this smile as one of support, so he really started to talk. While they debated back and forth, Kam Kim-ah alone was occupied with his thoughts. He was thinking about putting some money aside and taking care of Crazy Ts'ai properly. Seeing her standing off in the distance, he experienced such a strong desire he couldn't sit still. He felt like laughing, but why he couldn't say. He picked up snatches of the conversation going on around him: "You're way off the mark! You haven't got a prayer of ever getting into the issue of society—the first qualification is to have two good eyes!" Know-it-all got to his feet and, aping One-eye's manner of tossing his head back and forth, walked back over under the eaves where Scabby Head and the rest of them were waiting.

Scabby Head didn't even look up at Know-it-all, but before he had even sat down, Fire Baby began to rail at him: "What the hell did you come back for?" The meaning behind this question escaped Know-it-all, who sat down very ostentatiously. Fire Baby glared at him, then jabbed him with his elbow: "We don't need your kind over here!"

"Fuck you! One-eye's single eye is fiercer than other people's two eyes!" He still hadn't grasped the meaning behind Fire Baby's comments. "Society, society, corporation, society.* Now what's bigger, society or a company? Do you know or not?" He paused for a moment. Actually, he didn't know himself. "If you want to know, I'll tell you. My hernia here is the biggest!" With that he took the wind out of the other man's sails.

Fire Baby laughed in spite of himself. He jabbed his elbow into Know-it-all, who turned around to look at him. Fire Baby's tone had lost its edge as he said: "What the hell did you come back for?" Scabby Head cut in before Know-it-all had time to answer:

"After this, if you line up on Kam Kim-ah's side, you don't have to come back over here." Know-it-all was stunned. "You've gotta learn to choose between your friends and your enemies." Scabby Head looked across the street, casting an icy look of warning from his seated position.

"Kam Kim-ah is an ambitious schemer." Fire Baby explained to Know-it-all the conclusions that he, Scabby Head, and the others had arrived at regarding Kam Kim-ah. Know-it-all bit his lower lip and nodded repeatedly, his eyes cast downward. "And so, don't let yourself be used. If old Hernia and old One-eye want to go over there, that's their business; we don't care about them."

"That's right, he's a schemer," Know-it-all agreed.

"If he wasn't, then why didn't he hang around with us once he

---

*The Chinese words for "society" and "corporation" are composed of the same two characters, with the order reversed.

got here instead of walking all over the place by himself, doing whatever it is he does?" Fire Baby asked.

"That's the truth. I could see that too. Just a while ago when we came over here, he didn't want to stick with us, but went over there across the street to be by himself."

"Then why did you go over there with him?"

"I just felt like chewin' the fat, that's all."

"Open your eyes a little."

Know-it-all kept nodding his head. Blockhead was standing off to the side giggling. Scabby Head was staring fixedly at Kam Kim-ah. Wanting to get into his good graces, Fire Baby commented to him: "Just look at Kam Kim-ah! I wonder what sort of scheme he's cooking up for us now?"

"You afraid of him?"

"Afraid of him, with you here? Afraid of a prick like that?"

Out of curiosity, they followed Kam Kim-ah's gaze.

"Hey!" Fire Baby poked Scabby Head and Know-it-all with his elbows. "Now I know what he's hatching in that head of his."

"I know that. What do you think I've been watching him all this time for?" Scabby Head narrowed his eyes as he glared at Kam Kim-ah.

"I can tell too."

"Tell what?" Know-it-all asked.

"Just look at Kam Kim-ah."

"That lousy rat! Has he got his eye on Crazy Ts'ai?"

"Now do you see?" Scabby Head said coldly. A feeling of uneasiness settled over the men. They stopped looking at Kam Kim-ah and, like him, riveted their attention on the mad woman, as a heated emotion gripped their hearts.

Make Your Best Move

Scholar Yang's funeral procession, from the vanguard to the mourners, stretched a distance equivalent to thirty or forty shops.

Kam Kim-ah was one of the banner bearers, carrying a blue banner representing the great grandchildren's generation. Immediately following him were Scholar Yang's image altar and his coffin. The mourners slowly made their way toward the busy part of town, and the men had heard that they were going to parade up and down several streets. Kam Kim-ah had a jittery feeling he couldn't shake. The route of the procession would surely take him past the stores owned by Stony, Prosperity, and Longevity. What if they spotted him? *Shit! They're sure to cut old Kam Kim-ah down! If I cover my face with the banner, the cloth is thin enough so that I can still see where I'm going.* This thought perked him up considerably, but as he walked on, a sudden apprehensiveness flashed into his mind. He quickly turned back to look at Scholar Yang's image altar. The look in the clouded eyes of the portrait was still one of peace with the world. *I know I had nothing to do with this.* He looked back one more time. *Scholar Yang, go in peace.*

When the funeral procession passed by the open-air turntable, even though his face was completely hidden behind the banner, Kam Kim-ah could still see Longevity's store behind the bobbing heads of the crowd of onlookers. Then he saw Longevity himself, dressed in a vest, his arms folded in front of his chest so that his tough, hardened muscles glistened in the sunlight. "Damn him!" he cursed under his breath. There was a distance of no more than ten steps or so between him and Longevity, and the worst thing was that they were on the same side of the street. Longevity was looking his way, his eyes fixed on Scholar Yang's image. Kam Kim-ah was afraid that Longevity would recognize him there. Then an idea popped into his head: he began to hobble along like a cripple. This so surprised Hernia, who was walking alongside him, that for a moment he was speechless. Kam Kim-ah was now directly opposite Longevity; he closed his eyes and began to chant: "Oh, Earth God, oh, Matsu, Goddess of the Sea, please bestow your protection on Kam Kim-ah." When he opened his eyes again he was terrified to see that he had strayed from the procession and that the onlookers were laughing at him. He ran back into the pro-

cession like a shot, completely forgetting that he was supposed
to be hobbling like a cripple. "Damn it!" He could almost feel
Longevity's eyes on his back, and a shiver ran down his spine. He
wished he hadn't feigned being a cripple. He wanted to rectify the
situation, but as he walked down the crowded street, each time he
decided to make things right, somehow he found that he lacked
the determination he had had when he first saw Longevity.

"Kam Kim-ah, what's wrong with your leg?" Hernia asked
impulsively.

"Got a damned cramp in it."

"Oh! The poor damned legs!" Hernia's glance moved from Kam
Kim-ah's leg up to his head. "Why are you covering your face like
that?"

"Don't you feel the heat today?" He kept his face covered. "This
makes me a lot cooler."

"Yeah, it's hotter'n hell." Hernia covered his face the same way.
"Hey, it is a lot cooler!"

The dramatic troupe came clamoring down the road, tooting
horns and beating drums, making a lot of noise. Altogether there
were some twenty different types of musical instruments—the two-
man great brass gong, the bass drum, the hand drums, cymbals,
bells, trumpets, three-stringed fiddles, two-stringed violins, flutes—
and the chorus of cacaphony produced by all these instruments,
which were being played for all they were worth, assaulted the
ears of everyone within range. Without straining his ears at all,
Kam Kim-ah could hear the muffled sound of the gong as it was
struck by one of the musicians at the head of the procession. That
was the only other gong like the one now lying beneath Kam Kim-
ah's bed. He listened and he thought, and as he did so, the gong
rang out loudly and blended in with his reveries:

Bong! Bong! Bong!
The gong beater's coming your way—
Listen everyone, here's what I have to say—

A call for all pilgrims at the Ch'i-ting Temple of
    the Patriarch—
Tomorrow afternoon at two o'clock—
Fire dancers will be there, tallies will be drawn—
Bong! Bong! Bong!
Calling all the Buddhist faithful—
Get ready your spirit money, your crackers and your
    candles—
Everyone off to the Ch'i-ting Temple of the Patriarch to
    burn incense and bow to the gods—
Bong! Bong! Bong!
Listen carefully, one and all—
Women in their period, or pregnant, cannot go—
People in mourning cannot go—
Bong! Bong! Bong!
Everyone who goes will be given a tally—
To take home and paste over the door for protection—
    Bong! Bong! Bong!

"Should we prepare a sacrifice?" a woman asked him.

"It's a lot better if you can. But if you've never made a vow for blessings received from the Patriarch, then there's no need to. All you need is some spirit money, crackers, and candles."

"Is it okay to bring fruit?"

Kam Kim-ah found himself surrounded by the neighborhood women.

"Sure. Fruit and clear tea are fine, but it's important to go with a pure heart."

"Is it okay to go if you've had a baby within the month?"

"Oh! If the month's confinement isn't up, you're not clean; so you can't go."

"Did you say two o'clock? Two in the afternoon?"

"Two o'clock tomorrow afternoon." Kam Kim-ah was kept busy turning from one woman to another answering all their questions.

If he didn't get away from them pretty soon, he thought, as the number of women increased, he'd find himself answering the same questions over and over. He started beating his gong, made his way forward through an opening in the crowd, and walked off. Naturally, some of the people stayed behind to pass on the news about the Patriarch to the late arrivals, as though they had been invested with some authority.

Bong! Bong! Bong! Beneath the same bright sun, the heat of summer growing more intense, his reveries dissolved back into reality, and as he looked out through the cloth in front of his eyes to see the faces of all the people gathered to watch the festivities, each and every one of them familiar to him, he was truly frightened that someone might spot him carrying a funeral banner. He heaved a long sigh and the emotional excitement he had been experiencing turned into a great, heavy stone that weighed down on him.

"Gold Clock," he called out. Hernia had long since stopped covering his face with the cloth banner. "Have you ever seen me out beating my gong?"

"I've . . . seen you, of course I have." He was walking with his legs far apart so as not to cause pain to his hernia.

"How'd you think I was at it?"

"I never could figure out why you gave it up." Gold Clock cocked his head to look over at him. Kam Kim-ah had by then already edged over to him until they were shoulder to shoulder. "Beating a gong has got to be a lot more dignified than carrying a funeral banner."

"Dignified, you say?" With his back to the man, Kam Kim-ah smiled an ambiguous smile; he didn't dare even look at Gold Clock.

"Yeah! I just can't figure out why you'd give it up."

Kam Kim-ah laughed a dull laugh, which Gold Clock found even more difficult to figure out.

The reverberations from the gong, almost illusory in effect, floated in waves of scorching heat and reached Kam Kim-ah's ears in pulsations. Thus it went until the entire procession was gathered at the oil shop at the end of the street, leaving room for the pall-bearers to carry their burden into the graveyard. All of the banner carriers were resting on their haunches beneath a red banyan tree. Scabby Head coughed dryly several times, then cursed: "Shit! Well, we're all here. Scabby Head, Rotten Ear, Blind Man, Hernia, and the Cripple. Have I missed anyone?" It suddenly dawned on Kam Kim-ah that what he was holding in his hand was not a gong mallet.

"Don't forget me, Blockhead! Hee-hee . . ." Blockhead added his name to the list, which broke the others up and lightened their mood. As for Kam Kim-ah, this round of laughter seemed to isolate him off to one side, and the barren scene before him produced an anguish that no amount of appeasement could drive away. He was beset by self-pity that had lost all its significance. Feeling terribly depressed, he was thinking that the only way to remove this anguish was to show contempt for these men. Because of this decision, their every action, the way they had isolated him, nothing could bring him any pain. "A bunch of old bums, lower than pigs!" he cursed inwardly. But he was still put out of sorts by their laughter. He raised his hand to rub his chest, then said, looking for sympathy: "Mongrel, you guys really hurt me—I'm still sore." He followed this with another inward curse: "They're worse than pigs."

"What's that! Didn't they turn you into a cripple?" Scabby Head queried in mock seriousness.

"I'm sore all over."

"Hey, Mongrel, he says you banged him with your head so hard he hurts all over. Go a little easier next time! Mongrel, Fire Baby." Scabby Head nodded his head with real satisfaction, as the other men burst out laughing, having understood the intent of his comments.

No matter what, it's a lot better to argue with them than just sit here all by myself. So he fired off one comment after another, though nothing came of any of it, and their interest flagged. In the midst of his bewilderment, he suddenly thought of some dirty stories that rescued him from his predicament.

Eventually Scabby Head broke in on his story: "Kam Kim-ah, the musicians are coming back. How much longer is this story of yours? Why don't you wrap it up for now and finish it some other time."

The words "some other time" were particularly pleasing to Kam Kim-ah's ear, so he stood up and brought his story to an end: "Of course you all know that when the woman laid down in the grass, her bound feet, which were sticking up in the air, kept moving up and down, until her husband saw them and shouted happily: 'Ah-mei! I caught the turkey! I caught the turkey! I can see its head.'" He still held his audience, and even though they all got to their feet, picked up their banners, and fell in behind the musicians in a big hurry to get back to Scholar Yang's home for a free meal, Know-it-all, Mongrel, and some of the others pushed Hernia out of the way and moved up alongside Kam Kim-ah to hear some more of these stories. But all the while they kept an eye on Scabby Head to watch the expression on his face.

"Kam Kim-ah," Scabby Head said with a smile as he turned back to look behind him, "these guys can't hold onto their money as it is, and if you keep it up, tomorrow they'll all be broke."

Know-it-all and the others detected a note of approval from Scabby Head that they were with Kam Kim-ah. So Hernia pushed by the others, yelling: "So you want to listen, do you? Well, so do I!" Kam Kim-ah's heart was warming up. His mouth was split in a broad grin and he was laughing, though not a sound emerged. His face looked as though it had been stamped right on the rays of the sun.

The Nightmare

After several uneventful days had passed, everything returned to normal: the second rice harvest had been completed, and no dreams invaded his sleep. His life had taken on a fixed routine: rising with the sun, he prepared a simple breakfast, then went over to the kadang tree, joined the funeral banquets, argued, chatted amiably; meanwhile resentment filled his heart more and more deeply. Even his limited supply of dirty stories had been exhausted, and it was unnecessary for him to observe the cold looks in the others' eyes or listen to their conversation to know that in this circle he had lost that certain something. If the situation didn't improve, before too long it wouldn't make much difference whether he was here or not. But what could he do? he asked himself. He had been born a person of integrity, and there was no way he, Kam Kim-ah, could stoop to supporting another man's balls as he crossed a threshold! *Who does Scabby Head think he is? I wouldn't even let him wash my feet.* He was fighting mad, and the more he thought about it, the more his heart froze. Every time Kam Kim-ah's turn to help in the kitchen rolled around, Scabby Head and the others said that he wasn't a real member of the group, so they skipped him and went on to the next in line. Whenever Know-it-all returned from helping in the kitchen, in obvious high spirits, he would make a big show of saying to the others in front of him: "Wow! There was a piece of lean meat this big," using his hands to describe it. Or he would say: "I dipped it in soy sauce and in garlic paste and had it with a bottle of wine—oh, shit! Just imagine eating like that every day!" As he carried on like that, his eyes never left Kam Kim-ah.

Ptui! These guys were all raised by pigs, and this big liar here is saying, "Hai! Just think what it would be like!" Fuck him and all his ancestors! Why don't you guys go to the open-air stalls in front of the Temple of the Patriarch to ask about me, about my good old days? What makes you think a lousy piece of lean meat would be such a temptation to Kam Kim-ah? That really makes me laugh. Back in those days, whenever I went over to the Temple of the Patriarch, Pine Root, Woody, and Righteous Virtue would call out to me, asking me this and that, to get on my good side. They'd shout, "Kam Kim-ah, we've already warmed some wine for you." "Kam Kim-ah, we've got some goose liver here for you." Humph! I serve no master, and if I feel like it I can eat shark skin!

Bong! Bong! Bong! Somewhere along the line, it seemed, a gong
had come to exist in his mind. It resounded—*Bong! Bong!*—on its
own. In the middle of the night it was so persistent that it caused
him great uneasiness and made his ears ring. He sat up straight,
his nerves so taut that his eyes were fluttering. He looked at the
darkness all around him, as though he wanted to stare a hole in it
to get a better look. He felt the walls closing in tightly around him,
and eventually came to the realization that he knew the source of
this pressure: the darkness all around him was congealing into a
hard lump and was about to freeze him solid there in the shelter.
He was breathing with difficulty, until from the depths of his confusion, with an agility born of terror, he leaped frantically off his
bamboo bed. As he knocked two empty bottles over, the noise tore
through the oppressively thick atmosphere, which quickly swallowed the sound up again. He stumbled headlong through the
shelter entrance, his outstretched arms supporting him against the
two concrete walls. "Come here!" he yelled. "Scabby Head, if
you've any guts, come here! Come here, all of you! Fuck ya all!"
His neck was straining to support his drooping head, when suddenly he felt the cool air of an autumn night, and just as suddenly
the faces of the men under the kadang tree appeared superimposed
on his mind, particularly their cold, hard eyes; he was powerless to
drive away those looks. "I told you to come! Didn't you hear me?
If you had any guts you'd have come!" Lines of laughter began to
appear at the corners of their eyes.

"If you don't believe me, there's nothin' I can do. But don't look
at me that way. Let's hear you say something. Let it out, curse me
if you want to."

But they just sat there lazily, though they continued to look at
him coldly, occasionally exchanging glances among themselves.

Kam Kim-ah looked at each of them in turn, but he could not
detect the trace of a kind look.

"You all know well enough how Crazy Ts'ai was deflowered
beneath the pork butcher's counter in the marketplace. I just felt
sorry for her, that's all" A look of exasperation that confused the

men appeared on his face. "What do you want me to say? I feel sorry for her."

The others all glanced over at Scabby Head, who smiled back at them. They turned their cold looks back on Kam Kim-ah as they heard him mutter: "I know why you guys are suspicious of me: you're thinking about how I take her food whenever we have a funeral banquet, and that I do it on the sly. I know you won't believe what I say, but I just feel sorry for her." He saw that they were looking at one another, conversing with their eyes. "But," he continued, "I did it on the sly 'cause I was afraid you guys would get the wrong idea. In all good conscience, may heaven strike me down with lightning if there's been anything between me and that woman."

But no matter how sincerely he said it, opening his very heart up to show them, knowing glances passed among the men, giving him an even more unpleasant taste.

"I really didn't do a lowdown thing like that!" He felt as though he were being tortured into self-revelations, one after another, under the unchanging looks of doubt in their eyes. He continued: "You all want me to own up to it, but . . . " He stopped, finding it difficult to say what was on his mind. This created a moment of tense anticipation. Finally, in nervous embarrassment, he admitted: "If it's my thoughts you want to know, well, it did occur to me several times, but when the time came and I saw her, I ran off, afraid to go through with it. I might have had the same thing on my mind when I took the food over to her, but the moment I laid eyes on her, I just put the bowl down on the ground, turned, and ran off. I was thinking of her. I *was* thinking of her!" This came out almost unintelligibly and had something of a sob about it. Scabby Head and the others laughed. Sensing that he was still not being believed, he cited another instance: "The night before last, she came to the park alone late at night—it must've been at least eleven o'clock, when there was no one in the park." A clarity suddenly came to his voice and his mood grew extremely serious. The faces of the men around him were frozen with the attentiveness of people listening fearfully to a ghost story, unwilling to miss a single word. "When I saw her I was scared and pleased at the same time. I looked all around to make sure we were alone. 'Crazy Ts'ai,' I said to her, 'you come with me to the air-raid shelter and I'll give you somethin' to eat.' And she did, she followed me quietly back to the shelter. I was really gettin' the itch then. I looked around again, and there was no one, not even a stray dog." When he reached this point in his narration, the other men began to squirm uneasily, as though they would burst just waiting for the climax.

"Now you all know that even though Crazy Ts'ai's got a big belly, she still ain't bad. I was constantly on the alert to see if there was anyone nearby. Although she seemed to know what I had in mind, she didn't resist. I figured she needed it too, since she already had some experience. As the saying goes: 'A man enjoys it three parts, a woman seven.' When I was sure we were alone, I . . . I reached out and touched her arm, but then I drew back like it'd been struck by lightning. I give you my word—all this time that she's been on my mind, the night before last was the first time I ever touched her." His listeners' faces showed how displeased they were that his narration wasn't going into enough detail. "I started to get scared," he went on, "and I told her to leave—started pushing her away, in fact—but not only did she stay where she was, she even headed into the air-raid shelter by herself, which scared me so much I just climbed up onto the grass covering of the shelter and waited there anxiously till dawn."

When Scabby Head and the others heard this, they showed their utter disgust, born of disappointment and a sense of having been cheated, with looks that seemed to show that they wouldn't give him the satisfaction of getting angry. And their disappointment proved a disappointment to him.

"I *did* think of her," he yelled. "Who hasn't? I'll bet all of you have. But that's all it was—thoughts. If you say I was wrong, then the only thing I did wrong was touch her once the night before yesterday. But I let go of her right away. I really did let go of her right away. Because I was too scared!"

At this point, not only was he subjected to cold looks from these men, he was now the target of silent looks of bitter loathing. He voiced his feelings of injustice by yelling: "If you don't believe me, you can call her over and ask her yourself! If anything happened between me and her, you can do anything you want to! If you want you can take me around to all the town gates, where I'll beat my gong and admit my guilt in front of everyone. How's that?"

Scabby Head expressed all of their sentiments with a hateful snort. This was an ambiguous response as far as Kam Kim-ah was concerned. He was feeling terribly dejected, unable to understand why he was having to give these men so many explanations. He regretted having told them about the incident of the night before last, and of having let out his secret thoughts for Crazy Ts'ai. In sum, he regretted having said any of this to these men.

Kam Kim-ah bought two bottles of 25-proof cheap wine and headed home to his air-raid shelter, making up his mind once again not to go back, ever. *Who cares that there'll be food to eat tomorrow at the funeral at K'e-lin! I'll just drink these two bottles of wine and get a good night's sleep.* He was mentally exhausted to the point that all desires had left him. He just hid out in his shelter and drowned his sorrows in the wine. Before he passed out, the mosquitoes that were feeding on him had all fallen drunkenly to the ground without even getting their fill of his blood. A kerosene lamp constructed of a tieband from a pair of shorts, lying in a small plate and supported by a single split chopstick, burned unwaveringly all the way down to the plate until the supply of kerosene was exhausted.

The sound of a gong being struck resounded in his ears, but no matter how hard he tried, he could not lift his head. It drooped forward until it could go no further, and then it rolled back again. In like fashion, no matter how hard he tried, he could not wipe away the persistent images of those cold looks. It eventually got so bad that they gave him shivers. Things had deteriorated with Kam Kim-ah until all he could do was shout in confusion: "Come on! Go ahead and look, what good does it do? Anyone, anyone with any guts, come over here . . . " He raised his arm and waved it in the air, causing him to lose his equilibrium as he stumbled several steps out the door. He lay prostrate on the grass, continuing to mumble in an unbroken stream. He was soothed by gust after gust of cool night air in the open park. Like an infant sleeping soundly at its mother's breast, he noiselessly sucked in the breath of life.

A road, the most familiar one of all, stretched out before him. Faces so familiar that there was no longer any need to consciously record their names lined the brightly lit sides of the road, eagerly awaiting the public announcement of some vile deed committed in the town. With this sight in front of him, Kam Kim-ah balked. The gong in his hands felt so heavy he could barely hold it; even the mallet seemed as heavy as a boulder. His mind was busily engaged in reflecting on ways of dying. He gave it some serious thought for a while, but found that he lacked both the knowledge and the courage. He realized that there were things more fearful than death. But all of these impressions, ill-defined though they were, took the shape of a torturous anxiety. He turned back to beg for mercy, but, seeing pair after pair of staring, frightening eyes, he was rendered mute. Turning back around, he felt those cold glares boring into him until his backbone seemed to recoil. Apparently the only option available to him was to follow through on his vow. In this critical moment, he still had thoughts of changing the wording of his defense, but no matter how simple he made it or how reserved, he would still have to say something along these lines: "The gong beater's coming your way. Listen everyone, here's what I have to say: I, Kam Kim-ah, have committed the unpardonable sin of seducing Crazy Ts'ai . . . " He wanted so badly to beg for mercy, or for death. Met by the same cold, unrelenting stares, he had no choice but to screw up his courage and walk forward, beating his gong and shouting: "The gong beater's coming your way. Listen everyone, here's what I have to say: I, I . . ." He could not go on as the full awareness of his discomfort hit him.

His mind was still clouded and confused when he opened his eyes, and he was in a state of total shock. He had no idea why he had walked into the woods—then it gradually dawned on him that the rice stalks that rose unevenly about him as he lay on the ground had made him believe he was in the woods. As he reached a state of awareness, the first emotion he experienced was the self-congratulatory happiness of one who realizes that a calamity has turned out to be only a nightmare. But this short-lived happiness only increased the mournfulness of his self-pity.

Today was the grand funeral of the rich man, Chen from K'e-lin, and there would be food to eat. He had heard that the Chen family owned nearly ten acres of land. Kam Kim-ah was through with making vows. He wanted to go over to the kadang tree. "If they don't believe me," he thought as he walked, "then they don't believe me—if the roots of the tree are solid, there's no need for the branches to fear a typhoon. How could people like that ever understand me, Kam Kim-ah? They think I'm just the same as them. That makes me laugh! Like that episode yesterday when Scabby Head and the others gave me those cold glares." He was not going to give that a second thought. His thoughts moved on to the rich Mr. Chen's ten acres of land, the golden grain, the piles of money, the funeral arrangements, the meat on the tables, the generous packets of spending money. And even if the image of Scabby Head and the others should occasionally flash into his mind, he had only to silently curse "Fuck 'em," and that took care of that. As he passed over Southgate Bridge, the canopy of the kadang tree came into view once again. His thoughts having turned to the tree, he spat on the ground. "Ptui! Fuck 'em!"

The Rainbow With No End

"Ah!—" Mongrel seemed to be trying to wrap up all of their comments into a general conclusion: "In shallow water the dragon is laughed at by the shrimps; in the open plain the tiger is at the mercy of dogs."

"What's that!" Know-it-all jumped up shouting. "Is that an admission that he's a dragon, or a tiger? And we're a bunch of little shrimps, and mutts? If you don't know how to make comparisons, then keep your mouth shut. You're the mutt, and who wants to be associated with you?"

The others all looked at Know-it-all and nodded their heads, some of them voicing their agreement with "That's right!" or "Good point!"

"Ai! Why make a big deal out of it? Why do that? I'm only here on a temporary basis, you know." Gold Clock the herniated was making fun of Kam Kim-ah by mimicking his manner of speaking. He glanced over at Scabby Head, then at the others. He was seldom in such high spirits, for it seemed that he never did anything right in the presence of these men. But this time, not only did he escape being yelled at and called "Hernia," he was actually rewarded by their light-hearted approval. "Temporary, I say, just temporary. You know what I mean?"

"Oh, no, don't be temporary! Stay here with us," Mongrel cut in, like an actor on the stage.

But Gold Clock was so beside himself with the joy of not having angered the others that he completely missed the opportunity to engage Mongrel in a mock debate. He just sat there, his arms clasped around his knees, as he rocked back and forth. Mongrel was growing a little impatient, but before the moment had passed, Fire Baby said, in imitation of Kam Kim-ah:

"No, no, when I say temporary I mean temporary. I'm not like you guys." He had all of Kam Kim-ah's little movements down pat, and the others all laughed at him. They constantly looked over to see if there was any reaction on Kam Kim-ah's part. As though he had some magnetic effect that kept drawing their eyes back to him, they seemed powerless to keep from looking over his way.

Kam Kim-ah sat alone in the spot where normally they all sat in a group, while the others had picked up and moved away from him to a spot under another kadang tree, some three or four trees removed from him. Their conversation was intended to drive him away. Their every sentence reached his ears and penetrated deeply into his heart. It was all over for him, he thought. His only recourse was to stay put, whether they wanted him there or not, and see what they would do. He just shrugged off the knowledge that it was a very undignified way to do things. Each time a peal of laughter floated across, he seemed driven by his curiosity to turn around and see what was going on. But with all the strength he could muster, he forced his will upon his seemingly rebellious neck. When all he could hear was a series of unintelligible mutterings, broken suddenly by an explosion of laughter, the strain was so intense that a soreness developed in his neck. He rested the point of his chin between his knees as he squatted there, not allowing his curiosity to get the best of him. He simply didn't know how else to handle the situation. More than once he was so agitated by what they were saying that he was on the verge of jumping to his feet and cursing them soundly before walking off and washing his hands of them. But for reasons even he did not know, he was unable to jump to his feet, powerless to curse out. He just stayed as he was, squatting motionlessly on his haunches, until his buttocks, his legs, and his back were numb with soreness, and eventually all that was left to him was the remorseful anger that filled his still-alert mind.

He made up his mind that if he heard any more talk or laughter that distressed him he would leave at once. But immediately after making this decision, he heard Mongrel say something about "hatching an egg." This produced a round of side-splitting laughter. His resolve of a moment before slipped away and lay there steaming. He began talking to himself: "I'm not stupid! Leave? That's exactly what they want. So I'll stay put and see what they do about it." He hugged his knees more tightly. Fearing that he wouldn't be able to follow through with his latest resolution, he forced his chin down hard, closed his eyes and, with all the will-power he could muster, resisted whatever it was that completely enervated him; thrills of victory came in waves to salve his wounded heart, which in turn inspired him with even greater courage to continue the struggle. This in turn increased his fatigue, while simultaneously causing him to experience the intoxication of a tragic hero as he held onto this particular spot.

Another burst of laughter hit him like a bayonet thrust. *Could they be laughing at me because I've got no guts? Fuck 'em! To hell with 'em! What can they do if I don't leave? So what if I don't have any guts? No! I don't have any guts if I do leave. Right! I don't have any guts if I do leave.* He hugged his knees tightly, pressed his chin down hard, and closed his eyes, as the *bong-bong* sound of a gong rang in his ears. Nowhere, not on any street or lane of the town, was there a cruel face, nor a pair of cold expressionless eyes. His throat was as parched as if he had been shouting at the top of his lungs. He noticed that his hands were hanging loosely, as though the left one were holding a gong, the right one grasping a mallet, and both were quivering slightly. After hurriedly and forcefully stopping these involuntary movements, he glanced at the thumb of his left hand, which was roughly stroking the callus on the inside of his index finger. This callus had been caused by the constant rubbing of the rope handle of the gong he used to carry. He smiled grimly.

As for Scabby Head and the others, although they had gained the upper hand by expelling Kam Kim-ah from the group, now as they watched him sit there so composed, appearing unaffected by what they were saying, conflicting emotions of triumph and defeat assailed them as well. The only difference was the source of these emotions: for them it came from a sense of superiority; for him, of inferiority. It was a stalemate. As it turned out, Kam Kim-ah was able to minimize the effects of this particular stalemate, for he had analyzed his own present situation and the deterioration of what had originally been good relations with the others. Scabby Head and the others, on the other hand, after spending a good part of the day poking fun and directing heated criticisms at Kam Kim-ah, found that he was unaffected by it all. Eventually, without being aware of it, they began to lose interest, even though no one was willing to bring the episode to a close. So they let things run their course, waiting for their interest to peter out naturally. Even the comments of Mongrel, Fire Baby, and Know-it-all, who continued to take their pleasure in heatedly baiting and poking fun at him, could no longer get a rise out of the other men. Gradually they, too, quieted down. But they didn't let Kam Kim-ah off the hook completely, for in addition to openly isolating him, they were already contemplating what they would subject him to next. In the meantime, Kam Kim-ah was no longer exposed to the laughter that so unsettled him.

Suddenly a new thought came to disturb him as he sat there in solitude. *What would happen if someone came now to make some funeral arrangements? Should I go along with the others? Or shouldn't I? Why should I sit here and meditate? Wouldn't I feel a lot better if I stood up and gave them hell, then just walked away? If I were to go along with these heartless bums, who knows what trouble they might dream up for me?* He thought and he thought, but to no avail. Concerned that some bereaved family member might turn up across the street to buy a coffin, he hoped desperately that it wouldn't happen today at least.

A leaf from the kadang tree fell to the ground right in front of him. He felt like someone who had run into a friend so intimate that all formalities could be dispensed with, someone he could welcome or ignore, as he pleased. He looked at it lazily, then picked it up and put it up to his mouth to lick it. He focused his gaze on the leaf, until his eyes grew crossed; his face was gaunt and slack. His thoughts turned to his present predicament, the source of which could be traced initially to the death of Scholar Yang. But it was his relationship with Crazy Ts'ai that had had the most direct effect. At first it had all been a simple misunderstanding. But after her belly had begun to swell, things started to turn bad. *What a joke! Blockhead can do it, so why can't I? Besides, I only* thought *about it.* More giggling from Blockhead's pursed lips, but he couldn't tell if it came from across the way or was a figment of his imagination.

Blockhead was giggling. "Don't, Mongrel. My ears are splitting."

"Tell us, what did you do with Crazy Ts'ai?"

"Don't. What did I do?" Blockhead stammered. "I . . . I only
. . . I only took a piss in her, that's all." Mongrel let go of Blockhead's hand, joining the others in side-splitting laughter. After
that, whenever they wanted to have a laugh at Blockhead's ex-
pense, they had only to grab hold of one of his ears and ask him
what he had done with Crazy Ts'ai. He would say that he had
taken a piss in her, that's all. Later on, by merely grabbing hold
of his ear, he would blurt out the same thing before even being
asked the question.

One day, Scabby Head suddenly asked: "Kam Kim-ah, haven't
you really ever had anything to do with Crazy Ts'ai?"

"Me?" Kam Kim-ah was momentarily speechless. Then he giggled and said: "I only took a piss in her, that's all."

At first a few of them chuckled at this, but when they saw the
hardened looks on the faces of Scabby Head and one or two of the
others, the laughter died as quickly as it had begun. What had
been intended as a joke had backfired, resulting in Kam Kim-ah's
complete isolation from that day on.

Crazy Ts'ai's belly had now become *the* topic of conversation
among most of the people in town, particularly the women. Kam
Kim-ah was terribly worried that his name would be drawn into
the talk. As a result, bearing his vague anguish as best he could, he
stopped bringing her food. And yet, whenever she saw him, she
continued to greet him with that idiotic smile of hers.

He had unconsciously chewed the kadang leaf into a pulpy mass,
and the slightly bitter juice from the leaf entered his stomach,
swallow by swallow. He thought, without being totally aware of
it, that if that piece of growing flesh inside Crazy Ts'ai's belly was
his, then . . . *Wow! Wouldn't that be something! I, Kam Kim-ah,
would gladly jump into a vat of boiling oil if I had a child. I could
endure any amount of suffering. That heartless woman of mine,
if she'd had any feelings at all, Ah-hui would be over twenty by
now. Shit! But then, what good could have come of it? It served
her right, being killed by that guy. It just proves the saying that*

evil is repaid with evil, good rewarded with good; nothing is left unrecompensed, and your day will surely come. This thought served to smooth away the feelings of injustice that filled his heart. Except for the sense of lonely isolation, the clamorous sounds that floated over to him were no longer a cause of concern. The rules of Heaven were the guiding principle in the ways of life. He who obstructs another person will be visited by Heavenly reprisals. He believed strongly in this principle of retribution and was convinced that in the future, Scabby Head and the others would get their just deserts. This brought a momentary feeling of comfort to him, and the melancholia brought on by fleeting memories of past incidents was swept cleanly away, while the inner strength he had mastered in his struggles dissipated. At this moment, he felt himself truly at rest—body and soul.

"Kam Kim-ah—" A strangely familiar sound from Scabby Head's direction came to him. As though shaken out of a sleep, he turned and looked over his shoulder, where he saw Mongrel jerking his chin upwards and pointing his nose at him, saying to a neatly dressed man: "Isn't that him over there?" All the men, including the stranger, turned their eyes in the direction Mongrel was indicating to look at Kam Kim-ah. This threw a slight scare into him. The man stepped onto the pedal of his bicycle and pushed himself over toward Kam Kim-ah.

"Kam Kim-ah, are you still beating your gong?"

He simply could not believe his ears. He got to his feet, feeling both flabbergasted and elated. Stooping slightly, he didn't know what to do with his hands, putting them first behind his back, then clasping them in front of him. "Do you mean...," he asked cautiously. But before he had gotten the words out, the other man butted in impatiently:

"Well, yes or no?"

"Yes, yes, yes," Kam Kim-ah answered him with a sense of urgency. "Um-hm, um-hm!" Although he didn't know what the man had in mind, he didn't dare ask any more questions.

"Meet me at the District Headquarters at two tomorrow afternoon. I've got a job for you." Then he added impatiently: "I'll need your services for three days."

"Yes, yes, yes . . .," Kam Kim-ah stammered, nodding with each word. He kept it up until the man was out of sight. Then it came to him—the District Headquarters. No wonder the man looked so familiar; in the past, he was the one who had always hired him when the District Headquarters had an announcement. "This head of mine is really something—I even forgot him." As he watched the man's retreating figure, the gratitude and happiness brought by this unexpected opportunity had the effect of slowly straightening his slightly crooked back, like a vine growing at night. Enough time passed while he was in this state of mind to vex the men looking on; then, sensing something in the air, he became aware of several pairs of eyes staring at his back. But there were no more cold shivers up his spine. He coughed dryly, sending the stares back where they came from, then turned around and gave the others a sweeping glance. Much to his surprise, these men whom he had endured for so long, whom he had feared to anger, and whose arrogance he had catered to, now resembled little more than a mass of dead cinders. Some of them were blinking involuntarily. Sickened by what he saw, Kam Kim-ah opened his mouth and released his long-pent-up anger.

"What's wrong with you? Look! Don't you know who I am? Since you want to look, get yourselves an eyeful. I'm different from bums like you, who spend your whole lives gnawing on coffin boards!" So saying, he rolled his sleeves way up, and with his arms—both as thin as rails—at his waist, he struck the pose of a scarecrow. Suddenly realizing that this outburst had included him in its invective, he added: "Don't you get the idea that I'm a bum like the rest of you. Maybe I'll just go and marry Crazy Ts'ai, and what of it! If I want to take a piss, I'll take a piss, and what of it! I'll take it wherever I want to, and what can you do about it? All you can do is swallow your own spit." And yet, for some reason, he was still intimidated by them. Almost instinctively, he maintained a guarded distance of as much as three or four kadang trees from them.

Scabby Head and the others were speechless, looking as though someone had smashed some valuable object of theirs when they weren't looking, and they didn't know what to do about it. At the same time, they were suddenly struck by the feeling that a livelihood of gnawing on coffin boards really wasn't a very respectable occupation (prior to this, the thought had evidently never crossed their minds). This impression, however, was only a shallow, fleeting one, and did not enter their relative consciousness. Self-demeaning looks appeared on their faces, but these were nothing more than instinctive shows of self-protection meant to illicit sympathy from the other party and help them over this critical moment.

Marry Crazy Ts'ai? Even Kam Kim-ah was shocked by this. How could he have said that? He felt a need to explain, both to himself and to the others. "I . . ." He sputtered for a while, but could never get past the word "I." Finally, growing impatient with himself, he blurted out: "I, Kam Kim-ah, mean what I say. If I say temporary, I mean temporary. My teeth aren't made to gnaw on coffin boards like yours are." But no matter how satisfying all this was, he couldn't shake the emotional discomfort caused by his comment about marrying Crazy Ts'ai. He was afraid they would take it in all of its despicability and turn it on him. "Of course, I wouldn't actually marry her; what I meant was *if* I did, what could you guys do about it?" But that didn't make him feel any better. *If I feel like marrying her, that's what I'll do! Having a baby is easy, but rearing a child is a deed of kindness; anyone can father a child, but a parent is one who rears a child, whoever's seed it may be!*

Blockhead, alone among the group of men, walked back and forth, totally unconcerned about what earth-shaking incident may be occurring in this circle; he simply continued doing what he did best, which was to giggle foolishly. But on this occasion, he was unable to draw any laughter from the others.

I've got to hurry back and get everything ready. I'll have to polish the gong with ashes, and the mallet—I may not be able to find it at all, and even if I do, the cloth head has probably rotted away. But the thought that he was going to let these men off so easily was an irritation, and he was tempted to level one more hateful blast at them. He thought for a moment, then:

"You guys come over to my place when you're not busy. I won't be able to provide too much, but at least you can have some rice wine and smoke a cigarette or two—no problem there. Now I mean it—you come on over. Kam Kim-ah here will be waiting for you." His intent was to mock them, and as he saw the embarrassed looks on their faces, he knew he had accomplished his goal. He spat once loudly, then turned briskly on his heel and walked off.

Later on, if I can really manage it, I'll treat them to a sumptuous meal in one of the open-air stalls in front of the Temple of the Patriarch. Then I'll give 'em each a pack of Long Life cigarettes and see if that doesn't make 'em feel just terrible.

The Gong Goes *Bong! Bong! Bong!*

"Hey, it's time to get up." He stretched out and reached beneath the bed to take out the gong that he had been using as a catch-all. He looked it over carefully. "Wow, you sure have slept for a long time; you've even got a dead lizard in here!" He stared intently at the sunken eyes with the tiny specks of white showing through the lizard's carcass. Then he picked out a nail from the junk inside and used it to flip the lizard's carcass onto the floor, after which he turned the gong upside down and dumped everything into a heap beneath his bed. At that moment he realized that he was holding in his hand a real, but badly tarnished, gong, and his heart was pounding uncontrollably. He turned the gong over and over in his hands, brushing the dust off as he did. He spat on it, then rubbed it with his fingers as he walked out of the shelter. He looked it over carefully once more in the natural light, as the sun glinted weakly off the spots he had rubbed with saliva. He could envision the gong in all its shiny luster, and its sound, which was in his mind always, seemed now to be pounding in his ears.

Bong! Bong! Bong! The gong beater's coming your way . . ." He
was talking to himself under his breath: "Once I fall on better
days I'll show 'em. Where do they get off looking down on me?"
He had pulled up a handful of wild grass from atop the air-raid
shelter, and with it he scooped up some ashes from the incinerator,
then gently rubbed the face of the gong. Although this gong had
the scars of two cracks where the hanging straps went, they had
been carefully polished, and a tiny crack as wide as a grain of
rice had been made, so that when the gong was struck the sound
wouldn't reveal any trace of the flaw, nor would its resonance be
affected.

"Shit! Damned good-for-nothing!" He remembered the day
those cracks appeared as though it were yesterday. It was on the
day of the Matsu festival: following the procession he had been
asked to stay over for a meal by the owner of the incinerator, and
he must have drunk a great deal that night, or else how could his
gong have fallen on a cobblestone? Never before, in all the time
he had been beating the gong, had Kam Kim-ah dropped it. He
had replaced the rope straps about once a month. *What a damned
good-for-nothing!* As he polished the gong, he cursed to himself,
though even he didn't know what the object of his cursing was.

As the gong began to shine once again, the lost days of Kam
Kim-ah's past returned in all their vividness, giving a scintillating
boost to his spirits. He reflected on the past: how, because of the
cracks in the gong, he had manipulated his wrist action as he
wielded the mallet and struck the gong at just the right spot so
that the sound had the same beauty and resonance as when it had
been whole and perfect, and so that the cracks did not grow any
longer. He knew the course of these two cracks by heart: where
they met near the middle, a tiny triangular section of brass was
about to fall off. In the past he had taken pains to guard against
this eventuality, and he would have to continue doing so from
now on. As he was relishing these thoughts of the past, his wrist
was twitching involuntarily. He could clearly see his reflection in
the gong; he laughed inwardly.

"Oh-oh!" He raised his head to discover that someone was standing there watching him. This stunned him momentarily. "What time is it?"

"I don't know exactly; I just came from the marketplace. I noticed by the clock at the District Headquarters that it was about eleven-thirty."

"How long ago was that?"

"I just came from there. Why? You back to beating the gong?"

"If I didn't, who would?"

"What's the occasion?"

"You can be sure there's an occasion. You go on and tell everyone to keep their ears open." He saw another fellow—a young man—walking down the road. He stood up and called out: "Hey, elder brother!" The young man turned around. "Elder brother, do you know what time it is?"

"No, I don't," he said, shaking his head. "I'm on my way home to eat lunch."

"Eat lunch? Then it must be somewhere around noon," he said to himself. He was greatly relieved.

Returning to the shelter, he got some rags and his old mallet handle, then went outside into the sunlight, where he began making a mallet head. Every once in a while he asked the time of day from a passerby, and by the time he had formed the mallet head out of the rags, he had already asked three people. Time seemed to be standing still. He looked for, but could not find, a piece of taro root to twist into a strap for the gong; then he was reminded of the tieband that served as a belt. He hadn't used it long, so it was still serviceable. He went back into the shelter to get the tieband from his black trousers, which were draped over the head of his bed.

He knew that he ought to eat something, but he wasn't the least bit hungry. He had brief thoughts of life under the kadang tree, of Crazy Ts'ai, and of the days that were to come, but all of these were cut short and superceded by the presence of "two o'clock" in his consciousness. Before actually meeting that man at the District

Headquarters at two o'clock, there was nothing else he could concentrate on. Should he go to the District Headquarters at one-thirty to wait for the man? No, one o'clock would be even safer.

Having reached the District Headquarters gate well ahead of the appointed hour, Kam Kim-ah paced back and forth in front. He watched the people returning to work inside, one after another, until he grew a bit anxious. Just about everyone who worked there had returned, so where was the man who had agreed to meet him there? Toying with the idea of going inside to ask around, he found he was much too frightened to do so.

"Kam Kim-ah!" someone behind him suddenly called out. He turned around, and there was the man. He told him that he had been there for an hour already, but the man, devoid of expression, simply told Kam Kim-ah to follow him.

"Are you all set?"

"I was all set a long time ago."

"Didn't you bring your gong with you?"

"I'll get it right away."

"No need." Every word the man spoke to Kam Kim-ah was uttered with a total absence of emotion, as if he were impatient with him. Kam Kim-ah was so guarded that he didn't even dare breathe hard. "You see this thing," the man said as he pointed to a placard leaning against a wall, on which some words were written (the thing was made of tin). "Well, I want you to carry it around and beat your gong. Do you know what it says?" For the first time he was looking directly at Kam Kim-ah, who forced a smile and shook his head embarrassedly. "Okay, then you just announce that this year's property tax and income tax are due by the end of the month."

"Yes, yes, I understand: the propriety tax and . . ."

"What do you mean, 'propriety tax'? Humph! I'm not talking about taking a woman to a hotel for some hanky-panky, you know," the man said, unable to keep from smiling. But he quickly regained his composure and said with a scowl: "It's property, not propriety."

"Oh! Property, property," Kam Kim-ah repeated with great effort.

"Right! Property, hm!"

"Excuse me," Kam Kim-ah said, cautiously trying to get into the man's good graces, "do I have to pay property taxes?"

"How should I know? Do you own a home?" he asked impatiently.

"I live in an air-raid shelter, the one in the park."

"Then you ought to pay an air-raid tax," he answered, holding back his laughter by closing his mouth tightly.

"When is that due?"

"Ai, what a chatterbox! Just go out and beat your gong and we'll let you off the hook."

Kam Kim-ah's response was an embarrassed smile.

"How much do you want for three days' work beginning this afternoon?"

"Don't worry about that." He didn't mind making sacrifices this time, for what mattered was that the man hire him again. "Forget it; I'll take whatever you want to give!"

"I can't do that."

"Then make it the same as I got in the past, and we won't count this afternoon."

"In the past?" He reflected for a moment, as Kam Kim-ah lifted up the placard, rested it on his shoulder, and started to walk off.

"Hey, hold on, wait a moment. Do you remember what you're supposed to say?"

"I know. This year's property tax and income tax are due by the end of the month."

"Now, that's property, not propriety! Remember that. Okay, go ahead and start beating."

Kam Kim-ah walked off carrying the tin banner, which made a twanging noise in the air. The feeling this gave him was nothing like the one he had experienced when he was carrying funeral banners. He was struck by the changing fortunes of life: when luck was not with you, it was like being tied in a knot that could not be undone; the more you tried to free yourself, the more tightly you were bound. But when fortune smiled on you, like a magician's sleight of hand, a "one-two-three-presto!" and all the loosened ends of the rope were laid out in straight lines.

Fortune did not smile upon a man many times in his lifetime, so it was essential that he take full advantage of his prospects this time. He had to make sure that his services would be needed in the future by producing greater results with his gong than the loudspeaker pedicab ever could. Over the next two and a half days, he thought, his beating the gong to urge the populace to pay their taxes ought to result in everyone in town's doing so by the end of the month. *I know what makes these people tick: if they think they can put it off, they will, and if they can get by with forgetting it altogether, they'll do that too. For people like this, who never cry until they actually see the coffin, the only way is to scare the hell out of them.*

In the days following the second rice harvest of the year, the sun bores into one like the bite of an autumn tiger. Kam Kim-ah, hoisting up the placard and holding his gong, hesitated for some strange reason; like a child standing naked on the edge of the shore, about to go swimming in strange waters, he lacked the final spark of courage. In the end, even this child doesn't know at what moment and in what manner he has entered the water.

As he passed through the gate of the park and went out onto the street, he reminded himself that he must do a good job. His thoughts returned to his brief rehearsal of a few moments earlier and the deftness with which he had struck the gong. When he reached Northgate Street, he could not gauge his feeling of the moment—was it excitement or apprehension? Many of the people on the street stopped in their tracks before they even heard the sound of his gong. Kam Kim-ah quickly went over in his mind several times the text of his announcement: "Property tax, not propriety tax, property, property . . ."

The first sound of the gong accompanied his first step onto the asphalt road. But he was given a shock; with an inward shout of alarm, he quickly hugged the gong closely to his body—he didn't want any new cracks to appear because of the powerful blow he had struck the trembling gong. No one who observed the look of panic on his face could figure out what he was doing. He made a mental calculation to determine the proper force of wrist action to strike the gong again and raised the mallet high, but then his arm froze in the air—he couldn't follow through. He let his arm fall slowly. He made some more mental calculations. Then—*bong, bong, bong*—three beats of the gong that, weak though they were, nonetheless were loud enough to bring several people out of their houses.

"The gong beater's coming your way—
"Listen everyone, here's what I have to say—"

He took a deep breath as he puzzled over why he seemed so breathless.

"This year's property tax—"

He stopped for a moment; assuming he had said it right, he continued:

" And the income tax—
"Are due by the end of this month—"

He was extremely disappointed in how it sounded. This was the sort of announcing that had done him in in the first place. If you didn't put a scare into these people, who understood nothing of the importance of paying their income tax, they'd simply ignore you.

The people in this small town, seeing that the gong beater had reappeared in their midst, were brought out by their curiosity. The sight of all the people he was attracting pleased Kam Kim-ah, but he was frantically trying to think of a way to add some zip to his announcement. Then his furrowed, troubled brow suddenly went slack. Following three beats of the gong that sounded quite satisfactory to him, he shouted out in a loud, confident voice:

"The gong beater's coming your way—

"Listen everyone, here's what I have to say—

"This year's propriety tax and income tax—

"Are due by the end of the month—

"If it has not been paid—

"You know how this government office is: they'll come down on you like a chicken butcher—"

The bystanders began to laugh. Kam Kim-ah beat his gong three times to drown out the sounds of laughter, then said:

"Laugh? You can laugh after you pay your taxes—

"Don't you dare take any chances—

"If you don't believe me, see what happens when the time comes; if I, Kam Kim-ah, am deceiving you with my words—

"I, Kam Kim-ah, will gladly let everyone here slap my face—"

He paused. *That should just about do it.* In half a lifetime of beating the gong, this was the very first time he had experienced a situation like the one today. No matter where he walked he had a teeming audience, and the more they laughed and carried on, the higher his spirits soared. He was secretly pleased. *Let's see the loudspeaker pedicab match this! Without me, Kam Kim-ah, to beat my gong, the thing wouldn't get done. I've had all I can stand of days like this. Now I'll show Scabby Head and the others how I've got it made, and I'll be surprised if they don't die of envy. I'll be able to avenge myself in my own lifetime. I'll treat them to a real feast. I'll even give them each two packs of Long Life cigarettes.*

By the time he had passed the shops along half a block of North-gate Street, he had made his announcement five times, and there was already a long line of curiosity seekers in his wake, all waiting to hear this comical speech a few more times. He turned his head

to look at this crowd of public-spirited citizens and was given a
shot in the arm by what he saw. *Just wait until I pass by the kadang
tree and they witness the prestige I've gained—what'll they think
then?* He had a pretty good idea what the motives of the people
in his wake were, and his mind was working at full capacity: as far
as he was concerned, the announcement he had been told to make
was of less importance than the embellishments he himself had
added. *Oh! I know what to say now!*

A feeling of wonder and joy gushed from his heart, as three
gong beats rang out in what was now practiced fashion. He said
what he was supposed to say, without missing a single word, although he had the feeling that he might have said propriety rather
than property. But, what the hell—property, propriety, what's the
difference—it's all about the same thing anyway. Then came the
important part. First three beats of the gong, then:

"If it has not been paid—
"You know how this government office is: it'll come down
   on you like a chicken butcher—"

Hearing the roar of laughter that these comments evoked, he
responded with a serious warning:

"You people may have never slaughtered a chicken, but
   you've seen others do it—it's no laughing matter—
"When the time comes, if I, Kam Kim-ah, have lied to
   you—"

Bong! Bong! Bong! Three more beats of the gong.

"I, Kam Kim-ah, will let you cut off my head and use it as
   a chair—"

He very complacently wiped the spittle from the corners of his
mouth, feeling that this oath carried great force—how could a slap
in the face compare with cutting off one's own head? Yes, this is
what he would say. How stupid he had been in the past, believing

that he had carried out his duties by merely repeating what he had been told to say by his employer. If all along he had done his job like he was doing it today, using his imagination to improve upon what he had been hired to say, he would never have fallen so low as to take himself to the kadang tree and live off coffin boards, not to mention all the abuse he had taken from that bunch of pigs.

The tin placard he was carrying on his shoulder, dignified though it may have been, was a lot heavier than a funeral banner. The wooden pole resting against his shoulder hurt like hell. He shifted it over to his right shoulder, thereby blocking his vision to the right side. When he looked off into the distance he noticed a round lacquered sign above a shop to the left with the word "wine" on it. He realized at once that this was Stony's store. His first impulse was to shift the sign back over to his left shoulder, but then the self-confidence he had so recently regained won out, for what did he have to fear now that he had his gong to beat? He didn't owe Stony too much money, and besides, he wasn't as heartless as Longevity. *As for Longevity, let's see what he can do now! I'll be able to pay him what I owe—I'll be a customer now!* But even with his courage pumped up, he was not totally unconcerned: his eyes never left Stony's store.

Before he had taken but a few more steps he was directly in front of Stony's store. Seeing Stony himself, he called out to him: "Stony, I'll pay you off tonight." Then with a show of how busy he was, he turned away, even though he was frightened stiff, and beat his gong right where he was standing. He said what he had been hired to say, then followed it with his oath. The laughter from the bystanders grew in intensity. Forcing himself to look over toward Stony, he was relieved by what he saw. Stony was certainly no Longevity: one look at his face showed you that he was a man with whom you could deal. He was thinking (actually, he was making plans, not just thinking): Crazy Ts'ai, Taiwanese opera, good rice wine, outdoor stalls, Scabby Head and the others . . . His mind was flooded with these disconnected thoughts, coming one upon the other. Sweat poured down his face and both of his sleeves were soaked from wiping it away. He had exerted himself to the utmost, but didn't feel at all tired. He continued walking until he had passed by another twenty shops or so. Preparing to strike his gong again, a piercing screech that hung heavily in the air brought him to a stop. A dark image had darted in front of him, and he found his way blocked by a bicycle. The person on the bicycle was none other than the man from the District Headquarters.

"Kam Kim-ah, stop at once! Go back to the District Headquarters immediately!" The man had anger written all over his face, and when he finished he stepped down hard on the bicycle pedal and rode off in the direction from which he had come.

Kam Kim-ah looked like a man who has sustained an electrical shock; he stood there dumbly for a brief moment. Then as he watched the retreating back of the man, he yelled as loudly as he could, so that the man on the bicycle would hear him:

"What's wrong? I beat the gong! Not only that, I really made a special job of it!" His voice was so shrill it nearly cracked. But the man's figure was lost among the crowds of people on the road. Kam Kim-ah felt weak all over; he turned and mumbled to the crowd of laughing people around him:

"I beat it, I really did a good job. You, any one of you can bear me out on that. I beat it . . ." What he mumbled after this no one could say for sure. He just stood there, his head hanging down, his eyes cast to the ground. Both his left hand, which was holding the placard as well as his gong, and his right hand, in which he was holding the mallet, drooped downward like falling drops of water. He was soon surrounded by row upon row of curious onlookers, as an atmosphere of seriousness moved outward from the center, infecting them all.

Kam Kim-ah listlessly took a few plodding steps forward, the crowd immediately giving way for him. He stopped in his tracks after just a few paces, raised his gong, much to the surprise of everyone, then lifted up his mallet and beat the gong loudly three times, momentarily forgetting all considerations of what he was doing. As the third and final beat of the gong faded away, a small triangular piece of brass fell to the ground. He seemed oblivious to everything as he called out in a voice tinged with madness:

"The gong beater's coming your way—
"Listen everyone, here's what I have to say—
"This year's propriety tax and income tax—
"Are due by the end of the month—"

By now the sound had become a wail. He fought hard to enunciate each and every word, but it was impossible.

"If by that time you don't . . . you don't . . ."

His voice was now quivering so badly that the words were unintelligible, although his mouth continued to move as if he were still speaking. He opened and closed it with great effort. Before long there were no more sounds, but by reading his lips, the onlookers could pretty much tell that he was saying, over and over:

"I, Kam Kim-ah . . . I, Kam Kim-ah . . ."

Ringworms
· · · · ·

The moment Ah-fa walked in through the door of his house after getting off work, his wife handed the baby over to him. Seemingly very uncomfortable cradled in his father's arms, the baby began to cry. Ah-fa quickly and clumsily rocked him back and forth for a moment, which produced the desired effect of stopping his crying. But the baby was not so much lulled into stopping as he was frightened by the violent rocking. Edging a short stool over with his foot—actually, it was nothing more than a block of wood—Ah-fa sat down, lay the baby across his legs, and began fumbling through his pockets for a cigarette. Then he remembered that he had smoked the last one after getting off work and had crumpled up the empty package and thrown it on top of the lime pit. It all came back to him now. There was some happy news he wanted to tell his wife, but before saying anything he decided to tease her a little first. This somewhat sinister idea had popped into his mind when he discovered he was out of cigarettes.

Ah-fa's wife was busy cooking dinner, running from one end of the kitchen to the other. Just then her still-rounded buttocks appeared directly in his line of vision, and as he watched her wriggling rear end his normal enthusiasm at being home was considerably increased. All of this weighed heavily on him, making him feel a little uncomfortable.

"Ah-kuei, I'm out of cigarettes." He knew he was just asking for trouble.

"You can worry about that tomorrow." She kept busy with dinner, not even turning around to look at him.

"Not on your life. I want a smoke now."

"If not smoking will kill you, then you can just go ahead and drop dead!" The spatula in her hand clanged loudly against the iron cooking pot.

"Take it easy, will you! What if you break the pot? I could buy a lot of cigarettes with the money it would take to replace it."

"We could buy all the pots we needed if you stopped smoking for a year."

As his wife leaned over to scoop some water out of the vat, her rump stuck up under her trousers, a sight which greatly amused Ah-fa. Since there was no water in the vat, the ladle merely clanged against the sides.

"Are Ah-chu and the kids out getting some yams?" Ah-fa asked.

"She's a lot better than you are. Yesterday she brought back a whole sackful plus half a basketful."

"Did Ah-hsiung go with them?"

"That's the only way I can get him out from underfoot."

"He's still small. Have you forgotten he's only three?"

This brought an angry scowl to her face; she picked up the wooden bucket and marched outside to fetch some water.

Ah-fa sensed that he should get on with telling her the good news, because if she got much angrier things might get out of hand.

His wife returned, carrying a bucketful of water.

"This time luck's with us," Ah-fa said. "When this job's finished the day after tomorrow, Ah-tsu wants me to go with his group to a job that will last a full three months." He riveted his eyes on his wife's face so that he could see her frown turn into a smile. But she pretended she hadn't heard him and busied herself with pouring the water into the vat. He continued anyway: "The pay is thirty-five dollars a day, five more than I'm getting now. This time I won't have to sit around all day with nothing to do." As his wife walked outside with the empty bucket, he saw that her face was still tightly set, and frustrated anger began to well up inside him. This is going a little too far, he thought to himself, and he decided to give her a taste of her own medicine when she returned.

It seemed to him that the stool on which he was sitting had grown thorns, making him fidget. He stood up and began pacing back and forth, growing angrier by the minute. *Everything was just fine at first, but she had to go and put me out of sorts! What's so bad about smoking a pack of cigarettes every once in a while? Since I'm the one who's earning the money, I can spend it any way I please.*

How long does it take to fetch a bucketful of water? She should have been back by now.

He walked over to the door and looked outside, but there wasn't a trace of her anywhere. He turned back and resumed his pacing, but just as he was turning away from the door, his wife entered the house with the bucket of water. Then as he turned to face her, a pack of cigarettes landed on top of the baby in his arms. But what caught his attention was the expression on her face: the warm, apologetic smile she wore quickly melted his heart.

Boy, that was close. I damn near ruined everything.

Laughing and giggling as they came, the four children brought back a big load of yams in baskets and in bags thrown over their shoulders. When they were all dumped in a pile on the floor, they presented a real sight. Ah-fa looked at them with mixed emotions.

"Where did you find that many yams?" he asked the children. "You didn't go and . . ."

Ah-chu, the eldest daughter, cut him short, saying: "It rained hard today, so the yams in the freshly plowed field were sticking out of the ground, right in front of our eyes."

"Oh! That's fine, then." Still he was a little apprehensive, thinking that the children might have stolen the yams. How could such a huge furrow of yams have gone unnoticed?

Number Two was about to say something, but one look from his elder sister quickly changed his mind.

"Okay, let's get ready for dinner," Ah-fa announced to the children, who were proudly gathered around the pile of yams. "Ah-ts'ang, go and buy half a bottle of wine for Daddy, and get a dollar's worth of peanuts."

"With what?"

"Get the money from your mother."

"What kind of wine should I get?"

"Hai! What a dumb question! Rice wine, of course!"

Ah-ts'ang quickly went out and bought the wine, then got eighty cents worth of peanuts, kept twenty cents for himself, stuffed some of the peanuts into his pocket, and hurried home.

Dinner had already started. Number Three stared blankly at the bowls filled with yams and screwed up his mouth. His mother scolded him loudly:

"You don't want any? So don't eat! Anyone who's born into this family can just count on eating yams. What makes a crooked-beaked chicken like you think you can eat rice?"

The child stealthily raised his head to look at his mother. He knew it was futile to argue with her, and if he didn't think he could get away with something, he didn't try. He knew that if he didn't stop, he was in for a beating. But in order to salvage a little face, he put on the airs of a spoilt child and said he wanted some peanuts.

"All right, you can all have a few peanuts. Now hurry up and eat," their father said, dividing the peanuts among them. "In two more days it'll be the second of the month, and after we've paid our respects to the local god, we'll all sit down to a good meal."

The children finished their meal on their best behavior. Noticing the gleam in her husband's eye, Ah-kuei knew there'd be activity in bed tonight. Lately, after several visits by Miss Li from the Happy Family Planning Association, Ah-kuei had begun to develop some misgivings over all this bedroom activity; with the knowledge she had gained, she now possessed a greater understanding and a new outlook regarding sex. But she was troubled by many concerns, and her feelings regarding the matter were mixed; there were even times *during* sex when her mind was on several related and quite scary things. Naturally, they were all things that Miss Li had told her, and she didn't know whether she should be grateful to Miss Li or bear a grudge against her.

As always when they were eating yams, the children—all but the baby—did so spiritedly, pointing at each other and giggling, none of them willing to acknowledge a fart. They sang the children's game "Striking the Gong" to determine who the farter was, pointing to a different child with each word:

> Bong-bong, strike the gong loud.
> Who farted by the doorkeeper, be not proud.
> The doorkeeper's mother picks up a steel pole,
> And drives the little fart right out the bunghole.

The song ended on Number Two, who loudly proclaimed his innocence. But the other three were adamant in their accusations and so a loud argument erupted. Finally their father stepped in to settle matters.

"It was me," he said. "So what!"

They all broke into gleeful laughter. Their mother cleaned off the table, giving instructions to Number One:

"Ah-chu, go help your brothers wash up and get them off to bed a little early."

Ah-chu was only nine, but she was everything an elder sister ought to be. She knew instinctively that her parents were going to do you-know-what tonight, and, for that matter, so did Number Two.

The entire family shared one large bed—all seven of them sleeping together. But ever since that humorous incident with Number Three, the parents felt that with the children growing up, they would have to put a divider in the bed. What they did was place a screen made of sugar-cane pulp down the middle of the bed. It was low enough that if they sat up they could still see whether the children were covered or not. But even the simple matter of placing a divider in bed was possible only after Ah-fa had gotten hold of another tattered old comforter, for their single large comforter was just big enough to cover them all if they slept bunched up close together. As for the humorous incident with the child, Ah-fa made a big joke out of it without the slightest embarrassment, telling everyone around him during rest periods at work. This is what had happened:

One night he and his wife had startled Ah-hsiung awake as he was sleeping beside them. When the little boy saw what was going on, his face had contorted with terror. Ah-fa quickly said to him: "Mama hit you today, didn't she?" The boy nodded his head. "Okay, I'm trying to crush her to death." Naturally, this was an exciting prospect to the child, who then got up, saying he wanted to crush her too, and sat astride his father. Ah-fa could tell this story so immodestly because it was clear from their normal conversation that all his co-workers had experienced more or less the same thing themselves.

Ah-chu put all the children to bed, then started to recite "The Old Tiger-Woman" to them again. Number Two complained that it was just like their daily fare of yams—she had told them the same story hundreds of times before. But Number Three said he wanted to hear it, and Number Four had no objections, so Ah-ts'ang simply buried his head under the bedding and ate the peanuts he had stashed in his pocket earlier. Ah-chu began the story: "Once upon a time . . ."

"There was an old tiger-woman . . .," one of her brothers cut in.

Their parents were still in the kitchen washing up for bed, and when they heard Ah-chu telling the bedtime story, they whispered proudly to one another:

"Listen to Ah-chu telling a bedtime story to her brothers."

"She's just like a little mother to them."

"If she'd been born into a wealthy family, at this age she'd still be doted on by her parents."

"That's a bunch of rubbish!" Ah-fa said. "Except for the fact that children from poor families aren't blessed with much of a fate, they're no worse off than anyone else in lots of ways. Poor children know how to do more things! Look at me—I was taking care of my mother when I was thirteen. Everyone else has to rely on their old grandparents to get by, but we rely on the sweat of our own brows!"

"That's because of all the rewards the other people have built up in former lives, so what's there to be surprised about?"

"Well, if that's the way you want to look at things, what can I say!" Ah-fa had the feeling that his tone of voice didn't quite fit what was about to happen, so he changed the subject. "Next month we can buy a piece of sheet metal to put over the leak in the roof. Then when it rains you won't have to wear a bamboo hat to cook."

"Like hell! Your hands start getting itchy the minute there's any money around!"

"Now don't make fun of me, okay? This time I really mean it."

"I'll believe it when I see it."

"Besides, I usually win at dice!"

"Win! Then where's all the money? Besides, it's all the same whether you win or lose!" Ah-kuei's tone of voice grew harsher: "If you lose, then there's no money. But if you win, you go on a binge."

"Aw, why keep bringing up the past?" He dumped out the water, then wiped his feet dry as he said in a softer voice: "Let's not talk about the past. And if you want to know the truth, I just wanted to win so we could have a little extra money around the house." He knew at once that this wasn't the right thing to say, either, but . . .

"Let's drop the subject!" Ah-kuei said sternly. "All I know is that you're a hopeless case." This was followed by a steady stream of low grumbling.

Ah-fa sat there without making a sound, waiting for his wife to finish. "Come on," he said finally, "you don't have to stop everything just to talk."

The strangest thing of all was that the desire he was feeling for his wife suddenly increased considerably. To him, a woman who was not genuinely angry was very sexy; or maybe his curiosity was aroused by this unusual fancy of hers. Whatever the case, he was growing impatient over his wife's stalling.

"Hey! Come on, hurry it up."

Sensing a somewhat pitiful ring in his comment, Ah-kuei figured that the time had come to put forward a condition:

"The burden of raising five children is already heavy enough," she said, "and if another one comes along, it's going to be more than you can handle."

Ah-fa knew she was right, though it was a topic he did not like to discuss. He was worried that she might not accept him tonight, and an unpleasant look appeared on his face. Ah-kuei knew well enough that this would make him unhappy, so instead of rubbing it in, she continued in a gentle voice:

"Why don't I have a 'loop' inserted? Miss Li said that once I had a 'loop,' we'd be free from worry." She gazed hopefully at him, but he simply sat there staring at the wall without making a sound, his brow furrowed as he puffed fiercely on his cigarette.

"Well, what do you say?" Ah-kuei asked after giving him ample time to think the matter over.

Just as he had done the last time she brought this up, Ah-fa turned and stared at her. But this time his overall reaction was markedly different. Previously he had felt that she was going too far, that the whole idea of inserting the "loop" was more than he could bear. Did she think he was unaware that the health center doctor who inserted the "loops" was none other than Ah-sheng's son? *No matter what, Ah-kuei is my—Ah-fa's—wife!* But this time was different. *Damn it, go ahead and have it inserted and don't tell me about it! How would I know the difference? Oh-oh, hold everything! If she didn't tell me, wouldn't that be the same as taking a lover?* . . . He simply could not arrive at a decision on something as serious as this in the brief time he had to think it over, and there was even less chance that he would actually change his position on the matter. So he continued to stare at Ah-kuei, all the while trying to come to some decision. For it was not just contradictory feelings that bothered him—his self-respect was at stake here.

Ah-kuei lowered her head and said softly, as though talking to herself: "It's for your own good. What difference does it make to me if I have a few more kids? There were eleven of us girls in my family before Mom finally stopped having kids. I'm sure I could do the same. But if you fall into the children trap you'll never be able to climb back out. It's up to you. We'll do whatever you say. It's really no concern of mine, and I'm not going to bring the subject up again. It's not easy for me to talk about this either, so just forget it!" She raised her head briefly to sneak a look at him, then lowered it again. There was no sense in redoing something that had already been taken care of.

All of this had gotten through to Ah-fa, but Ah-kuei had completely misread his opinions on the matter. Actually, how could there be any misreading when he hadn't even made his feelings known to her? He really had no opinions on the matter, so what was there to talk about? He stared at the wall with an angry, troubled look, for not only did the mere mention of the subject put him out of sorts, he felt too that his wife didn't know when to stop. He had been in a happy mood until his wife ruined everything with her nonstop chattering.

"Now get out of here," she said. "I want to wash my feet."

Ah-fa turned and walked into the adjoining room, after which Ah-kuei put the piece of wood up to block the doorway. When he heard the soft sound of the makeshift doorway being put carefully into place, he surmised that she wasn't really angry, and it pleased him to know that the situation hadn't soured after all. Not that there was any reason for it to, since the thought of having any more children was just as disagreeable to him. "*Should I insert it or not?*" *What a stupid woman!* Just then he heard the sounds of splashing water as his wife washed her feet on the other side of the partition, and he felt himself giving in completely. He wanted to let her know that he was no longer angry, so he called out in his normal tone of voice: "Ah-kuei!" He listened very carefully to her reaction.

"What?" She could guess the expression on his face from his tone of voice.

"Are you in there smelting gold or something?"

Although Ah-kuei didn't answer, both she and her husband had a good laugh over this remark.

The children all appeared to be fast asleep, but Ah-kuei sat there for a moment looking at them uneasily.

"They fell asleep long ago, so what are you looking at?" Ah-fa asked with some impatience.

"I'm worried that the baby might catch cold. He's already coming down with something."

"You can hold him when you go to sleep in a little while."

Their daughter, Ah-chu, grew tense every time this situation presented itself. She lay there now, her eyes opened wide, her ears pricked straight up. But her parents were speaking in hushed tones that made it very hard for her to hear anything at all. She very carefully rolled over and stuck her head out from under the bedding then, holding her breath, peeped through a hole in the partition. She was suddenly aware of a slight movement behind her. Turning back to take a look, she discovered that Number Two was also awake. Ah-ts'ang put his finger to his lips as a sign for his sister not to say anything. Ah-chu squeezed her eyes tightly shut and twisted her mouth frantically as a sign to her brother to go to sleep. Eventually the two of them struck a compromise; by then they could make out what their parents were saying.

"What in the world is this?" It was their father's voice.

"It's a ringworm!"

"How did you get one here?"

"It had to have come from you," she said in an accusing tone.

"Ugh! What a disgusting thing!"

The minute the kids heard the word ringworm, the ones they had on their bodies began to feel itchy. Ah-chu scratched hard at her neck, while Ah-ts'ang began scratching his head for all he was worth.

"Where else do you have those things?" Father asked.

"Here."

"Here?"

"A little higher."

"Oh! You've got 'em all over!"

"Not as many as you. Oh, that itches!"

"Don't scratch 'em. They're filthy!"

"What do you think you're doing?"

"I . . . I . . ." He couldn't say it.

" ' I . . . I . . . ' " Ah-kuei repeated, mimicking his embarrassed reply. "You act like some kind of tyrant who plays with fire but won't let anyone else even light a lamp."

"These awful things!" he complained as he scratched with all his might.

"I really feel sorry for the kids. The baby's only a few months old and he's already got some."

"Just when did we start having ringworms around here?"

"Who knows. It's been years."

"Really? Yeah, I guess you're right."

"Of course I am. The next time we have some money around the house, don't bother about sheet metal—what we need is ringworm medicine."

"It's not like I never bought any before."

"Buy some good stuff next time!"

"Good stuff! Do you know how much it costs? We can't afford it."

"You know, it's strange. I've never seen any rich people who had ringworms, so why is the medicine so expensive?"

"If we buy a lotion, it only stops the itching for a little while. Besides, if you took all the ringworms in this family and laid them out on the floor, they'd cover a whole tatami mat. Buying a couple of bottles of lotion is about as much use as rolling around on the tatami."

"So what'll we do?"

"It's just our rotten luck!" Ah-fa kept scratching out of a sense of exasperation. "Ouch! Ouch! I'm sure I broke the skin. It's all wet and sticky!"

"Mine too."

"That's no good! Is there any water left in the pot?"

"Not much. I'll go boil some more."

"Boil some more, you say! If it's too hot, it'll burn me to a crisp! Ouch! Ouch!"

"It's all your fault," Ah-kuei said.

"What'd I do?"

"If you hadn't mentioned them a minute ago, everything would have been all right. As long as you don't talk about ringworms, or think about 'em, or touch 'em, then there's no problem."

Ah-fa had to agree with her. "Well, it's not that big a deal. For poor people ringworms are just part of the family. Go ahead and boil some water!"

Ah-kuei was suddenly struck by a fact of life. "Aha! Now I understand. This is just how all our kids were born."

"What do you mean, this is how they were born?"

"If the kids are going to come, then just let them come. As long as you don't think about it, mention it, or touch it, then there's no problem."

"That's what you say!" Ah-fa was getting a little irritated. "Tell me what all this has to do with boiling some water?"

"Then will you let me have a 'loop' inserted?"

Ah-fa's building anger made him seem like a walking time bomb. It was so still in the room it was as though everything had frozen to a halt.

The two children slipped back into their places feeling terribly disappointed. They were both scratching themselves without letup.

The Taste of Apples

· · · · ·

The Accident

During the early morning hours as the thick layers of clouds were beginning to send their moisture downward, an automobile accident occurred at the intersection where the road from the eastern outlying areas enters the city. A dark green sedan with foreigner's license plates crashed into a rickety old bicycle like a wild animal pouncing on its prey, crushing it on the other side of the yellow dividing line of the two-lane highway. A hot-food tray was still securely fastened to the rear bicycle rack, which protruded out from under the car, but the contents of the tray—mainly rice—had been scattered all over the street, and the solitary salted egg that had accompanied the rice was lying smashed along the edge of the safety island.

The rain was coming down harder now, and the puddles of congealed blood in front of the sedan were being washed away by the falling rain. Several foreign and local MPs were there busily trying to determine the circumstances of the accident.

The Telephone Call

" . . . he won't be in this morning . . . Um-hm . . . don't worry about it; a junior secretary like me can easily handle a matter like this. Um . . . Huh! Now hold on a moment, listen to me. Don't forget, we're in Asia now! The other fellow is just a laborer . . . Huh? Well, isn't he . . . That's right, he is! So there . . . he can't cause any trouble. Hmm? Let me finish what I was saying. This is the country in Asia with which we have the closest cooperation and ties of friendship. Besides, it's the most secure. Huh? . . . Would you let me finish what I'm saying? America has no intention of jumping with both feet into the middle of a quagmire. Our President and our people all feel that way. Now look, let's not say anything more on the subject . . . just send him there . . . Um! All right, I'll accept the responsibility . . . okay, I'll call right away . . . right . . . right, that's how we'll do it. Goodbye!"

The Labyrinth

A young foreign affairs policeman led a tall, burly foreigner up to a district where tiny illegal shacks made of wooden crates and sheet metal were located. There were no clearly delineated streets or byways here—everything was laid out in capricious disorder. The two of them made their way through the area for a while, as if they were meandering through a labyrinth. "Boy, what a great place for a game of hide-and-seek!" said the foreigner with a laugh as he walked behind the foreign affairs policeman.

"That's what I was thinking." The policeman detected some sinister meaning in the comment, even though it had been said as a joke. He wondered if the foreigner was mocking him for not being able to find the house they were looking for, questioning his qualifications as a policeman. He was stung by the injustice of it all. The foreigner was probably unaware that the foreign affairs police only assist the local precinct police in incidents in which foreigners are involved. He regretted bringing him here straight away instead of first checking in with the local police. Now even he was in the position of having to find his way through all this confusion.

He lowered his head slightly to look for some numbers on the tightly packed doorways. The foreigner behind him was a whole head taller than any of the shacks in the area, so that about all he could see was a mass of rooftops made of sheet metal and plastic covers, plus some old tires and bricks that were used to hold down the roofs. Some of the roofs also sported an array of wooden crates, bird cages, and the like. The policeman turned around to look at the foreigner surveying this landscape, and said in a not-very-convincing tone:

"Their new homes are nearly completed—those apartments alongside the river are the ones. Once they've moved these people out they're going to put up a high-rise here." He felt pleased with himself over his alert reaction, but at the same time was uneasy about lying. If the man hadn't insisted on coming personally to pay his respects to Chiang Ah-fa's family, the policeman would never have brought a foreigner to this kind of place. Appearing to be attentive to his companion's responses, all he really heard was the American-style conversation pregnant with ambiguities and sinister connotations. In order to show that he was, in fact, listening, he responded with an "um-hm" from time to time. Meanwhile, his efforts to determine what was on the foreigner's mind distracted him from his painstaking search for house numbers. They had continued on several paces without exchanging a word when they met a little girl standing in the lane with a baby strapped onto her back. The policeman asked her a question, but the moment she opened her mouth, he was dumbfounded. The foreigner, standing off to one side, uttered a muffled "Oh, my God!" The little girl, it turned out, was a mute.

They walked off, and as the mute watched their retreating backs, she let out a stream of incoherent grunts, accompanied by a flurry of hand motions.

The Rainstorm

The rain, which had momentarily stopped, began to fall again. Large drops of rain beat down on the myriad materials that served

as rooftops, producing a resounding tattoo and increasing the anxieties the young foreign affairs policeman was experiencing. Just
as he was contemplating recommending to the foreigner that they
enlist the aid of the local precinct—right in the midst of his embarrassed indecision—he suddenly discovered that the house number directly ahead was 21-7.

"Here it is!"

"You don't say!" the foreigner blurted out spiritedly.

Just then the rainfall turned into a downpour, and without a
thought for the niceties that ought to accompany a visit by civilized people, the two of them burst in on Ah-kuei and her daughter, who abruptly raised their heads from their work by the pickle
barrel to find themselves face to face with this uninvited foreigner.
Even with the kindly, embarrassed look on the foreigner's face, as
the mother and daughter witnessed the policeman and foreigner
rush in upon them like this, they imagined for a fleeting moment
that something momentous was about to happen; a shadow of
terror settled upon them.

The rain beat down hard on the sheet metal roof, producing such
a clamorous noise inside the room that the policeman was forced
to shout as he translated what the foreigner was saying. Since Ah-
kuei didn't understand Mandarin, all she saw was the policeman
energetically opening and closing his mouth. The motioning of his
hands caused her to look even more apprehensively toward her
daughter, Ah-chu, hoping that she would let her in on what was
happening. But when she saw her daughter's lip tighten with a look
of alarm and sadness, she asked in a terrified voice: "Ah-chu, what's
wrong?"

"Ma . . ." Opening her tightly pursed lips to speak, the daughter
burst into tears.

"What's wrong? Tell me quickly!"

"Pa . . . Papa's been run down by a car . . ."

"Oh! Papa . . .? Where? Where is he? . . ." Ah-kuei's mouth contorted involuntarily. "Where is he? . . ." This was followed by a
stream of incoherent babbling.

The policeman tried to comfort her by saying in halting Taiwanese: "Don't worry, don't be frightened." Then he reverted back to Mandarin, saying to the young girl: "Tell your mother not to be so upset, and don't you cry either. They've already rushed your father to a hospital emergency ward." The foreigner stood off to one side with a remorseful look on his face and said something, which he then asked the policeman to convey to the others.

"This American says that he'll take full responsibility, and he urges your mother to stop crying." The foreigner walked over and put his hand on Ah-chu's head, nodding repeatedly to make his point, hoping that she would understand.

At that moment the little mute girl with the baby strapped onto her back burst in through the doorway, dripping wet. Unaware of what was happening inside, the moment she entered to discover the policeman and the foreigner she had run into a short while before, her eyes widened and she began making loud grunting noises, accompanied by hand gestures. All the while Ah-kuei continued to moan almost witlessly: "What'll we do? What'll we do? . . ." When the little mute realized that a pall of grief had settled over the room, her grunting quickly subsided and she walked softly over next to Ah-chu.

"Is she your sister?" the policeman asked in disbelief.

Ah-chu nodded her head. Feeling ill at ease, the policeman said to her anxiously: "Hurry up and untie the scarf—the baby's soaking wet." Then he turned to the perplexed foreigner: "It's her younger sister," he said.

"Oh, my God!" the foreigner softly muttered for the second time.

In the Rain

Ah-chu covered her head with a piece of transparent plastic and walked out of the area of tiny shacks in a great hurry, heading toward her younger brothers' school.

The heavy rainfall continued, so that the clothes stuck to her body on the side of her back that was soaked through. Had she draped the plastic more carefully over her back when she was leaving home, she wouldn't have gotten so wet. She was accompanied on the way by her thoughts: *If Papa can't work, then there'll be no money for the family, and this time Mama will have to adopt me out.* It would be different than before, when her mother had tried to frighten the girl by saying: "Ah-chu, if you don't behave yourself, I'll sell you off!"

But this time she wasn't frightened at all. She never wavered from the conviction that she would be a perfectly behaved, obedient adopted daughter, accepting any and all hardships that came her way. Then her adopted family would have no cause to mistreat her and would even allow her to return home to see her younger brothers and sisters. By then she might even have a little money saved up to buy a toy gun for her brothers and a ball and a doll for her sisters.

But even though she wasn't frightened by this prospect, the more she thought, the faster her tears fell. Before she knew it, she was standing in front of her younger brothers' school.

Civics Period

During the morning civics period, not a single student's voice emerged from the classrooms, only the sounds of several loud, shrill-voiced teachers, which could be heard even from a distance. The old principal, his hands clasped behind his back, moved stealthily down the hallway outside the classrooms like a shadow.

The woman homeroom teacher of the third grade White Horse class was standing at the podium with a pointer in her hand, leveling it at Chiang Ah-chi, who was being made to stand in the corner to her left as punishment.

"This semester is almost over," she was saying to everyone, "and Chiang Ah-chi still hasn't paid his tuition." She turned back to look at Ah-chi: "Chiang Ah-chi!" He quickly raised his head to look at her. "You have to stand there every day during civics period," she continued. "Aren't you ashamed of yourself?" He quickly lowered his head. "Lin Hsiu-nan paid his today, so now that leaves only you standing there—how do you feel about that?" The children all turned to look at Lin Hsiu-nan, who first lifted his head and smiled back at them proudly, then dropped his head bashfully. "Hm, Chiang Ah-chi, when can you pay it?" The teacher walked to the edge of the podium, drawing closer to Ah-chi, then tapped him lightly on the shoulder with her pointer. "Well?" He raised his head to give her some kind of answer, but the instant he looked into her eyes, he lowered his head again. The teacher tapped him once more with her pointer: "Ah-chi, when are you going to pay?" she asked.

"To—tomorrow," he answered softly.

"Huh—?" the teacher exclaimed loudly. "Just when will this 'tomorrow' of yours ever come?" Everyone in the class laughed. "I don't put any stock in what you say anymore. I'm not asking you to pay tomorrow; next Monday will be fine. Don't you get the idea that all you have to do is stand up there all semester to get by without paying. Don't forget that if you don't come up with the money, your teacher has other means. Remember now, you must have it by next Monday! Do you understand?" Ah-chi nodded his head. "Fine, as long as you understand."

Bowing his head very low, Ah-chi ran toward his seat without looking up.

"Hey there!" the teacher shouted. He stopped in his tracks in the midst of his classmates and turned back to look at the teacher. His classmates were all laughing. "What are you doing? Just *what* do you think you're doing? Come back here! Since you haven't paid yet, you've got to keep standing! If you can bring the money tomorrow, then you won't have to stand anymore. Otherwise, I would be very unfair to Lin Hsiu-nan, wouldn't I?" The children turned around in their seats again to look at Lin Hsiu-nan, who felt both proud and sheepish; he lowered his head because he didn't know what else to do.

The matter concerning Chiang Ah-chi had just about run its

course, so the teacher returned to the podium and asked the students seated below: "Little friends, what moral lesson have we learned from this week's civics period?" She scanned the seats in front of her briefly as every child raised his hand. "That's fine. You can put your hands down; let's say it together."

"Co—op—er—a—tion!" they said in unison.

"Right, cooperation. Take Chiang Ah-chi, for example: everyone has paid his tuition except him. Can we call that cooperation?"

"NO!" Once again the class responded loudly in unison.

Ah-chi, who had just breathed a sigh of relief, grew tense again as he heard the teacher mention his name. He thought of himself as an uncooperative child. The very mention of this tuition brought with it the memory of his father staring down at him. Then he thought longingly of the rural elementary school down south. He couldn't figure out why, when they were in the south, his father had kept telling his mother how good things were up north. Down south if they were late in paying their tuition, his teacher, Mr. Yang, wouldn't punish him by making him stand in the corner.

When Ah-chu reached the third grade White Horse class, the first thing she saw was Ah-chi standing in the corner. Quickly moving up alongside the window, she called out with undisguised trepidation: "Ah-chi!" His heart skipped a beat and he immediately hung his head low. The momentarily startled teacher rushed out of the room, as all of the children turned to look outside the classroom, those at the rear standing up to do so.

"Is Chiang Ah-chi your younger brother?"

Ah-chu nodded, then said: "Our papa was run down by an American's car."

"How bad is it?"

The classroom was all astir.

"I don't know," she said, beginning to cry.

"All right, now, don't get worked up." The teacher turned and walked back into the classroom, as the students clambered back to their seats. "Chiang Ah-chi, hurry up and go with your sister to see your daddy." Ah-chi didn't seem to be any more upset over the news than he was over having to stand in the corner. He bowed deeply to the teacher, then walked slowly back to his seat to pick up his books.

From that moment on until he walked out of the classroom with Ah-chu, the eyes of all the children in the room followed his every move and action.

"Where's Ah-sung's classroom?" Ah-chu asked him.

"Over there," he said, pointing to the door at the end of the hallway.

On the Overpass

The rain still hadn't let up; Ah-chu squatted down and arranged a plastic cover over Ah-sung. "You oughtta be able to put this on yourself!" As she thought again about her being sold into adoption, she drew back one of her hands and wiped the tears that were streaming down both sides of her face. "Don't feel sad; I'll come home to see you sometimes." Actually, neither Ah-chi nor Ah-sung displayed the slightest trace of unhappiness; they were in a daze, and Ah-chu's words served only to confuse them more. "Let's go! Hurry now, Mama's waiting for us." Ah-chu took Ah-sung by the hand, Ah-chi walked alongside her, and the three of them passed through the front gate of the school together.

When they reached the intersection near the school they watched the cars passing by in both directions, waiting for a chance to dart across. The shrill sound of a whistle came to them from the car-stand across the street.

"Ah-chi, we can't cross, there's a policeman over there. Let's use the overpass."

Ah-chi walked on ahead and lightheartedly jumped up onto the steps. Ah-sung cried out anxiously: "Hey, wait up."

"You're the one who's walking so slow. Why should I wait for you?"

Ah-chu looked up at Ah-chi, who had turned back to face them, the sky above him serving as a backdrop: "Ah-chi, wait for your brother," she said. Then she lowered her head again: "Hurry up," she urged. "Ah-chi's waiting for you."

While Ah-chi waited for his sister to catch up, he looked down at the cars passing below him. Then he turned back to look at his sister and Ah-sung, who were five or six steps behind him.

"Sister," Ah-chi said with a tone of sadness creeping into his voice, "I don't want to go to school anymore." Ah-chu stopped where she was and gazed up at him, while Ah-sung continued climbing up the steps.

"Ah-chi!" she said, her head lowered in deep thought as she started up again behind Ah-sung. "Ah-chi, what would Daddy and Mommy think if they heard you say that?" She grabbed hold of the now silent boy and together they all walked across the overpass.

"We can't afford the tuition."

"Wait till Daddy has some money, then we can pay it."

"But the semester is almost over . . ."

"That's all right," Ah-chu comforted him. "Wait till I've been adopted and I'll give you the money."

"Is somebody going to adopt you?" he asked in astonishment.

"Uh-huh!" Even though she answered him firmly, tears began to course down her cheeks faster than she could wipe them dry.

"Does Mommy want to adopt you out?"

"I'm afraid this time it's for real. Daddy was run down by an American's car . . . ."

Ah-chi still didn't understand what his daddy's being run down by an American's car had to do with their future. As a matter of fact, his attention was momentarily caught by the fact that Ah-sung wasn't there beside them. "Hey! Where's Ah-sung?" They jerked their heads around and spotted Ah-sung squatting down alongside one of the railings in the middle of the overpass, watching the automobiles passing beneath him.

"Ah-sung!" Ah-chu called out.

"Ah-sung really makes me mad! He does this every day when I take him to school. He even throws pebbles down on the cars!"

"Ah-sung!" Seeing that he was paying no attention to her, Ah-chu ran over angrily.

The sight of Ah-chu dragging Ah-sung over toward him made Ah-chi laugh.

"I'm going to tell Mommy when we get home that Ah-chi said you do this every day!"

"He does too—he started it!" Ah-sung said as he glared at his brother.

"Who said so?" Ah-chi was still laughing.

"Come on! Let's go! Mommy's probably worried to death. It's taking us all day just to cross an overpass!"

"Sister, carry me down on your back," Ah-sung said when he reached the head of the steps leading down.

Without saying a word, Ah-chu squatted down to let Ah-sung climb up onto her back.

In the Sedan

Heedful that her husband had lost a lot of blood and was now undergoing emergency treatment, Ah-kuei cried helplessly and muttered reproachfully: "I told him that jobs are the same every-where, but he wouldn't listen to me. He kept saying we should go up north and try our luck there. Now look at the luck we've found! My God! Just what kind of luck have we managed to find? . . ."

She was still crying as they approached the highway, though she wasn't even aware that they had reached the street—she simply followed Ah-chu wherever she led her.

The policeman and the foreigner were standing alongside a big black sedan, signaling to them with their hands.

"Mama, there's the American. Ah-chi, take the others over there."

When the foreigner saw them walking toward him, he jumped into the car and started the engine. The policeman jumped in be-side him. As she walked up alongside the car, Ah-kuei began crying even more loudly, more than likely intending to make this American aware that he had brought her family to ruin.

The policeman stuck his head out the window: "Get in!" he said.

Ah-kuei simply stood there and wailed, while Ah-chu stared at the closed door, not knowing what to do. While everyone stood there indecisively, Ah-chi reached out and grabbed the door handle. Nothing happened. So, putting his left foot against the car, he used both hands and pulled on it with all his might. Still nothing. Just then the foreigner, suddenly realizing that they hadn't yet opened the door, turned halfway around in his seat with a grunt, reached over, and opened the door from the inside, nearly sending Ah-chi sprawling backwards.

Ah-kuei and the children couldn't possibly have managed to seat themselves if the policeman hadn't told them all just where to sit. Fortunately, even with her lack of experience and her apprehensions, Ah-kuei bumped her head only slightly as she climbed into the car, and was merely startled. That and the unexpected opulence of the car interior combined to bring her crying to an abrupt halt.

Before they had driven very far, Ah-kuei realized that she had stopped crying as she was seated in the car, making her mournful cries of a moment earlier seem a bit contrived. She soon recommenced babbling and sobbing, and before long was giving rein to her grief with loud wails.

The policeman, unable to endure her mournful crying, turned around and said: "There, there, Mrs. Chiang, there, there! Don't cry so hard. Who knows, maybe Mr. Chiang was only slightly injured. But if you cry too hard, you might make him even worse—he could even die! Now, stop crying." At first he was feeling pretty badly himself, but this little speech of his nearly made him burst out laughing. He quickly turned around and faced forward biting down hard on his lower lip.

Ah-kuei was crying out of a genuine sense of grief, to be sure, but not understanding clearly what the policeman had said to her, she figured that they must all be in sympathy with her, so she cried even more bitterly, mumbling as she did: ". . . how are the five children and I going to live? How are we going to live . . .?"

The policeman wanted to give her more counsel, but as he turned around he saw her crying so hard she was trembling, and the words stuck in his throat. He could think of nothing to say that might stop her crying. Looking at the situation from a different angle, he realized that for an impoverished woman to give rein to her grief this way wasn't necessarily bad for her emotional health. As this thought formed in his mind, he was struck by his own selfishness.

Ah-chu, holding the baby in her arms, was pressed up close to her mother, though her thoughts were only of what might happen after her adoption. Ah-chi, Ah-sung, and the mute girl were all kneeling on the back seat, looking at the scenery out the back window and giggling. For them, their father's accident had quickly been left far behind around one of the curves in the road.

As the car followed a gradually winding mountain road, the three children on the back seat pressed up against the side window that separated them from the scenery outside. They watched the houses at the base of the mountain grow smaller. Ah-chi and Ah-sung kept pointing to things for each other's benefit, excitedly telling one another in soft voices to look here and there. Even the little mute girl was exuberant, but when she tried to speak, it came out in loud grunts: "Ai ya! Ba, ba, ba, ya . . . ."

The White House

A clean, white, medium-sized hospital stood on the scenic mountaintop. Although the parking lot beside it was filled with cars, there were no people walking around. Several white sedans and ambulances were parked among the cars, and there was a short white fence surrounding a patch of Korean grass made dazzling by the recent rainfall.

Ah-kuei was still crying bitterly as the car drove into the parking lot.

"All right," the policeman said to her "all right. We're here now, so you'd better stop crying."

But with the cold, white hospital there in front of her, and not another soul in sight, Ah-kuei was confronted by a series of images. She knew her husband was inside. Was he dead? Crippled? Or what? Suddenly she could no longer restrain the emotions that she had been able to keep more or less under control thus far. Covering her face with her hands, she let herself be led along by Ah-chu, the wailing sounds of her uncontrollable grief sticking in her throat and making her sound a little like a dying animal.

When Ah-kuei and the others followed the foreigner inside the hospital, the grief that had been surging unchecked within her was brought under control by the stern atmosphere of the hospital. Having regained control of herself, she looked around at her children, who seemed to be frightened by the strange, new environment. She gathered them all together, then squatted in front of the mute girl. Using sign language, she pointed to her own mouth, then to the mute's mouth, indicating that she wanted her to quiet down. The mute nodded her head, then grunted loudly. She realized that she had done something wrong when she saw the angry glare in Ah-kuei's eyes. She tried her best to scoot backwards, but Ah-kuei pulled her up close and made hand motions of sewing the girl's mouth closed. The frightened mute shook her head spiritedly.

The policeman walked over from the reception desk and told Ah-kuei: "Mr. Chiang isn't in any danger—only his legs were broken. He'll be coming out of surgery soon."

From the policeman's expression and tone of voice, plus the few words she could understand, Ah-kuei had a rough idea of what he was saying. She glanced over at the reception desk just as the foreigner, a comforting smile on his face and a foreign nurse beside him, walked over to her. He began talking to them feverishly, bending over at the waist and making hand motions first against his left leg, then against his right; then he nodded his head. Just then, much to everyone's surprise, the mute girl, seeming to comprehend what he was saying, walked up in front of him, patted his leg, and began grunting and gesturing. The foreigner smiled and nodded to her.

The foreign nurse took them into an empty ward to wait for Chiang Ah-fa. With the knowledge that her husband was in no immediate danger, Ah-kuei felt considerably relieved and, like her children, began to scrutinize the hospital and the people walking around in it. Being sick in a place like this might not be all that unpleasant, she thought to herself. After the foreigner and the policeman had left the ward, Ah-chu asked Ah-kuei: "Mama, Papa's going to stay here, isn't he?"

"I don't know."

"How long will he stay?" Ah-chu asked with growing interest.

"You little rascal! What are you so happy about?" She was nearly laughing herself.

Ah-chu could tell that her mother wasn't really angry, so she said bravely: "I have to go to the bathroom."

To her surprise, her mother said with a laugh: "Me too. I've held back ever since this morning. This is awful! Where can we pee in here?"

"I dunno."

"This is awful!" Just as she was bemoaning the situation, Ah-chi and Ah-sung ran into the room. "Where in the hell have you two been?"

"We went to the bathroom," Ah-sung answered.

"Where is it?" she asked impatiently.

"Over there!" Ah-chi pointed casually. "Go out here, then turn, then turn again, and there it is."

"You little brat, aren't you afraid of anything? Where do you think you are? What's the idea of running all over the place! Now, where is it? Take me there."

"Over there!" Ah-chi gleefully threw open the door and started out.

"Wait a minute! Slow. down . . . and stop shouting."

Ah-chi and Ah-sung took Ah-kuei and the others to the toilet, then the two of them ran back to the empty hospital room.

"Hey, everything in the place is white," Ah-sung noted with amazement.

"This is an American hospital."

"Their clothes are white, and so are their hats and shoes."

"So is the room." Ah-chi looked around as he continued: "The sheets are white, and the blankets, and even the bed. So are the windows and the walls . . ."

Ah-sung was getting a little anxious, since everything in sight, everything mentionable, had already been covered by his brother. He rolled his eyes as he thought hard, then blurted out: "The place where we peed was white too!"

"Besides, there's the . . ." His thought was interrupted by the return of Ah-kuei, Ah-chu, and the mute. Ah-kuei began scolding the moment she walked through the door. "You little rascal, you! Someone would think that you were having a baby instead of just taking a leak, you were in there so damned long! There was some American man in there who kept saying 'Noh! Noh!' or something like that. What the hell does 'Noh! Noh!' mean? He had me so nervous I darn near died." Then she changed her tone of voice and asked: "How did you pee?"

"Aren't you supposed to sit on it?"

"You sat on it?" Only after she saw Ah-chu nod her head did she say with a sense of relief: "Me too." Then she happened to notice a bulge around Ah-chu's chest. She reached out and grabbed it: "What's this?"

Unable to back away quickly enough, Ah-chu just let her mother reach inside her blouse. "It's great toilet paper!" she said awkwardly.

"Ai! What a rascal you are!" She pulled a big wad of clean white toilet paper out from under Ah-chu's blouse and straightened it out a bit. "Really!" she said. "What if someone found out about this?" She turned around with her back to the children and put the neatly folded toilet paper together with that which she had taken from the toilet. Seeing that it made her belly protrude far too much, she reached over and took the baby from Ah-chu and held it kind of low to cover the bulge. Then she said: "What's wrong with this kid today? She's sleeping like a corpse." She looked herself over and straightened up her clothes a bit.

Just then the policeman rushed in. Ah-chu and Ah-kuei were so rattled that even the policeman noticed it. He quickly tried to comfort them by saying: "Don't be frightened, please don't be frightened, there's no danger. You can see him in a few minutes. Take it easy." He had barely finished when the foreigner and a nurse rushed in together, looked things over, and said something to the policeman, who translated for them: "Everyone out of the room for a moment."

Ah-kuei led the children out into the hallway, after which two male nurses entered the room and wheeled out the empty bed. Before long a bed carrying the unconscious Chiang Ah-fa was rolled past them and into the room. This sight was enough to cause Ah-kuei and Ah-chu to weep softly. Ah-chi, Ah-sung, and the mute stood in the doorway staring dumbly inside the room watching the nurses' bustling activity. The children simply could not believe that this was their daddy. Except for his closed eyes, and his nose and mouth, he was completely swathed in bandages.

Unable to shake his suspicions, Ah-sung gently tugged on Ah-chi's sleeve and asked him in a soft voice: "Brother, is that white thing our daddy?" Then he just stood there, his eyes and mouth opened wide.

The Winged Angel

By now there was no one in the room but members of Chiang Ah-fa's family, including Ah-fa, who was still under the anesthesia. Ah-kuei was again seized by a sense of sadness, but this time it was not caused by imaginary fears. She felt genuinely sad for the head of the family, upon whose existence they all depended. Both of his legs were broken, his head and arms had been injured, and it was quite possible that he would become a cripple. What were they to do? Just what were they to do? She mumbled as she sobbed, looking straight into Ah-fa's eyes and hoping he would soon come to. Ah-chu was holding the baby and crying, thinking of all the hardships she could expect as an adopted daughter. She no longer reacted as bravely as she had that morning when these thoughts had first occurred to her while she was walking with Ah-chi. She was so frightened she nearly began to wail out loud several times. As for the other three children, when they saw their mama and eldest sister feeling so unhappy, they didn't dare run about or cause a commotion. They stood there quietly, looking here and there, and even when they wanted to ask something, after thoughtfully looking the situation over, they held back.

After a while, a nurse in a Catholic nun's habit walked in, looked at the patient, then at Ah-kuei and the children, and asked: "Has he come to yet?"

With the exception of the mute girl, they were tremendously surprised by this; they simply couldn't believe their ears. Sensing from their facial expressions why they were all so shocked, the nun said with a smile: "I can speak Taiwanese. I'm a Catholic sister. I was working at Saint Mary's Hospital, but in accordance with the wishes of my Lord, I've been temporarily assigned here at the American Hospital to take care of Mr. Chiang." She glanced around the room at Ah-kuei and the children: "Is your whole family present?"

Ah-kuei didn't know what to do except nod her head. If she hadn't been so upset, the sight of a foreign woman, who bore no resemblance at all to herself, speaking the local dialect with such fluency would surely have seemed comical to her. The children were all staring in amazement at the woman, smiles adorning their faces. They were reminded of the winged angels they had seen on greeting cards. Somehow or other, the appearance of this nun suddenly caused everyone in the family to feel that their world had grown somewhat larger. And that was why Ah-kuei felt compelled to try to make the woman appreciate her dilemma. But how? After giving it some thought, the old tried-and-tested method seemed the best: having been grief-stricken from the very beginning, she abruptly reverted back to the way she had been before the arrival of the nun, looking dispiritedly at Chiang Ah-fa's face, rubbing his hands, sobbing and mumbling: "What'll we do? Oh, what'll we do? Here we are, seven of us, no food to eat, no clothes to wear . . . Ai! What are we going to do? Why didn't the car hit me instead? Why did it have to hit you?" She grew visibly sadder as she went along, and all of the nun's attempts to calm her were in vain; in fact, the nun's admonitions proved an added stimulus to cry. The nun was well aware of the effect this kind of situation had on a woman like Ah-kuei: faced with the cruel realities of a difficult situation, her ability to go on would quickly be fortified. And so, taking advantage of Ah-kuei's sobbing, she quietly slipped away for the time being.

Ah-kuei was by then weeping over her own predicament: "Woe is me! What'll we do? What'll we do now?"

"Mama, Mama, the nun's gone," Ah-chu said tearfully.

Ah-kuei raised her head and looked around, then stared at Ah-chu with eyes red from crying, and said in a pained and angry voice: "So what does that have to do with us! Why tell me?" Seeing Ah-chu lower her head, she continued: "Now you've all seen how your daddy was crippled in an accident, and from now on I expect every one of you to shape up. Keep your eyes open a little wider for my sake."

Ah-chu's thoughts turned once again to her adoption. She hadn't imagined that her mother would get so angry just because she had told her that the nun was gone. She had had the best of intentions, thinking that her mother had been wailing for the nun's benefit. It wasn't fair! These thoughts produced a steady flow of tears from Ah-chu's seemingly inexhaustible supply.

"Ah-chi! Ah-sung!" Seeing the state Ah-chu was in, Ah-kuei felt she had been too harsh with her, so she turned her attention to the others: "And the same goes for you two! Your daddy can't work any more, so you two will have to work in his place."

For reasons unknown, Ah-chi was so tickled by all of this that he had to lower his head and bite down hard on his lower lip to keep his mother from noticing. Ah-sung, who was standing off to one side, listened to his mother's threat that he would have to work in his father's place, and, unexpectedly, he turned very serious, answering obediently: "Yes, ma'am."

Ah-chi could hold back no longer, and as his mouth opened, he began to giggle. Even Ah-kuei's angry curses of "What's this? That's just great! You can drop dead, you crazy child! Hurry up and drop dead!" had no effect on his laughing, which would stop only when it had run its natural course.

Blessed Are the Believers

The combination of the anesthesia wearing off and Ah-chi's laughter brought Chiang Ah-fa around. He let out a soft moan, bringing a sudden change to the atmosphere in the room. Ah-kuei placed her hand on his chest: "Don't move," she said. "Especially your legs."

Ah-fa lay there, straining to raise his head so that he could see his legs: "What's wrong with my legs?"

"They're broken."

When he heard that his legs were broken, Ah-fa's head dropped weakly back onto the pillow, and he let out a sigh. "I thought I was dead for sure." He grew silent as he looked up at the ceiling, his eyes still clouded, then he asked: "How about the kids?"

"They're all here, right beside you."

"Papa," Ah-chu called out softly. Ah-chi and Ah-sung also called out, and although the mute made no sound, she quietly lined up with the others alongside the bed opposite their mother. As Ah-kuei stood there watching Ah-fa cast a silent glance at each of his children, she was moved to tears. The whole family seemed to have turned into a bunch of idiots, standing dumbly by unable to say a thing. And the longer this situation persisted, the worse everyone felt, as each of them desperately hoped that someone would break the ice and say something. Just then the baby in Ah-chu's arms began to bawl.

"Give her to me," Ah-kuei said, so Ah-chu walked around the bed and handed her over. "This little imp seems to know that something's happened to you. She hasn't cried a bit all day, ever since morning. She's got to be hungry now." So saying, she exposed one of her breasts and began feeding the baby. The sounds of the sucking baby were the only ones to be heard in the stilled room.

Thoughts of his own injuries and of all these people around him made Ah-fa feel miserable. He wasn't absolutely convinced that he was still alive. *Why haven't I died? Why not just get it over with? Otherwise, how will they manage if I continue to live in this condition* . . . "Where am I?" he asked with a start, as though the question had just then popped into his head.

"An American hospital."

"Huh? An American hospital? Where . . . where's the money coming from?"

"I don't know. We were brought here to see you by an American and a policeman," Ah-kuei answered.

"Where are they now?"

"They said they'd be back in a minute."

Ah-fa didn't say another word, but just lay there looking as though he had a great many things on his mind. The expression on his face alternated between one of concern and one of relief, which led Ah-kuei to assume that, to some degree at least, he was reproaching himself. So she said: "Have you given any thought to how we're going to manage through the long days ahead?" As she uttered these words her nose began to ache and tears started to fall. "I told you before," she continued with a note of resentment creeping into her voice, "but you wouldn't listen. I said that if it was work you wanted, you could find it anywhere. But you didn't believe me; you said women just don't understand, and that we should try our luck in a big city. Finding work isn't the same as opening a business—what kind of luck is there to try? No, there's luck, all right! And we've just found our share, haven't we . . . ."

"Mama, that's enough," Ah-chu cried out anxiously. She saw her father's face turning livid with anger, though he didn't say a word, and she knew that if her mother kept it up much longer, he would explode with rage, after which nothing could calm him down. Ah-chu had witnessed such scenes many times—this was the way their arguments always started. Ah-kuei herself was well aware of the fact, but whenever matters reached this stage, she was powerless to avoid the inevitable results. This time, at least, she stopped her monologue in the nick of time, and, in the silence that followed, the only sound to be heard was Ah-fa's labored breathing. Remembering the nurse's instructions to press the buzzer by the head of the bed if she needed anything, Ah-kuei pressed it, and almost immediately the courteous and friendly nun came rushing in.

"Ah, he's awake," she said when she saw Ah-fa. Then she walked over to his bedside, put her hand on his forehead, and asked: "How do you feel?"

Just like the others before him, Ah-fa was shocked to hear a foreigner speaking the local dialect.

"That's fine, his fever must have broken." She took a thermometer out of her pocket, shook it a few times and looked at it. "Open your mouth and put this under your tongue." She put the thermometer into Ah-fa's mouth, then cast a darting glance around the room, taking in all the others. "Are you still afraid, hmm?" she asked with a smile.

"It doesn't make any difference whether we're afraid or not," Ah-kuei answered her. "We're still worried."

"Do you believe in God?" Seeing that Ah-kuei had nothing to say, she continued: "There are blessings for those who believe!"

Just then the American and the policeman entered with several bagsful of things in their arms. They exchanged greetings with the nun, and the affairs of God were put aside for the moment.

They put the things on the table one at a time: "Here are some sandwiches, and some milk, and here's some cola, and here . . . here's some canned fruit; then we have some apples here," the policeman said, identifying each object. "You can eat this for lunch."

The children looked at the bags, absorbed in their contents. The nun took the thermometer out of Ah-fa's mouth: "That's fine," she said after looking at it, "he doesn't have a fever." Then she went to the foot of the bed and made an entry on the chart hanging there. The foreigner and the policeman drew up closer to Ah-fa, smiling at him. Bewildered, Ah-fa returned their smiles.

"This is Colonel Grant. It was his car that hit you," the policeman said.

Colonel Grant reached out and grabbed hold of Ah-fa's hand, as a constant stream of unintelligible mutterings poured from his mouth. From his facial expression, Ah-fa could tell that the other fellow was feeling somewhat remorseful.

The policeman acted as interpreter: "He said he's terribly, terribly sorry, and he begs your forgiveness. He said he's prepared to assume all responsibility, and he hopes he can become a friend of your whole family."

Like Ah-kuei, Ah-fa did not understand Mandarin, but he had figured out that it was Grant's car that had hit him, so he said angrily and accusingly, accompanied by moans: "Aha! So it was you! You oughta be more careful. I saw your car coming a long ways away, so I pulled over to let you go by—I never thought you'd come right at me. Aiya! When you smashed into me, you also smashed my whole family to pieces . . . ." Wanting very much to know what Ah-fa was saying, Colonel Grant looked over at the policeman, who returned his look and shook his head. Eventually it was the nun standing behind them who conveyed Ah-fa's words to Mr. Grant.

From that point on the nun acted as Colonel Grant's interpreter.

". . . In addition to the insurance company compensating you, Colonel Grant considers it a matter of personal honor, and for that reason, as well as for official reasons, his organization is willing to assume full responsibility in guaranteeing that you will not suffer financially because of Mr. Chiang's incapacitation. Additionally, he hopes that you will permit him to send your mute daughter to a school in the United States." Everyone quickly turned to face the mute, throwing a scare into her. If Mr. Grant hadn't just then placed his hand on her head and rubbed it, she would probably have been frightened to death. Ah-kuei and Ah-fa looked at one another. The nun quickly added: "No hurry—we can talk more about this later. But for now here's twenty thousand." Grant gave her an envelope, which she placed on Ah-fa's chest: "You can use this to live on for the time being, and there will be more later."

Twenty thousand! This nearly made their heads swim, but since the money was right there in front of them, something had to be said. But what, what should they say? All this indecision gave them both the uneasy feeling that they had done something wrong and offended someone.

The policeman, who had been standing off to one side, suddenly broke the silence:

"This has been a stroke of good luck for you," he said, "being run down by an American's car. If it had been anyone else, you'd probably still be lying in the road, covered with a grass mat!"

Ah-chu bent down near Ah-fa's ear and told him what the policeman had said. Ah-fa suddenly said through tears of emotion: "Thank you! Thank you! I'm sorry, I'm so sorry . . ."

The Taste of Apples

They ate sandwiches and drank cola as they chatted happily; the Chiang Ah-fa household had never been as harmonious as it was at this moment.

"Ah-kuei, when you go home, make sure you don't tell anyone how much money we got."

"What makes you think I'd do that!" Then she turned to the children and said: "Now all you kids got the message, didn't you! Whoever goes and shoots off his mouth will find it sewn shut by me!"

"I wouldn't dare."

"Neither would I."

"Papa, I want to keep these soda cans," Ah-chi said.

"So do I," said Ah-sung.

"I don't want any of you kids losing these pretty soda cans," Ah-kuei warned sternly. "I'll flay the skin off the bones of anyone who loses them!"

"We know," the children shouted out gleefully.

Ah-fa was experiencing an unusual feeling, one completely devoid of cares or worries. It was written all over his face, and Ah-kuei noticed it with a strange sensation; she had never dreamed that Chiang Ah-fa, this man for whom she had borne five children, was capable of such an attractive expression. Seeing that he wasn't watching her, she moved her head back a little and stood there staring at him. *Just look at him! When has he ever looked as dashing as he does today? Today he really looks like a human being.*

Ah-fa stole a glance at Ah-kuei while he was drinking some milk. He was wondering why she hadn't started in again with her grumbling. He was even hoping that she would repeat that sentence, "You said let's go up north and try our luck; now just see what you've run into!" *Just wait till she says that, and I'll come back with "Well, if this isn't called luck, I'd like to know what you call it!" Ha-ha, I could sure take the wind out of her sails with that!* Ah-fa took another look at her at the very moment that her eyes were on him. Knowing smiles spread across both their faces.

The happy atmosphere the family was enjoying was interrupted, but not unpleasantly, when Grant brought the foreman and the workers' representative, Chen Huo-t'u, to call on the injured man.

The foreman and Huo-t'u entered the room without a single consoling word; as always, they merely giggled and laughed and said things like: "Wow! What a life, Ah-fa—nothing but lying in bed, eating and crapping. As for the rest of us, nothin's changed. We're still working like animals. Who could have it better than you! Ha-

ha-ha! Hey, hey, we'll all depend on you from now on!" the fore-man exclaimed.

All of this greatly puzzled Ah-fa and Ah-kuei.

"Hey, Huo-t'u, what are you two talking about? You're getting me all confused."

"Don't put on an act with us. Do you think we don't know? This American fellow told us all about it. They're even going to send your mute daughter to a school in the United States. Not only that . . ."

"Who said?" Ah-kuei asked.

"There must be a hundred of us at the job who know all about it."

"That's only right! Otherwise, how could we know if one of our brothers was being taken advantage of. Isn't that right?"

"Sure, that's right. This Mr. Grant sure knows how to treat peo-ple," Ah-fa said.

"Hey!" Huo-t'u shouted, then asked conspiratorially: "Hey, Ah-fa, did you do it on purpose? Ha-ha-ha . . ."

"Damn you, Huo-t'u, you had to say it, didn't you? No goddamn kidding . . ." There was nothing Ah-fa could do; not knowing whether to laugh or cry, he simply cursed at Huo-t'u with the trace of a smile on his face. Nonetheless, everyone was laughing.

"Huo-t'u, if you think it's so great, why don't you go do the same thing?" Ah-kuei teased him.

"Me? I could never be as lucky as you. Look here. With a pointy chin like this, where would I find that kind of luck?" Everyone burst out laughing again.

Because of the jobs waiting for them, the foreman and Huo-t'u let this count as paying their respects and departed.

"Damn it, what's a guy supposed to do with a bunch of nutty people like that?" All of a sudden Ah-fa's legs began to ache. "Ow! My legs are hurting."

"Call the nurse."

"Hold on. She was just in here; we don't want to put them to too much trouble." He saw the children looking longingly at the apples, so he said: "If you want an apple, take one—one apiece." The children quickly reached out and took them. "And give your mother one!"

"No, I don't, I don't . . ." But Ah-chi had already put an apple into his mother's hand. "Why don't you have one too?"

"My legs hurt too much for me to feel like eating."

"Shall I call the nurse?"

"I already said you don't have to—weren't you listening?" Ah-fa said a little irritably.

Everyone was holding an apple, turning it over, not quite knowing just how to eat it. "Go ahead and eat them!" Ah-fa said.

"How?" Ah-chu asked bashfully.

"Just like they do on TV," Ah-chi said, then took a bite to show them.

While everyone was watching Ah-chi take a bite, Ah-fa said: "For what one apple costs you can buy four catties of rice—and not a single one of you even knows how to eat them!"

Following this remark, the children and Ah-kuei all began to eat their apples. The silence of the room was broken by the crisp sound of apples being bitten into, gingerly, one after another. As they took their first bites they said nothing, although they felt that they weren't quite as sweet as they had imagined; rather they were a little sour and pulpy, and when chewed they were frothy and not quite real. But then they were reminded of their father's comment that one apple costs as much as four catties of rice, and the flavor was suddenly enhanced. When they took their second bites, they spiritedly bit off big chunks, with the result that the sickroom was filled with a chorus of loud munching.

Ah-fa, who hadn't wanted one at first, finally succumbed to the temptation: "Ah-chu," he said, "give me one of those too."

The Two Signpainters
· · · · ·

1

Following revisions in the building code, the eleven-story Insurance Building was no longer the tallest structure in Ch'i-shan, a city that lies along an earthquake fault surrounded by volcanoes.

The twenty-four-story Silver Star Hotel rose up steeply on the southwest corner of Sheng-sen Avenue where it crossed the Ai-pei River, completely occupying the grounds of the former Chi-p'eng Middle School. A huge wall facing east paralleled the west side of the road that ran alongside the Ai-pei River. Though it had been built slowly, brick by brick, by the time it finally reached its present massive proportions it gave everyone the impression of having suddenly appeared out of nowhere.

It also created an illusion to people in cars crossing the Sheng-sen Bridge from the train station, for the moment they began their descent of the span, this massive gray wall in front of them seemed about to topple over on them, which made their hearts tremble. After having experienced this once, they would mentally prepare themselves for the sight, yet when they actually came down off the bridge a momentary panic would seize them. People to whom this happened often would unmindfully look up at this massive gray wall with vague, helpless grins on their faces.

Before long, there was more activity at the wall: the Chi-shih Cola Company decided to make use of the wall by painting a semi-nude mural of VV, the most popular starlet of the day, to advertise their product. The job was commissioned^{contracted} to the Giant Sign-painting Company, which in the past had only done five- or six-story-tall ads or had painted the names of factories on chimneys. They were investing all of their capital and technical skills into this one big job.

It took them two full weeks to complete the white base coat, only to discover that legal action was being taken against them. Newspaper reports said that the three-hundred-plus families who lived opposite the huge wall had signed a petition, complaining that with the wall painted white, it was as though their homes, which faced west, were now facing east, for they were blinded by the early morning glare of the sun's rays off the wall. One of the families was suing the company, alleging that one morning as the grandfather was pointing his cane at the wall and swearing, covering his eyes with his other hand, he suddenly collapsed in a faint and never regained consciousness. The newspaper report concluded with the observation that the wall seemed to be a living thing.

2

Ah-li and Monkey were suspended at the seventeenth story. They had been working on VV's huge breasts for three or four days, without making much headway. Monkey unceasingly brushed on the paint mechanically and evenly, an old folk song from Eastern Taiwan on his lips. How many times had he sung that same song since starting work? Over and over he sang it, with such enthusiasm that one would think he could keep it up until nightfall. Ah-li was sick of hearing it and thought of telling him to stop, but that's as far as he went—thinking about it, never bothering to actually say anything.

Although the white base coat had drawn complaints from the residents opposite the wall, the two men, who were wearing dark sunglasses as they worked, noticed nothing out of the ordinary.

But once they began to apply color they could no longer wear their sunglasses. The heat of the sun beat down on their backs, its glare reflecting off the painted wall into their eyes; not a drop remained in their water bottles, and the water in their bodies oozed out through their pores, dripping to the ground below or evaporating into the air. Getting another drink of water was not going to be easy. In the three days since they had been applying color they had lost their appetites for everything but guzzling down tea and water. Their bodies had turned dark in the sun, the pounds melting away.

What distressed Ah-li the most was the job before him. They were supposed to be painting VV's breasts, but who could tell? The breasts alone were several stories tall, while the two men were plastered up against the wall endlessly slapping on paint, until finally they began to wonder just what they were doing up there. Bucketful after bucketful of paint went onto the wall, but when they looked back they could see several white spots showing through the places they had just covered so evenly. In the past, whenever they put on a base coat they had always used a brush to smooth out the rough surface of the wall. But this time they had sprayed it on to save time, with the result that the roughness of the wall showed through all too clearly. By the time the boss realized the seriousness of the problem, it was already too late. It had taken them several days just to paint the rounded outline, and now that it was time to start adding the color, they'd just have to use a little more paint and a little more time.

Ah-li's vision was getting blurred. Each brush stroke took great effort, but he was still unable to tell at a glance how it looked. Working like this made him feel that he was being cheated and that he was cheating himself. Sometimes it seemed to him that a spell had been cast on him, that he was engaged in a meaningless struggle in a vast, illusory fantasy world. Not far from him, Monkey kept on with the same folk song, though now he was only humming the tune. It still got on Ah-li's nerves. He felt like telling Monkey to shut up, but then he decided to let him continue a while longer.

If he didn't stop soon, though, maybe then he'd tell him. He finally just stopped what he was doing and watched Monkey. The man acted as though he was having an easy time of it, his brush never stopping. Ah-li would have loved to know what was going on in Monkey's mind. He looked up above him, then down below: there were more than twenty men on the wall, each of them steadily manning his brush. *Aren't they also wondering what they're doing up there? And the boss told me that since I do such good work, I was responsible for painting the breasts.* The boss had said that they were the hardest to do, and that they were the essence of this particular ad. He had put his hands up to his chest and made the motions of giving a woman's breasts a hard squeeze. The men standing around waiting for their work assignments had had a big laugh over this, producing an embarrassed look on the face of Ah-li, the man assigned to paint the breasts. He couldn't tell for a moment whether they were laughing with him or at him. Monkey was laughing the hardest of anyone. So when the boss had said that he could choose his own assistant, he had unhesitatingly picked Monkey, though Monkey had loudly protested—No, no, no . . .

The sight of Monkey wielding his brush alongside Ah-li now struck Ah-li as funny. Somewhere along the line he had picked up his brush and started painting again, and the bucket was soon empty. He hooked it onto the rope, then gave a few tugs as a sign to the men below. The empty bucket was slowly lowered to the ground. The few puffs on a cigarette he could manage while the refilled paint bucket was being hauled back up would constitute his rest break. He lit a cigarette and reflected on what the boss had said. *Good work? How was my work good? On such a ridiculously large thing as this, what difference could "good work" make?*

Monkey had voluntarily stopped singing his folk song for a moment, but now he started up again. Ah-li couldn't imagine what was so good about a folk song that the man could sing it for hours on end without ever growing tired of it. Both he and Monkey were from Eastern Taiwan, and this was an old folk song from their district. Although it gave him a warm feeling, he had grown sick of hearing Monkey sing it today. But as Monkey picked it up again, the irritable feeling Ah-li had had when he was about to tell him to stop a moment before surprisingly disappeared. He was amused by the sight Monkey presented. Before he knew it, he too had begun singing along with Monkey, who turned around with a smile on his face, nodding at him as he sang loudly to let him hear the correct melody and help him over the unfamiliar lyrics. Ah-li paused momentarily to listen to Monkey and quickly got the hang of it. For reasons he could not comprehend, this filled him with a refreshing happiness. Monkey in turn was delighted by the look of happiness on Ah-li's face.

"So you sing too?" Monkey edged his way over next to Ah-li.

"I caught it from you," Ah-li said with a smile.

"I thought maybe you were a mute or something."

"Don't make fun of me, all right?"

"You know yourself that these last few days you've been like a zombie, not saying anything and not eating. Every time I saw that scowl on your face I wanted to come over and slug you."

"Slug away."

"Don't think I won't," Monkey responded. "You wait and see."

Ah-li merely sighed.

"What good does it do to sigh? You ought to tell your old mother the truth."

"Did you read my letter?" Ah-li was a little shocked.

"Didn't have to. The same old problem, isn't it?"

"You really didn't read it?"

"Who the hell wants to read your letter!"

"I'm not calling you a liar." He suddenly felt that there was no need to give an explanation. "You know, there's really no way I can send it this month. I borrow two hundred dollars from you every month and I've never paid any of it back. It's been over a year now. How much do I owe you?"

"Whose idea was it to tell her you made two thousand a month?"

"If I didn't tell her that, she'd want me to go back and work on the farm!"

"Yeah, but just think: there's a big difference between twelve hundred and two thousand!"

They were silent for a moment, then Monkey continued: "You still oughta tell your old mother the truth."

"Oh! No!" Ah-li shouted, terror-stricken.

"Then what're you gonna do? You only make twelve hundred a month, and if you're gonna send five hundred of it home, how are you gonna live? What choice do you have?" Monkey looked at the downcast Ah-li, then continued: "I'll tell her if you don't want to."

"Don't worry about your money. I'll pay you back sooner or later." For some mysterious reason Ah-li was angry.

Monkey was hurt by this. He turned to walk away, then stopped and said in measured tones: "Ah-li, if we weren't old friends, I wouldn't take that kind of talk from you." Then he walked off humming the folk song as though nothing had happened.

Ah-li had regretted the words as soon as they were out of his mouth, and hearing Monkey say they were old friends made him feel even worse. He couldn't quite muster up the courage to apologize, although several times he came close. He attacked VV's breasts with his brush. He couldn't recall when he had first begun to be so afraid of his mother. At the mere mention of her name, he could picture her tear-stained face as she said over and over: "You shouldn't treat me this way! When your father died, you were only three and your sister was two . . ." He wouldn't let his thoughts go any further. He felt very, very guilt-ridden. *But what can I do?* Her letter had stated point-blank that they really needed a cart for transporting things, and she wanted him to send a thousand dollars home, since she had already put down a two-hundred-dollar deposit. This was what was on his mind, and he felt like going over and telling Monkey that this time his mother wanted a thousand, not five hundred. He figured that Monkey might forgive him when he heard that. As he looked over at Monkey, he desperately hoped he would turn around. There was no discernible expression on his profile, and it was impossible to judge his mood merely from the way he was singing.

Before Ah-li had used up a third of his last bucket of paint, it was time to knock off for the day. The other men working began to edge their way carefully along the wall. He continued to apply the paint, one brushful after the other, once again feeling that a spell had been cast on him and that he was in a vast fantasy world engaged in an endless struggle. Monkey moved over and asked: "Want to call it a day?"

"I still have more than half a bucket left."

Monkey picked up a brush and began to work alongside him. Ah-li was fervently hoping that Monkey would keep talking so that he could explain things to him. But Monkey remained silent, and Ah-li grew impatient. "What are you thinking?" he suddenly blurted out.

"What's there to think about?"

"Are you still mad?"

Monkey looked over at Ah-li, then said rather helplessly, a pained smile on his face: "I've got problems too, you know. You don't feel any worse than I do. You believe me?"

"Haven't you been singing all day?"

"This kind of work really makes you feel miserable. It's terrible. After a few days of painting like this, you start to get a little crazy. I'm not even sure now just what it is I'm painting."

"You're painting VV's breasts!" Ah-li was secretly pleased— Monkey was just like him after all.

"Ah, come on! VV's breasts is what everyone says, but I'm not sure we can really paint anything like that." Monkey took a vicious swipe with his brush.

"I thought all along that you were having a great time the way you were singing."

"I've been singing to keep from crying!"

"Then why have you been singing our old hometown folk song about the centipede, the toad, and the snake?"

"I don't know. That's just the one that came to mind."

"Homesick?"

"Are you kidding? You can be sure I'd never miss that place in eight lifetimes. I made a promise I'd never again set foot on the land my uncle shit on."

"But you've been singing the same song all afternoon."

"Yeah! Funny, ain't it? Once I started singing, it was like I was hooked on it and couldn't quit. I stopped and gave myself hell a couple of times, but before I knew it I was humming the same song again. I don't know what damned power it had over me. The more I tried not to sing it, the more it kept popping into my head, until I couldn't stop singing it. Hai! Funny, ain't it?"

"I thought you were happy."

"Happy?" Monkey nearly shouted.

"I tell you, if we keep on painting like this, I don't know who's gonna flip his lid first."

"Can't you take this painting any more either?" Monkey seemed surprised.

"You have to ask? No one could stand this!" He slopped on some paint with disgust. "What . . . what . . . what are we doing here?"

"What do you suggest we do?" Monkey started slopping the paint on like Ah-li was doing.

"What *can* we do? Paint! Who the hell cares how it turns out, as long as they remember to pay us when it's finished!"

"Don't mention money. As soon as I hear the word I get a funny feeling all over. We've worked for Giant Signpainting Company for two or three years now, and it's been a year and a half since they raised our pay to twelve hundred. Do you know how much the eleven temporary workers hired for this job are making?"

"Do you?"

"A hundred a day."

"That much?" This came as a shock to Ah-li. "How do you know?"

"One of 'em told me."

"That's ridiculous. What does that make us?"

"Now you know!"

A little paint remained in the bucket, which the two of them carelessly slopped onto the wall.

"Let's go," Monkey said.

"Go where?"

"Down!"

Ah-li thought for a moment. "Let's go up."

"What for?"

"We're on our own time. Let's go sit up on top."

"What about the brushes and buckets?"

"Take 'em with us."

They cautiously climbed up on top of the scaffold.

"Let's just sit here," Ah-li said.

"Since we're on our way up, why stop here? We might as well go on up to the roof."

"There's nothin' up there."

"So what. Let's go! Follow me. There are some girders sticking out over there. We can climb up over them."

"Take it easy. Don't fall from here all for nothin'."

"If you fall, your old mother won't get a penny," Monkey teased.

"Stop talking and watch where you're going!"

"No problem," Monkey responded confidently.

"Here, hand me your bucket." Ah-li took the bucket and watched Monkey climb. "Secure that rope. No, on your right."

Monkey made it to the top. "Here, give me the buckets."

Ah-li turned and looked down to the street. "Wow! We're out over the Ai-pei River!"

"Come on up before you look."

"How're we gonna get back down?"

"The same way we got up."

"I don't think it's gonna be all that easy." Ah-li climbed up onto the roof, then looked down to the street. "Wow! If you fell from here it'd be worse than being in a plane crash."

"Don't keep looking down. Let's just find a place here to sit and talk."

"There's nothin' here."

They looked all around the unfinished roof of the building. "The wind's sure strong!" Ah-li commented.

Monkey walked over toward the front of the building. "Ah-li, let's go up there." He pointed to a thick steel pipe that stuck out some two or three meters and was supported in the middle by another steel pipe that jutted out from the wall at a forty-five-degree angle. A heavy steel mesh construction basket hung from the end of the pipe. Beneath it there was nothing but street.

"What?" Ah-li's eyes were wide with wonder. "You mean you want us to climb up onto that floodlight?"

"If we climb into that steel basket that'll make it worth coming up here."

"Forget it. It's too dangerous."

"Dangerous? How do you think they're gonna hook up the lights there? Come on." Monkey got down and started to crawl over.

"Monkey!" He stopped and looked back at Ah-li. "Let's just forget it. What's wrong with just sitting here?"

"It's a snap." Monkey started to crawl, then stopped suddenly and said to Ah-li: "Most people consider what we do as being dangerous, but we don't think so. It's the same thing here. Come on. I'll go first and you follow." With that he slid on down, wrapping his arms and legs around the support pipe, and crawled carefully upside down.

"Ah-li, hurry up and come over!" Monkey stood up in the steel basket. "Now this is really something! You won't believe what a thrill it is! Leave the buckets and rope there. When you look out from here, it really looks like you're right over the Ai-pei River. Come on."

Ah-li hesitated for a moment, not really wanting to do it.

"Don't be such a coward! What do you say?" Monkey shouted.

"Don't call me that. If you say that again, I won't go for sure."

"Okay, okay, I won't say it."

Like Monkey before him, Ah-li wrapped his arms and legs

around the steel pipe, thinking to himself that if he were to fall from here, it'd be all over. It was so high! He suddenly felt a chill up and down his spine. Then he could hear Monkey—he was singing again, damn him. *He's turned into a singing machine.* He swore at Monkey under his breath as he stole a look down below.

"Yo! Monkey, we really are right above the Ai-pei River!"

"What's wrong with you? Why do you keep looking down from there? Get on over here quick, then you can look all you want!"

"I'm here, aren't I?" Ah-li said with a weak laugh. "You're the one who's scared."

"Stop talking and get over here." Monkey couldn't take his eyes off Ah-li as he crawled over.

Ah-li looked down again. *Damn! What the hell am I doing looking down all the time? I wouldn't have noticed if Monkey hadn't mentioned it.* He climbed in. Monkey breathed a sigh of relief and said with a smile: "Well, what do you think? Great, isn't it? Now you can look to your heart's content."

"There are some electric wires here. Wonder if they're hot?"

"Probably not, but don't touch 'em."

"Think they'll come looking for us?" Ah-li looked down at his feet on the steel mesh floor of the basket. He fantasized that he might shrink so small he would slip right through a hole in the mesh or that he would turn into water and drip through.

"Don't be such a damned fool. We're on our own time now, so they can't tell us what to do."

Ah-li was still looking down at the street below, his hands tightly gripping the edge of the basket. "Monkey, do you think anyone can see us?" Ah-li spoke in hushed tones, unconsciously fearing that the steel basket was overloaded. Monkey didn't hear him. He tugged on Monkey's clothes, and as Monkey turned around, the steel basket swayed with the shift in weight. "Aiyo! Don't move, Monkey!" Ah-li spoke almost as though he were afraid to breathe.

The look on Ah-li's face made Monkey laugh. The basket swayed more violently, but now Ah-li wasn't as frightened as he had been a moment before.

"Monkey," he said calmly, "don't laugh at me like that." Although the basket was still swaying slightly, he kept telling himself not to be afraid. But this forced him to be even more attentive to the movement of the basket. Noticing that Ah-li was dead serious, Monkey stopped laughing and even felt a little embarrassed.

"Okay, I won't laugh. What did you want to tell me when you tugged on my shirt?"

"I was just wondering if anyone can see us up here."

"What're you afraid of?" Monkey knew at once that this was the wrong thing to say. Ah-li got to his feet, having huddled there in the basket ever since crawling over from the balcony.

"You think I'm a coward. Well, let's just see how brave you are, all right?" He had a wounded look on his face.

When Monkey saw him like this he no longer dared to make fun of him.

"Not me, not me," he said again. "I wasn't making fun of you."

"You weren't? That's exactly what you *were* doing."

"No no no, I swear!" Monkey raised his hand as a sign of his oath, but he presented a ridiculous sight.

Ah-li could barely keep from laughing: "You've got the nerve to swear?"

"I swear. May the pipe holding this basket snap in two if I meant to make fun of you."

That did it—Ah-li burst out laughing.

"Yow! That shows what kind of friend you are! You'd swear another man's life away!"

"I'm in the basket too, you know!"

"You sure are."

"What difference does it make, since we're pals!"

They were both laughing happily by now. Ah-li sensed that the basket was swaying more violently than ever; forcing himself to keep his fear in check, he couldn't stop laughing. He cast a quick glance below when Monkey wasn't looking.

"Look down there," Monkey said.

This threw a fright into Ah-li, who thought that Monkey had noticed him. But Monkey continued: "We're directly above the roadway up here, so the people and cars down there are closer to us than anyone else. They don't even know we're here. What chance is there that we could be spotted by anyone off in the distance?" The two men's attention was on the ground below.

"Look, the people down there are just specks, and the cars are like matchboxes. How could they possibly see us?"

"What do you think, doesn't everything down there on the ground look like the works of some kind of machine? That's it! It looks like the works of a wristwatch. Some of the parts are big, some are small, some fast, some slow; back and forth they go, each moving in its own sphere. Hey, have you noticed how neat and tidy everything down there looks from up here?"

"Of course it does," Monkey said with a laugh. "Even if a man and a woman were up here stark naked, I'll bet no one would even notice."

"Give it a try."

"You try it. You first."

"I didn't say it."

They both laughed again.

"You're afraid someone might see, aren't you?" Monkey asked.

"You mean afraid they'd come up and stop us?"

"Never happen."

Ah-li paused a moment to think, then said: "I wonder what my old mother would do if she saw me up here."

"I think she'd probably faint."

"Let's drop the subject—it bores me."

"Got any cigarettes?" asked Monkey as he searched his own pockets.

Ah-li took out a pack and handed him a cigarette. They lit up and lapsed into silence. Finally Monkey pointed over to the train station and said: "The train from our hometown is just about due at the station."

Ah-li looked off into the distance to see the train slowly pulling into the station.

"How long have we been here?" Monkey asked in a muffled voice. "I've always hated figuring out time."

"What?" Ah-li couldn't make out what Monkey was saying. He too was speaking in muffled tones.

"What I said was, how long has it been since we left home together and came to Ch'i–shan? It's been a long time, hasn't it?" Monkey took a long puff on his cigarette. "It's gone by so fast. We arrived at just about this time of day. I remember it turned dark soon after we stepped off the train."

"It's been two years and seven months."

"That long?"

"You figure it out. When do the anemones bloom at home? You remember you told me to meet you early in the morning in the clump of anemones behind the temple? I waited so long for you to show up that I'd picked almost all the flowers along the riverbank. When you finally did show up you told me your uncle had lost back all the money he'd won two days before, and had even lost your aunt's bracelet in the game, so there hadn't been any money for you to steal." Ah-li paused before continuing: "I asked you 'What're we gonna do?' and you answered me by asking the same question." They both laughed.

"Damned if you don't have a good memory."

"At the time, we made plans to sign on as deckhands on the boat my uncle worked on. But then I asked you how we were gonna get to Ch'i-shan on the little money we had between us. What would be left after we bought the train tickets?"

"No problem! Didn't you say we could look up your uncle?" Monkey spoke excitedly, his voice filled with confidence and hope.

"That's it! That's just what you said then, and exactly the way you said it. You've got it down perfect!"

Monkey gave Ah-li a heavy slap on the shoulder and laughed heartily.

"And then what?"

"And then . . . and then we became signpainters," Ah-li said uneasily.

"Let me tell what happened." Monkey was watching Ah-li puff incessantly on his cigarette. "We looked for your uncle for three days without finding him, until our money finally ran out. You said you wanted to go home, and we started to argue. Since we didn't have the money to return home, I said we should keep looking for your uncle. But then you told me you'd never actually seen him, that you'd only heard your mother talk about him. So then we became signpainters and now we've paid our dues. The boss has us working on the biggest painting in the world, and has given the two of us the most important part of the whole thing." When Monkey was at his happiest, his laughter sounded like someone pounding a table.

"You said you didn't hold it against me."

"I don't—I'm only trying to be funny."

"I'll bet there are lots of young people like us who are treated badly at home and run away to follow some pipe dream."

"Look there! I'll bet there are some on that train from our hometown. They step down off the train, bundles in hand, mouths wide open as they stare blankly all around. That's just about what they all look like." Monkey was struck by the humor of this scene he had painted.

"Off the train and onto a ship of thieves."

"What ship of thieves?"

"Once you get on 'em, you can't get off! You go where they take you."

"All you know are a bunch of expressions you've picked up from the old-timers. The other day you used one that I was gonna ask you about, but I forgot."

"The old-timers' expressions may be corny, but they say it best."

"What do you mean, say it best?"

"I mean they're right on target!" Ah-li said. "Just leave it at that!"

"How come I'm not aware of it?" Monkey teased him. He flipped his cigarette away toward the riverbank. "Give me another cigarette."

"I'm not sure myself, but that doesn't matter." He fished out another cigarette and continued: "If you told me to go back east and live in the mountains again, I couldn't do it. I don't think I could stand it for a single day." He took out his matches, and since there was some wind, he lit his own cigarette first, then took a deep puff. "A cigarette up here sure tastes good." He handed his cigarette to Monkey to light his own off of. "Could you do it?"

"Didn't I already say that I, Monkey, would never again set foot on land where my uncle had shit?" He passed the cigarette back.

"That's not what I mean." But he didn't know how to express what he meant. "The first time I went home they treated me like a man from outer space, crowding around and asking me a thousand questions. The village chief even said to me: 'I'd be very grateful if you'd try to find a job for my Ah-mu when you go back.' You wouldn't believe it, but they seemed to respect me. It didn't seem right. I never figured that the second time I went home, over New Year's, that the village chief would ask me in all seriousness if I had found Ah-mu a job yet. I felt just terrible. They think we've really got it made here."

"If that's the case, then why can't you go back?"

"That's hard to say." Ah-li was feeling somewhat troubled. It wasn't that he was afraid to say why, but that he didn't know how to express what was in his heart. "To give you an idea, I've got this feeling that I can't go back till I've made some money. But with the way things are, there's no chance of that, and if I went back broke I'd lose face." Noticing the disapproving look on Monkey's face, he quickly added: "That's not the only reason, of course, but I can't find the words for the others right now."

"Forget it! What's the use of only talking about boring things like that?"

The sky was growing darker, the winds had picked up, and the empty paint buckets were rattling and sliding around with each gust of wind. Monkey unmindfully began humming the folk song about the centipede, the toad, and the snake.

"Ah-li, let's quit this line of work, okay?" Monkey suddenly said, coming out of his deep thoughts.

"Why?"

"I knew you wouldn't go along with it," he said despondently. "Forget it, just forget I said anything."

"How do you know I wouldn't go along with it?"

"The boss is really counting on you on this job."

"Didn't I just say that if we keep going on like this, I'll be surprised if we don't go crazy? Have you forgotten that?"

"That only goes for this job. Once it's finished, won't you be in good shape? There won't be any more jobs like this afterwards. But for me, this lousy painter's job just doesn't suit me."

"To tell you the truth, I'm not sure I'll even be able to finish this job."

"Have you got somethin' in mind?" Monkey asked, happiness written all over his face. "You thinkin' of quitting?"

"Nope."

"Well then, say what you mean!"

"All we can do now is let things take their course. I don't know what's gonna happen."

"Then what did you mean when you said you wouldn't be able to finish this job?"

"Who knows what can happen when you run into a dumb job like this that can drive you nuts?"

"Maybe we'll really go crazy. Maybe we'll be so fed up we'll up and leap to our deaths."

"It's not *that* bad," Ah-li said with a laugh. "Who knows, maybe someday we'll just say the hell with it all and quit. Either that or we'll just keep puttin' in our time and see how things turn out."

Monkey reflected for a moment, then said: "Ah-li, let's not worry about doing everything together, okay? I think I might just quit tomorrow!"

"Don't jump off the deep end." Ah-li couldn't think of anything better to say. "All of a sudden you're jumpin' off the deep end. Of course, if you had a better job lined up, I'd shut up, but I know you haven't."

"If I don't show up anymore, you and I are still best friends. And besides, we're still roommates."

"That's not the problem. Do you think you can just do anything you want?"

"Hey! Now?" Monkey cried out resentfully. "As I see it, nothin' we do for the rest of our lives will be our own choice!"

"Didn't we leave our hometown together and come to Ch'i-shan?"

"That's the only time. And just look where that got us!" Monkey was getting angry. "I don't care—I'm quitting tomorrow."

"What then?"

"Who cares!"

"How could things be as easy as that?" Ah-li said with a laugh.

"I said who cares, and that's that!"

"Everything is just fine, so why get so touchy all of a sudden?"

Neither man said anything for a moment.

Ah-li took out his cigarettes. "One left. Here, you take it." Monkey shook his head. "Then let's split it," Ah-li said, breaking the cigarette in half. Instead of giving half of it to Monkey, he put the two halves in his mouth and lit them both. Then he handed one over to Monkey. "Boy, was I dumb a minute ago; this is the way I should have lit 'em." Monkey took his half of the cigarette, but didn't take a puff right away. Ah-li smoked his cigarette as he watched Monkey closely.

"Let's climb down after we finish this cigarette."

Just then a strong gust of wind blew one of the paint buckets over the ledge. Ah-li let out a yell, but Monkey was struck dumb with fright. They stared blankly at the bucket as it was tossed by the wind past them and down to the ground. For what seemed to be an eternity they were in a state of fearful shock, staring down at the bucket and at the pedestrians on the street below. The bucket shrank to the size of a small speck, then, when it had nearly disappeared from sight, a crisp clank resounded from the street. They looked at one another.

"It didn't hit anyone, did it?" Ah-li asked.

"It didn't look like it did," Monkey said, staring downward with wide eyes.

"No, it didn't. If it had, someone would be lying on the ground," Ah-li said. "A few people have walked over to take a look."

"It didn't hit anyone." Monkey seemed to be reassuring himself. "Did you hear the sound it made when it hit the ground?"

"Yeah. *Clank.* It wouldn't make that sound if it had hit someone."

"It couldn't have hit anyone. Those damned people down there, why are they stickin' around? Here come some more. Look at 'em!"

"I see 'em. Goddamn 'em!"

"Look at 'em! They're not leaving. What're they looking at us for?"

"I think we'd better climb down."

"What're you afraid of? It didn't hit anyone."

"More and more people are gathering down there."

"Who cares!" This "Who cares!" was said with the same anger as a moment earlier. Monkey suddenly thrust his head out over the edge of the basket and shouted down at the top of his lungs: "Get away from there! If you don't watch it, I'll jump and squash you all!"

These shouts startled Ah-li. "What the hell are you doing, yelling like that?" He was getting mad.

"Look, they're moving away, aren't they?" Monkey said triumphantly.

"Moving away? There are more people than ever now. How can you say they're movin' away?"

"Damn them!"

"The ones in the center are moving back, but more and more people are gathering around the edges. Look over there! Cars are stopping too. We're in trouble now."

"We didn't hit anyone."

"Look, there's a clearing opening up right beneath us."

"Damn them, they think we're gonna throw somethin' else down."

"No, they think you're gonna jump."

"Me!?"

"Isn't that what you just yelled down?"

"Let 'em wait!" Monkey said.

3

Before long, traffic on the road running alongside the river was completely snarled at the intersection of Sheng-sen Street. More people continued to crowd around until there were even groups forming along Sheng-sen Bridge and on the opposite bank of the river. A police car drove up to the area, sirens screaming and lights flashing.

"Here come the busybodies," Monkey said.

"Let's get outta here."

"Let's go!"

When they looked back up to the roof they saw four men come running up to the ledge from the stairwell. This gave them a start, and before they knew it, the four men had reached the edge of the roof. One was a uniformed policeman, two were stocky men in civilian clothes who looked like judo experts, and the fourth was also in civilian clothes, but much slighter than the other two.

"Now, you two stay put," the policeman blurted out. The other three men, who seemed to be surveying the situation, were speaking in normal voices. Monkey and Ah-li couldn't have heard them, for with the howling wind, one could only be heard by shouting.

Ah-li and Monkey were terrified, though they forced themselves to present a calm outward appearance.

The apparent lack of concern on Monkey's face made the policeman especially fidgety, for experience told him that such a calm expression was the kind worn by a person who disdained death. As a result of his flustered state, the first thing he said to them was: "Why do you want to commit suicide?" He was a couple of meters away from them, but he had to shout to be heard over the gusting winds.

"We're not suicides!" Monkey answered him.

"What? Speak louder!"

"We're *not* suicides!" Monkey shouted.

"Not suicides? That's fine! Stay put!" The policeman turned and said: "Mr. Chi, come over here and talk to our friends."

The slight man walked over and said very politely: "What's the problem, my friends? Maybe I can help."

"We are *not* suicides!" Monkey shouted again. He was beginning to lose his temper.

"Don't listen to 'em," interjected the policeman, who was on his haunches nearby hooking up a radiophone. "Whether they're suicides or not, it's always safer to treat 'em as though they were."

"I know you're not suicides," the slight man said.

"Then you guys stand back and let us climb over there," Monkey said.

"Uh, hold on now, just hold on." The policeman quickly put down the radiophone and turned around. "We're going to help you in just a moment," he said. "Now please don't move."

"Hey, why don't you say something?" the man asked, pointing to Ah-li.

"I've got nothin' to say," Ah-li answered him lazily. They couldn't possibly have heard him.

As the policeman rigged the radiophone antenna, he kept his eye on Ah-li, saying in a low voice to the man named Chi: "Keep a close eye on the silent one there."

"What are your names?"

"What?" Monkey asked.

"I said what are your names?"

"We're both named Chin," Monkey answered him. "Now if

you'll let us climb over there, we'll be happy to answer all your questions." He turned back to Ah-li and said to him in a normal speaking voice: "What'll we do? They don't seem to believe us."

"What *can* we do? About all we can do is sit right here and let 'em do whatever they want with us."

"What can they do with us? Come over and carry us on their backs?" Monkey turned back and shouted to the men: "Since you won't let us climb up there, do you plan to come and carry us over on your backs?"

This gave the men on the roof a scare.

"That's the same tone of voice the guy who jumped off the Insurance Building used."

"That's right. Be very careful. If another one jumps, it won't look good for us—and this time there are two of 'em!" the policeman commented.

"The way things look up here the two strongmen we brought along won't be of any use," Mr. Chi said. "The fire trucks and ambulance haven't arrived yet. See if you can hurry them up."

By this time more people had begun to congregate on the rooftop, some of them reporters with cameras hanging around their necks. They pressed up to the edge of the roof as close as they could to the two men and started taking pictures.

"What's your full name, Mr. Chin?" the slight man asked Ah-li.

Monkey nudged Ah-li with his knee: "Ah-li, he's talking to you."

Ah-li rested his chin on his arms and looked at the man, but said nothing.

"His name is Chin Ah-li. Mine's Chin Wang-ken, but most people usually call me Monkey."

The people on the roof laughed.

"So that's why you're not afraid to climb up so high," a reporter chimed in. But they couldn't hear him.

"Gentlemen, would you cooperate by letting us ask the questions, please. I'd rather you didn't ask anything just now, since there are people's lives at stake here. This is no laughing matter, so please cooperate," Mr. Chi said to the reporters.

"Are you brothers?"

"No."

"Then it's just a coincidence that you're both named Chin."

"In Chin Village on the east coast, everyone's named Chin," Monkey said.

They could hear the bells and sirens of the fire trucks below. Ah-li and Monkey looked down to see several men descend from the three fire trucks and begin rigging a safety net directly beneath them. An ambulance was parked over to the side. Everywhere they could see there were throngs of people.

"Mr. Chin," the policeman shouted.

They raised their heads and looked back up at the roof.

"Don't worry about all that, it's just there to protect you."

"We're not worried!"

"That's fine."

Monkey began to feel somewhat depressed. He noticed that the roof was nearly packed with people. The man who had been talking to them so pleasantly was now surrounded by a group of reporters, and though he could see him gesturing, he couldn't make out what he was saying.

"Do you have any relatives in Ch'i-shan?"

"No."

"How about him?" he asked, pointing at Ah-li.

"He doesn't have any either."

"Where do you work?"

"At the Giant Signpainting Company. We painted those huge breasts on VV on that sign down there."

The policeman asked Monkey all the routine questions he needed for his report. Monkey was getting annoyed with it all. Ah-li asked him softly: "Do we have to answer all their questions?"

"I guess so."

"We're gonna be famous. We're sure to make tomorrow's headlines."

"To hell with the headlines! We haven't done anything wrong."

"How much longer is this gonna take?"

"Who knows? I never dreamed there'd be this many people with so much time on their hands."

"What'll we do?"

"What'll we do? We sure can't climb up there now, so we'll just have to see what they have in mind for us."

"Yep, that's what we'll have to do!" Ah-li was in complete agreement.

The sky was now completely darkened and two lights were shining down on them from the roof. The ladders from the three fire trucks below extended only up as far as the fourteenth floor. Spotlights were aimed at the two men from three separate angles. The only thing that Ah-li and Monkey could see clearly was each other. Just as they were beginning to grow uneasy and impatient from the effect of the lights, another bright light appeared right in front of their eyes. Two objects suspended from the end of a bamboo drying pole slowly inched toward them.

"What's goin' on?" Monkey yelled out.

"Don't be afraid! They're only microphones for the Ch'i-shan and Sheng-sen television stations." The voice came to them through a loudspeaker. "Don't worry, we're not going to hurt you."

"Damn it, don't let 'em trick us," Ah-li said softly to Monkey.

"I promise we won't hurt you. We're here to protect you. We're not about to trick you." The voice over the loudspeaker was crisp but soft.

Ah-li and Monkey were startled.

"Can they hear us?" Ah-li asked.

"That's right, you're coming through loud and clear. Didn't you hear me when I said that those things hanging from the bamboo pole are microphones? We can hear every word you say." The voice through the loudspeaker continued: "Now do you believe we're not going to trick you? I told you we were using microphones. Now we won't have to strain to talk to each other."

Flashbulbs were popping, one after the other, and there was a great deal of activity on the roof. Some of the background noise was picked up by the loudspeaker.

"Chief Tu, would you give us an interview? We're from Sheng-sen TV."

"All right."

Another bank of lights suddenly flashed on the roof, and Ah-li and Monkey could see some of the people up there. Chief Tu, the policeman who had talked with them, was surrounded by a group of reporters and was answering their questions. Mr. Chi had resumed talking to Ah-li and Monkey through the loudspeaker, but they were still able to overhear some of the interview going on behind him, things not meant for their ears.

"Chief Tu, do you think that the situation will remain at an impasse?" a reporter asked.

"I'm sure it won't," Chief Tu answered with assurance.

"What do you feel is the safest means at your disposal?"

We'll do everything we can."

"Chief Tu, we need more concrete answers. You understand that both Ch'i-shan and Sheng-sen TV cameras are on you right now, and that people all over the country are waiting in front of their sets for your answer."

The reporter's comment brought Chief Tu up short; after a momentary pause, he stammered: "Er ... um ... this is how it is. Uh ... ever since they started putting up high-rises, uh, suicides have, uh, steadily increased. Over the past several years, uh ... a dozen or more people have jumped to their deaths. We've, uh, managed to save two people ..."

"Chief Tu, could you be a bit more specific, please."

"Very well, uh, one of them we rescued by using a ladder, the other was saved by a net. But, uh, there's always some danger with a net. We missed several, who fell to their deaths, and one who hit the net, but was killed when he bounced off. Um ..."

"What's going to be done to protect these two men?" a reporter asked.

"Uh, as I see it, the ladders are out, since they only reach up to the fourteenth floor. We're twenty-four stories up right now ..."

"*Camera! Take* a shot of the ladders!"* the reporter hollered.
Then he turned and asked Chief Tu: "Since the ladders are out,
will you use a net?"

"Not if we can help it. Uh, we're going to try to find out why
they want to commit suicide, then we, uh, we'll try to help them
solve their problems so they won't have to jump."

"Chief Tu, just a while ago they said they had no intention of
jumping," a newspaper reporter rejoined.

"Hmph! You can't believe anything a potential suicide says.
We've seen this before. They say they're not gonna jump, then the
minute you let down your guard, they're over the side. Heh-heh-
heh, this, uh, is a heavy responsibility we have."

"What if they're really not going to jump?"

"How can we be sure?" Then Chief Tu added: "Even if they're
not planning to jump, we have to operate on the premise that they
are. Don't you agree? Uh, that's the humanitarian way to go about
it. Don't you agree with that?" He gave a satisfied look into the
camera.

They continued talking, Ah-li and Monkey overhearing every
word, and growing terrified when they heard Chief Tu say that a
tranquilizer gun was one of the means at their disposal.

"Would you tell us your names, please?" Mr. Chi asked.

"Didn't you just ask us that?" Ah-li responded impatiently.

"Yes, of course. And you answered everything just fine. But, well,
it's like this. Everyone here is very concerned about the two of
you, so I'm asking you some of the same questions for our TV
audience. Please don't be angry."

"Are we on TV?" Monkey asked in amazement.

"We're gonna be famous," Ah-li said. "Monkey, who said we'd
never make a name for ourselves?" Ah-li's emotions were producing feelings he could not express. At least now he had a desire
to talk.

"How long have you been in Ch'i-shan?"

---

*The first two words are in English in the original.

"Monkey, you did all the talking last time, so now it's my turn to give the answers."

"Go ahead!" Monkey too felt a change in himself. "Ah-li, it seems that being on TV makes me feel like talking."

"Me too."

"You go ahead."

"What should I say?"

"Hey, Mr. Chin and Mr. Chin, you haven't answered my question yet," the loudspeaker blurted out.

"What question? Go ahead and ask!" Ah-li answered.

"How many years have you been in Ch'i-shan?"

"Two years and seven months."

"You have a good memory." Then the loudspeaker asked: "What have you done in those two years and seven months?"

Just as Ah-li was about to answer, he heard the voice of someone in the background over the loudspeaker.

"It still doesn't appear to me that those two are set on committing suicide." It was one of the reporters.

"I don't think so either," another agreed.

"Don't you be fooled by their cheerful manner. That's just an indication that a man who's been thinking of suicide has made up his mind," Chief Tu said to them.

Since the loudspeaker was pointed straight at them, if Ah-li and Monkey strained they could hear the soft voices of the people talking in the background. And the people standing on the edge of the roof heard part of what was being said, but since they were hearing it unamplified, they never dreamed that Ah-li and Monkey could overhear the interview.

"Hm? What have you been doing these two years and seven months?"

"We've been working together as painters the whole time," Ah-li answered. He was trying to hear the interview taking place in the background.

"Not bad. You two must have painted a lot of houses in that time."

"Now you know better than that, so what's the big idea!" Ah-li

said testily. He sensed that the interview going on in the background was important to him, and he strained to pick up some
secrets. "I told you that we're signpainters. For instance, we did
those big billboards in front of the train station." He was growing
impatient.

"There's some fine work there, like the ads for White Oil, Rose
Soap, and for the refrigerators," the voice over the loudspeaker
praised. "Then you two are artists!"

"That's fine with us. Call us whatever you like."

"Really, that's good work. A lot of artists' work goes unnoticed,
but just think how many people see your artistry every day!"

More snatches of the ongoing interview filtered through:

". . . of course there are things we can do, like offering them some
food, for instance." Chief Tu was answering a reporter's question.
"Then we could lace the food with knockout drops or something
. . ." The remainder of his comments were drowned out by the
loudspeaker.

"I'll bet there are a lot of people around town who know that you
two painted those beautiful billboards in front of the train station,"
the loudspeaker said.

". . . let us reporters interview them?" One of the reporters was
making a request of Chief Tu.

"You'll have to understand that there's a purpose in our chatting
with them. We must avoid spooking them. We're trying to keep
them calm."

When Ah-li heard this part of the interview in the background
over the loudspeaker, he shouted out: "We want to talk to the
reporters."

A commotion broke out at once on the rooftop.

"All right, but first answer a few more questions, then you can
talk to the reporters," Mr. Chi said through the loudspeaker.

"No! We want to talk to 'em now," Monkey said.

Chief Tu led the reporters away from the microphone and talked
to them for a while, after which one of them came over and took
the microphone from Mr. Chi.

"I'm a reporter from the Sheng-sen Television Station," he said. "My name is P'an Ming."

"Mr. P'an, how many years have you been a reporter?" Monkey asked. His question took Ah-li by surprise. He stared hard at Monkey. The question also took the people on the rooftop by surprise.

"Not long, just a couple of years."

"During those two years have you covered any hot news items?"

"Um . . ." While the reporter P'an was puzzling over his answer, some of the people beside him urged him to say "yes" while others told him to say "no."

All of this greatly displeased Monkey.

"Well, yes or no?"

"No!"

"So today's your big chance, isn't it?"

When Chief Tu saw that the tables had been turned and that the reporter was stuck for an answer, he grabbed the microphone, nearly ripping it out of the man's hand, and said: "Let's not get into all this. Let's change the subject, all right?"

"No! I want to talk to reporter P'an!"

P'an reluctantly took the microphone back; he was coached by Chief Tu: "Tell him that this isn't a hot news item."

So P'an said, without giving it any thought: "No! This isn't much of a story."

"Oh, I understand. It's only a big story if I jump." He turned to Ah-li and said: "Ah-li, they're disappointed, did you know that?"

Ah-li was confused by Monkey's remarks and was growing uneasy. Just then an argument broke out on the rooftop. ". . . just who's interviewing who around here?" Chief Tu was noticeably distressed. "Will you take the responsibility? I certainly won't!"

"Monkey, what's on your mind?" Ah-li asked.

"I'm not sure. I'm all confused. One minute I think this, and the next minute something else."

"Me too."

"I wonder if my uncle ever bought a TV set," Monkey said pensively. "I really doubt that he could afford one with his gambling problem."

"But someone else might have one."

"As I recall, your folks don't have one either, so they'd have to go over to the neighbors to watch TV."

"Oh God, I hope my mother isn't watching this!" Ah-li said.

"I'm sure she is."

Someone on the roof was talking to them again: "Now just what are your problems?" It was Chief Tu.

"Problems? I've got nothing but problems!" Monkey said. "How about you, Ah-li, any problems?" Ah-li had been stunned by the issue of his mother, and was so distraught he couldn't speak.

"Just tell us your problems and we'll help any way we can."

Seeing the despondency on Ah-li's face and the complete dissipation of his spiritedness, Monkey responded lethargically: "What good would it do to tell you?"

"Try us and see."

"We've boarded a ship of thieves." When the words were out, even Monkey himself didn't know what he meant. They had somehow just slipped out.

"What does that mean? Make yourself clear. I'm sure we'll be able to work things out for you."

"Ask Ah-li, those are his words." Fatigue was setting in on Monkey.

"Ah-li, tell us, please, what were you referring to when you said you'd boarded a ship of thieves?"

Ah-li ignored Chief Tu's question. He imagined that his mother was seeing everything on TV, and he was not going to answer any more of Chief Tu's questions.

Tension was growing on the edge of the roof.

"Wang-ken, you tell us your problems, okay?"

"Didn't I just say we'd boarded a ship of thieves?"

"All right, all right, can you tell me how much you earn a month?"

"Monkey! Don't tell 'em!" Ah-li blurted out. When Monkey saw

how tense Ah-li had become, he swallowed the words he was about
to utter.

Someone standing behind Chief Tu said: "Get to the point. The
best idea is to get them to talk about their problems."

"Do you make three thousand?"

They didn't answer.

"Two thousand? Well, how much?"

"Don't ask us that!" Ah-li shouted. He was visibly agitated.

"All right! Let's talk about something else."

"We'll talk about nothin'!" Ah-li spat out.

Ah-li's outburst had brought the whole situation to an impasse.
Monkey didn't know what to do. Several times he wanted to ask
Ah-li what was going on, but he stopped short each time. The reporters' flashbulbs kept popping. The winds howled around the
rooftop.

*"First, zoom in, zoom in."** The speaker must have been one of
the live-coverage reporters. There was a sudden heaviness in the
atmosphere, the pressure was starting to build. Everyone in the
area was finding it a little hard to breathe. Ah-li began to sob, a
heartrending, uncontrollable sob. The photographers clambered
up to the edge of the roof. Monkey was muttering to himself, but
no one could understand him.

"Ah-li . . ."

"Leave me alone!" Chief Tu was just about to say something to
save the situation when Ah-li unexpectedly started to scream hysterically. He got to his feet, stared up at the roof, then began wailing pitifully and uncontrollably. By this time, Monkey's mutterings
had become intelligible: he was saying over and over: "I don't
care, I'm going down, I'm going down, I'm going down . . ." Without a break in his muttering, he rose to his feet, grasped the edge
of the steel basket, preparing to go back down the same way he
had climbed up. Ah-li knew he was going down. Monkey raised
his leg to hook it on the edge. The loudspeaker blared out: "Wang-

---

*English in the original.

ken—Wang-ken . . ." The whole area was lit up brightly by the frantic popping of flashbulbs. Monkey shielded his face from the glare with his arm. Chief Tu was shouting for all he was worth. Monkey suddenly released his grip and stood up straight in the basket. An ear-splitting "AHHH" of disbelief rose from the invisible crowds below and reverberated against the mammoth wall— Monkey had fallen. At that instant, Ah-li shouted hysterically for them to douse the spotlights, and the ensuing darkness engulfed him as though he were a child in the womb, moaning softly. The wind that had been howling around them could hardly be heard now above the frantic screams of the people on the roof. But through it all, the shrill cry of a television reporter shouting *"Camera! Camera! Camera! . . . !"** was heard as it pierced the heavens.

---

*English in the original.

Sayonara • Tsai-chien

• • • • •

Human Requisites

I cannot help feeling pleased with myself when I reflect on how I handled two onerous affairs over the past couple of days. The first was taking seven Japanese men out whoring with some of my countrywomen, the other was constructing a false bridge between those seven Japanese and a Chinese youth: that is to say, the perpetration of a gigantic hoax.

This is how it all came about: Late yesterday morning the general manager of my company placed a long distance phone call to Taipei from our branch office in Kaohsiung, telling me to be at the airport by 12:10 to meet a Mr. Baba and six other Japanese. He told me repeatedly and in no uncertain terms to treat them very well, as they had extremely close business ties with our company. He said that they had decided to leave the airport directly for a pleasure excursion at the hot springs in Chiao-hsi. I recommended that since Chiao-hsi was so far out of the way, it would be better to take them to the hot springs in the resort town of Peitou.

"Everyone knows that Chiao-hsi is way out in the country; besides, the girls there aren't as pretty as those in Peitou, and their tourist accommodations leave a lot to be desired. But you see, they're looking for something a little different. Baba and his bunch

---

The title is the Japanese and Chinese for "goodbye." The four sections of the story are titled after popular Japanese films.

are a 'Sennin giri kurabu,' a so-called 'Thousand Beheadings Club.' They've been to Taiwan five times already—this makes the sixth—and Baba wrote that he wanted the hot springs of Chiao-hsi on their itinerary."

"How about this, sir: Why don't you ask the assistant manager, Mr. Yeh, to accompany them? I've got lots of work to do."

"No, no! Chiao-hsi is your hometown, so I want *you* to take them."

"But . . ."

"This is company business, and urgent business at that," the general manager said very seriously. Then he started to laugh. Most likely it struck him as funny that he was turning pimping into urgent company business. At least that's what I figured.

At first I didn't think there was any way I could refuse, but when I heard him laughing I mustered up my courage to try to somehow get out of it. Just then the telephone exchange time signal blared in my ear and the operator cut in: "Do you want to continue your conversation?" The general manager and I answered almost simultaneously: I said yes, he said no. Unfortunately for me, it was his call, and he responded by hanging up. I distinctly heard the click, but I automatically shouted "Hello! Hello!" several times before finally replacing the receiver with feelings of disappointment. Unless I decided to just give it all up and go home, it looked like I was slated to act as a pimp.

In my wildest dreams I had never imagined that I would someday be engaged in pimping. But in fact, this turn of events was neither as lightly achieved nor as simple as it sounds, for at the time I was in the throes of a painful psychological struggle.

As I slammed the receiver down on the hook, Assistant Manager Yeh and my office mates all turned to look at me. Assistant Manager Yeh already had an inkling of what had transpired, especially since I had mentioned his name during the conversation, and as soon as I had finished talking, he deliberately raised his voice to say: "So the general manager wants you to take a group of Japanese to the hot springs at Chiao-hsi, huh?"

"He wants me to be a pimp!" I said angrily.

Except for two office girls who lowered their heads, all of my other co-workers in the room burst out laughing. I felt from their looks that they had thrown down a challenge. Under normal circumstances they all considered me to be the most principled and straitlaced person among them, and in my speech and actions that was how I wanted it to be. So it seemed to me that they were eagerly waiting to see how I was going to handle this pimping business. I hadn't expected to be put into such an awkward position by the looks of people like this, who revel in the misfortunes of others. Actually, it wasn't simply a matter of doing a little pimping, for if that had been all there was to it, I could easily have laughed at myself then and there and let it go at that. I'm sure I could have managed that without any damage to my principles. The problem was that not long ago, a newspaper article had spurred me into viciously attacking the Japanese in front of these people in a fit of nationalistic fervor. Now here I was, expected to meekly take a group of seven Japanese men out whoring around with some of my countrywomen. I was acutely aware that my colleagues would prefer to see me throw up my hands and quit. They would then give me looks of respect and envy, and even be so magnanimous as to honor me with a round of hearty praises. Naturally, some would only be going through the motions, pretending they were really intent on my staying on.

I knew that if I went ahead stolidly and met those Japanese, my image would plummet in their eyes, and even my work in the office would be affected. But all of this was nothing compared to the deep-seated struggle within me as I tried to face myself.

My position as a Chinese who has an understanding of modern Chinese history has led me to abhor the Japanese. I was told that my grandfather, whose stories I used to love listening to, had his right leg smashed by the Japanese when he was young. Then there was my middle-school history teacher, an unforgettable man whom we all respected, who had tearfully related to us episodes from the 1937–1945 War of Resistance against Japan. He told how the Japanese invaders came to China with battle songs heralding their heavenly mission of rooting out the unrighteous, and euphemistically gave this vicious and evil war of aggression against China the title of "holy war." Meanwhile they swept across China murdering and brutalizing untold numbers of innocent civilians. This history teacher, who was himself from Nanking, showed us a foreign magazine with photographs of the "rape of Nanking." We saw decapitated Chinese, pregnant women whose bellies had been slit open by bayonets, and, most unforgettably, lines of Chinese, including mothers clutching their children, walking hand in hand into huge pits to be buried alive. I recall that my entire body grew rigid and hard as stone when I saw those pictures. Our tears flowed as we listened to what he was telling us, and we hated ourselves for being too young to have participated in the eight-year War of Resistance to search out the "Jap devils" and avenge our countrymen.

Who could have predicted, with all the changes in the world situation and the transformation of society in the twenty years that followed, that the seeds our history teacher had planted in our hearts as part of his historical mission would reach the present stage of development. Though I could feel an occasional embryonic movement, no opportunity for the seeds to sprout forth ever presented itself; or perhaps this awareness of mine had long since been washed away by the tides of time. Still, there is no way that something so deeply rooted in my conscience could ever be completely eradicated.

Now, however, not only couldn't I be hostile to Japanese, but, on the general manager's orders, I was being forced to accompany them to the hot springs at Chiao-hsi and keep them well entertained. Granted that any Chinese would have felt the same sort of contradictions if he were given such an assignment, but my position as someone from the town of Chiao-hsi added yet another layer of ineffable difficulty. What could I say to my hometown friends when they asked me my purpose in coming home? The general manager had emphasized over the phone that he wanted me to take them *because* I was from Chiao-hsi.

Damn it, I'll just quit!

Quit?

Since coming to Taipei ten years ago, I've already changed jobs more than twenty times, and every time I've done just as I pleased. Several times during that period I didn't even have enough money to pay the rent, and there were occasions when I had to pawn things to get money to take my sick baby to see a doctor. The clouded expression that had settled upon my wife's face during those fearful days has not to this day completely left her. If I refused to take this assignment, where could I find another job? Then there are the chest pains that have been bothering me in recent nights. I can no longer cope with these things as easily as I could in the past. In all honesty, the job I have now has given my small family its first chance for stability. And the clouded look on my wife's face, which up till now had been the picture of fear and foreboding, has gradually given way to wrinkles of laughter with our child's beginning attempts to speak and his other new tricks. Even our son's chronic bronchial infection seems to have disappeared.

Damn it! I've got to stay on!

Stay?

These principles, which I've held onto so tenaciously for many years, and which have formed my unique personality and temperament, were they to be cast aside now? Then why have them in the first place? It would not seem like the real me. I knew that all my close friends would be surprised if I did this thing, and after having grown accustomed to hearing their praises, what would I do if their vision of me lost its luster? I figured that the hardest compromise to strike would be with myself, for if I put aside my principles, what would I have left?

But on the other hand, if I took that stance, wouldn't I be placing my ego above everything else? Wouldn't that be the shortsighted way to look at things? Am I so great that I need not sacrifice anything at all, even for my family? Especially since my wife and child don't necessarily share my principles. For even though my wife is an adult who can understand her husband's principles and their worth, and can even support these principles regardless of the strain they impose upon her, what about the child—that child who understands nothing at all? When he's hungry he has the right to open his mouth and cry for milk. When he's sick he has the right to demand medical attention—he has the right to demand of the world that he be allowed to grow up and become independent. I know that I could not bear to shortchange my own child, for who knows, he may someday accomplish something great, and if not him, maybe his children. And it might be that the key to his future rested solely on whether or not I did this thing.

When my thoughts reached this point I suddenly discovered what a bastard I'd been in the past. The greater part of those so-called principles of mine could in fact be summed up as a game of esteeming myself by looking down on everything else and prizing only those things that elevated and satisfied my own ego.

"I guess I've got to do this pimping job after all," I said in answer to the stares of those in the office who eagerly anticipated a quick resolution. Although I said it jokingly, I had actually come to this decision with great seriousness. I knew what they were all thinking, so I had to construct a ladder and let my self-respect descend carefully if it was to remain intact. "Don't laugh. I've got to try my hand at being a pimp. Why not?" It seemed that I didn't really care whether they were even listening—I just had to finish this simple though important speech. "If I don't take those seven Japanese today, someone else will. One way or another, seven of our country-women will be put on the chopping block." At first they were speechless, then they exploded into laughter.

"Hey! Hwang, what's wrong with you! We're not an anti-prostitution commission or anything like that, so why talk to us that way all of a sudden?" This statement by Assistant Manager Yeh was followed by more laughter all around.

"Now, wait a minute. Listen to me, will you?" I really didn't have anything else to say, but I couldn't just drop the subject there either. "As far as I know, there isn't one of those girls who has willingly fallen. They're all victims of their environment—sacrificing themselves for their families. Since I'm going to be their pimp, I'll show them how to bleed those Japanese. You all know that the price of women shows how developed a place is—the cheaper the women, the more backward the place. For example, there are several countries in South America where a girl earns only eight pesos for a day's work picking coffee beans, whereas a fourteen-year-old girl can earn sixteen pesos by sleeping with a man, the exact price of a cup of coffee in one of the big hotels. Don't laugh, that's the truth. In the eyes of the Japanese we're also a backward nation. Even though we've actually made great strides, they hold us in contempt. Damn it, when I see them coming to Taiwan with all their airs of superiority, it makes my blood boil!"

"And so you're going to take them for some fun at Chiao-hsi?" This daring response from the shy Miss Chen came as a complete surprise. It sparked another outburst of laughter; I also laughed, though in fact I was troubled by the comment. For after all my efforts to build a ladder in order to lower my self-respect more gently, the bottom had suddenly been kicked out from under me.

I couldn't let Miss Chen's comment pass, but what was I to say? My sole reaction was a series of "Uh-huh's." It must have seemed pretty comical, since the others all laughed.

Just as I was finding myself falling into a state of total embarrassment, a sudden inspiration came to me; I replied to her question by asking: "If the general manager had given you this assignment, would you have taken it?" My heart let out a secret cry of alarm when I said this, for if she were to say no, then what would I do?

But before I had time to give it any more thought, Miss Chen responded with alacrity: "Since I'm a girl, the general manager wouldn't ask me to."

During the laughter that ensued I quickly shifted the object of my attack: "Assistant Manager Yeh, would you have done it if the general manager had asked you to?" He stammered something as he laughed, and I continued: "During our phone conversation just a moment ago he said that this was company business, and urgent business at that!"

Assistant Manager Yeh snickered. "There's no question about it. No one would dare refuse, would he?" As I stood looking at them with those smiles frozen on their faces, I was clearly aware of just how sneaky a person I had become.

The Seven Samurai

By midday I was standing at the airport exit holding up a large piece of white paper on which I had written "Welcome Mr. Baba" in big letters. I was waving it feebly and with considerable embarrassment in front of the arriving passengers. Before long a Japanese came up and looked at the sign in my hand, gave me a smile, then turned around and shouted in Japanese: "He's come, he's come. He's over here!" Out came four more, all of whom gathered around the first man, then turned to look back inside. I could hear them jabbering to one another:

"What about Baba *kun* and Takeuchi *kun*?"* asked the first man out.

"They're still at customs."

"I wonder why they're giving us so much trouble this time."

"It looks like they're only nitpicking with us Japanese."

"They're real bastards!"

"They even checked inside my pants."

"Me too!"

"Really? Ha-ha . . . they didn't check mine."

"Come on now, they checked all four of ours!"

"Did they really check your crotches?"

---

*The Japanese word *kun*, like the word *san*, means "Mister," though the former is much less formal, and is used by friends.

"Um-hm. They made you take down your pants too. What's so embarrassing about that? Why not admit it?"

"Heh-heh . . . now, if it had been young Taiwanese girls doing the examining, I'm sure we'd all have been happy to oblige."

The whole bunch of them laughed delightedly, laughter that appeared to wash away the anger caused by the inspection.

They were standing diagonally across from me, separated by a railing and five or six steps. I figured that since we had already made contact, I might as well fold up the piece of paper and put it in my back pocket—I could still see myself standing there a moment ago waving it in the air. "I was making a goddamned fool of myself!"

The one who had emerged first thought I was talking to him: "Baba *kun* hasn't come out yet," he said. "Wait a moment, please."

Once again they seemed agitated by something or other.

"Do you think Baba might have run into some trouble?"

"How could he? He wasn't carrying any contraband in."

"Could it be on account of those nylon stockings and panty hose?"

"No, of course not! We've brought them with us several times before without running into any problems."

"Maybe so, but we brought in eighty pairs this time!"

"Those things are dirt-cheap. If they want them, they can have the whole lot as a gift."

"This is such a letdown."

"Those sons of bitches!"

" . . . "

" . . . "

" . . . "

Since we were separated by some distance, I couldn't make out all of their grumblings, so I wasn't sure just what they were talking about.

The other passengers from their flight had debarked and passed through, and they were still waiting for Baba and Takeuchi. One of them started over my way to say something to me, but just then a couple of the others called out at the same time: "They're coming out!"

Two short, stocky Japanese, their faces set tightly, emerged.

"Any problems?" asked their friends.

"What kind of problems could there be? They were just trying to make things tough for us. Damn, that makes me mad!"

"Oh, Baba *kun*, he's here," the man said, pointing to me.

A smile quickly appeared on Baba's face, and he led the others over to where I was standing. We exchanged name cards across the railing.

"Mr. Hsü is in Kaohsiung . . .," I stammered.

"Never mind, we're all aware that your general manager is henpecked."

"No, honestly, he really couldn't make it back from Kaohsiung this time."

"What difference would it make if he could, since he's so henpecked?" Baba asked with a chuckle. "But the trip won't be wasted as long as we have Hwang *kun* to accompany us."

"No, . . ." I didn't know how to respond to him. Although not intended, Baba's words had reminded me of my role as a pimp. Troubled as I was, I managed to say: "Well, I'll do my best, but I'm afraid I might disappoint you."

"Just looking at you, so young and handsome, we know you won't."

Damn, that sounded terrible! I wondered what they were thinking.

"Baba *kun*, what are we waiting for?" they pressed him.

"Nothing at all!"

"Well, let's go then."

"Let's go!" Then Baba said to me: "Hwang *kun*, the success of this trip depends on you."

Their luggage was very simple: each of them had a bag slung over his shoulder, a parcel containing two bottles of imported liquor in one hand, and in the other hand another small bag. Since there were eight of us in all, we hired two taxis and headed directly from Taipei Airport for Chiao-hsi.

Although we had exchanged name cards at the airport, I still wasn't sure who was Ochiai, who was Tanaka, and who was Ueno. The only ones I knew were the last two to come out—Baba and Takeuchi—and Sasaki, whose name I learned later. I remembered him because he had a particularly long face, and because he had been the first one out of the airport, the one who had nodded to me. I was in the first taxi with Baba and two others, whose names I didn't yet know, while Takeuchi, Sasaki, and the others were in the second car.

"Hwang *kun*, how far is it from here to Chiao-hsi?" Baba asked.

"Well, if we don't run into any rain or fog on the mountain roads, two and a half hours should just about do it," I said.

"That's pretty far!" said one of the others—the bald-headed one.

"How's that?" the man sitting between Baba and the other blurted out with a laugh. "It looks like Ochiai *kun* is getting kind of impatient!"

"Bullshit! You're the one who's getting impatient!" But he was laughing.

"If you want to know the truth, Tanaka *kun* is getting impatient too," Baba joined the others laughing.

I turned around in my seat in front and said: "No, I'm afraid that Baba *kun* isn't telling the *whole* truth. He ought to have said that *everyone* is getting impatient."

All three of them roared with laughter as they shouted out their approval.

"I was right, wasn't I? This trip won't be wasted as long as we have Hwang *kun* along with us," Baba said. "He knows exactly what's on our minds."

Damn him! Goddamn him . . . I cursed to myself, though my face was all smiles. I was completely conscious of the fact that in ten years of working in the business world I had acquired the habit of masking my true feelings, a habit I had always despised in others. Nonetheless, this kind of societal influence on an individual's habits was no different than the instincts of camouflage, protectiveness, alertness, and imitation that animals have developed in order to survive.

From our light banter of a moment before I learned that the bald-headed man was Ochiai, and that the other one was Tanaka. As the taxi passed around the statue on Tunhua North Road and onto Nanking East Road, Tanaka looked behind him and said: "Have him slow down a bit. The other taxi can't keep up with us." The others turned around to look.

"He's caught up—he's right behind us now."

"Take it easy," I said. "The drivers both know the way."

The three of them turned back around in their seats and quieted down for a moment. Baba blew out a puff of smoke.

"What's going on with the Taipei Customs people lately?" he asked exasperatedly. "They're coming down pretty hard on us Japanese."

"Yeah, I wonder why!" asked Ochiai.

"It's a case of Tel Aviv guerrilla-phobia," I said reproachfully.

"Tel-a-what? What phobia is that?" asked Ochiai as he leaned over.

I could see that neither Baba nor Tanaka had understood either, so I said: "Last month at Israel's Tel Aviv Airport, wasn't it four of your young countrymen who . . . ?"

"Oh, that!—We know . . .," Tanaka said in a subdued voice, while the others leaned back in their seats and nodded.

"That damned bunch of animals murdered all those innocent people in just a few minutes." Then I added, controlling my anger: "So who can blame the customs people here?"

"Oh, of course," Baba said, "of course. But still it seems like they're more sensitive here in Taipei . . ." Even though Baba, Ochiai, and Tanaka tried to conceal their distress, I could still see it in their faces.

"If they're so sensitive in Taipei, then why didn't they just refuse to let you off the plane?" I paused for a moment, then continued:

"Tel Aviv guerrilla-phobia is a worldwide phenomenon these days."

"Um, you've got a point there," Baba said in a low voice.

"The Japanese youth of today are absolutely lawless." The look on Ochiai's face showed me that he was trying his utmost to absolve himself of any blame. "Day in and day out they're shouting their opposition to one thing or another. All Japan is in a state of mass confusion. As I see it, if the situation continues the way it is, the end result is going to be chaos."

As Ochiai finished I felt an urge to settle some old accounts by reminding him that the previous generation of Japanese wasn't much loftier than the youth of today. The blood and stench of their aggression in China had left an indelible stain on the annals of history. But after seeing the unhappiness on their faces and a complete absence of the looks of superiority that Japanese people usually bring with them to Taiwan, my thoughts went unspoken and I just let the matter drop. Instead I smiled and asked: "Why so serious?" I paused. "Did they confiscate anything of yours?"

"As a matter of fact, they didn't."

"We certainly didn't bring any contraband in with us."

"Then everything's all right. I was afraid they'd confiscated your swords," I said in jest.

"What swords?" Baba cried out nervously. The others stared tensely at me without making a sound.

"Hwang *kun*, don't make jokes," said Ochiai. "What swords are you talking about?"

Seeing how edgy they had become, I laughed even harder. "What swords do you think?" I asked. "The swords you use in your 'Thousand Beheadings Club,' of course."

They exploded into laughter as they caught the joke.

"Ha-ha . . . that's right, our 'thousand beheadings' swords! Ha-ha . . ."

"We couldn't hijack an airplane with those swords, could we? So naturally they wouldn't confiscate them! Ha-ha . . ."

Baba felt himself ostentatiously below his waist: "I'd better feel, just in case," he said. "Maybe mine was confiscated without my knowledge."

To be honest, no matter how mischievous I was feeling, or how much I wanted to get their goats, this still struck me as very funny.

Then Baba assumed the pose of a stage comedian and shouted out in the loud and peculiar voice of a Japanese samurai:

"The Way of the sword is the Way of man;

"With the sword there is man;

"As the sword perishes, so perishes man."

Ochiai and Tanaka were sitting beside him laughing. Ochiai told me that what Baba was incanting were the final lines of their "Thousand Beheadings Club" manifesto. Their mood had changed to a happy one.

"How many years have you had this 'Thousand Beheadings Club'?"

"Eight years. We seven are the only members," Baba answered.

"Why are there only seven of you?"

"Well, the seven of us were schoolmates in elementary and middle school, then we were together in the army, and now we're business associates. What do you think of that? You don't see that very often, do you? A lot of people want to join us, but we won't let them."

"This club of ours may not have a very large membership, but in Japan we're famous," added Ochiai with great pride.

"Does this so-called 'thousand beheadings' of yours have any special significance?" I asked.

"Of course it has!" Baba squinted his eyes knowingly and said: "In former days all samurai had but one wish, and that was to kill a thousand men during their lifetime."

"I don't imagine any of them ever made it, did they?"

"No, but this was the samurai's ideal, and anyone who didn't subscribe to it was not a good samurai. And so, in order to kill his thousand men, he had to constantly practice his art."

"Then what's the significance of your 'thousand beheadings'?"

I already had a pretty good idea, but I asked just in case there was something else.

"Heh-heh." Baba let out a cunning laugh, then said: "The days of the Samurai Code are gone forever, and we can never again wander over the earth wearing swords, killing and being killed. Besides, we wouldn't be samurai even if we could. What we mean by our 'thousand beheadings' is that we hope during our lifetime to sleep with a thousand different women. Heh-heh, do you follow me?" Baba looked smugly at the other members.

I was suddenly struck by how loathsome they were, but a smile must still have shown on my face, or they wouldn't have been so openly licentious. The terrible thing about it was that I didn't have to consciously feign the expression on my face.

"Have any of you reached your goal?"

"Not yet!" Ochiai blurted out. "A thousand doesn't sound like too many, but in fact it's difficult as hell . . ."

"A thousand is our ideal, so every time we get the chance, we travel: South America, Southeast Asia, Korea, Taiwan . . . these are places we often visit."

"Oh, then you must spend a lot of money!"

"We weren't born with any, and we can't take it with us, and as long as you look at it that way it doesn't seem so bad. Since life is short, you have to take your pleasures when and where you can. Isn't that right? This is another point all seven of us agree on." I never imagined that such a thing as they were talking about could be supported by a tragic-heroic philosophical foundation. Baba had given this explanation in complete seriousness.

"That's not all. We have a principle that except for our own wives, we can never sleep with the same woman twice," added Ochiai.

"Does it count as a breach of the club's rules?"

"No, but you see, there's a limit to every man's vitality. Just doing it a thousand times is no mean task, so in order to achieve our club's objective, this sort of self-restraint comes naturally."

Even Tanaka, who had been sitting quietly in the corner of the seat, leaning back with his arms folded and a smile on his face as he listened to the others, added a comment of his own: "Hwang *kun*, there used to be a basement coffee shop in the downtown area by the name of . . ." He thought for a moment. "I can't remember the name. Let's see, did it have a barber shop upstairs . . . right, it was a barber shop. Do you know if that coffee shop is still there?"

"Hm, a basement coffee shop . . ." I pondered for a moment: The Barbarian doesn't have a barber shop upstairs, nor does the Literary Salon; then there's . . .

They sat there talking as I pondered. Baba looked over at Tanaka and asked excitedly: "Do you mean the place where Akiko worked?"

"Right! Akiko's place." Tanaka, too, was growing interested.

"Hwang *kun*, you listen to me and you'll know right away what place he means," said Baba as he tapped me on the shoulder. "There's a very narrow door next to the barber shop," he said, using his hands to help describe it, "that's very easy to miss. That door is the entrance to the coffee shop. Now, do you know where I mean?"

I shook my head. "No, I can't place it."

"That's strange!" Baba replied. "It's really a famous place. It's very well known in Japan! How could you not know it?"

"I'm sorry, I just don't. What makes the place so famous?"

"Heh-heh-heh. There are girls there from all over, and they can do absolutely everything. Are you sure you don't know?"

"No." I really didn't know. Baba and Tanaka eyed me with knowing looks on their smiling faces.

In his role as the upholder of fairness, Ochiai said: "I believe Hwang *kun* when he says he doesn't know. In matters of this kind, tourists are always better informed than local residents. Places like that cater to tourists, not local people, so it's not so strange after all."

By rights I should have been grateful to him for getting me off the hook and saving me from embarrassment, but it seemed to me that he had attached entirely too much importance to the whole affair. What was the great loss of honor in not knowing about such a place? In fact, in Chinese society, this knowledge was in itself a loss of honor. I wondered how Japanese looked at things like this. I experienced a mild passing anger.

"Ochiai *kun*," I said, "there's no need for you to make explanations for me like that. If you were to ask me something like where the Palace Museum was, or the Historical Museum, and I couldn't tell you, then I might feel embarrassed. But in matters like this, well . . . ha-ha-ha . . ." I laughed then because I sensed that I was being too somber and that my words seemed to make them a bit tense. They nodded their heads repeatedly, expressing their agreement with what I was saying.

"Hwang *kun*, you're right, of course. But we didn't mean any harm."

"That's right, we didn't mean any harm."

I was quite adept at pretending. I laughed loudly as if it were something very funny, and gradually they were affected by my laughter. I was even able to squeeze out a few tears of laughter, and as I wiped my eyes, I said: "So? Now who's being serious, you or I? I'll tell you the truth," I said with a smile, "I do know that basement coffee shop you're talking about. It isn't there any longer. It was closed by the police a while ago."

There was nothing the three of them could do but look at me and smile. Ochiai seemed about to say something, but just as he started to speak, something told him to let it pass. He just sat straight up and then fell back against the seat.

"Hwang *kun*," Baba said, "you're really something!" Afraid that this would lead to another misunderstanding, he added: "What I mean is, I really admire you."

"No, no . . ."

They began talking among themselves.

"I was right, wasn't I?"

"That's for sure."

"Oh, come now," I said.

Tanaka still sat there in his corner, smiling and nodding his head.

I was generally pleased with things so far, having gotten in at least a couple of licks.

"There are three of you ganging up on just one of me," I said jokingly. "That's not fair." I looked at my watch. "We still have more than an hour before we get there, so if you can sleep, you ought to try—you need to conserve your energy."

"No, I'd rather chat with you. But maybe you feel like sleeping," Baba said.

"No, I'd just as soon chat too."

"Hwang *kun*, if we say anything out of line, don't let it get under your skin," said Ochiai with a grin.

"I won't, and the same holds true for you."

As the taxi was passing through the mountain area known as Sea of Clouds, the driver placed a new cassette in the tape deck, another Chinese rendition of a popular Japanese tune.

Most likely due to the effects of the music, Tanaka looked out at the mountain scenery and exclaimed: "Look at that! This place looks just exactly like Aomori Prefecture!"

"I was just thinking the same thing myself," said Ochiai a little incredulously. He lowered his head and looked out the window. "Except that there aren't any apple orchards by the roadside here."

"Even the song the driver's put on is just right," I said.

"That, and your perfectly fluent Japanese," added Baba with a smile.

Damn it, that does it! I cursed to myself out of anger and a sense of injustice. If Baba's comment had been a calculated one, then I had lost this round. I secretly observed his expression to see if he had any intention of wounding me or not. If he had, then I would have had to respond with some verbal jabs of my own. But my observation told me that he had no such intentions, even though I still felt uncomfortable. I couldn't help thinking that in their subconscious they still considered Taiwan one of their colonies.* No, not only in the subconscious, but in reality the Japanese business-men who come to do business in Taiwan, with their haughty and disdainful attitude, strut around just as though Taiwan were their economic colony. I turned back around in my seat and looked at the mountain road ahead; throughout the trip I had been troubled by feelings of loathing. Baba and the others in the back talked and laughed as before, and although it seemed that they were talking about me, I didn't pay any attention to them. As I sat there with anger boiling inside me and a meek expression on my face, it didn't concern me whether they were talking about ordinary things or if they were engaged in that disgusting conversation of theirs.

Damn it! A pimp! I'll quit!

Quit?

I should have put my foot down the moment I finished my conversation with the general manager in the morning. But how could I just up and quit then?

The psychological struggles that had raged in me after the morning phone call were upon me once more. Unable to bear the pressure of these contradictions, I rolled the window down, stuck my head out, and let the wind beat against my face. After taking a few deep breaths, I felt a little more comfortable. The taxi was just then passing above a mountain valley with a stream running below. I began taking in the scenery: I could see the floor of the valley below and the long, narrow mountain stream as it flowed along. The strange thing was, the sight of this threadlike river flowing far down on the floor of the valley somehow brought vague thoughts of history to my mind. History? Whose history? I didn't know. I felt as though the stream down there was flowing through my heart, bringing with it feelings of depression and sadness.

Baba patted me on the shoulder and said after I pulled my head back in the window: "Hwang *kun*, would you please ask the driver

---

*Taiwan was occupied by Japan from 1895 till 1945.

to stop. We have to relieve ourselves." As our taxi pulled to a stop, the car behind us with Sasaki and the others also drove up. Giggling and laughing, they all got out of the cars, formed a line at the side of the road, and began relieving themselves. I stayed in the car, watching them, and as I noticed two tour buses approaching, I began to be a little anxious for them. But just as the tour buses, which were full of passengers of both sexes, passed by, not only did the men continue to leisurely joke and talk, some of them even turned around as they were taking a leak and smiled at the passengers on the buses. Years before, whenever people of the older generation had talked to me about the Japanese, they had told me how the men loved to piss by the side of a road. At the time I hadn't thought it was such a big deal, but seeing the men standing there in a row, oblivious to everything but taking a leak, I finally understood why the older generation had been so preoccupied with this idiosyncrasy, and why the Chinese called the Japanese "dogs" or "the four-legged ones."

After the tour buses had passed, the men were laughing loudly, and I could even hear Baba shouting out in that strange voice:

"The Way of the sword is the Way of man;

"With the sword there is man;

"As the sword perishes, so perishes man."

Yonjimbo

It was already three-thirty in the afternoon when we arrived at the Evergreen Hot Springs Lodge in Chiao-hsi. After they had picked out their rooms the seven of them debated for a while over whether to eat first or to take a bath. Ultimately they agreed to have dinner and wine served in Baba's room.

Two middle-aged women wearing uniforms and wooden clogs quickly and efficiently brought a large round table into the room, after which they moved in the right number of stools. When they came in again carrying the dishes and chopsticks, they brought with them three seventeen- or eighteen-year-old girls.

"These three are on duty," the waitress, whose name was Ah-hsiu said to me. The three girls stood apprehensively off to one side. Ah-hsiu pointed to the nearest one: "Her name is Hsiao-wen, the one next to her is Ah-yu, and the last one there is called Ying-ying." As their names were called out the girls nodded for lack of anything better to do, then crowded together and began to giggle.

I gave a cursory introduction all around. The seven men looked the girls over from head to toe, causing them no little embarrassment. Hsiao-wen lowered her head and seemed to be looking at her own unattractive feet, with their short, stubby toes and painted nails, trying her hardest to draw them back in. My experience told me that these three young girls were fresh from the countryside; the deep suntans they had acquired from years of working out in the sun hadn't faded much at all. Also I had an occasional glimpse of the dark scars left by bites and sores that appeared all over their calves. Though they were professional girls now, their timid expressions produced an effect of freshness in the eyes of those seven Japanese battlefield heroes. I could hear their muted discussion:

"Not too bad."

"Nice and earthy," said Baba, "but that might be just what we're looking for."

"They're all pretty young."

"They look to be about sixteen or seventeen."

Sasaki said something—what, I'm not sure—that made the others laugh, and laugh hard. The three girls stayed huddled together and even looked a little frightened, though for some reason they couldn't keep from laughing along with the men. The one called Hsiao-wen even turned around and pinched Ah-yu and Ying-ying on the legs, causing both of them to scream out. Puzzled and startled, the Japanese asked me what was going on.

"You three dimwits," Ah-hsiu yelled to the girls as she set the table, "why aren't you over here helping me! I'll raise hell with you if you don't watch out!"

"Hsiao-wen here pinched us for no reason at all!" complained Ying-ying as she reached her hand out toward Hsiao-wen's leg. "I'll get even with you!"

"Help! Don't . . . !" Hsiao-wen screamed and ran over toward us.

"Madame! Look! Look here at your Hsiao-wen!" Ah-hsiu yelled at the top of her lungs.

The waitress who had come in with Ah-hsiu joined the conversation, saying very earnestly: "If you're not going to help, then at least sit down and behave yourselves. What do you think you're doing? These Japanese men here are guests, you know!"

The girls then calmed down.

"They're still children," Baba said with a smile.

"Look here," Ochiai said as he embraced Hsiao-wen, who had just run over to him. "She's got quite a body. I want her." He lowered his head and looked at her cradled in his arms: "I like you. Do you understand?"

Hsiao-wen nestled softly in Ochiai's arms and asked me what he was saying. I told her. Suddenly she lifted her head and pointed up at him: "You can drop dead!"

"Hsiao-wen! Watch what you're saying!" Ah-hsiu warned.

Ochiai's curiosity was piqued. "What?" he asked.

"I was just teasing him," Hsiao-wen said.

Ochiai asked me again. "She said you're a sex fiend," I told him.

He and the others laughed when they heard this. "That's right, I'm a sex fiend." Then he gleefully pointed at the others, one at a time: "And so is he, and so is he, and so is he . . . all seven of us are sex fiends."

Sasaki, who was standing next to Ochiai, nonchalantly reached over to feel Hsiao-wen up, but she quickly pushed his hand away.

"What makes you think you can do that?" she said. Then she struck the pose of a comic character in a Taiwanese opera and said with a smile: " 'A man takes no advantage of a good friend's wife.' Don't you know that?"

"Oh, you're a wicked one, you are!" Sasaki said with a laugh in response to her actions.

"Hwang *kun*, what's this child been saying?" Ochiai asked.

When I told him what she had said, he was, of course, delighted, and he proceeded to hug her even more tightly. "She really is a good girl!"

Sasaki, amused by all of this, reached out again and touched Hsiao-wen on the thigh. She promptly hit his hand, and they went back and forth like that while the others looked on with amusement.

"You can drop dead!" Hsiao-wen shouted. She wanted Ochiai to come to her defense, but he was trying to get her to hit Sasaki.

Naturally, Hsiao-wen hadn't meant anything in particular when she said "A man takes no advantage of a good friend's wife," but she wouldn't let any of the others except Ochiai even touch her. I thought to myself: "Hsiao-wen is, after all, Chinese, and even though she's a prostitute, in a contest to see who was more civilized —Hsiao-wen or the Japanese—they wouldn't be her equal." This is probably why we Chinese deride the Japanese by calling them "dogs."

Before too long Ying-ying and Ah-yu were also in someone's arms. It was then that the situation arose that caused me more discomfort and embarrassment than any other in my whole life. I was expected to translate all their meaningless small talk, and not just for one, but for all of them. Besides, for someone not personally involved in a sexual liaison, most of what they were saying was terribly grating on the ears. Nonetheless, I had to translate all their comments for them. We have a saying in my hometown that goes: "The pig-stud farmer earns his pleasure." It means that someone who raises a boar to service others' pigs does not earn much, but he at least can get some vicarious thrills. In a rural society this kind of occupation is not looked upon as a respectable means of livelihood, and a person who engages in it is usually an old man who lives alone. Although he doesn't have a wife or children to keep him company, while the pigs are mating he remains alongside them, assisting in the process, using his hands to keep everything running smoothly, an event that can arouse him. Well, that's where this local saying comes from. Now that doesn't mean I'm using rural

standards to look down on pig-stud farmers, for they can at least
get aroused by their work. What was I going to get out of mine?

Damn it! The more I thought about it, the angrier I got. But
then, how could I lay all the blame at their feet? Actually, they
weren't forcing me to do what I was doing. On the contrary, they
had treated me with politeness and courtesy. Their constant
"Hwang *kun* this, Hwang *kun* that" was more or less designed to
get on my good side. Then just what was it that made me feel I
had to do it? Normally my understanding of society's influence on
the individual is more theoretical than practical, but this time my
comprehension came from personal involvement. Just as I was
squaring off with Gargantuan society, unhappily it sneezed, blowing me away to the very heavens as though I were caught up in a
violent windstorm. Naturally, before me was not society in its
entirety, only that portion under the control of Japanese economics.
I think that must be why the Japanese come here with such feelings of superiority.

"Hwang *kun*, have them send in a few more girls," Takeuchi
said.

"Have them all come in. Tell them we have presents for them,"
said Baba as he turned around and picked up a bag. "Look, we
have all these presents."

I told Ah-hsiu to send them in, and she said they would be coming right away, just as soon as the meal was served.

As promised, as soon as the first course arrived, twenty or so
girls came up to the room—some stood inside and some remained
just beyond the door. Ah-hsiu played the director, calling out to
them: "You girls inside the room, step in closer. You girls outside,
come on in." Then she said to me: "The three duty girls are already
agreed upon. In addition to them, why don't you all choose one
more apiece. You might as well have a few more." As she finished
she noticed there were still some girls who hadn't come into the
room, so she yelled out: "I told you to come in, but you just stand
there! Well, don't accuse me of playing favorites when it's too
late!"

Although several moved inside the room, at least seven or eight remained outside. The girls' faces were generally expressionless, but I could still tell who among them had been successful in their occupation and who had not. The ones inside the room manifested more confidence and pride than those outside. As I went out to ask the others to come into the room I spotted one leaning up against the wall, her head lowered as she toyed disinterestedly with her fingernails. When she noticed that I was coming out of the room she raised her head to look at me, then dropped it even lower than before and turned her face to avoid looking at me. In that brief moment I had a good look at her face—one side of it was covered with a dark green birthmark. I vacillated for a moment, for if I asked her to come in, her inferiority feelings would be even stronger than they were then, but if I didn't ask her, then she'd be thinking: "The customer doesn't like my face," and would feel even worse than she did now. What was I to do?

In the midst of my indecision, not knowing how best to handle the situation, I took her hand gently and said to her: "You're mine. Now won't you come on in?" I saw the look on her face—she was both startled and pleased—and in that instant her mind seemed to be cleared of many of its contradictions. Taking courage from this, I spread open my arms and very affectionately herded all seven or eight of the girls into the room. My attitude toward them seemed to erase even the feelings of inferiority they usually carried with them.

Baba was standing on a chair and weaving back and forth, causing everyone to laugh lightheartedly. He unzipped the bag draped around his neck and pulled out several pairs of nylon stockings, which he held up over his head as he shouted: "Is everybody in? Come on over! There's a pair here for everyone."

I urged the girls to go up and take them, but I never figured that as they all surged forward to grab a pair, the six Japanese sitting on the floor would jump at the opportunity to join the fray. Twelve hands suddenly reached out and began feeling the girls up at random, resulting in a great deal of laughter and shouting. The

men could not have been busier or happier, saying to themselves
proudly as they kept feeling around:

"Aha! I felt it."

"Hey! Don't run away, those are nice titties."

". . ."

I went up and grabbed several pairs to pass out to the few girls
who wanted some but didn't have the nerve to go up and get them.
They were all so delighted to get their hands on these things that
even the ones who were molested during the handout felt it was
worth it. Actually, stockings like those weren't all that different
from the ones sold in little stalls near the supermarkets in Taipei
for about twelve dollars a pair—the packaging was a little nicer,
and that's about all. Whatever this exchange between the Japanese
and the girls constituted—whether it was to be a part of the whole
deal or just a welcome gift—I couldn't help but be reminded of
their countrymen's posture in so-called Sino-Japanese economic
and technical cooperation. *Damn it*—as these thoughts crossed my
mind, I started feeling uneasy about myself again.

It was during all this grabbing and feeling that each of them
selected the girl of his choice and began embracing her. Baba had
his eye on one for himself, so he jumped down and threw his arms
around her. The girls who remained, knowing that they hadn't
appealed to anyone, started to drift away.

"Hey, wait a moment!" Ah-hsiu called them to a stop, then said
to me: "Ask the Japanese to select a few more to join the fun, since
they're all so cute." Then she turned to the girls and shouted to
them: "Just look at you—about as much life as bumps on a log.
You don't laugh, you don't cry . . . you know, I'm not going to
starve if you don't earn enough money, and I'm not going to get
fat if you do. I've got a bigger heart than any of you . . ."

Baba responded to the suggestion by saying that there were already ten girls, including the three who had been assigned, and
that they didn't want any more. At this the girls started walking
out of the room again. One of them mumbled as she passed through
the door: "I could have told you they wouldn't want any more, so

why did we have to stay behind and lose face . . ." I didn't hear the last part of the sentence, since she was walking out of the room as she said it, but Ah-hsiu, who had been helping inside, dropped what she was doing and ran after them:

"You bunch of tramps!" she screamed from the doorway. "You're all a bunch of sluts!"

They asked me what Ah-hsiu was yelling, but how could I translate that for them? All I could say was: "She told them to have the kitchen hurry up with the food."

"Oh, I thought it was an argument. Japanese is still the best-sounding language, especially when spoken by women. Hai! It's just beautiful," said Ochiai proudly.

"That's for sure," agreed Sasaki. "A lot of foreigners feel that way. How about you, Hwang *kun*?" The others were nodding their heads in agreement.

I'm afraid that even if an enlightened Japanese were to come to visit Taiwan, one of his ex-colonies, it would still be most difficult for him to keep from exposing his feelings of superiority. How much more so then for Baba and the others of his generation, who come here, do whatever they please, attain their goals with money, whore around with our countrywomen, and even have bad things to say about our language! With a forced gentleness to my voice, I said: "That's right, your Japanese language is just the same as your packaging designs—very attractive. Japanese has a nice sound to it, but its application is a whole different matter."

I stopped and looked at them for a moment. I could tell that they didn't understand what I was trying to say. I was about to explain myself when another idea came to me; I said to them jokingly: "There's another facet to the Japanese language: take, for example, sexual intercourse. Here in the countryside the people use the word 'screw,' while our soldiers say 'shoot your wad,' both of which you feel lack elegance and sound simply awful. But if you say 'have sex' in Japanese, or just use the foreign term that has been imported and swallowed whole, *'meiku rabu'* (make love), then you think it's both elegant and romantic-sounding."

I could see that this had struck them as funny, so I continued: "But in fact, with 'screw,' 'shoot your wad,' 'have sex,' 'meiku rabu,' aren't we still talking about the same thing? Can it be that if you say 'meiku rabu' you're talking about doing it a different way? Or maybe it lends the act respectability? Or perhaps it means that you can join bodies and souls as one and rise to the heights of supreme bliss?"

At first I had secretly reminded myself to sound as friendly as possible, but as I went along I grew more excited until I couldn't hold myself back. Fortunately the only parts of my discourse they paid any attention to were the vulgarities and the humor, so they laughed even harder. I didn't think it was all that funny, and it suddenly occurred to me that this analogy should not be used to criticize the Japanese language. It should be used as a criticism of the ego-pleasing and phony conduct of the intellectuals. When I saw that they had mistaken my comments as a joke, treating them as a laughing matter, it gave me an uneasy feeling. But something inside me told me to just drop the matter.

When the food arrived the topics of conversation began to expand. The girls sat down next to the men and started pouring wine and serving bites of food to their customers. The girl with the birthmark on her face who had been standing the farthest from the room was now sitting beside me and seeing to my needs with great enthusiasm. It occurred to me that I had a moral responsibility as far as she was concerned, since her intimate feelings toward me had originated when her opinion of herself was at its lowest, and I had said: "You're mine, now won't you come on in?" She had been moved by that. For someone like me, who feels very hostile toward Japanese, having to play the pimp in order to keep my job, and making arrangements for them to whore around with my own countrywomen, had created immense inner conflicts. If I hadn't had the capacity to mask my feelings with a happy exterior—much like a clown—I'm sure I could not have withstood such a bitter struggle. Under conditions like these, how could I have any desire for a woman?

My own heart cried out with the injustice of it all. If I didn't have her come to me that night, she would feel slighted, for even though she was a prostitute, if I were to disappoint her after my actions had stirred up her emotions—even if it were only a one-night stand—I would still be guilty of trifling with her. I turned and looked at her. She returned my look shyly, then quickly turned her face away again in what seemed to be a manifestation of her inferiority complex. Seeing how simple and unworldly she was, I didn't have the heart to disappoint her. *Okay, I'll see what happens tonight.*

A little while earlier, before the girls entered, I had acted as interpreter for the conversation among the three girls—Hsiao-wen, Ying-ying, and Ah-yu—and the men, and I was absolutely fed up with this role. Suddenly I had an inspiration: I would open a provisional language course to teach the Japanese some Chinese and the girls some Japanese. But I would only teach them the words for "good," "no good," "yes," and "no," and they could all learn them together. As soon as I mentioned my plan they all promptly agreed, and within three or four minutes they had mastered their lessons. They were having a great time: a constant, uninterrupted flow of "yes," "no," "good," "no good" emerged from their mouths until they got so noisy I found it hard to continue my own conversation. I stood up, clapped my hands loudly, and shouted everyone down:

"Okay, now," I said, "all of you can say the words. From now on you can communicate verbally and with hand and body language. So please, I beg you, don't bother me any more." Things really began to heat up then. Even the most taciturn among them decided to try their hand, and as a result, whether they were getting through to each other or not, this became the entertainment that went with their food and drink. The sounds of laughter alternately rose and fell, and even I was laughing so hard my sides were splitting. The girl sitting on the other side of me said to Ochiai: "You're a son of a bitch."

"Good, good." Ochiai nodded his head vigorously to show how

happy this made him. The girl, whose name was Mei-mei, was so overcome by laughter that she collapsed over onto me. Ochiai asked me what she had said. "Didn't you just say 'good'?" I asked. He said he guessed that what Mei-mei said must certainly have been interesting.

"It most assuredly was," I answered. "She said that you were a little on the heavy side, but still cute."

Ochiai was so happy that he grabbed Mei-mei's hand and said: "Really? Hee-hee-hee, you're pretty cute yourself." There were many more of these comical exchanges, until soon they all began to suspect that they were being made fun of. And so I was once again interpreting every sentence for them.

"Hey, friends," I said to the Japanese with a smile, "treat me like a human being too, all right? I can't just sit here and watch you have a good time, can I?" I reached over and put my arms around Ah-chen, the girl with the birthmark on her face, to give her a hug. Then I held out my winecup and said: "I'll drain this cupful to express my apologies to you gentlemen." So saying, I drained the cup.

"Won't this make it difficult for us?" Baba asked good-naturedly.

"How could it? Doesn't your 'Thousand Beheadings Club' roam the world relying only on your swords?"

"Hwang *kun*, you are the sharpest person we've ever met among the local people. We're no match for you."

"You flatter me." I picked up my winecup again: "Here, let this cupful represent my gratitude for your flattering remarks." Again, I drained the cup.

I could sense that from our first meeting at the airport up till now their attitude toward me, or at least insofar as their speech and their conduct reflected it, had undergone quite a transformation. By this time they no longer exhibited any sense of superiority in front of me, and even Baba seemed a little intimidated by my presence.

As I observed them at the meal I could see that they were not inhibited by the language barrier and had even turned it into a form of entertainment. And the knowledge that they were in a foreign country made them feel like they were floating on a cloud. Because of this they began to get the itch. Squinting his eyes and holding Ch'iu-hsiang in his arms, Baba said to me: "Hwang *kun*, I'm afraid we can't avoid imposing upon you now. Do you know their price?"

I asked Ah-chen, but she only stammered and was unable to say anything. Eventually, the girl sitting next to Tanaka, Pai-mei, was pushed forward by the others to speak for them.

"Are you interested in a 'rest' or a 'mooring'?" she asked. Actually, she had no idea of the real significance of the Japanese words *kyukei* and *teihaku*, which were remnants from the Japanese occupation. In this context, a "rest" meant a "short time," and a "mooring" meant an "overnighter."

"How much for a 'mooring'?"

"It's like this: if it's one of our own people, it's two hundred." Then she looked at the Japanese and asked me softly: "They really don't understand what we're saying?"

"Not a word. Say whatever you want as loudly as you like."

Nonetheless she continued in a low voice: "For Japanese it's four hundred."

"All right." Then in a loud voice I said: "We'll make it a thousand for a 'mooring.'"

"Aiya! Not so loud!" one of the girls blurted out. The others all laughed.

"How much of it do we have to give you?" Pai-mei asked.

"None."

"How can that be?" several of them asked in unison.

"Don't worry about it." Then I said in Japanese: "One thousand for the night, and that's not a bad price. You can use your revalued yen and enjoy both convenience and economy."

"All right, let's make up our minds," Baba nodded to the others with his head cocked to one side, indicating that he was asking for their opinions, although the inference was that he had already made the decision for them.

"Baba *kun*, you still haven't asked Hwang *kun* to take care of the arrangements for our trip to Hualien, have you?"

"Oh, I almost forgot," Baba said, striking himself on the forehead. "Hwang *kun*," he said to me, "I'm going to have to ask another favor of you. We've heard that in Hualien you can find real aborigine girls . . . ."

"I'm not sure," I answered calculatedly.

"You really don't know? Heh-heh-heh . . . ?" Ochiai asked teasingly.

"It doesn't make any difference. Hwang *kun*, we plan to stay in Taiwan for a week, and Hualien is one of the places we want to visit. Make a long-distance phone call to your company for us now and have someone buy eight tickets for the noon flight tomorrow."

"Don't you mean seven tickets?" I asked.

"The eighth one is for you."

"I'm afraid I have things to do tomorrow."

"Don't you want to go along with us?"

"It's not that. I really do have things to do. But don't worry, if I can't make it, the company will send someone else to accompany you. Okay, I'll go make the phone call," I said as I walked off.

"Sorry to trouble you."

When I returned to the room after placing the long-distance call, nearly all the girls had left. Only Ying-ying and Hsiao-wen had stayed behind to clear the table.

"What's up? Where is everyone?" I asked.

"We asked them to leave for a while so we could make our preparations," Ochiai said to me with a mysterious grin. "Hwang *kun*, don't you have to make preparations too?"

"What preparations would I have to make?" I already had an inkling of what they meant. I smiled, and Ochiai and the others smiled back.

"What about the phone call?"

"The plane leaves tomorrow at 12:30. We'll leave here in the morning on the 9:31 train."

"Fine, no problem." Baba looked at the others. "That's it then."

Ochiai reached into his pocket and pulled out a little gold object that looked like a lipstick, only slightly larger. "Ever see one of these?"

I took it from him and opened it up. They were all standing around snickering as I examined it.

"Isn't it a cologne atomizer?" I asked, putting my thumb on the button.

"Hey! Don't press it!" Ochiai yelled. "Don't press it!" They all laughed.

"Just what is it anyway?" I hadn't a clue.

"Haven't you ever heard of the magic oil of India?"

"No."

Ying-ying and Hsiao-wen, thinking it was a cosmetic of some sort, dropped what they were doing to come over and take a look. "What's that?" Hsiao-wen asked.

"Hey! Don't let them find out." Ochiai grabbed it away from me, but then he must have realized that they couldn't understand what he was saying. When he continued, he appeared to relish talking about it while they were present in order to add some new effects to the drama. He said: "An hour before we get to work, we spray a little of this stuff on the turtle's head—just a little. Hai! There's nothing like this stuff—the pleasure it brings is almost endless!" He smiled lecherously at the girls: "You know what I mean?"

Hsiao-wen reached over to take it, but I snatched it away. "This is an ointment for aches and pains," I said to her. "Hurry up and clear away the dishes." The girls walked away feeling somewhat disappointed.

"Hwang *kun*, you can try a little if you'd like," Baba said.

"I don't think so," I said, handing it back to Ochiai. I experienced a strange kind of anger.

"Hwang *kun* isn't like us, he's still young. He probably doesn't need it."

By then they had finished the food and wine, so everyone headed back to his own room. Most likely they were all in the midst of making their so-called preparations. I went back to my room and lay down on the bed to sort out my feelings. My thoughts went round and round without ever coming together. Then they turned to Ah-chen, the girl with the birthmark. I was sure that if I summoned her in the evening she would be happy to come and would treat me well. Beginning to get aroused, I suddenly recalled that I would be doing this thing along with the Japanese, and my anger was rekindled. *Shall I not call her then? As self-debasing and simple as she is, she must certainly think that I want her tonight. If I don't call her, she will be hurt, and this hurt will go beyond just the missed chance to earn some money.* I thought and thought about it. *Damn it, I'll wait till tonight and see what happens!*

Just as I was lying on the bed feeling miserable, Baba knocked on the door and came in.

"Excuse me, Hwang *kun*, sorry to disturb you."

Whatever the situation, they were always polite and courteous. But I was still disgusted with him. If politeness and courtesy become habits and lose their spontaneity, what you have then is blatant superficiality. He had a grin on his face as he said to me: "Shall we call the girls now!"

"Right now?" I sat up.

Baba looked at me and nodded his head. I glanced at my watch. "But it's only a little after six o'clock!" I said.

My somewhat startled reaction seemed to cause him some embarrassment. "You're right," he said with a smile, "it is a little early, but we've already finished our preparations."

"You mean you've already sprayed on your magic oil of India?" Though there was a smile on my face, I wasn't feeling very happy.

He nodded: "And some other stuff as well. You see, since the potions are effective only for a period of time . . ." The smile on his face suddenly retreated and was replaced with a pathetic look.

"They don't have any bad effects on your body, do they?" My expression of concern for him was a complete fabrication.

"Of course they do if you use them too often. But think about it—we're all in our fifties, and a thousand 'beheadings' is no simple task." As he said this the final trace of a smile disappeared completely.

I stood up and patted him on the shoulder. "All right," I said, "I'll go."

"I'll go back to my room." The smiling countenance that he had entered with started to make its return. But I knew that the smiles on their faces were dependent on the support they received from the magic oil of India and other preparations.

I walked out of my room against my own inclinations. Had there been someone behind me forcing me on, no matter how strong his arms, I would have unquestionably turned back to resist, even if I were to die in the attempt. But when I turned my head back there wasn't a thing in sight, and in that blur of time the cold, still corridor—almost deathlike—gave me a fright. In that fleeting moment I seemed to have moved suddenly from a strange and distant place back to reality. Unwilling though I was, I had no choice but to walk downstairs. At the desk at the foot of the stairs I ran into Ah-hsiu, who had been serving us just a while before.

"Hwang *san*," she addressed me in Japanese style, "what can I do for you?"

I was momentarily speechless, for I suddenly realized that I could not avoid asking her straight out to have the girls go right away to sleep with those Japanese. A little while earlier, when I was negotiating the girls' price, I hadn't felt so keenly what I was involved in, since I was able to more than double the going rate. On the contrary, I even experienced the stirrings of a national consciousness—the illusion of serving my fellow Chinese. Whether or not such behavior and feelings were justified, I still experienced the thrill of dealing a defeat to my enemy. But not at this moment. As I stood there before Ah-hsiu, I knew as clearly as could be that the moment I opened my mouth to speak I would be a bona fide pimp. "Damn it! That bunch of Japanese say they want the girls to come to their rooms now," I said to her angrily.

"Huh! Now? They can't go now. Why, it's only . . . what time is it?" She looked up at the clock on the wall, then at the girl behind the counter. "It's only six o'clock. How can they go now? Our girls aren't here to serve them exclusively."

"I know that, damn it! But . . ." I couldn't finish.

"We're not trying to take advantage of anyone," Ah-hsiu said, "but the general rule is that a 'mooring' is from midnight on."

"We can't do that. No one ever expects a girl to spend the night with him starting this early," added the girl behind the counter.

"That's right! I know that," I said.

"I'll tell you what. We'll have the girls go to them half an hour early, at eleven-thirty—how will that be?"

"That would be fine, of course, except . . ." I paused for a moment. "Would you go upstairs with me and tell them to their faces? Just tell them what the general rule is."

"You'll have to be my interpreter."

As we walked upstairs Ah-hsiu said to me: "The girls here say you're a good person." After a pause, she added: "Aren't you originally from Chiao-hsi?"

"Who said so?" I answered with a start.

"Your home is next to the temple, and you're Uncle Yen-lung's eldest son. Am I right?" She smiled.

"How did you know?"

"All the older people in our place recognized you."

"Damn!"

"It doesn't matter." Then she asked me in a very lighthearted tone: "Did you go to Taipei right after you quit teaching? What sort of business are you in now? You must be doing quite well."

"Not really. I just work for a company."

"It's been several years already, but Yü-mei still talks about you. She says you were the best teacher she ever had."

I stopped in my tracks and asked in a trembling voice: "Who is Yü-mei?"

"My eldest daughter. You were her fifth- and sixth-grade teacher."

I remembered her, and in some respects I felt somewhat relaxed.

"Oh! So Chen Yü-mei is your eldest daughter! Where is she now?"

"She's in her first year at a girls' high school. She's changed quite a bit since you knew her. She's grown quite tall, taller even than me."

"Mrs. Chen, I have a favor to ask of you. Please don't tell Yü-mei that I came here," I said awkwardly.

Mrs. Chen thought this was pretty funny. "I won't, but what difference would it make?"

"No, please. Just say you ran into me somewhere—anywhere."

"I won't tell, I won't breathe a word," she said with a giggle.

We talked for a while longer at the head of the stairs. I still felt a heaviness in my heart, though I was a lot more at ease than when Chen Yü-mei's mother had first told me she knew who I was.

I took Mrs. Chen to find Baba and informed him of what she had told me.

"So that's how it is!" he said. "What a damned nuisance."

"I'm terribly sorry, but those are the rules around here." Mrs. Chen nodded her head apologetically.

"How about this, then: suppose we throw in a little more money, could we have them come now?"

"I'm sure that would be all right, but I'm afraid it would place a hardship on you."

I asked how much more each one would have to give to have the girls come now.

"At least two hundred."

"Let's tell them five hundred. After all, the Japanese are so rich they won't miss a few hundred."

After I informed Baba, he said: "Well, if that's the way it is, then we have no choice. I'll go ask the others."

He knocked on each of the doors and called the others out into the corridor; once they were all there together he opened the discussion. When they arrived at their decision Baba represented them: "I guess that's how it has to be. Hwang *kun*, tell them to come right away." When it came to business and money, the Baba who had up to that moment given me the impression of someone who treated others politely had been transformed into a person just like everyone else.

Before long, all of the girls they had requested, excepting Hsiu-hsiu, whom Takeuchi had wanted, arrived in the rooms. Mrs. Chen and I took the thoroughly displeased Takeuchi downstairs to the girls' resting quarters to select another girl who appealed to him. After the longest time he very begrudgingly settled on a girl named Mei-chün. It seemed to me that my conduct had been abruptly and severely restricted ever since Mrs. Chen had told me that most of the people in the hotel knew me. Moreover, I experienced an unremitting anxiety; had I said or done anything out of line in the presence of my fellow villagers before that moment? *Damn it, here I am, with Takeuchi picking out a girl as though she were a piece of goods.* He continued the process for a while longer. By rights, I should have been trying to do something for the benefit of the girls, but seeing the exasperated look on Takeuchi's face, I stood frozen off to the side, embarrassed to death.

After Takeuchi walked off with Mei-chün, Mrs. Chen came up behind me: "Hwang *san*, how about you?" she asked with a smile. She actually had the best of intentions, for if I had wanted the company of a girl, she wouldn't have thought anything of it, working as she did in such a place. But her smile gave me a feeling of unbearable discomfort. I knew what she had in mind.

"No, not for me."

"You don't have to be such an honest man. Ninety percent of those who take it on the chin are honest folk."

Hai! I had to laugh inwardly. *God only knows if I'm an honest man.* But all I said was: "That's all right. This has nothing to do with being an honest man or not."

She laughed and let the matter drop, simply following me upstairs. Naturally this took me by surprise, as I had hoped she would press the issue, giving me the opportunity to ask her advice on how to handle the matter of Ah-chen, the girl with the birthmark.

"Mrs. Chen," I said, pausing at the bend in the staircase, "I'm sure that Ah-chen is under the impression that I want her this evening. But actually . . ."

"Don't you worry about it. I'll find a nice one for you."

She had misunderstood me. Of course, I'm no saint, but in my complex and totally self-contradictory state of mind, I couldn't come up with a single decent idea.

"No. I think I'd like to give her five hundred and not have her come to my room tonight."

"That's not necessary. I'll tell her and it'll be all right."

"But I . . . I already made arrangements with her earlier." This was the best way to handle it. If I were to say that I was fearful of injuring Ah-chen's self-respect and adding to her low opinion of herself, Mrs. Chen might laugh at me, I thought. At the same time I was terribly afraid of running into Ah-chen. I took five hundred dollars out of my pocket and gave it to her.

"If that's the way you want it, you don't have to give so much. One hundred is plenty." She kept one of the bills and gave me four back.

I took three and handed back one. "Let's do it this way. Give her two hundred."

"Ha-ha! She makes a hundred percent profit just like that," she said with a laugh as she took the money.

I went back to my room, lay on the bed, and stared blankly at the ceiling. I had nothing to look forward to but a long evening alone in my room, and I didn't know what to do with myself. How could I go to sleep so early in the day?

Since I'd been away for a long time, I gave some thought to going home to have a look around.

But Father would ask me when I had arrived and what I had come home for. If I told him the truth, that I was accompanying some Japanese on a pleasure excursion to Chiao-hsi . . .ai! I wouldn't even try. I would only be looking for trouble. Earlier, when I chose not to take over his brokerage and even quit my job as a teacher, a scene had erupted that left a lingering bad taste. If I were to tell him now that the job I had gone to Taipei for was bringing Japanese here to the hot springs to whore around, nothing I could say would make any difference; even plunging into the Yellow River could not wash the stains away.

I didn't want to dwell on it any longer. There was no going home!

Instead of going home, I thought of other places I could take a walk to.

But wouldn't it be the same? If I ran into any friends, wouldn't they also ask my reasons for coming home? They might even let my father know, and things would be even worse. To travel to Chiao-hsi and not even come home! It would be just like two years ago when he had screamed: "When the ancient sage emperor Yu was taming the Yellow River, he passed by his home three times without entering. But you! Who the hell do you think you are!" If he were to fly into another rage because of me, this time I was afraid he might die of apoplexy. No, that was no good either. I decided to just lie there.

I rolled over and noticed a photograph of a foreign pinup girl hanging on the wall. She was straddling an overturned chair and cradling her chin in a waiting pose. As I was looking at it my train of thought quickly turned in a new direction. I figured that those Japanese—*Damn them*—were just then reaching their climaxes. I wondered what effects the magic oil of India had. Who knows, if I hadn't been recognized by Yü-mei's mother, maybe Ah-chen would already be lying beside me. There is a saying that men have: "Ugly women are great in bed." With her low opinion of herself and my expression of interest in her, I'm sure she would have shown me a terrific time. *Damn it! I wonder what she's doing right now.* But no matter how overcome by my own desires I was, something inside me maintained its awareness. It was this awareness that kept me from daring to face myself, and the less I dared to face myself, the fewer my chances of escape. As a result, I felt ill at ease and so pained that I jumped violently to my feet. I lit a cigarette and paced the floor. Suddenly I noticed the telephone. I reached out and took it off the hook; the girl at the desk answered the phone:

"Front desk, may I help you?"

"Oh, I'm sorry, it was nothing." I hung up the receiver. But I was immediately aware that what I had just done was without doubt very unusual, and if the girl at the desk were to mention it later to anyone else—especially Yu-mei's mother—not only would it be the object of a lot of speculation, even my private thoughts in the room would be common knowledge. Ai! More cause for embarrassment! I figured the best thing to do would be to leave my tiny room.

I went downstairs, gave my apologies to the girl at the counter, went into the restaurant, found a table and ordered some food and a bottle of beer. I sat there thinking, trying to figure out what sort of lie I could tell my wife to avoid having her suspect me of being unfaithful. Thoughts that had sprung from my own imagination and those that had their origins elsewhere came to me one after another for some time. Eventually I was like a lonely long-distance runner who was undergoing slow and agonizing physical and mental torture; I had finally reached the finish line, dead drunk and empty.

Japan's Longest Day

When I opened my eyes the following morning I saw Ah-hsiu, Baba, and the others standing around my bed. In my dazed state of mind I was shocked awake by the anxious looks on their faces and by their apprehensive comments of "Hwang *kun*, there's nothing wrong, is there?" I sat up with a start.

"What's happened?" I asked.

"You scared us. We thought you were sick."

"No, I'm fine. Look!" I sat up and threw a couple of punches in the air. "There's nothing wrong."

They all laughed. Then Mrs. Chen told me that they had knocked repeatedly on my door without being able to awaken me. They couldn't even get me up by ringing my telephone. Finally they had asked her to bring the passkey.

"It's getting late," Baba said. "Didn't you say we'd be taking a train a little after nine o'clock?"

"Mrs. Chen, did you buy the tickets for us?" I asked.

"Yes, for the 9:31 train. I'll get them in a minute."

"Hm, 9:31." I looked at my watch. "There's no problem, since we still have about an hour. The train station is nearby." Then I said to Mrs. Chen in Taiwanese: "Will you get our bill ready, please. Have they paid the girls?"

"Yes."

I took out another two hundred and gave it to her as a tip.

"My goodness, it's embarrassing to be taking a tip from Teacher Hwang. Thanks a lot," she said as she left.

"Hwang *kun*, you must have had a good time last night, eh."

"Um, I had a good time." In matters of this kind, no one will believe you if you say you didn't do anything. And if you do manage to convince them, then you'll be laughed at and suffer a loss of face. So it's far better just to come up with a positive answer.

"No wonder you were so spent you couldn't even get up. You must have had quite a time—a night of pure enjoyment!"

I grinned at them, delighted that these dimwits were so easy to fool.

"How about the rest of you?" I asked.

"Not bad!"

"Well, I didn't enjoy myself!"

A voice, full of displeasure, came from somewhere near the window behind me. The others were convulsed with laughter, but it took me aback. It was Takeuchi. He stood there looking out the window, keeping his back to us.

"What's the matter, Takeuchi *kun*?" I asked him.

"It won't hurt to tell him, will it?" Baba asked.

Takeuchi turned around with a forced smile on his face as Baba said with a laugh: "In the years since we founded our 'Thousand Beheadings Club,' we've made one discovery. Most people, maybe even you, would probably call it superstition, but what happens is that whenever one of us encounters bare skin . . . uh . . . a bare surface . . ." He grinned as he paused. "What I mean is, if he makes a girl without any pubic hair, then unfortunate things begin to happen to him."

"Can that be true?"

"Last year, after I had one in Hong Kong, I lost a thousand American dollars. Ochiai had one, after which his factory caught fire. Sasaki had an auto accident and spent two months in the hospital. And then there was . . ."

"That's enough!" Takeuchi interrupted.

"Yes, that's enough," I agreed. "These are all coincidences. You don't really believe in such superstitions, do you?"

As I was talking I observed Ochiai looking for something in his bag. Carefree as can be, he pulled out a little memo book with a red sateen cover, walked over, and flipped through the pages in front of me.

"Take a look at this," he said.

I took it from him to look through it, and was startled when I realized what the thing was. I began to silently curse them. This little book, it turned out, was a record that they kept for the "Thousand Beheadings Club." Each page had on it the time and place, the name of the girl, a description of her figure, how the lovemaking went, and what happened, followed by a critique. The bottom half of the page was left blank, so that they could use a piece of transparent tape to affix one of the girl's pubic hairs.

"Now do you see?" Ochiai said with a grin. "Takeuchi's page for today won't . . ."

"All right, all right, I guess you're happy now!" Takeuchi shouted.

I couldn't understand why he was so angry. It must have been something I didn't understand about their "Thousand Beheadings Club."

Later I found out that each of them had one of these little notebooks, which they used when they discussed their experiences. If they made some sort of discovery this way, then everyone could perform some experiments based upon it.

Once they were on the train they began discussing their experiences of the night before, holding nothing back.

"Hey!" I interrupted. "You should realize that there are people all over Taiwan who speak better Japanese than I do, maybe right here beside us."

"We're not discussing politics," Baba responded.

"I know you're not, but we Chinese aren't accustomed to talking about sex openly and are embarrassed to even hear such talk in public places." I knew that my words were a little inflammatory, but what the hell, those are the breaks! It wouldn't do any good to suppress my feelings any longer. But I still had a smile on my face.

They were speechless for a moment, then Baba said with a nervous laugh: "Hwang *kun*, you're not angry, are you?"

I could only say with a laugh: "What's that? If I were angry, I'd keep my mouth shut. It's just possible, however, that someone might be offended and come over and slug you."

They were frightened by this prospect, at least a little, and after taking a look around them, they turned back to me.

"Could that really happen?" Sasaki asked softly.

"We don't have to worry about such things in Japan," said Ochiai.

"But that's Japan—this is not Japan!" I said.

"Naturally," said Baba, "but I don't agree with what Ochiai *kun* just said. We too . . ." Baba was obviously trying to salvage some dignity for his country, but he realized at once that he was on shaky ground, so he paused momentarily.

Ochiai picked up the conversation, saying with some displeasure: "Baba *kun*, is that necessary?"

I turned to the attack, responding to what Baba had been about to say, remembering to keep a smile on my face.

"Baba *kun*, no matter what the situation, if there is something that embarrasses you in Japan, or something you don't dare do for fear of injuring others, then you shouldn't do it when you go abroad, at least in regards to what we're talking about. Isn't that right?"

"No, wait a moment, Hwang *kun*, I didn't make myself clear. What I meant was . . ."

"Hey, that's enough, Baba *kun*, that's just about enough. Let's everybody speak for himself. Who asked you to be a spokesman for Japan?" Then Tanaka said to me: "Hwang *kun*, please don't take things so seriously. Heh-heh . . ."

I laughed along with him. "Tanaka *kun*, who's taking things seriously? But you make it sound improper for someone to take things seriously. Besides, since you're Japanese, under certain circumstances or in certain situations you can't avoid representing Japan. But I agree with what you say—everyone should speak for himself."

"You see! From the beginning I said that Hwang *kun* was the sharpest Taiwanese we'd ever met, didn't I?" Baba said.

"Let's just forget it," I said. "Let's all take it a little easier."

"How can we take it easy now? Hwang *kun*, you're really something. It was you who created the tense situation, and now you want *us* to take it easy!"

"You've got it all wrong. But all right, you just do whatever you want." Then I added: "Don't have any thoughts for me, but in case something happens, I'll still be here beside you."

"Then we can put our minds at ease," Baba said.

Nonetheless, after my warning, they seemed to have run out of things to say. Each of them sat there like a block of wood. I hadn't a clue what they were thinking. When the train pulled into Ting-shuang-hsi, Ochiai asked: "How long before we get to Taipei?"

"Another hour."

"We still have that far to go?"

"Um-hm."

A young man who had evidently boarded at T'ou-ch'eng moved over beside us, and I noticed at once that he was very attentive to our conversation. I had cautioned them not to talk about their sexual experiences on the train partly because I felt they were being much too open about it and partly because I had noticed this young man beside us who was engrossed in their comments. As our eyes met, he smiled and nodded to me. I nodded back.

"Excuse me, sir, you're Chinese, aren't you?"

"Yes, I am."

"It's hard to believe that someone as young as you can speak such fluent Japanese."*

"You're too kind. I barely get by."

"My name is Chen, and I'm a senior in the Chinese Department at Taiwan University. After I graduate, my father is going to find a way to send me to Japan for advanced study. So could I trouble you to ask these Japanese a few questions for me?"

Just as I was thinking to myself that he might be a little too brash, he asked abruptly: "What do those men do in Japan?"

Damn this young fellow! If I ask them some of the questions he has in mind, they might laugh at the presumptuousness of our young people. Besides, isn't it all topsy-turvy for a student of Chinese literature to leave China and go abroad to do advanced study? Then I had an inspiration. Why not take this opportunity to hurl a few barbs at the Japanese and teach my young friend a lesson at the same time? The prospects of a little sport nearly made me laugh out loud. Serious though the matter at hand may have been, I figured this would be a good chance to have some fun.

I told the young man that they were a fact-finding group of Japanese college professors.

"Oh, that's just perfect!" He was delighted. "Would you mind helping me out, then?"

Though the others couldn't understand what we were saying, they were watching our expressions closely and with great concentration, especially when the young man was speaking.

When I turned back to the Japanese, the young man nodded to them, and they timidly returned his gesture. "He's a college senior," I said. "His field is history, and since he's writing a thesis on the

---

*As a rule, only Taiwanese educated before 1945 speak Japanese.

eight-year War of Resistance, he'd like to discuss a few things with some Japanese."

They were momentarily speechless. Then one of them said confidentially: "As businessmen, we don't know anything about that."

"That doesn't matter. I don't even know what he's going to ask." I turned to him. "They'll be pleased to answer your questions, though they're afraid you might not find their answers satisfactory. Also, before you begin with your questions, they'd like to ask you something first. They want to know why someone studying Chinese literature would want to go to Japan to do his research."

"I've heard that there are a lot of original editions there," he said.

I felt very uncomfortable over this answer and wanted to respond to him right then and there. But I kept my feelings in check and pretended to give his answer to the Japanese.

"He'd like to know if you were born around 1916," I said.

They looked at one another with shocked expressions on their faces, wondering how the young man could have guessed so accurately and why he seemed to be investigating them. Actually, I already knew this information from when I had registered them at the hotel.

"What does he want to know that for?" Baba asked with an expression of displeasure. "Hwang *kun*, this can't have anything to do with the thesis he's writing. Besides, that's personal."

Seeing that the young man had observed the look of displeasure on Baba's face, I quickly told him: "Professor Baba is quite disappointed with your response, and even a little upset. He said that research in any field of knowledge doesn't depend upon the edition one uses. For example, if you're doing work on the *Book of History,* using both an original and a later edition, will you gain a deeper understanding from the former?"

"But your mood and feelings while you're doing the research won't be the same. Also . . ."

"Hold on there," I interrupted him. "If you say too much at one time, I won't be able to interpret for you, so let me tell them what you just said first." I turned to the Japanese. "He offers his apologies for asking this sort of question, but he just wanted to gain an understanding of the background of those days, that's all. He'll understand if you don't feel like answering him." Then, speaking for myself, I said: "Were you, as a matter of fact? What difference could telling him make."

"Well, if that's all it is, as a matter of fact all seven of us were born in 1917. We're from the same town and we were classmates in elementary and high school." When Baba finished, the others stared intently while I spoke to the young man.

"Many people who do research in Chinese are under the impression that they're doing research on Chinese words. But what's really worth researching is Chinese society and the great Chinese thinkers. He said that your wanting to go to Japan to do research in Chinese literature is actually just a pretext, isn't it?"

An embarrassed smile appeared on the young man's face. "No, it isn't a pretext. I really want to go to Japan to study. But what the professor says is certainly worth thinking about. Could I ask if he's a Sinologist?"

"No, he's a professor of Japanese literature, but anyone in Japanese literature has a solid foundation in Sinology." I was beginning to get a little flustered. I hoped I wouldn't forget what I was supposed to be asking the Japanese, and wind up giving apple answers to questions about oranges.

"My papa's always telling me that Japan is a pretty good place, so I'd like to see it for myself."

Baba and the others were looking at me, waiting to hear what was being said. I turned to them: "He said you must have been just the right age to be drafted into the army and take part in the war of aggression against China, right?" I looked first at the pale face of Ochiai, then at the composed Baba. I said with a laugh: "This fellow doesn't care much for others' feelings. But then there's no harm done. Ochiai *kun*, you seem a little more touchy about this than the others. What's wrong?"

"Nothing's wrong." He paused for a moment, as though troubled. "In those days everybody was drafted into the army except for the disabled. Naturally, we were no exception."

"A great war certainly isn't something caused by common folk. I don't care if you call it a war of aggression, because it was started by the Japanese Imperial Government in power. Me, I was only someone who followed orders." Baba looked at the others. "Isn't that right?"

"To listen to you now, you'd think that you opposed that war right down to your marrow. But what about in those days? Weren't you right in there singing about how you represented the Way of Heaven in its destruction of the unrighteous, marching onto the continent of China as you sang, and calling it a 'holy war?' " Then I forced a smile and said: "If I'd been in your shoes, I guess I'd have done the same thing."

Suddenly feeling as though a great weight had been lifted from their shoulders, they all laughed nervously.

"Then you've all been to the China mainland? When you were in the army, that is?"

"All except Takeuchi *kun*."

"It seems I've suddenly gotten interested in the subject myself, but actually these are all his questions." I smiled, then turned to the student and said: "The professors hope you'll forgive them if they sometimes seem impolite by being critical of your thoughts in this matter."

"Oh, don't worry about that. I should be thanking them," he answered.

"They say it's understandable that your father has good feelings about Japan, because people of his age grew up under a Japanese educational system that kept them ignorant. But someone of your generation shouldn't have such thoughts."

"It was my papa who told me . . ."

"Let me finish. Professor Baba also said that supposing Japan is a fine place, or that America is a fine place, or that somewhere else is a fine place, what you seem to have in mind is to go to a fine place somewhere to enjoy yourself, or perhaps just to escape from reality. What he wants to ask you is this: Granted that Japan is a fine place, but just what have you done for Japan? If the answer is nothing, then you'd best not make plans to go and reap the benefits of her accomplishments." I smiled. "But the professor says that this is just a personal reaction to your comments, and if you really want to go to Japan, he says you'd be welcome."

"I wouldn't go there just to have a good time! I'd be going to study!"

"Going to study is fine, and that's your business. What the professor says is not intended as a criticism of you, but is aimed at today's youth and their dissatisfaction with reality, which makes them all want to run off to a better country that exists only in their imagination. These are the people he's talking about. Only you know whether or not you're one of those people."

"What he says is right, and I respect him for it. How many days will they be here looking things over? It would be wonderful if they could come and speak at our school."

I'll be damned! So this is what our young students have come to. This is the sort of common-sense talk you can hear anywhere. But in the mouth of a foreigner it somehow gains credibility. *Hmm. "Only monks from afar really know the Scriptures!"* Although it struck me as funny, it unnerved me a little as well. I had started out just wanting to poke a little fun; how could I have guessed that I'd soon be attacking both parties? I knew that I didn't have enough understanding of these matters to keep it up forever, and sooner or later I'd let the cat out of the bag. I figured it was time to put on the brakes. But how? Since I didn't know, I had to keep it up until the young man got off the train.

The strange part was that I hadn't expected that in using my limited knowledge of history to settle some accounts with the Japanese I had actually induced these men with their superior airs to simply acknowledge a debt by slowly nodding their heads.

"This student has made his position clear, and I think we can accept it."

"I hope that in his thesis he won't use our viewpoint as a critique of Japan."

I was elated to hear Sasaki say this, for I could see that little remained of the pleasures they had bought the night before. But I wasn't quite ready to let them off the hook yet. I wanted to turn their pleasure into anguish, no matter how ephemeral it might be. "I don't think he will," I said. "To draw general conclusions from an isolated situation is taboo in scholarly work. I'm sure that a college student understands that."

"I hope so," Sasaki said. Then he continued: "Not long after the war, when television came to Japan, we were able to witness the past in films about the war we had been involved in . . ."

"Did you see any of the fighting in China?"

"Sure! Quite a bit, as a matter of fact." He looked at his friends. "Isn't that right? It was then that we were able to really see what kinds of things we had done."

I feigned a confused expression. "How could you have a clear picture of what you had done after seeing filmed records?"

"Oh!" Ochiai, his face looking drawn, showed signs of real discomfort. As for the others, although they glanced back and forth at one another, the focus of their attention never strayed from our conversation. Sasaki blurted out almost painfully: "We saw scenes of the rape of Nanking, we saw bodies floating on the Whampoo River, we saw the bombing, we saw . . ."

"Sasaki *kun*, that's enough," Baba said, shaking his head, "that's enough, that's enough."

I agreed that he had said enough. They had been parties to it, and if they had truly seen films giving irrefutable proof of their ruthless persecution of the Chinese, there was no need for me to pursue the matter any further. This reminder that I had given them was all that any humane, conscionable human being could stand. Seeing the mental anguish written on their faces, I could tell that I had achieved the desired effect. But what could I say at this juncture to the young fellow beside me who seemed so terribly eager to know what was going on?

I continued having my sport with both parties for a long while.

"Young fellow, please don't be angry."

"I won't."

"Just now they wanted to ask you something else. You told them that you had never been to the National Palace Museum, and that came as quite a shock to them. They expressed real disappointment in you. You say you're a college student and that your major subject is Chinese, and that you even live in Taipei. Then why haven't you taken the time to go and have a look?" I could see that he was still swallowing the bait; he lowered his head slightly with an expression of shame. "They said that even though they have come to Taiwan for a visit of only a few days, they've already been to the museum twice. They said that their minds have been constantly troubled as they wonder how a magnificent race of people that was able to produce the cultural treasures in the museum could in recent years have dried up so completely."

"Mr. Hwang, I feel so ashamed."

"But then, you're too honest. When you meet foreigners who are so concerned about China, you should lie to them and say that you've been to the museum. And if that sort of thing embarrasses you, then why don't you just go to the museum some day and take a look for yourself? But no matter, what's happened today is no real loss of face—at least you're sincere. But isn't there something you'd like to ask them about Japan? Before you could even start, their questions kept you from asking them anything."

"I did have some questions, but after listening to what they've had to say, my questions don't seem so important any longer. I feel this has been a lucky day for me—I've learned at lot."

"As a matter of fact, you can often hear people here saying the things they were telling you today. It's strange that if your own people say something, it's like a fart in the wind, but if a foreigner says the same thing, it's like a message from the gods. Isn't that right?"

"But, honestly, I've never heard any of this before."

"Sure, I know. I'm saying that this happens a lot."

I glanced over at the Japanese; they were sitting there as though they were about to hear a judge pronounce sentence on them. When I turned to talk to them, they changed their posture slightly to concentrate on what I was saying.

"I hope you'll forgive this brash young man . . ." I didn't have a chance to finish.

"What do you mean? We couldn't respect him more!"

"Youngsters his age are a little on the romantic side and are generally more patriotic. I already told him not to ask any more questions, since it's all history anyway. You've come here to enjoy yourselves, and talking about the past like this can only cause you unhappiness." I paused for a moment. "But the young man did say that after the Japanese put down their guns, they switched to economic aggression, where they don't have to see their victims' suffering. I told him he shouldn't say that, but he said it *is* economic aggression, and from certain angles . . ."

"Hwang *kun*, that's enough," Baba said, shaking his head, "that's enough!"

Sasaki said agonizingly: "Hwang *kun*, I'm so sorry."

"Why should you be?" I said with a smile.

"We all feel very guilty. Please tell this young man how much we respect him. If the postwar Japanese youths were at all like him, then I think there'd be hope for our country." From the very beginning I could sense that Sasaki was more deeply affected than the others. The situation this time, in which their reveries had caused them such pain, had also started with him and then spread to the others.

The train pulled to a stop at Pa-tu. The young man broke in on our conversation.

"Mr. Hwang, I'm getting off at Pa-tu. Thank you, thank you all." He bowed very respectfully to me and to the others. This so unnerved the Japanese that they jumped to their feet and returned his courtesies, almost as if they were being cowed into it.

"This is where he gets off," I said.

"Sayonara!" It had never occurred to me that the young fellow knew a word or two of Japanese. This was the first time they had not gone through me. They were actually communicating with each other.

"Tsai-chien!" Nor had I suspected that these Japanese had learned to say a word or two of Chinese.

Each of them shook hands very gravely with the young man as they parted.

"Sayonara."

"Tsai-chien."

The young man left, and they all sat down. Sasaki, very much moved, sighed: "There's a Chinese youth you can be proud of."

"And how about me?" I asked playfully.

There was a hint of returning smiles as they said: "Naturally, you are too."

Ah, God only knows! This struck me as quite funny.

"I was right, wasn't I? You have to be careful of what you say in public places here. If that young man had been able to understand Japanese, things wouldn't have turned out as they did."

"Hwang *kun*," said Baba, "let's not talk about it anymore."

They leaned back lazily against their seats. Ochiai asked: "Hwang *kun*, how much longer?"

"About thirty minutes."

"There's still thirty minutes to go?" he blurted out as though the remaining half hour of our trip would take forever.

Bibliographic Note

Hwang Chun-ming's earliest short stories were published primarily in the literary supplement to the *United Daily News* (Lien-ho pao) and in the literary magazine *Yu-shih wen-yi*. Several of the stories translated in the present volume first appeared in the literary quarterly *Wen-hsüeh chi-k'an*. Hwang's first volume of stories, entitled *His Son's Big Doll* (Erh-tzu te ta wan-ou), was published by the Ta-lin Publishing Company in 1974, and includes four of the stories translated here: "The Fish" (Yü), "The Drowning of an Old Cat" (Ni-szu yi-chih lao-mao), "Ringworms" (Hsien), and "His Son's Big Doll." In March 1974, two volumes of Hwang's stories were published simultaneously by the Yüan-ching Publishing Company: *The Gong* (Lo), which, in addition to the title story, includes "The Two Signpainters" (Liang-ko yu-ch'i chiang); and *Sayonara • Tsai-chien*, which was the source for that story and for "The Taste of Apples" (P'ing-kuo te tzu-wei). In March 1975, the collection *The Little Widows* (Hsiao gua-fu) was published by Yüan-ching. In the latest published volume of stories, *I Love Mary* (Wo ai Ma-li), published in 1979 by Yüan-ching, only the title story is new; it will appear in translation in an anthology of Chinese fiction from Taiwan, to be published by Indiana University Press.

"The Gong" is included in the first anthology of Taiwan stories to be published in the People's Republic of China, which appeared in 1979.